1

Office workers bustled between cubicles, the floor noisy with phones and printers, the hurried conversations between co-workers, and the echo of construction from the renovation of the floor above. The corner office on the thirtieth floor of Gaines, Shirp, and Mott offered a beautiful view of the spectacular architecture of the Chicago skyline.

Sunlight filtered through the floor-to-ceiling glass office windows that overlooked the busy streets of downtown, shining on the office's simple, modern, and sparse furniture, which encompassed: a desk, a large drawing table, and a bookshelf that stretched just as wide and tall as the wall behind it.

A jacket hung lazily over the back of a chair behind the desk, which was stacked with piles of magazines, books, papers, and photographs, arranged in hazardous attempts at organization. The desk phone had been removed from its perch, the cord wrapped around the device, and was tucked neatly in the corner next to a pair of black heels.

Wren Burton stood in her white blouse, pencil skirt, and stockings, hunched over the drawing table, pencil in her right hand while her left gripped an engineering scale, both working seamlessly together over the trace paper. Her hands stroked the lines and curves effortlessly, every motion breathing life into her creation, challenging the skill and knowledge of those that had come before her, as she offered her own monument that would stand the test of time.

A single strand of hair broke loose from her ponytail, and she brushed it back, the smudges on her fingertips staining her pale skin with the silver grey of her pencil. She took a step back then circled the sketch, a master examining her work with an unyielding gaze, examining every angle, every inch, to ensure its perfection. She returned to the front of the drawing table and gave an approving nod. *It's finished.*

A deep vibration rattled her desk, shaking loose a few pieces of paper stacked too high, which floated gracefully to the floor. Wren wiped her fingers on a napkin, transferring the smudges of lead from her skin to the white of the half crumpled paper, and checked the name on the caller ID of her cell phone. She curled her slender fingers over the device, dulling the incessant buzz, hesitant to answer, before finally succumbing to the caller's persistence. "Hey."

"Did you forget?" The voice's tone on the other end of the phone was irritable and short.

Wren wedged the phone between her cheek and shoulder, quickly reaching for the sketches and filing them hastily into her bag in the seat of her chair. "You know I didn't forget."

"It's not that you forget to pick them up, it's just you usually forget to pick them up on time." The tone switched from irritated to superior, as if the words were meant to enlighten her of her own flaws.

Wren leaned on the edge of the desk, her head tucked low between her shoulder, her patience tested with an irritating itch she desperately wanted to scratch, but she did her best to keep her tone amiable. "I'm leaving now. Is that on time enough for you?"

An exhausted sigh whispered through the phone's speaker. "Look, I've got to go. There's a call coming in. Are we still going to talk tomorrow morning when I get home?"

Wren pulled on her jacket. "Yeah."

"All right. Tell the girls I love them."

"I will." Wren ended the call and tossed the phone back on her desk more forcefully than she intended. She scratched the thin, circular tan line on her left ring finger then opened her desk drawer. Amidst the chaos of sticky notes and pens rested a diamond ring. She pinched the silver band between her fingers then twirled it around her thumb and index finger, the gemstone catching the sunlight. After a few turns, she clamped the ring in her fist then shoved it in her jacket pocket.

Wren slid on her bag's shoulder strap, and one of the documents sticking through the opened compartment brushed her elbow. When she looked down, the words "Petition for Divorce" glared back at her. She forcefully shoved the papers deeper into her bag then zipped it shut.

Once she arrived at the elevator doors, Wren tapped her foot impatiently, checking the time on her phone, when an unwelcome hand grazed her hip. "Wanna grab those drinks tonight?" Dan asked, his fingertips trailing around her waist as he circled her, his lips grazing her strands of hair. "Then maybe head back to my place?"

Wren wrenched her body away and twisted Dan's wrist hard enough for him to wince. "No. And touch me like that again, and I'll make sure it's me who gets fired for aggressive advances." The elevator doors pinged open, and Wren flung Dan's arm away, leaving him red-faced and rubbing his wrist.

The stifling heat of the elevator only fanned the flames of anger, and when she made it to her car in the parking garage, she violently flung her bag in the trunk then slammed it shut. Her knuckles flashed white from the grip on the steering wheel, and she screamed, all of the frustrations bellowing out in the quiet of her sedan until she deflated, her forehead touching the crest of the steering wheel. She reached for the inside of her jacket pocket, removed the wedding ring, then twisted it back over the pale circle of flesh.

Traffic was heavy but not standstill. Wren drummed her fingers on the steering wheel as the clock on the dash flashed three thirty. She cursed under her breath then slammed her foot on the brake at another red light.

The parent pickup lane was empty upon Wren's arrival at Lakeside Elementary, and her daughters were the only kids left. Addison was entranced by the video recorder she'd received for her birthday, while her younger sibling, Chloe, twirled and danced next to her. The chaperone grabbed their attention and opened the rear passenger car door, Chloe climbing in first, with her sister close behind.

Wren rolled down the window, and the chaperone hunched down to meet her. "Thanks for staying with them, Mary."

"You're welcome, Mrs. Burton. Enjoy the weekend."

Addison helped Chloe buckle her seat belt then turned back to her camera, her small fingers fiddling with the buttons on the side. The device caught Wren's eye in the rearview mirror as she pulled out of the school and back into the thickening rush-hour traffic. "Making another movie, sweetheart?"

"It's an assignment for school," Addison answered, not looking up. She fumbled the device awkwardly in her hands. The camera was much larger than she was equipped to handle.

Wren shifted lanes and turned her attention to her youngest daughter. "And how was your day, Chloe?"

"Fine." Chloe's sharp blue eyes absorbed the world outside, watching the cars and buildings pass, her young mind discovering new things, and always enthralled with the experiences.

Another traffic light flashed red as the car's Bluetooth signaled a call, and a massive semi-truck blocked her view of the traffic ahead. "Hello?"

"Mrs. Burton?"

"Yes, this is she."

"This is Guidance Counselor Janet Fringe at University High School. Your son, Zack, was paired with me at the beginning of the school year. I just wanted to let you know that any future absences will require a doctor's note."

Wren disengaged the hands-free device and picked up her phone. "I don't understand. Zack hasn't missed school at all this year."

A pause lingered on the other end. "I see. Well, I have at least ten notes here dismissing him from class with your signature."

Wren nearly dropped the phone. "Ten?" *I'm going to wring his neck.* "And Zack is not in class now?"

"No, Mrs. Burton. Today's note simply stated that he wasn't feeling well."

Wren knocked her head into the driver side window, her eyes shut and nostrils flaring. She gritted her teeth then tried to regain her composure with a soft exhale. "Thank you, Ms. Fringe. I'll be sure to provide the proper documentation moving forward." When the call ended, Wren slammed the phone into the passenger seat. "God dammit!" Chloe's lowered head caught Wren's glance in the rearview mirror, and she turned around, gently shaking Chloe's foot. "Hey, I'm sorry. I didn't mean to raise my voice."

"Are you mad at Daddy again?" Chloe asked, those piercing blue eyes wide and watering. She understood more than a mind of five years old should comprehend.

"No, that's not what this is about. And that's not something you should be worried about, okay?"

"You guys fight all the time," Addison said, her tone indifferent to the situation, as she played with the camera. "Are you getting a divorce like Brittany's parents?"

A horn blared, shifting Wren's attention to the green light and open road. She accelerated, searching for the right words to explain the complexities that accompanied a marriage to a pair of children. "Your father and I, we... sometimes we don't tell each other everything. But it's something that we're working on. And it's definitely not anything the two of you should be thinking about." Wren eyed Addison in the rearview mirror. "No matter what Brittany says." The speedometer pushed fifty, and Wren's mind wandered to every place except the driver's seat. *Eighteen years together; all of those memories. How did this happen?*

Tires screeched, and a horn blared. The collision from the minivan jarred the entire car and thrashed Wren about in her seat. The sedan spun, and Wren's hands flung from the steering wheel as the air bags exploded, her seat belt digging into her chest and shoulder, keeping her from ejection. Tiny pellets of shattered glass scraped her skin and whirled around her head.

Just when the spinning stopped, with Wren's head swimming in confusion, another neck-snapping jolt knocked the car backward. Her limbs flew forward, and her forehead smacked the steering wheel, a knife like pain thrust into her skull.

Sheet metal crinkled like tin foil, and the bits of glass clinked along the hood, roof, and pavement as the jarring motions finally ended. Through the sharp, high-pitched whine in her ears, she heard more horns blaring in all directions along with the thunderous collisions of metals echoing down both sides of the road.

Wren slowly lifted her head from the steering wheel, her vision doubled, a warm trickle running down her cheek. She gently tapped her forehead at the source of the pain, wincing at the touch. She squinted at her fingertips, wiggling them back and forth, a crimson shimmer flashing in the light.

Wren maneuvered her arms aimlessly, her lack of coordination reaping fruitless action. Her fingers fumbled over the seat belt buckle, her arms and shoulder scraping against the now-deflated airbags.

A breeze gusted through the open space where the windshield once rested. She squinted, her vision fuzzy and strained as she examined a lump on the hood of her car. The longer she stared, the more the lifeless form took shape. When the bloodied head came into view her heart skipped a beat. The top of the victim's head had caved in, and his limbs were twisted awkwardly where he lay.

The sight of the carnage snapped Wren from the confused haze, her body stiff and irritable as she turned around to check the backseat, a sharp pain radiating from her left shoulder upon movement. "Chloe? Addison? Are you guys okay?"

Addison came into view first, her eldest daughter brushing bits of glass from her hair. "I feel dizzy."

"It's okay, baby. Mommy's going to get you out." The steering wheel pinned her legs. She shimmied and squirmed, finally freeing herself. "Chloe?" Her gaze shifted to her youngest daughter who lay motionless. Blood ran down the side of her cheek. "Chloe!"

Wren shouldered her door, which obstructed her escape after only clearing six inches of space. She looked out the broken window to the twisted metal that had warped along the side, which barred her exit. She pushed herself over the steering wheel and through the broken front windshield.

The hood buckled under the weight of Wren's hands and knees, glass bits jumping up from the ripple of metal and the corpse offering a mummer's attempt at life. All around, people stumbled from their cars, some quiet, others screaming, but everyone bewildered. Wren leaned against what was left of her twisted car frame for support as she clawed toward the rear driver-side door. "Chloe!"

Wren yanked the handle, but the door offered the same resistance as her own, the hinges warped and twisted beyond function. She fought through the pain and planted one foot against the side of the car, both hands on the door handle, and pulled. The door hinges squeaked, the metal creaking along with her joints. Her face reddened, and her hands ached from the stress. She offered one last tug just as her arms felt like they would pop from their sockets, and she fell backward, the door relinquishing its seal.

Wren scrambled from the pavement, half crawling and jumping toward her daughter. "Chloe, can you hear me?" She gently patted her daughter's cheek, careful not to try to move her. She placed her palm under Chloe's nose and felt the light flow of air. Addison had tears running down her flushed red cheeks as she stared at her bloodied sister. Wren reached for her arm. "Addy, can you unbuckle your seat belt?"

Addison nodded stiffly. "I think so." Her fingertips scraped against the metal as more glass fell from her shoulders. After a few failed attempts, she finally freed herself then scooted closer to Chloe, her sobs increasing the nearer she drew to her sister.

Wren patted her pockets, looking for her phone, her concentration wavering between her daughter and the erupting chaos of angered shouts and curses that carried on the wind.

A passenger from the van that had collided with the front of Wren's car stumbled out, her eyes glued to the man's body on the hood. "Jason!" she screamed, her sobs so powerful, they pulsated her body as she wavered left and right, her coordination affected by either injury or grief. She collapsed onto the hood, her hands groping the man's shirt as he lay unresponsive, screaming his name over and over.

All around, similar scenes unfolded, and the entire

highway was blocked with wrecks stretching as far as Wren could see, none of the traffic signals working. She spotted her phone on the pavement and retrieved it with a shaky hand. Her finger wavered over the numbers on the screen, struggling with the simple task of dialing 9-1-1.

Wren crouched by Chloe, checking her daughter's breathing again. A few rings, and the number beeped a busy signal. "Come on." She hung up and redialed but was offered the same result. "Shit!" She punched the side of the car, and a knifelike stab rippled through her shoulder.

Suddenly, Chloe stirred, her eyelids fluttering open and closed as she rolled her head from side to side. Wren dropped the phone and the screen cracked against the pavement. "Chloe, can you hear me? Sweetheart?"

"Mommy!" Addison shrieked, thrusting her finger at the bloodied corpse on the hood, her eyes wide and her small chest heaving up and down in labored breaths.

Wren quickly grabbed Addison's cheeks, forcing her daughter to look at her. "Addison, it's okay, sweetheart. Don't look at it. It's all just pretend. I need you to be brave for me, okay? I need you to be brave for your sister. She needs our help." Addison nodded, and Wren stroked her hair then reached for her phone once more, scraping the grainy asphalt off it and checking for a signal but to no avail.

A sudden fear washed over Wren, the uncertainty in the surrounding chaos pulling her toward a darkness that she couldn't see, couldn't feel, and couldn't hear. And then, just before the fear reached a fever pitch, red-and-blue lights flashed to her left, where an ambulance struggled to push through the traffic.

2

Addison wrapped her arms tightly around Wren's neck as they followed the paramedics into the emergency room. Even with the added sixty pounds hanging from her neck, Wren kept pace with the stretcher, the paramedics barking information at the nurses.

"We need to get this girl an MRI scan immediately. Possible concussion and fractured radius, breathing but unresponsive." The paramedic passed Chloe off to the nurse, who helped lift the stretcher onto another bed.

"What's your daughter's name, ma'am?" the nurse asked.

"Chloe." The entire ER was bursting with new admittances. Everywhere she looked, someone screamed, someone bled, and voices dripped with helplessness.

The nurse guided a needle into Chloe's arm then tore her shirt open and placed circular white stickers across her chest that ran wires to a machine that beeped with the vertical rise and fall of her daughter's pulse. "Ma'am, I'm going to have to ask you to leave while we run some tests."

Another nurse gripped Wren's arm and pulled her backward. Addison clung tighter to her neck. "What tests? No, I need to be here when she wakes up." Wren strained against the bodies removing her from the room. She looked to Chloe, still motionless on the cot, and the team of doctors surrounding her.

The doors were shut and locked, and Wren was forced to watch behind the thick glass of a window until one of the nurses pulled a curtain, engirding the staff in privacy. Addison cried into Wren's shoulder, and she cradled her daughter's head, rocking her back and forth. "It's all right, sweetheart. Your sister is going to be fine."

One of the nurses escorted Wren to the trauma waiting room, away from the mayhem of the ER. The waiting area was small, chairs lining the walls. The seats were filled with nervous friends and family members, anxiety etched on their faces as they stared at the floor with blank eyes, bounced their knees, and fidgeted their fingers.

Wren found that she wasn't immune to the apprehensive pathology as she paced back and forth, constantly glancing down the halls. Her stomach twisted in a knot every time one of the nurses walked by. Lost in her own worry, she felt a light tug on her shirtsleeve, and Addison looked up at her. "Mom, I'm hungry."

A vending machine hummed just outside the room, and Wren grabbed a bag of chips. Addison munched noisily as Wren took a seat. The television bolted to the ceiling in the corner of the room was turned on, but only the emergency broadcast signal played on its screen. The high-pitched whine of the signal was just as constant as the bright, multicolored lines on the monitor.

Wren pulled her phone out, and her heart leapt as one of the signal bars appeared on the screen. She immediately dialed her son, but the call went straight to voicemail. Then she tried her husband and received the same outcome. She went back and forth, dialing each of them over and over, their voicemails repeating the monotonous message in her ear. The din of the emergency signal in the background grew louder. More voicemails. *Pick up your phone.* She clenched the phone tighter then dialed again. *Voicemail.* The television's constant din tipped her anxiety over the edge until it finally burst from her lips. "*Can someone turn that off?*"

Every head in the room turned. Addison cowered in her chair, discarding the bag of chips. Wren massaged her temples, her nerves frayed and the frustration of the unknown slowly taking control of her reason. Her son was missing, Chloe was unconscious, and she couldn't get a hold of their father.

A sudden quiet overtook Wren's mind, and she realized the television's ringing had ceased. The multicolored scrambles had been replaced with a news anchor flipping through notes on his desk. He looked to his left. "We're on?" He stacked the notes together and cleared his throat. "Good afternoon. I'm Rick Cousins, and this is a Channel 4 News special update. The Chicago city power grid has been down for the past thirty minutes, affecting transportation and communication efforts across the metropolis area. We've received reports of activity at the power plant just south of the city, but we have yet to receive any confirmation about the cause of the outage."

Wren shifted in her seat, leaning toward the monitor. *If the power is out across the entire city, then Doug is most likely out on calls.*

"Emergency services have been overwhelmed with an influx of callers, and we've learned that Mayor Chalmers has declared a state of emergency, seeking federal assistance through the National Guard as well as state aid." The anchor placed his finger to his ear. "I'm being told that we have some video feed coming from one of our traffic helicopters. Tom? What do you see up there?"

The screen cut to an aerial view of the city. The once-flowing veins of life that were the city's roads and highways had frozen like rivers of ice. The camera zoomed in on specific pileups and the struggling emergency vehicles attempting to navigate through the chaos. People poured out of stores and shops, the crowds wandering the streets in dazed confusion. "As you can see, traffic is shut down. Hardly any movement along the roads here as authorities scramble to try to restore order, and—wait. Go back there. Did you see that?"

The camera jerked sharply, the operator zooming in and out, the pixelated image blurring out of focus. The pilot and cameraman whispered to one another, and the picture suddenly returned to the news anchor. "With all of the confusion on the ground, I'm sure it's been difficult for police and rescue personnel, and we here at Channel 4 would urge everyone to remain calm."

Every face in the waiting room was glued to the television, the sheer size of the chaos around the city too much to fathom. *Zack is out there somewhere.* She jumped from her seat and turned to Addison. "I need you to stay here for a second, okay sweetheart?"

Addison protruded her lower lip. "Where are you going?"

Wren kissed the top of her head. "Just stay put. I'll be right back. I promise." She stepped out into the hallway, the right leading back into the emergency room where the double doors swung back and forth as staff members shuttled patients down the hall, while her left led toward the trauma and operating units where Chloe was being tended to.

Noise spouted over the intercom with requests for doctors and nurses. Wren dodged out of the way of speeding paramedics, the hall densely trafficked with the sick and wounded. The emergency lighting had kicked in, offering the hallway an eerie glow from the hospital's backup generators. Finally, she arrived at the nurses' station. "Excuse me."

Piles of papers were stacked high, engulfing the nurse in small towers. She kept her head down, the two phones on her left blinking with calls as she scribbled notes, oblivious to anything beyond the paper under her nose. Wren waved her hand under the nurse's face, which triggered an agitated sigh, and the nurse finally looked up. "Can I help you?"

"I need to get in contact with Doug Burton. He's a paramedic with station—" The nurse held up her finger then answered the phone. The thin wire of patience holding Wren's civility frayed then snapped as she reached across the counter and yanked the phone from the nurse's ear and slammed it back onto the receiver. "My son is missing, and I need to speak with the police."

The nurse angrily picked the phone back up. "Ma'am, you can have a seat, and I'll speak to you when I'm done."

Wren slammed her fist on the counter, knocking over a pen holder and spilling them to the floor. "No! You'll speak to me now!" Wren's voice silenced the noisy hallway, her outburst drawing the attention of everyone within earshot. "Now, I know you can contact dispatch, so what I need you to do is pull your head out of your ass and do something that actually matters!"

"Mrs. Burton?" The touch that accompanied the words was as light as the voice. "Your daughter is awake. You can see her now if you'd like."

The anger fled from Wren's mind as quickly as her disappearance from the nurse's station as she followed the other staff member into the recovery rooms, where she found Chloe propped up on a cot with a cluster of pillows. Her daughter's head was wrapped in a white bandage, her left forearm was in a cast, and her lips and mouth were stained purple from the popsicle dripping down her right hand. "Hi, Mommy."

Wren gently pressed Chloe's head to her chest. A doctor hovered close by with a clipboard in his hands and a stethoscope hung over his neck. He extended his hand. "Mrs. Burton?"

Wren reached over to greet him. "Is she going to be all right?

The doctor smiled. "Well, as long as she cuts back on her diet of popsicles, I think she'll pull through."

"No way," Chloe said, taking a big lick up the side.

While her daughter enjoyed the playfulness, Wren's mind still wandered the dark corners of fear she'd been worrying about since the wreck. "So sh—"

"She's fine." The doctor smiled, the tone in his voice oddly reassuring. "A minor laceration to the head, which we stitched up. No concussion. She had a fractured radius, so the cast will have to stay on for at least six weeks. Other than that, she's healthy as an ox." He gently brushed Chloe's hair back. "And from the look of that popsicle, she eats like one too."

Chloe flashed another grin, her teeth stained the same harsh purple as her treat. Wren let out a sigh, the tension slowly melting away.

"I'll be back to check on her in another hour," the doctor said. "If you need anything, just flag down one of the staff, and they'll be able to help you."

"Thank you." Wren shook his hand then was left alone. She knelt beside the bed, stroking Chloe's hair as she finished her popsicle and pointed to the cast on her arm. "You know, we could get people to sign that."

The idea perked Chloe up. "Really? Can I draw on it too?"

A welcome laugh escaped Wren's lips as the corner of her eyes crinkled. "Sure, we can do that." She kissed Chloe on the cheek. "I'm going to get your sister. She can be the first to sign it."

Chloe frowned. "Okay, but do I have to share my popsicle with her?" She batted those blue eyes, pulling the treat closer to her.

"No," Wren answered. "That's all yours." Wren left Chloe to her snack then found a nurse just outside the hall. "Could you watch my daughter for a moment while I go and get her sister?" The nurse obliged and Wren took another look at her daughter propped up on pillows, the popsicle juices draining down her hands, before leaving.

The hallways were even busier than before, the rooms she passed so full that some of the injured were forced to seek treatment in the hallways. Wren did her best to keep her gaze away from the moaning, screaming patients that lined the halls.

When Wren turned into the waiting room, she found that all the seats were empty, save for Addison in the corner. Everyone else was huddled around the television, which still aired the news broadcaster from earlier. She watched the crowd curiously, as they were seemingly entranced by the images on screen.

Addison looked up from her seat, the tiny lines on her face forming the worried look reserved for mothers and others far beyond her age. "Is Chloe okay?"

"She's fine," Wren answered. "Do you want to go and say hi?" Addison nodded, and Wren scooped her up, heading for the door. But just before she left, the panicked tone of the broadcaster stopped her dead in her tracks.

"I repeat, anyone in the downtown area of the city, please lock yourselves inside your homes, and do not venture into the street. We have eyewitness accounts as well as footage from our traffic chopper of masked individuals roaming the streets, armed with assault rifles, targeting anyone in their path. Police have warned that these individuals are incredibly dangerous and highly unstable. And— Wait. We have some new footage coming in from our traffic chopper. Tom, what are you looking at?"

Wren inched closer, her shoulders brushing against the tightly packed group, all of them drawing in a collective breath.

"Rick, a group of the terrorists are making their way

down Roosevelt. People are running, we're seeing— Oh my god, did you get that?" The camera zoomed in on three individuals circling around an elderly woman on her knees. One of them placed the tip of their gun to the back of her head and squeezed the trigger.

Wren gasped and shuddered with the rest of the huddled masses, using one hand to cover her mouth and the other to keep Addison's face away from the images.

"Tom, do the authorities know what these people want?" the news anchor asked.

"No. I've radioed with a few of the police choppers in the area, helping keep an eye on things for the law enforcement on the ground, and they haven't received an explanation as to who these people are or their demands."

Another shot of the chaos in the streets flashed, and Wren found herself drawn in to take a closer look. The background images on screen were oddly familiar. A tingling sensation crawled up the back of her spine as her mind returned to the words the traffic pilot uttered. *Roosevelt.* The next image on the screen revealed a building close to the hospital, and Wren realized where the terrorists were heading. *The medical district.*

3

Wren quickly backpedaled out of the waiting room, still carrying Addison on the way, and made a beeline for Chloe's room. They needed to get out of the hospital. *We need to get out of the city.*

The rest of the people in the waiting room were frozen in place like the traffic outside, but if the murderers on the television were looking for a place for mass casualties, then there wasn't any better location than the hospitals that comprised the medical district. Wren hastened her pace, her shoulders smacking into unsuspecting hospital staff members on her way to Chloe.

The nurse Wren left to keep Chloe company had her daughter giggling when she skidded through the door, her voice catching in her throat as she struggled to breathe. "We need to go. Now." Wren reached for her daughter's hand, pulling her from the cot as the nurse stepped aside, confused.

"Mrs. Burton, the doctor said he'd like to keep her under observation for the next twenty-four hours." She positioned herself by the door, blocking Wren's exit. "We just want to make sure Chloe is okay."

Wren set Addison on the floor next to her sister then took a quick step forward, the nurse recoiling from the speed. "You need to put this facility on lockdown. Immediately."

Chloe and Addison clutched Wren's legs, burying their faces into her skirt. The nurse placed a hand on Wren's shoulder. "Mrs. Burton, you've been through a lot. Why don't I have Doctor Avers come have a look at you?" Her fingers went to the bandage on Wren's forehead. "You've had some head trauma yourself."

Before the nurse had a chance to try anything else, Wren shoved her aside into the doorframe, wiggling past with Addison and Chloe in tow. She hurried down the hallway, the nurse shouting after her. "Mrs. Burton, stop!"

Wren ignored the stares, the shouts, and the staff members she passed who tried reaching out a hand to stop her, which she swatted away. While some of the staff tried to intercept, amidst the chaos of the bustling hospital, one more patient leaving opened up time and resources.

The nurse finally ended her chase, and Wren followed the exit signs that led her back to the emergency room, but she stopped at the nurses' station attached to the main hallway. She realized she had no car and, with the city in its current condition, no other transportation.

The phones on the nurses' desk blinked, and Wren looked around to see if anyone was watching. When she determined that the coast was clear, she pushed through the small double-door barriers and looked for the unit codes to get in contact with Doug. She shuffled through the papers, looking for the notebook she knew rested somewhere under the piles of junk.

Three quick, sharp pops sounded down the hall, and the noise stopped everyone in their tracks. Wren's heart froze as she stepped around the station's corner, the busy ER hallway becoming eerily quiet, like the calm before a storm. She shoved Chloe and Addison behind her, her pulse racing and her breaths cutting themselves short.

Machine-gunfire erupted, and screams broke through the dam of silence. The ER doors burst open, bringing a flood of people and the deafening sound of gunshots with it.

Wren scooped up both girls, trying to stay ahead of the masses spilling into the hallway, turning into a tidal wave of bodies careening around the corridors. She stumbled twice, the heels of the stampede smashing her feet, but she kept her balance even with the added pounds of her daughters swaying her center of gravity.

Patients and staff ducked into nearby rooms, slamming doors behind them, no doubt locking them, but she knew the standard hospital locks could easily be bypassed. She needed to find another place. Something more secure.

Wren's left leg cramped, and she saw others passing her. More gunshots thundered, and Wren flinched in reflex, ducking her head, the noise too close for comfort.

The next gunshot brought down a man to her left, and Wren felt a warm sprinkle of liquid hit her cheek as the man collapsed, but she didn't stop. She only kept eyeing the corner up ahead. *Just keep moving.*

The cramp in her leg loosened a bit, and Wren dug her heels into the tile, the gunfire popping like fireworks now. She turned the corner, hoping to find an exit, but the hallway only led her to an interlocking maze of more hallways. She tried a few of the first doors on her left as she passed, but they were locked. The only signage led her back into the path of the armed terrorists.

Addison and Chloe trembled in Wren's arms, their bodies vibrating in fear and shock. The back of Addison's head had bits of red speckled into her strands of black hair. Wren's heart wrenched, her concentration scattered across her mind, which raced with the tenacity of a sports car.

People rushed past, their faces showing no coherent

thoughts other than *Run*. As Wren stood there, gripped by the same icy fear that had consumed her girls, she shut her eyes, a shudder running through her at the sound of more gunfire. *Where do I go?*

The memory of a long night at work illuminated the dark recesses of her mind, and Wren snapped her eyes open, rushing toward signage down the hall on her right. She frantically scanned the labels, shifting her weight from side to side impatiently. *Where are you?* And then she saw it, nearly at the bottom, in white uppercase lettering. The ICU.

Wren turned on her heel, ricocheting against the flow of bodies that cursed and violently slammed into her, trying to shake loose her grip on the girls. "No, you're going the wrong way! Follow me!"

But Wren's voice was cut off by gunshots. She twisted her body around just in time to see one of the terrorists stepping into the hallway, firing into the crowd running in the opposite direction.

A lightness overtook Wren's body as she broke into a sprint, a few of the people around catching wind of her flight, although she wasn't sure if they meant to follower her or simply reacted to the gunfire. Regardless, when they came upon the next hallway, she pointed and veered, ten of the fleeing victims breaking off with her. "Hurry, just down here!"

The ICU was up ahead, and Wren felt a well of hope rise within her at the sight of the steel-reinforced doors she knew could withstand a heavy assault. She skidded to a stop and reached for the handle to pull them open, and the brief ray of hope quickly withered away as the door remained locked. "No, no, no."

The girls suddenly turned to lead in Wren's arms, dragging her down. The people that followed pounded on the doors in a flurry of arms and fists, screaming to be let inside. An electronic badge lock rested on the adjacent wall, close to a small nurses' station. Wren pushed past the panicked group and set the girls down, searching for any key card that would let them inside.

Wren ripped the desk apart, her fingers scouring every square inch until more gunshots echoed down the hallway, freezing her movements. The people clamoring at the doors quickly turned around as well, two of them sprinting back down the hallway in hopes of escaping the gunman, while three others collapsed to the floor, crying. The remaining five continued to pound the steel with their fists, their voices cracking from their piercing screams.

A jacket rested on the back of the chair, and Wren ripped it off, searching the pockets. Her finger grazed the thin edge of plastic, and she yanked it from the white coat. Wren glanced at the picture but not long enough to examine it thoroughly, just hoping the badge would work.

Wren seized Chloe and Addison by the hand and pulled them from behind the desk just as another bout of gunfire blanketed their hallway. The vicious echo triggered Wren to thrust Chloe and Addison back behind cover as she watched two of the people that followed her get gunned down. The others quickly jumped over their dead bodies, huddling behind the small cove of the desk.

All nine bodies shivered in one collective unit as the hallway grew silent. Wren was in the front and watched the blood slowly drain from the bodies on the floor, staining the bleached-white tile red.

"*Yuhzir!*" an angry voice shouted, his words bouncing down the hallway as violently as the bullets from his rifle. The light thump of boots sounded, followed by the click of metal. "*Al khuruj kamu jahat mamamatik!*" The voice kept the same virulent tone from before as the proximity of his words drew closer.

Wren eyed the keypad. She had no way of knowing whether the badge clutched in her hands would work, and the moment she stepped out from the cover of the wall, she'd be shot down. She looked back down to her girls, both of them sobbing silently and clutching her legs as they huddled close, their tiny bodies trembling over one another.

Wren kissed the tops of their heads, looking each of them in the eye as she said, "I love you both. So very much." She grabbed the arm of the only person in the huddle who didn't wear an expression that looked as if it would shatter into hysteria. "I'm going to make a run for the key pad. The moment you hear it beep, take my girls and run inside, got it?"

The young man couldn't have been older than her Zack. She noticed that he wore jeans with scrubs as his top. He took the badge from her hand, and for a moment she thought he was going to take her place, but he simply examined the plastic and handed it back to her. "It's an ICU badge. It'll work."

The badge lingered in the air between them before she took it, along with the fate she knew would follow. She crouched to the edge of the wall before her nerves got the better of her, and took one last look at her girls. She did her best to take in all of their features—the curves of their cheeks, the different-colored strands of their hair. She froze that image in her mind then sprinted to the keypad.

It all happened so quickly. The moment Wren made it around the corner, the access pad looked closer than before, and Wren stretched out her arm, the terrorist's shouts quick and unintelligible.

Two steps into her leap, Wren heard the gunshot. When her outstretched arm made contact with the access lock, she felt her body go limp. She collapsed, her face smacking against the floor. She wasn't sure if the badge had worked until she saw feet hurry past her line of sight.

Gunshots and screams filled the air, and Wren was afraid to look up. She was afraid to see one of her children join her on the tile, but she had to know before it was too late. She strained her neck as she lifted her cheek from the cold tile. Two more bodies joined her on the ground, but the figures were big—too big to be either Addison or Chloe.

And that was when Wren saw the two of them, carried by the man she'd left them with. She saw them only for the flash of a moment, their cheeks streaked with tears, looking down at her, their small arms and hands reaching out in desperation. Wren placed her cheek back down on the tile and smiled, knowing that her children were safe. Knowing that she'd done what she could. The cool of the floor was oddly soothing, and with her body numb, she closed her eyes.

The screams and gunshots sounded distant, and she felt herself drifting off to sleep, her fatigued mind swimming in a pool of apathy. But something kept prodding her, preventing her from submerging herself in the welcoming basin. The light tug turned to pain, and Wren became aware of her shoulder aching, followed quickly by a splitting pang in her head. A warm sensation filled her mouth, and suddenly she was awake, the taste of blood on her tongue.

A blinding white light hovered directly in front of her, and Wren knew she was lying down, her eyes squinting from the brightness. Shadowed figures penetrated her line of sight, and she heard their mumbled questions, but the piercing pain ringing through her body vanquished any attempts at answering.

Wren's body shifted and moved, though not by her own actions. Hands ran along her body, there were sharp pinches in her arms, her blouse was ripped open, and cold dots were placed on her chest. Voices drifted in and out of her consciousness, and Wren struggled to stay afloat in the churning sea of her mind.

They were shouting at her now, and Wren desperately wanted to tell them to leave her be, to let her die in peace. She wanted to go back to sleep, drift off into nothing. She was so close, so close to warmth and rest. She hadn't realized how much she needed it until now. *Just let me go.*

But then a pair of names reached her, and the names were accompanied by faces she recognized. Blue and hazel eyes shone through the darkness of her fatigue. She knew them. She... loved them.

"Ma'am, I need you to stay with me."

The voice penetrated Wren's thoughts but didn't match the eyes in her mind. They were children. They were her children. *Chloe. Addison.* The names struck her consciousness like lightning, and the wave of darkness was eradicated by the light of the room, but with it came pain—more pain than she'd ever felt in her life.

"Just hang on, Wren!"

Wren nodded, but suddenly she felt tired again. Except this fatigue was different. Her eyes shut, her dreams filled with memories of her daughters. Memories that she clung onto for dear life.

4

A dull ache in Wren's left arm disrupted her sleep. When she moved, it was as if every cell in her arm were slowly being ripped apart. A knife-like pain split her skull, and the same white light she remembered seeing before flooded her senses with brightness. She brought her right hand up to block the light and found a clamp on her index finger, a wire running from the end.

Confused, Wren examined the rest of her body and saw that her clothes had been removed and replaced with a hospital gown and that her left arm was cradled in a sling. She ripped the clamp from her finger and tossed it aside, triggering a loud beeping from a machine. She flung her legs over the side of the cot, her feet dangling as she struggled to balance on the edge.

Two hospital staff members burst into the room before Wren could stand and quickly ended the machine's rant. One of them placed a hand on Wren's shoulder. "Mrs. Burton, you need to rest."

Wren's mind felt heavy, as though her thoughts were forced to walk through thick piles of mud. "I need..." she started but lost the thought. She felt dizzy, the pain in her left arm subduing her speech.

"Mrs. Burton, do you know where you are?"

The question was asked innocently, but Wren couldn't help but notice a hint of condescension. She shook her head, steamrolling through the grogginess. "The hospital." She slid from the side of the bed, her legs wobbling and the wires attached to her chest under the hospital gown pulling her back. "My children." Wren yanked the wires out from the suction pads on her skin and stumbled to the door despite the nurses trying to restrain her. "Addison! Chloe!" She frantically spun in circles, the surroundings unfamiliar.

"Mommy!"

The voices came from Wren's left, and when she saw Addison and Chloe running to her, she collapsed to her knees, hugging both of them with her one good arm and ignoring the searing pain her body roared in defiance. Tears slid from the corners of her eyes unexpectedly, and she kissed both her girls feverishly.

Chloe gently touched the fabric of Wren's sling. "Did you hurt your arm too?"

"I did." Wren smiled, positioning her sling next to Chloe's cast. "Now we match."

"Not really," Chloe said, frowning. "Mine's all hard. Yours is soft."

"Sounds like you have a future doctor in the family."

Wren turned around and saw a man in a white coat hovering over them. He was tall, his hair thinning and showing streaks of grey and white intermixed with what stubborn brown refused to age. He knelt down beside the girls. "Hey, your mommy and I need to talk, so why don't you go play with Nurse Malla for a little bit?"

The nurse appeared, gently taking both girls by the hand. Both of them offered Wren one last hug, and she watched them disappear down the hall until they turned the corner out of view.

The doctor led Wren back to the bed, where she required help to climb back on the thin mattress. Whatever energy propelled her to leave her bed had evaporated, leaving her drained and hungry for rest.

"How are you feeling, Mrs. Burton?" the doctor asked, flipping through a few pieces of paper on a clipboard.

"Hurt." Wren laid her head back on the pillow, closing her eyes, but a gunshot wakened her. A brief rush of adrenaline surged through her, and everything came flooding back. The masked men. The blood. The bullets. Carrying her children through the stampede in the hallways until they ended at the ICU doors.

"It's okay." The doctor put his hand on her shoulder, easing her back down on her pillow. "Those men are still in the hospital, but we're safe here. The doors are reinforced steel. And that key card you found was the only one missing from our inventory after we locked the doors." He returned his attention to the clipboard. "It was smart making a run for it here. You've worked in hospitals before?"

"No," Wren answered, shaking her head. "I designed one in college." She cleared her throat. "I'm an architect." Although the pain in her arm made her wish she'd remembered the security procedures for a hospital lockdown sooner. "Federal guidelines require that all hospitals constructed after 2010 have security features built into all of their critically weak departments in case of contamination or terrorist activities." She looked at her arm. "I was shot?

"Yes. The bullet nicked your humeral shaft, but it went straight through." He aimed his pen at her head. "You smacked your head pretty good, though." He gingerly opened her eyelids, shining a light in each of them. "You have a concussion."

Wren eyed the badge hanging from the front of his coat,

and she squinted to read it. "Dr. Reyes, what's going on out there? Have you heard anything? Have the police arrived?"

"You don't need to worry, Mrs. Burton." The doctor's tone was dismissive. "We have protocols in place for things like this. The authorities are doing what is necessary. In the meantime, you and your girls are safe. Now, get some rest, and I'll be back to check on you in a little bit."

Before Wren had a chance to put in another word, Reyes was gone, and she was too tired to try to shout after him. Her mind raced with worry, but fatigue soon took over, and she drifted off to sleep.

* * *

WHEN WREN WOKE, her body still ached, but her mind had regained its plasticity. She flagged down one of the hospital staff and managed to change from the hospital gown into a spare T-shirt and pants one of the nurses had in her bag. Once dressed, she went in search of her daughters.

Wren found her girls tucked away in one of the empty patient rooms, busy entertaining themselves. Chloe had stumbled upon a few of the toys the ICU staff kept for the children of any parents they treated, and Addison was fiddling with her camera, filming anyone that granted her access.

The past few hours had seen the excitement of the hospital decrease dramatically. After the initial onslaught from the terrorists, most of the screams had ended, and only every twenty minutes or so was there another gunshot, the sound dulled by the tons of concrete and steel between Wren and her children. A chill ran through her as considered what those shots meant.

The ICU had a few doctors and nurses on staff, some of them already in hiding. Doctor Reyes, who had been in surgery, hadn't even heard the screams and gunshots until one of the staff came and told him. With his hands trying to save a man's life, he told them to lock the unit down.

Of the original ten that had followed Wren, only four remained alive: the man who'd carried Addison and Chloe inside, a middle-aged woman with dried blood still on her face who refused to speak, a young woman, and an older gentlemen with no hair except for the ring of white that stretched around the back of his head from ear to ear. Most of their eyes still held the same hollow emptiness, the shock of the attack fresh in their minds, torturing what shreds of sanity they had left.

Once Wren was up and about, she heard arguments between small groups of people about wanting to leave, while others were hell-bent on staying put. Most of the staff felt it was their duty to stay with the patients to make sure they were properly cared for. Most everyone who wasn't staff wanted out.

Wren walked to the main ICU doors, keeping away from the windows on her approach in case any of the terrorists were stationed nearby. The closer she drew to the entrance, the slower her steps became. Each door had a strip of thick-paned glass built in. She placed her finger on the cracked glass, the surface still smooth despite the thousands of tiny fault lines the bullets had inflicted.

It was nearly six o'clock, which meant she and the girls had been inside that hospital for nearly three hours. Despite Dr. Reyes's assurance that help was coming, she thought it would have happened by now. And if the roads were still blocked as they'd been before, there wasn't any guarantee the terrorists wouldn't find a way into the ICU before help arrived. *We can't stay here.*

Wren found Dr. Reyes with one of the nurses, knowing it was his counsel the staff had listened to in the first place. "Could I speak to you for a moment?" Specks of blood still dotted the doctor's coat and pants along with a few larger blobs on his chest. She wasn't sure why he hadn't changed.

"What is it?" Reyes's clipped his short as he sipped from a Styrofoam cup. Dark circles imprinted themselves under his eyes, which she hadn't noticed before.

"I understand your need to stay with your patients, but there are some of us here who need to leave. My son—"

"Mrs. Burton, I assure you we are safe." Reyes pointed to the front of the ICU, where the entrance had been redecorated with bullets. "The only way we go out those doors is when the police arrive."

"Doctor, I don't think you know what's going on out there. The city is gridlocked; I barely managed to get my daughter here in an ambulance. There isn't a guarantee the police will come, and if these people want some type of ransom, then—"

"Help is coming. Whatever's happening in the city will blow over. There are procedures that we have to follow." Reyes showered his wisdom like he was speaking to a child, the arrogance thick in his tone.

It could have been the doctor's words, the way he said them, the events that had unfolded over the past few hours, or the fact that she hadn't eaten anything all day, but she shoved the doctor as hard as she could, despite only being able to do so with one arm. "Those men shot at me and my *daughters.* They put to slaughter everyone in the emergency room. I will not sit here and wait for some person five hundred miles away to give an order about a situation they know nothing about! These people aren't taking hostages. They're spreading a holocaust."

Reyes chucked his coffee cup against the wall, the cold, brown liquid splattering against the blue paint. "Lady, there are thirty patients in this facility who are in critical, life-threatening condition and need attention and observation around the clock. I need my staff to perform at one hundred percent, and given the fact that you and your girls don't have the prospect of being in danger in the foreseeable future, I would have to tell you that I don't give a shit about what you do or do not feel, or what you think or do not think. We're safe where we are."

Wren noticed a crowd had gathered, drawn by the raised volume of their voices. "We're at the gallows waiting for the executioner to give the signal. We are *not* safe." She walked away, leaving the doctor fuming, and brushed past the hospital staff wordlessly. She didn't care what she had to do. She was getting her girls out of that building before it was too late.

"Hey."

The whisper came from a room on her right, and Wren saw the young man who had taken her girls inside the ICU. He motioned for her to step in, and she complied. He led her into a small room where one of the ICU patients lay unconscious, machines she'd never even seen before hooked up to the woman's body.

"You don't think anyone is coming?" He kept his voice low, even in the privacy of the room. He was shorter than Wren, and the fact that he stood with a hunch only lowered his stature.

"No. I don't." One of the machines beeped, and the nurse hushed her, waiting to see if anyone would come. But no one did. "And I don't think whoever has control of this place is going to let anyone live. What happened in the ER, I..." Sudden flashes of bullets, blood, and screams pulsated like a strobe light in her mind. "No one is coming."

"I told the doctor the same thing. But he's not all wrong. There *are* procedures for lockdown that we have in place, and we do have a procedure for hostage situations."

"This isn't a hostage situation."

"Yeah, I was getting that feeling too." The nurse paced

back and forth, cradling his chin in his hand, rubbing his skin raw.

Wren looked at the woman lying in the hospital bed, her head shaved, needles and wires stuck in her arm and tubes shoved down her nose and mouth. From the looks of her, she couldn't have been much older than Wren, but with her skin so pallid and her body thin from whatever disease inflicted her, it was hard to be certain. The woman looked so still and quiet, almost as if she were already dead.

"The moment I open those doors, Doctor Reyes will trigger a quarantine lockdown, and once that happens, no one is going anywhere. But there might be a work-around."

"Then hurry," Wren replied. "I'm not sure how much time we have left."

The nurse headed for the door, but before he was out of earshot, she called to him. "Do you know what happened to her?" She stared at the patient, unsure of what would kill her first: the disease or the madmen in control of the hospital.

"No."

"Can she even hear anything? Does she know we're here?"

"I'm not sure. I never worked in the ICU before. I only graduated nursing school a few months ago. This is my first week at this hospital."

Wren wondered if she had family, a husband, or friends that came to see her. If she did, she imagined the only reason they weren't here was because of the power failure. With emergency vehicles barely able to navigate through traffic, she doubted any non-emergency personnel would be able to move through that mess. Her mind suddenly drifted to Doug and the divorce papers. She knew he was out in the chaos, on a call, trying to save someone's life—perhaps a woman just like herself, trapped somewhere. But all of those calls, all of those long nights, had taken a toll on both of them.

Wren finally left, leaving the woman in peace and to whatever fate awaited her. She remained quiet on the walk back to the front of the ICU. She turned the corner to the main hallway, where the entrance doors were located, and saw Addison near the windows. Her first instinct was to scream, but she bit her tongue, afraid the noise would draw attention. She broke out into a hobbled, pain-filled sprint.

Addison was fiddling with her camera when Wren yanked her away from the doors in a panicked hurry, keeping the two of them low as her daughter dangled from her one good arm. "Mom! What are you doing?" Addison squirmed and fidgeted, clutching the camera in her hands.

"Addison, listen to me. You don't *ever* go near that door." Wren shook her daughter's shoulders. "You scared me half to death."

Addison lowered her head. "I'm sorry." She opened the camera and extended it to Wren. "I heard people outside the hallway, so I went to see them. I thought if I could get them on camera doing something bad like they do on TV, then it would help."

Wren's expression softened. She couldn't fault her daughter for trying. "That was very brave of you, but you have to be careful. These people will hurt you if they see you, so you have to stay hidden." She took the camera and rewound the playback.

The picture was shaky, Addison fumbling the device in her hands. Most of the footage was of the door, but when Addison lifted the camera high above her head, Wren saw two terrorists, one of them carrying a bag. The two were speaking quickly, their motions hurried.

Wren squinted at the tiny screen, trying to figure out what they were pulling from the pack, but the screen kept wavering back and forth. She paused the film then rewound it again and zoomed in for a closer look.

The devices were small, brick-like, and she had to watch it a few times before she realized what she was looking at. Once it struck her, she slammed the camera shut and dragged Addison back to Nurse Malla, who was still watching Chloe.

"There you are, Addison," Malla said. "We wondered where you ran off to."

"Keep the girls here," Wren said, ignoring the nurse's apologies, then turned to both of her daughters. "You two do *not* move. You hear me?" Wren kept her tone strict, and both of them nodded.

Wren clutched the camera tightly, searching the hallways for Doctor Reyes and the nurse she spoke with earlier. She found the doctor in one of the patient rooms, a cluster of nurses around him, all of them casting disapproving glares at her presence. "We have to get everyone out of here now."

Reyes didn't look up from his clipboard, scribbling down notes. "I told you before, Mrs. Burton, we have procedures in place for things like this. Everything will be resolved soon."

"I know. In fact, the people that shot up the hospital are taking care of that right now. And we need to get out of here before they decide to detonate the bombs they're placing in the hallways."

5

Wren tore apart the desks on the nurses' stations, looking for as many pieces of paper as she could tuck under her good arm along with a few pens then rushed to the conference room where Reyes had gathered the ICU staff.

While she spread the papers out over the table , her mind was already sketching the outline of the building from what she remembered of her entrance. "I need to know every staircase that you know of on this floor, where it leads to, and any other security doors that will be locked."

Wren stabilized the elbow of her wounded arm then drew perfectly straight lines without the aided effort of a ruler. The basic building structure took shape, and she noticed the quiet. Wren brought the pen in her hand to rest and looked to the strained faces, half of them pale and frozen, the others confused in disbelief, and none more so than Reyes. The shock from the video had stripped them all of the invisible shields of protocols and procedures. "Doctor."

Beads of sweat rolled down Reyes's temple as he stepped forward and knuckled his fists into the table. The same tremor in his arms also shook his voice. "The first available right turn out of the ICU doors is a hallway that leads to a corridor where the hospital's cardiac center is located. There won't be any security restrictions there."

"How many rooms?" Wren asked, offering a rough sketch of the unit and marking notes in the corner of the paper.

"Twenty-one," the doctor answered.

"Twenty-five." One of the nurses stepped forward, her voice no louder than a mouse's squeak. "I used to work that rotation before I was moved to the ICU. Twelve rooms on the left, and thirteen on the right. The stairway at the end of the hall will be locked, though."

"Keyless entry?" Wren asked.

The nurse shook her head, and Wren tightened her grip on the pen. Any door with a function beyond the doctor's ID card was useless. Wren finished the sketch, scribbling dead end over the unit. "That's good. What about the rest of the corridor?"

The doctor rubbed his forehead till his skin turned raw and pink, an exhausted sigh escaping his lips. "Everything leads back to the front of the hospital near the ER. It takes up nearly all of the first level. There's a staircase on the corner, but it's blocked off because of construction. The only way out is the way you came in."

Wren slammed her pen onto the table. Anger and adrenaline rocketed her thoughts into overdrive, and she ran through every possible design that an architect would have used for the hospital. And while she wrestled with the logistics of how to escape, the rumble of panic spread through the others like wildfire.

"They're just going to blow us up?"

"Somebody has to be doing something, right?"

"We need to get out of here. I can't die here. I won't die here!"

Every shrill outcry only compounded the next person's despair. Wren shut her eyes, turning every stone in her mind over for anything that could aid in their escape. The groans of despair rumbled louder, reaching a crescendo.

"Enough!" Wren's cheeks flushed red, and her roar rolled over the room, casting everyone in silence. "This is what they want." She pointed beyond the halls of the locked ICU doors. "We let fear take control of us, and we lose whatever reason we have left. They want..." *The bombs.* Wren pushed past the nurses and cleared a path back to her sketches. "We need to go down."

"Down?" Reyes asked. "We're on the first floor."

"I know." Wren extended her sketch below the ER, creating another level and stretching the staircases underneath the building. "We're going below it."

Everyone gathered closer, all of them clinging to the floating raft that was Wren's mind, watching her deft hands bring the paper underneath her palm to life. She sketched notes in different corners, labeling utilities and their functions, creating a path that would lead them to safety. She dropped the pen and smoothed the paper over the table. "Whenever a building is set for demolition, the goal is to have the building implode on itself, and a part of that strategy involves the foundation."

"So, what? These guys are looking to detonate the building safely?" Reyes asked.

"No, not with the placement of devices I saw in the hallway," Wren answered. "It's sporadic, flashy. If they do bring the building down, it won't be pretty. But"—she pointed to the subterranean level on her sketch—"this hospital has utility functions below the main floor. A friend of mine worked on this place, and he designed it to give the hospital more of a streamlined appearance in functionality. And every floor is required to have an emergency exit, even below ground. We get to the utilities room, and we have our way out."

"I've been in the staircases," one of the staff members said. "I haven't seen one that goes below the ER."

"Well, one of them does." Wren leaned back over the table, examining her sketch. "And we have to figure out which one."

With at least a chance of escape, the group exhaled a cloud of anxiety-ridden relief. Wren finished her sketches after a few quick interviews with the staff to add to her drawings then duplicated the maps by the number of staircases that they needed to investigate.

The cluster of radios at the nurses' station were checked for a charge then distributed among the six groups of five. "Make sure you're on channel six. The moment you get to the lower level, you let the rest of us know. Keep it short, and make it quick. If the terrorists are listening in, they'll know what we know." She looked back to her girls, still huddled by the desk, Addison stroking her sister's hair. "Surgical instruments." Wren looked back to the group. "We need something to protect ourselves."

A nurse separated himself from the group. "I'll take a look in the supply closet." The weapons were distributed to every group member, and as Wren went over everyone's route and role one last time, she noticed the tremor in every hand white-knuckled over the silver of surgical instruments.

"Wren." Reyes snuck up behind her, flanked by three nurses. For a moment, Wren thought he would try to stop her, and she wedged the knife between herself and the doctor. "We've chosen to stay behind."

The knife dipped in Wren's hand. "What? Doctor, I told you that whatever procedures you think—"

"It's not about procedures," the doctor interrupted. "I took an oath. There are still sick people in this unit, and I won't abandon them. Not when there's still a possibility of rescue."

"Doctor, these people, they—"

"I know." Reyes adjusted his glasses, straightening the bloodstained white coat, which he wore more like a suit of armor. The finality in the doctor's words marked his own grave, but Wren didn't push the subject any further. Whatever duty Reyes still felt he owed was his to fulfill, just as her duty propelled her to keep her children safe.

The groups quickly gathered by the door, and Wren cupped her one good hand around Addison's and Chloe's, keeping the knife gripped painfully in her left. "We're going to get out of here, okay girls? But when we leave, we have to be very quiet. We can't talk at all, and you always need to hold on to one another and stay with me. I know this is scary, but we have to be brave." She offered their hands a reassuring squeeze, their soft skin warm against the palm of her hand. "Let's go."

Wren's knuckles whitened over the blade's handle, and she struggled to keep a lighter grip on the girl's wrists. She peered through the small sliver of window the ICU doors offered and checked the hallway, the heat from her breath reflecting off the door and back onto her lips.

Blood and bodies lined the floor of the hallway, but the living were nowhere in sight. Wren shouldered the door open and kept low, pushing both Addison and Chloe's faces into her pants legs, trying to spare her daughters any more trauma. "Keep your eyes shut, girls."

Wren guided the three of them around the puddles of blood and outstretched arms and legs sprawled in every direction. The odor from the bodies on the floor mingled with the sterile stench of hospital disinfectant, and Wren tucked her nose into the crook of her shoulder.

Once they arrived at the corridor, the groups split, each heading in their own direction, huddling close to one another, silent through the halls save for the light shuffle of feet.

The body count only grew the closer Wren moved to the ER. Some lay face down, but the ones that faced up still had their eyes open, gazing into the false white light flickering above. Wren shuddered at the sight of them, and she felt the same warm spray of blood from the man who was shot in front of her. She involuntarily wiped her cheek on the sleeve in the crook of her elbow as though bugs had crawled on her face, their small legs tickling her skin.

A faint echo of voices froze Wren in her tracks, and she shoved the girls behind her and against the wall. Shifting the blade to her good arm, she aimed toward the sound's origins. Her breathing grew labored, and she looked behind her, debating whether to turn back. The hallway was door-free, leaving her completely exposed, with nothing but the gritty texture of the walls to claw.

Then, slowly, the voices faded, and the hammering in her chest subsided. Wren dropped her arm, and both Addison and Chloe sobbed quietly into her stomach, flinging their arms around her waist. "Shh. It's okay, girls." She kept her voice a whisper. "We need to keep moving." The girls offered little protest as Wren pulled them to the end of the hallway, where they passed more bodies and bombs.

Wren crouched low before she poked her head around the corner, quickly looking in both directions of the hallway's intersection. The trail of bodies grew thicker toward the ER entrance, where the door to the staircase just so happened to be positioned on the left. She turned back to the girls, both of them still huddled close to her leg, their little bodies trembling. She gently peeled their faces off her shirt, now sticking with sweat and tears. "Addison, do you remember that scary movie you saw over the summer that you watched at your friend Katie's house?"

Addison nodded, sniffling. "You said you didn't want me to watch it, but her parents said that I could."

Wren wiped a tear from her daughter's cheek. "And you

remember how everything you saw was just pretend? It wasn't real?" Again she nodded. "I need you to do that again. Whatever you see, just know that's it pretend, okay? You don't need to be scared." Wren turned to Chloe. "And that goes for you too. Everything is pretend. Now, stay close, and remember to keep quiet."

Wren wrapped her fingers around their thin wrists, coaxing them around the corner, her glance shifting between the staircase door and the girls. They both kept their eyes glued on her as Wren maneuvered them around the outstretched legs and arms of the dead. Chloe tripped over a hand, but Wren caught her, and when her daughter glanced down at the arm attached to it, soundless tears burst from her eyes.

The staircase door was only a few feet away but was blocked by a body with a smeared bloody handprint that stretched from the handle to the floor. Wren huddled the girls together next to the wall, and they clutched onto one another tightly, hiding their faces in each other's shoulders.

With her right arm, Wren grabbed the fallen nurse by the wrist, dragging him from the doorway. She strained against the heavy body, a trail of fresh blood smearing the floor with each pull. With the doorway finally clear, she reached for the handle just as harsh, foreign voices echoed from behind the ER doors.

In her panic, Wren let loose the door, and it clanged shut with a bang. She grabbed both girls by the hand, yanking them down the hall, jiggling the door handles along the way, each one of them locked. She tripped over a leg in her haste, twisting her ankle, and nearly fell but caught her balance with an outstretched arm. Her fingers grazed a door handle that gave way to her pull, and she ducked inside, shutting the door just before the masked men burst into the hallway.

The room was dark, and it took a moment for her eyes to

adjust, but when they did, Wren found they were alone. She hurried Addison and Chloe under the empty patient bed, covering them with whatever she could find as harsh, hasty-tongued words flooded the hallway.

"Stay quiet. And don't move. No matter what." Wren crawled to the door, locking it, still clutching the knife in her hand. She huddled herself in the corner, her fingers flexing against the handle. She pushed herself from the floor, the back of her shirt sliding against the wall. *Keep walking. Just pass by.*

The mumbled jargon stopped right outside the door, and Wren's eyes locked on the handle. She reached for it instinctively, locking her arm in place, raising the tip of the blade high above her head, every fiber of her muscles strung tight as a steel cable. A jerk rattled the steel handle, and her skin burst with sweat, the handle now warm and slick under her palm.

Wren tensed her shoulder and arm, shouldering the door to offer more resistance. The handle shook violently as more jargon spewed through the door cracks along the frame, until finally Wren felt the handle loosen, the grip on the other side given up. The muffled voices moved farther down the hall, and Wren slowly uncurled her shaking fingers from the levered piece of steel.

The two bumps that were Addison and Chloe underneath the blankets of the hospital bed poked out their heads then scooted hurriedly to their mother's aid. She grabbed both of them, squeezing them tight, and felt the hot burst of water seep from the corners of her closed eyes. She took slow breaths, forcing herself to regain control. It wasn't over until they were out of the building.

The radio in Wren's pocket crackled, followed by a faint voice. "Staircase three does not have a level below the first floor."

The small rock of hope that Wren stood upon fractured slightly at the news, but it refocused her will. She kissed both girls then rose, keeping her daughters behind her as she opened the door, checking the hallway.

With their path clear in all directions, she hurried down the hallway back to the staircase door, leaping over the corpses in the hallway and pulling the girls with her. Their feet scurried down the steps in the staircase. Wren looked up through the narrow shaft between the banisters that circled all the way to the top of the building but saw none of the masked terrorists.

Wren's heart rate returned to the jackhammer-like pace from before as they neared the bottom of the stairwell, her feet finding the steps faster the closer they moved. *Let it be here. Please.* When she pivoted left, her heart leapt as the staircase continued, leading down into the utilities level. She fumbled for the radio, pulling the girls down the steps. "I found it. Staircase two."

Static flooded from the speaker when Wren removed her hand from the talk button, and the acoustics of the staircase bounced the harsh tones around the walls. She quickly lowered the volume, and a quivering voice replaced the harsh static. "*Help.*"

Wren stopped, listening to the same words repeat over and over like a parrot. "Please. Help. Help me. Please. *Someone's coming.*"

Just before the last transmission ended, Wren heard the same foreign tongues from earlier. *Turn off the radio. Be quiet. Stay hidden.* But Wren's thoughts fell on deaf ears as the broadcaster continued their bumbling rant, heightening their hysteria with the growing voices of the subversives. "God, no, please, I don't want to die!"

The transmission ended with the ring of a gunshot, and Wren froze, the staircase echoing with the gunfire. She glanced back up the staircase to the doorway into the ER.

The door swung open and was slammed into the wall by three rifle-wielding terrorists in masks, and the moment their eyes found Wren, she sprinted through the utilities staircase door.

Both girls struggled to keep pace with Wren, their tiny legs too short for her long strides. She stopped, lowering herself so they could both wrap their arms around her neck. "Hang on tight!" When she lifted them off the ground, her left arm felt as though it would snap in half, but the growing voices of the terrorists in pursuit offered her the resolve to push on.

Wren pounded her heels into the floor, her arms and legs growing numb from the rush of adrenaline coursing through her veins. The heat from the equipment quickly soaked her in sweat as she weaved in and out of the large water heaters, humming generators, and buzzing electrical boxes.

Gunshots rang out, but the terrorist's foreign shouts failed to penetrate the raucous noise of the utilities. Emergency signs glowed on the walls, guiding her to salvation. More gunshots ripped through the air, and Wren shuddered with every percussive blast ricocheting off the heavy machinery.

Wren turned a corner, and the exit was in sight, a straight shot from her current location, less than twenty yards. The muscles in her legs burned as she used what energy remained to push herself the final stretch, giving it everything she had, her lungs on fire. Sparks flashed to her left in time with the sound of another gunshot, and she flinched, clutching Chloe tighter. She pivoted her hips, shifting her shoulder into the door's exit bar.

More bullets peppered the doorframe as sunlight flooded the utility room. Wren squinted from the brightness but refused to let up her pace and stumbled forward blindly. More shouts and bullets thundered behind her as her eyes adjusted to the light outside, the landscape slowly taking shape. She dashed behind cars in a parking lot, and for the first time looked behind her. The masked men had stopped at the door, screamed and fired into the air, then rushed back inside.

Wren collapsed to the pavement, Addison and Chloe falling with her, the flash of strength and stamina depleted. Both girls crawled over her, but Wren's mind was so fogged with exhaustion that their words were incomprehensible. She rested her head back against the hot metal of a sedan's door, feeling the heat of the sun beat upon her face. But the quiet was short-lived.

Explosives detonated in the building, splintering steel and concrete and shattering the glass windows, which transformed to shards of deadly rain. Wren grabbed both girls tight once more, feeling the rocking percussions shake the earth as if the very depths of hell had opened up. The explosions erupted quickly, like firecrackers. BOOM, BOOM, BOOM!

A high-pitched whine filled Wren's ears as she choked on the thin layer of dust that rained over her and the girls. She wiped her face with her shoulder but only smeared the dust around. She glanced back at the hospital, which was scarred and cracked from the detonations.

Smoke billowed from the broken windows, whose glass reflected the sun from the pavement. Fault lines ran up and down the side of the building like spider webs, some thick enough to lie inside. And then the building moaned, the cry bellowing from its core, and Wren knew it was coming down. "Girls, run!" Like the building, her voice cracked and faltered as the girls sprinted with her through the parking lot.

Thousands of tons of concrete and steel deteriorated to nothing but ash in a matter of seconds, the once-proud structure unleashing a cloud of dust that consumed cars, trees, and bushes. Wren glanced behind her, both Addison's and Chloe's arms stretched as she dragged them behind her, their short legs struggling to keep up with her pace. "Cover your mouths, and shut your eyes!" Wren kept her eyes on both girls as the dust cloud consumed them till she saw nothing but darkness. The only confirmation her girls were still with her was the touch of their hands.

6

Sirens. Screams. Shattering glass. Crying. Horns. Grinding metal. Confusion. Fear. All of it was too surreal. Whatever thin layer of order that kept the city from slipping into chaos had dissolved. Everywhere Wren looked, people were scrambling, running, hiding, looking for a safe place to wait it out.

Wren shook her hair, bits of dust from the hospital remains swirling from her head and shoulders to the ground. She walked down back streets, avoiding the chaos that was the main roads, her hand still clutching the small surgical knife. She caught a broken reflection of them passing an electronics store that had been looted, the shelves inside bare save for a few cords and smaller items.

She, Addison, Chloe were covered from head to toe in a layer of greyish-brown dust. They stumbled forward like ghosts in a dying city. Both her daughters hung their heads, their feet shuffling against the pavement, their small bodies exhausted and stretched beyond their limits.

"Mommy, I'm hungry," Chloe said.

"I'm tired," Addison added.

"I know, but we have to keep moving." *But to where?*

They'd walked ten blocks since the hospital collapsed, and she hadn't seen anyone resembling authority, only roaming crowds looking for safety they all hoped still existed.

The afternoon sky swarmed with helicopters above, the thump of their blades pestering Wren's ears like mosquitoes in the summer. She looked up, and their small figures dotted the blue sky like flies on paper.

Wren brought the girls to a stop at a street corner, where remnants of car wrecks littered the roads, some of which still blocked traffic. Everywhere she looked, the power was still out. No street lights, no signs, no televisions—anything that was plugged into the grid was shut down. She checked her phone, praying for a message from either her son or her husband, but the signal on her phone had died. She snapped it shut, cursing under her breath. *Think.*

Intersection signs rested just above Wren's head, and she took a step back to get a better look, squinting from the glare of the sun. *West Fifteenth and South Throop Street.* Less than half a block, and they'd run into South Blue Island Avenue. A fire station was just up that road, where her husband spent his first three years in the department. With everything crumbling around her, she figured that was as safe a place as any to start.

Wren approached the station wearily. Both bay doors were open, their spaces void of the massive rescue vehicles that usually rested inside. Attached to the bay garages were the living quarters, a two-story brick building with Station No. 18 engraved in gold lettering across the front.

Wren brought the girls inside the bay doors, praying that someone was still here. She reached for the doorknob that led from the garage to the living quarters, but it was locked. She pounded the door with her palm, dust shaking from her sleeve with every strike. "Hello! I need help! Please! Hello!"

Every unanswered smack and scream only heightened Wren's desperation. It was as though she were slowly being lowered into icy water, paralyzed and unable to swim. The water was inching up her chest, its frozen needles pricking the tender flesh of her neck, now gliding up her chin, touching her lips, freezing her tongue, filling her nose and lungs, the ability to breathe slipping away.

The lock on the other side of the door clicked, and the door swung open, and Wren felt herself pulled from the icy waters. "Wren?" A heavyset, mustached, middle-aged man stood in the width of the doorway. "Is that you?"

Wren fumbled for words, but when they escaped her, she simply flung herself onto Nathan's chest and squeezed tight. When she finally pulled herself back, the girls were still huddled behind her, staring up at the large man. Wren shook her head, trying to compose herself. "Nathan, I'm sorry, it's just... I didn't have anywhere else to go."

Nathan stepped aside. "Are you guys all right?" He gingerly examined the sling on Wren's arm as Wren trailed dusty footprints into the station.

Wren looked down at her arm, nearly forgetting the sling was there. "Yeah, I was at the hospital." The events blurred together in her mind. "We had a car accident when the power went out." The girls stuck close to her legs, and she tried peeling them off, but neither would budge. "My phone hasn't had any service, and it's... just been crazy out there."

Nathan took a seat next to the radio station. The sounds of emergency operators flooded through the speakers, and he turned the volume down. "Yeah, it's definitely been busy. I had to turn on the generators when the power went out. It's like that across the entire city, even stretching out into the suburbs."

So even if I went home, there still wouldn't be any power. Addison tugged at Wren's pant leg, more dust falling to the carpet. "What is it, sweetheart?"

Addison gestured for her to bend down then cupped her

hand and whispered into Wren's ear. "I have to go to the bathroom."

Wren looked around as Nathan barked codes through his receiver, and spotted the stalls down the hallway. "Okay, go on, sweetie." She pointed Addison in the direction and sat Chloe on the couch, while she went into the kitchen and wet a cluster of paper towels. "Close your eyes, baby."

The paper towels only smeared the dust around, but after a few minutes Chloe's cheeks returned to the soft, puffy white flesh that Wren recognized. "There, that's better."

"I'm still dirty," Chloe said, looking down at her clothes and rubbing her hands up and down the front of her shirt. "When can we go home?"

Wren stroked Chloe's hair back behind her ears, little smears of dust still streaking down her forehead. "Soon, baby." It was a lie she desperately wanted to be true, but if there were more of whoever assaulted the hospital, she wasn't sure if there would be a home to return to or not.

Wren found a blanket and tucked both of them on the couch together, their eyelids fluttering open and closed. "You two stay here while I talk to Nathan, okay? I'll just be right over there." Two sleepy yawns and nods later, and the girls were passed out on the couch.

Nathan smiled as Wren walked over. "How old are they now?"

"Nine and five." Wren took a seat in the second chair next to the radio equipment, fiddling with her hands. "I haven't been able to reach Doug. Can you—"

"I've tried." Nathan twitched his mustache upon answering. He swiveled in his chair, grabbing a notebook out of the drawer next to him. "But that doesn't mean he's not okay. It's been crazy out there, and even the city's backup generators have been wonky lately. I'm surprised the ones we had here started up." He flipped through the pages of the notebook, and Wren leaned over to get a closer look.

Hundreds of lines of small-four digit numbers lined the paper in columns, followed by texts explaining what each of them meant. Nathan flushed a bashful grin. "I'm not the normal dispatcher here. I'm still just volunteering. Heck, I haven't been called in since Doug worked here."

"Do you know what's going on out there? Have you heard anything?" Wren's first-hand experiences had tainted her viewpoint. For all she knew, the masked men who'd destroyed the hospital were the only terrorists left in the city.

"It's not good." Nathan's mustache lowered with his frown. He inched closer, the chair squeaking lightly under his girth. He hunched over and kept his voice down. "I have a friend who lives outside the city, who I met through my CB radio, and he says that whoever is doing this has been planning it for a while." A grin crept up the side of his cheek, and he pulled a map from behind him. "Here, look. Every circle you see is a report of shootings where paramedics have been sent. Look at the sights."

The red circles overlapped one another and nearly turned the entire map a shade of crimson. "Christ." She traced her finger over the wrinkled fold lines, examining each location. "Industrial district. Transformer stations. Water pressure lines." She looked up. "They're all public utilities."

"Exactly." The fire volunteer poked his pudgy forefinger into the map. "You think this is some ragtag team of gangs and thugs?" He wagged his finger and shook his head. "And whatever they have planned next will be even worse."

Wren collapsed back into the chair, her shoulders sagging, her mind racing through all of the possibilities. She shifted her gaze to her girls, asleep on the couch. "This is impossible."

Nathan shrugged, returning to his work at the dispatch. "Oh, it's entirely possible. And I'd bet my last dollar that all this is just a smokescreen for something bigger."

Wren jolted, her pocket vibrating from her phone. She

fumbled her fingers inside and quickly pulled the mobile out. Texts from her son pinged in, one after another, only one signal bar on her phone. She flipped through them, reading them hurriedly.

"Mom, help." "I'm stuck." "Can't move." "An explosion." "Please. Help me."

Wren covered her mouth, tears cresting at the bottom of her eyes. She answered quickly before her signal was lost again. *"Where are you?"* She gripped the phone with both hands, her eyes locked on the screen as she waited for any type of reply. The one signal bar on her phone disappeared, and with it, her son. "No." The cold waters of panic flowed through her once again. She rushed around the station, holding her phone, cursing, praying, thrusting the device in different directions in hopes of finding the signal once more. But after exhausting the area, her hands fell to her sides. *My son.*

Flashes of atrocities she'd only seen in her nightmares harassed her mind. Had the group that caused all of this taken him? Was he hurt? *Stop it.* The texts meant he was still alive, and she had to find him. She rushed over to Nathan, who was still busy relaying updated information to units out in the field. "You guys can lock in on cellular signals, right?"

"Um, yeah." His neck wiggled back and forth in rhythm with his uncertainty. "I mean, it depends if the phone is on and how many of the towers are still operational."

"I need you to find a phone for me. The number is four, seven, nine, eight, three, nine, one."

Nathan hesitated, the radio buzzing with chatter. "Wren, I'm sure Doug is fine, and I don't know if I'm even authorized to do this, and it's getting pretty busy—"

"Nathan, it's Zack. He's in trouble. He's stuck out there alone in all this." Wren gripped Nathan's arm. "*Please.* I have to find him."

More radio chatter blared from the speakers, and

Nathan's expression softened as he reached for a pen and paper, jotting down the first three digits of her son's cell. "What was the last part again?"

Wren's eyes glistened wetly, and she repeated it while she white-knuckled the back of Nathan's chair, nearly tearing through the cloth with her nails. Once the numbers were punched in his computer system, the screen lit up with pings on a gridded map of the city. "It'll take a minute to hone in, and like I said, that's only if all of the towers are still operational." He smudged a fat fingerprint on the screen. "See there? That one is down. And this one."

Wren drew in a breath. *Let me find him.* The computer pinged but then flashed an error message, and Wren's heart sank to the pit of her stomach. "What happened?" The words escaped her mouth like the final wish of an inmate on death row.

Nathan clicked the message, enlarging a portion of the map. "Well, it looks like we have a general location, but the program is having trouble locking it down."

A ray of light broke through the wall of cemented fear surrounding Wren's mind. She pushed Nathan aside, examining the location then finding the area on the map, and her brief moment of hope was crushed by a wave of realization. "Oh god."

Wren backed away from the screen, the map slipping from her fingers and falling to the floor. Nathan rolled forward, picking up the map, making the connection between the computer's coordinates and the red circles. Zack was in the industrial district.

7

Wren tucked the girls into Nathan's cot, the two of them still holding on to each other tightly, neither letting the other out of their sight. She kissed their foreheads gently. "I love you. You two will be safe here. I promise."

"Mommy, don't go," Chloe said, pulling the sheet up snug against her face.

Wren brushed the bangs out of her eyes and felt her heart crack at those words. "I have to, baby." She gave Chloe's arm a reassuring squeeze. "But I will come back for you."

"With Daddy?" Addison asked, mimicking the same motions as her younger sister.

Wren nodded and kissed them once more, catching the lump in her throat before it shook the confidence in her voice. "I love the two of you more than anything. Now, be good for Uncle Nathan, okay?"

"We will," they said, then huddled close to one another. Wren turned off the light on her way out and left a slight crack in the door.

Nathan waited for her in the kitchen, still shaking his

head in disapproval. "This isn't a good idea, Wren. Let me send someone out there to check."

Wren snatched the truck keys from the counter and tucked them in her pocket then picked up the box of medical supplies Nathan had put together. "You've been trying for the past thirty minutes. I'm not going to sit around and wait for someone to go and get my son when I know where he is."

"But you *don't* know where he is." Nathan pointed back to his dispatcher equipment, frowning. "That area is three square miles. You think you can find him in all of this? With what's happening out there? You've heard the calls I'm dealing with; it's Armageddon out there!"

"I have to try!" Wren slapped the words in Nathan's face so hard that he took a step back. Heat flushed off Wren's cheeks, and she felt her entire body grow hot. She gritted her teeth, gnawing the sour anger in her mouth. "I will not leave him out there alone. He's scared. He's hurt. He needs help." The resolve broke, and grief twisted Wren's face. "I have to try."

Nathan hugged her, rubbing her back. "I know." He looked down at her and grinned. "Just remember that whatever you do to the truck, I'm liable for."

Wren wiped the sorrow from her eyes and smiled. "Yeah, I'll try to bring it back with a full tank too." Nathan helped her out to the EMS vehicle parked behind the station and loaded the medical kit in the back. "Thank you, Nathan."

"I'll keep trying Doug." He opened the driver door and picked up the receiver on the radio, adjusting the dial. "I'm going to put you on channel nine so you can listen to what's happening out there. If I'm able to get a unit over to your son's location, I'll let you know through here." He placed the receiver in her palm and closed her fingers around it. "Be careful out there."

"I will." And with that, Wren climbed inside and put the fire station in her rearview, her eyes flitting to it long after it could no longer be seen. She kept off the main roads, following the path that Nathan suggested, and quickly discovered that the sight of the emergency vehicle painted a target on her back for anyone she passed. She kept the accelerator floored, only breaking for turns or traffic congestion. She twisted the grip around the steering wheel, the leather creaking back and forth. Her concentration split between the road and the radio, the chatter buzzing mechanically in their codes and emergency service nomenclature.

The deeper into the outskirts of the city she drove, the more decrepit her surroundings became. Mobs beat one another, and the random pop of gunshots jolted her with every unsuspecting explosion. All around the city was crumbling.

Wren cut hard on the next left, tires screeching as she refused to slow her pace on the final stretch to the outskirts of where the computer program had located Zack. She weaved around broken and abandoned cars, mounting the sidewalk, her arms and shoulders shaking from the vibrations of the tumultuous ride.

The broken houses she passed slowly faded into industrial complexes, many of which had been abandoned or shut down. Columns of smoke rose farther down the road, the faint glimmer of flashing red lights fought against the bright afternoon sun, and she hastened her pace.

Streams of water blasted from fire hoses onto rising flames that flickered and waved as high as skyscrapers. The hoses did little to calm the raging inferno as one of the smaller structures to the left collapsed. The flames reflected in Wren's eyes as she moved past the carnage. *Zack wasn't in there. He wasn't in there.*

"Wren." The radio under the dash crackled. "Wren, can you hear me?"

Wren fumbled with the receiver, dropping it on the floorboard before scooping it back up. "Nathan? I'm here." Her fingers clutched the radio like a footing on the side of cliff, her one lifeline as she dangled on the rocks, clinging for dear life.

"One of the cell towers came back online, and I've got a better read on Zack's location. Keep heading north on the road you're on, and look for a company called Mining Limited. It was shut down a few years ago, but the leasing information says it's currently empty. That's where the software narrowed its search."

"Thank you." Wren floored the gas pedal, the engine roaring. Her eyes scanned the signage running along fences on the side of the street until she spotted the mining company. The tires screeched to a halt as Wren mounted the curb of the sidewalk. She had half her body already out the door when she remembered the medical bag Nathan had packed. She snatched it from the backseat and sprinted blindly for the old factory's entrance, which was encased with a rusted fence.

"Zackary!" Wren scaled the old fence, struggling with only one good arm, the metal wiring rough and coarse against her skin, her hands and feet finding what holes they could on her way over, the medical bag slung over her shoulder. She twisted over the top fence railing then landed awkwardly on the cracked parking lot pavement and broke out into a sprint toward the building. Her feet pounded against the concrete, her mind and body pushing beyond the fatigue of the day, past her own limits. She skidded to a stop at the first pair of factory doors she saw, which were chained shut. She pulled, pushed, punched, and kicked but did nothing more than rattle the rusted gatekeeper refusing her entry. She pulled her hair back in frustration, digging her nails into the hard flesh over her skull. "Zaaaaaaaaack!"

The scream was bloodcurdling, Wren's throat raw and cracked. She looked up to the broken windows, too high for her to scale. She sprinted to the side, running down the shadowed portion of the building that blocked the hot summer sun, each door she passed locked with steel chains. "Zack!"

"Mom."

Wren stopped, her feet sliding in the loose, broken gravel. She clutched the chained doors, her ears pressed close to the crack in the middle. "Zack, honey, where are you? Zack!" She patted the walls with her palms, the brick of the building cool from the lack of sun. She jogged to the next pair of doors. Those were locked as well, but the chains sagging around the door handles offered some give. She slid the medical bag in first. She gripped the handle firmly, pulling backward with her right arm, the crack between the two doors widening with each strained pull. She thrust her left shoulder inside, ducking under the chains pulled tight across the narrow opening. Her stomach and back scraped against the sides of the door, and she drew in a breath, her face reddening from the tight space, and with one final push leapt inside, her wounded left arm smacking against the pavement, sending a thousand tiny knives through her body. Wren forced herself off the cold, dirty floor, shoving her pain aside.

"Zack?" The acoustics of the building echoed Wren's voice high into the ceiling. She squinted into the darkness and stumbled forward, groping for the medical bag. Her fingers found the cloth then the zipper, and she rummaged with her hand to the bottom until she found the flashlight.

One click illuminated the darkness. Wren drifted the oblong orb across the space inside, which revealed large cylinder vats, rusted tables, and overturned chairs. "Zack, where are you?"

"Mom."

Wren pivoted left, the cast of light following her. She hurried forward, sifting through the darkness, repeating her son's name over and over. Each time he answered, he sounded weak, tired. She rounded one of the large vats and saw that two had collapsed on each other, their rusted steel twisted, bent in angles that jutted out in every direction. She shined the light underneath, trying to find a way through. "Zack!"

"I'm here."

The light reflected off a shoe to Wren's left. She sprinted farther around, seeing an outstretched hand, fingers wiggling in the flashlight's beam. Wren dropped to the floor, smooshing her cheeks against the dirtied concrete, shining the light on Zack's squinting face. Zack's face, hair, and clothes were covered in dust, the whites of his eyes shining back at her brightly. Wren ran the light down his body and saw his leg was pinned behind him under a load of steel. It looked broken, but he was alive. "Are you hurt?"

"I can't move my right leg." Tears formed in his eyes. "Mom, my friends are under there, and I can't hear them." His words grew thick toward the end, and tears burst from the corners of his eyes, darkening the dust on his cheeks as he rested his head on the floor, sobbing.

Wren shifted the light to the wreckage behind her son, knowing that anyone underneath the tons of steel was already gone. "It's okay. Let's just focus on trying to get you out first, okay? One thing at a time. I'm going to take a look at the damage. I'll be right back."

Both vats had collapsed in on themselves, and the cylindrical structures weren't as much of a problem as the supporting beams that had twisted and tangled underneath, forming a jungle gym of rusty, broken steel. Toward the back, she saw a puddle of blood seeping out from under the heart of the collapse.

"Mom?" Zack asked, his voice still thickly coated with the glaze of fear.

"I'm here, Zack." Wren shut her eyes, fighting the cold shiver running down her back. *Just get him out.* Her spine stiffened, and she shined the light on every portion of the wreckage that she could spy. It was a mess. Any time she thought she would be able to move a piece of steel to give Zack the space he needed to crawl out, she found another bar tangled with it that she knew, if moved, would only worsen her son's predicament. *So don't remove it.* She shined the light on a path to Zack's leg. It was tight, but she could reach it.

Wren flattened herself against the floor, Zack squinting into the light. "I'm gonna get you out of here, honey. Just hang tight. I'm going to be right back."

"Mom, hurry." Zack's words were strained, the panic of the situation finally settling in. "I don't want to die."

"I won't let that happen." Wren grabbed his hand, her son clutching back like he did when he was boy. "I'm getting you out." She gave a squeeze then exited the building, barely wedging through the chained door, and sprinted for the truck.

The flames down the street still roared, with the firefighters doing their best to keep the inferno from spreading. She flung the trunk of the SUV open and peeled off the floor cover, exposing a spare tire, tire iron, and jack. She ripped the jack from its casing, leaving the trunk open in her haste.

Wren was squeezing through the doors when she saw a group of trucks and SUVs speeding down the roadway. She squinted, expecting the flashing lights of police and emergency vehicles, but saw none. Instead, the closer the caravan approached, the more she could make out some of the men in the back of the truck, wielding rifles and wearing black masks.

Wren disappeared inside the factory, the jack clanking against the concrete as she flopped to the floor next to it, the doors swinging shut behind her. Her fingers fumbled over the cool chunk of iron and she tucked it under her arm, the flashlight jerking in all directions as she sprinted back to where Zack lay trapped.

"Hang on, baby." Wren's hands shook as she set the flashlight down, angling it to illuminate her path along the metal death trap. She lifted her leg, stepping over the first beam, then was forced to immediately duck below a second. When her foot hit the floor, she had to twist her ankle awkwardly as the jack tucked under her right arm knocked against one of the mangled beams.

The trek was slow going, Wren's body contorting in the same extreme angles as the twisted wreckage. The cloth of her pants and shirt tore on the sharper edges, and more than once she felt the sharp pinch of tearing flesh, quickly followed by a warm trickle of blood.

Zack's leg was finally within reach, along with the beam that pinned it down. Wren's legs trembled as she struggled to keep the strength to steady herself while shoving the jack under the beam. "Zack, once I get this up and off of you, crawl forward as fast as you can." She looked to the thick beams that crisscrossed all around her, praying that her calculation of the shift in weight wouldn't bring the entire structure down upon her head.

Wren flattened the jack as low as it would allow her and rolled it under the beam, the two pieces of metal scraping against one another, each offering their own whining disdain of the other. She gave the jack a few more good shoves, making sure it was secure, then twisted the handle into place and pumped.

The iron handle could only move a few inches up and down in the narrow space, smacking against the metal bars, Wren banging her knuckles bloody with each hastened pump. But slowly, the steel beam lifted off her son's leg.

Zack moaned, and Wren wasn't sure if it was from pain or release. The beams cast shadows all around her from the flashlight, and it was hard to see the extent of the wound as the steel lifted, but once it was high enough, she watched the mangled leg wiggle forward and heard the scrape of Zack's clothes and body against the floor. "I'm out!"

The beams around Wren gave a dissatisfied creak, and she quickly slithered through the narrow openings and harshly angled gaps, feeling the shift of the unstable metals around her. The first steel beam gave way toward the middle, a sharp din ringing through the factory when she was only a few feet away from escape. Her hands clawed at the beams around her for support, her feet frantically slipping off of the angled steel, her elbows, knees, and head smacking against the metals on her manic escape.

The harsh din of collapse echoed louder, and through the ringing collision of steel, she heard Zack screaming, telling her to hurry. The beams shifted, but safety was less than a foot away now. Just as one of the steel rods to her right jerked sharply toward her head but stopped less than an inch from her eye, she used what strength was left in her legs through the opening, a sharp tear opening on her right thigh as she collapsed to safety on the floor next to the flashlight, which illuminated the mangled structure's destruction.

Wren lay back on the ground, her right hand fingering the warm blood fresh on her thigh. Any movement triggered a hot burn that rippled through her leg, but she forced herself to stand. "Zack?" She grabbed the flashlight and saw her son, red-faced, dirty, sweating, and staring at the mangled carnage that was his shin.

She collapsed to the floor next to Zack, each of them squeezing one another tightly, their light sobs echoing off one another. When she pulled his head back, her anger toward his situation returned. "What were you doing here? Do you know what's happening?"

"I'm sorry, Mom. We used to come here all the time to hang out. I didn't know this was going to happen. None of us did. I'm sorry." Zack leaned his wet, sobbing face into her shoulder. "I'm so sorry." He clawed at her arm, his body shaking with every wave of grief that ran through him.

Wren brushed her fingers through his hair, hushing him,

glad for the simple fact that he was alive. "It's okay. But we need to get out of here and get your leg taken care of." Wren had never excelled in her biology classes but knew that they needed to take care of the injury quickly. He could be bleeding internally or god knew what else. Priority one was getting him out of there.

Zack lifted his arm over Wren's shoulder and let out a cry as they pushed him off the floor together, his right leg dangling limply between them. Her son was taller than she was now and had a good thirty pounds on her, and with her own leg still dripping blood, each step forward forced her to extend what little energy remained in her body.

The flashlight wobbled back and forth in her hand with the sling, the shaky spotlight guiding them back to the doors she had managed to squeeze through.

"Wait, wait, wait." Zack stopped them. "Where are we going?"

Wren motioned the light over to the doors. "Out of here."

Zack gestured behind them. "There's already an open door in the back. It's covered up by some old equipment, but it's there."

The pair of doors that were chained together rattled loudly, sunlight breaking through the cracks and flooding the factory floor, accompanied by the thick foreign tongue that Wren had heard at the hospital.

Wren flicked the light off, casting the two of them back into darkness. "We need to move. Hurry!" She kept her voice a whisper. She turned them around and limped forward as fast as they could move together.

"Mom, what's going on? Who is that?" The panic in Zack's voice returned, and the banging doors and rattling chains grew louder with every step.

"Just keep moving, baby. And keep quiet." Wren found the wall, and they used it to guide them to the rear of the building where Zack and his friends had snuck in. *His friends.*

And what's left of them will rot under that steel. Their parents will never see them again, never hear them speak, never feel the warmth of their faces.

A loud clang sounded, and Wren turned around to see sunlight penetrating the dark facility. Two shadowed figures stepped inside, one of them barking at the other like a dog. Wren hastened her son's pace, practically dragging him deeper into the darkness.

"Right here," Zack whispered, pointing to a faintly darker rectangle.

The voices of the terrorists echoed louder, and when Wren fumbled for the door, the lights from their flashlights kicked up, sweeping the factory's landscape. She shouldered the door open, quickly getting both of them inside. "Where now?" The room was pitch black, and Wren feared moving too quickly and triggering a noise that would give away their position.

"Just keep going straight," Zack said, his voice still a wheezy whisper.

Light shone through the cracks in the doorframe as they shuffled toward freedom. "Hurry, Zack." They double-timed it, limping forward faster and faster, Wren's heart beating out of her chest, her mind aware of every pain radiating in her body. *Just keep going.*

They thudded against the door Zack described, and Wren thrust it open, sunlight blinding both of them. Zack stopped to catch his breath, but Wren pushed him forward. "We can't stop, baby. Let's go."

But when Wren's vision adjusted to the light, she saw just how bad Zack's injury was. The jeans were soaked and darkened around the area where the beam had pinned him, and while Zack could bend the knee, she noticed his foot hung loosely from the ankle and that his shin shifted slightly to the left. She looked to his face and could see the pained effort as he gritted his teeth with every step.

Wren stopped at the corner of the factory, knowing they'd have to pass by the exposed doors the terrorists had entered, and made sure the coast was clear. Gunshots sounded toward the emergency vehicles where the fire still raged, but her vehicle remained parked and unharmed.

They were forced to go all the way around the gated entrance, Zack too weak to climb the fence where she had entered. The moment her hand touched the passenger-side handle of the EMS vehicle, a scream pierced the open air behind them.

Wren turned to the sight of two masked men sprinting in their direction. "Hurry, Zack!" She opened the door and threw her son inside. She slammed the door shut, running around the front of the vehicle as gunshots thundered behind her. She jumped inside and started the car, slammed the shifter into drive, and floored the gas pedal as bullets thrummed against the vehicle, shattering the back passenger-side windows. Wren thrust her son's head down, keeping one hand on the wheel and ducking herself.

Another round of gunfire shattered the rear window, and Wren did her best to keep both eyes on the road, swerving left and right to avoid the machine-gunfire. She blew past stop signs and intersections, the wind whipping through the shattered window, flinging her hair in all directions. The speedometer pushed sixty, but she didn't slow her pace, putting as much distance as she could between her and the blazing hell behind her.

8

The radio in the truck spit sporadic crackles and pops as Wren twisted the dial, trying every channel to get back in touch with Nathan, or anyone. "Hello? Nathan, can you hear me?" But every time she took her hand off the receiver, all that answered was the steady buzz of static.

Wren viciously slammed the receiver against the dashboard and punched the steering wheel as Zack winced from shifting in his seat. She looked from the empty fuel gauge glaring back at her over to her son, who brushed glass from the shattered window off of his lap, and gave his hand a squeeze.

Zack laid his head against the headrest, closing his eyes. His face was slick with sweat, and Wren worried that he may have had a fever, or perhaps he was just delirious with pain. He needed a doctor, and with the seven circles of hell surrounding them, she wasn't sure if that help could be found.

"Can't we just go to the hospital?" Zack asked.

"It's gone, Zack." Wren wasn't sure why she told him, but she hoped that he was old enough to take the news, as she was desperate to share the burdens of the world with someone. "What's happening out there is bad. Your sisters are with Nathan at a fire station, and no one knows when this is all going to be over."

Zack glanced down at his leg, a quietness overtaking his eyes, his body consumed with stillness, and Wren watched his eyes as he processed her words. She gently grabbed his arm. "Right now there isn't anywhere that's safe. I know it's hard, but you need to understand what's happening out there. You need to know what we could face. There is nothing more important to me right now than protecting our family, but we have to be smart while we're out here, okay?"

Zack gave a quick nod. "Yeah. Okay."

"W—n." The radio crackled spontaneously, spraying a rush of static then incomprehensible chatter. "Wre- -r- -ou th-re?"

Wren reached for the receiver. "Nathan? Yes, I'm here. Can you hear me? Nathan? Are the girls okay?" She lifted her finger off the receiver, both she and Zack leaning closer to the device, waiting. Listening.

"Yeah, it's me," Nathan replied. "The girls are fine. Are you all right? Did you get Zack?"

Wren exhaled, smiling. "Yes, I found him, but his leg is broken. I need to get him to a doctor." And as if on cue, Zack winced. "He's in pretty bad shape."

"Let me see what I can find."

"Hurry." Wren set the receiver down and glanced out the empty space where the passenger-side window once rested. She had pulled off onto a random highway when the truck sputtered to a stop. She knew she was south of the city, and judging from the worn-down houses and open fields, it was farm country.

"Mom?" Zack asked, snapping Wren back to reality.

"What is it?"

"I know I shouldn't have been out there. I shouldn't have left school. I'm sorry."

"Absent ten times this semester?" Wren shook her head, her voice exasperated. "What the hell were you even doing out there? It's dangerous any day, let alone one like this. What is going on with you? You never talk to your father and me, and you've been elusive and defensive when we try to communicate with you. I know a lot of it is hormones, but you've got to let us in a little bit."

Zack kept his head down, his eyes on the floorboard. "I know you and Dad are getting a divorce."

Wren shook her head, floored at how her son could even know something like that. "What are you talking about?" She'd spoken to no one except her lawyer about it. She hadn't told her parents or her sister. It was something she'd kept to herself for the past three months.

"You guys don't talk to each other anymore. I can see it at the dinner table and how late you stay at work. You guys are barely ever in the house together." Zack looked up from his feet. "Why?"

Wren was on her heels, unsure of how to proceed, her mind drifting to the divorce papers she'd planned on giving Doug later that night, before all of this. Before the world went to shit. "I didn't realize you'd been paying that close attention."

"Addy and Chloe know something is up too. They don't talk to you about it, but they talk to me." Zack shifted uncomfortably, the lines on his face accentuated by the dirt and soot smeared on his cheeks. "Is it true?"

The hazel eyes staring back at Wren were wide, and though Zack was almost fully grown, easing into his father's features and shoe size, he looked at her like Addison and Chloe had in the hospital. "Zack, your father and I—"

"Wren, are you still there? Wren?"

Wren snatched the receiver back up and offered a relieved sigh, thankful for the interruption. "Yeah, I'm here." Zack sank back into his chair and looked away.

"I've found Doug. He just finished up with a fire at the downtown circle. He's bringing an ambulance to you with a paramedic team to work on Zack's leg. Then he's going to come and get the girls."

Zack turned back to the radio at the mention of his father, and the news brought a mixture of anxiety and relief for Wren. "Thanks, Nathan. For everything."

"Just hang tight. He has your GPS coordinates and should be there in fifteen minutes, assuming he doesn't have any problems getting to you. I'll be on here if you need anything."

The signal ended, and Wren set the receiver back on the hook. She looked at Zack, who still had his eyebrows raised, wanting his question answered. "Zack, your father and I have had some problems lately. He knows that, and so do I. We never meant for that to have an effect on you and the girls, although at some point I think we both knew it was going to happen."

Wren rubbed her brow, bits of dirt and grime falling. She felt the grainy particles on her fingertips, and the frustration at the forefront of her thoughts pounded her mind like a hammer on an anvil. "Your father and I have a lot to talk about." She kept her voice low but firm. "And that will be a decision between the two of us. But regardless of what happens with that, I promise you that nothing will stop us from loving you and your sisters. Nothing."

"Yeah. Okay." Zack rested his head back, reabsorbing himself into the cone of adolescence that he'd become so accustomed to in such times, ignoring everything around him.

Wren fell against the back of her seat, closing her eyes,

but found them opened every few seconds to check the clock on the dash, which seemed to be frozen as the minutes crawled by.

After the thousandth glance at the clock, she saw running headlights on a vehicle up the road. Zack tried getting out of the car but stopped once the pain from his leg thrust him back into his seat. Wren placed her hand over his chest. "Stay here."

Wren climbed out of the car, making her way around the engine and to the side of the road to get a better look. She squinted, the heat coming off the road giving the vehicle heading toward them a hazy, wavering image. *It could be anyone.* Her mind drifted back to the masked men she saw in the SUVs and trucks, armed to the teeth.

But when the flashing lights flickered on top of the vehicle, all of the tension coiled up in her body released. *Doug.* She waved her arms, moving down the side of the road to grab the ambulance's attention. It slowed to a crawl and pulled in right behind the EMS truck.

The back doors of the ambulance burst open before it came to a stop, and Doug jogged over, his clothes dirtied and dark with sweat, a breathlessness in his voice when he spoke. "Are you guys all right?" He stopped at Zack, clutching his son in both arms, Zack squeezing back just as hard.

Wren walked to him, hesitant, the coldness of their last interaction still fresh in her mind. She kissed him lightly on the cheek, in the end glad he was here and glad he was alive.

"Nathan said he'd been trying to reach me all day, but the damn radios have been so shoddy that we've barely been able to keep in touch with our own people." Doug stepped aside as two other paramedics wheeled a stretcher over and started inspecting Zack's leg.

"Doug," one of the paramedics asked, "mind giving me a hand here?"

"Sure." Doug helped Zack up with one easy lift under his son's shoulder, transferring him over to the gurney. Zack yelped in pain, but Doug made the move quickly. He gripped his son firmly, his tone a blend of father and firefighter. "We're going to have to cut the pants open and take a look."

Zack nodded, his breathing accelerated. One of the paramedics brought a blade up from the hem of the pant leg to the knee, splitting the jeans in two and exposing the black-and-blue skin, the bone of his shin dented and leg oozing blood. Zack looked away immediately, and Doug slid on a glove.

"We need to link an IV and set the bone." Doug ran his fingers up and down Zack's leg with a light touch, applying pressure along the joint to check for any other fractures. Every wince from Zack told Doug all he needed to know. "Feels like a clean break."

The other paramedic gathered the necessary devices, cleaning Zack's arm for the IV needle. A fresh round of sweat burst from Zack's face, his breathing accelerated. "Dad, I—"

"You can do this, Zack," Doug said, taking the brace and adjusting it to fit his son's leg. "It's going to hurt, but only for a little bit. We need to stabilize it so there isn't any more damage to your tissue. I'm going to do it on three, okay? One." But before Doug reached two, he snapped the bone back into place. Zack wailed in pain, falling back onto the stretcher, and passed out.

Wren rushed to her son's aid, gripping the gurney's railing. "Christ, Doug, you could've—"

"The sooner it happened, the better," Doug snapped, wrapping Zack's leg in the brace. He stopped and let the paramedic take over, brushing the hair that had matted on his son's forehead. Zack's head lolled back and forth in a pain-induced haze. He looked back to Wren, his features softening. "I'm sorry. I didn't mean to—"

"It's fine." Wren offered a weak smile, taking Zack's hand,

giving it a kiss, and holding it all the way to the ambulance, where the three climbed inside. The second paramedic rode in the passenger seat and the other drove.

The ride back into the city felt long, the ambulance swaying back and forth. It was the first time they'd been in the same room for longer than two minutes for more than a month. "Nathan tell you about the girls?"

Doug nodded, his eyes still on Zack, twirling the gold band on his left ring finger around the dirty, greasy stains. "Yeah, he told me."

"And you know what happened with the hospitals? With everything that his friend told him?"

Doug laughed, shaking his head. "Christ, Wren, you don't actually believe him, do you? His theories? His crazy-ass friends that live out in the middle of nowhere with their... whatever the hell they have? Everything I've heard so far said that this is limited to Chicago. There haven't been any reports anywhere else around the country of similar events happening. This will blow over."

Wren nodded, trying to shake loose the thoughts that had consumed her since the moment she saw those men at the hospital. The way they killed without hesitation or explanation. While she hoped that Doug was right, she knew that Nathan had one thing nailed down: whoever these people were had been planning this for a very long time. "Where are we going?" she asked, trying to change the subject.

"Since the hospital's collapse, the medical unit downtown has been relocating to smaller hospitals. We're heading to one of the Shriners on the east side of the city. From what we've heard on the radio, it's still standing. We're going to pick up the girls on the way, along with Steve's wife and son." He gestured to the driver.

"Shouldn't we get him to a hospital first?" Wren asked, taking Zack's limp hand.

"He's stable for now, and Nathan's station is on the way. It won't take long." Doug let go of the gold band around his finger and hung his head. "So, you still want to talk?" He glanced up, the stoic expression offering no hint of what *he* wanted.

"Not now, Doug." Wren rubbed her eyes, trying to ease the rising pressure in her skull. The last thing on her mind was her marriage. "We get the girls, we get him patched up, and then we go home. We can talk then."

"Sounds like the same record I've heard before."

Wren leaned forward, her face flushed red and her words a harsh whisper. "Well, I'm sorry that I don't want to talk about our marriage problems with our son passed out with a broken leg and our youngest daughter with a broken arm, huddled in a fire station with her sister while the entire city burns around us." She cocked her head to the side, nodding sarcastically. "Yeah, I think I'd like to skip that."

"Then when?" Doug matched her tone and resentment, his fingers curling to fists. "Every time I bring it up, you shut me down, so when?" He tossed his hands in the air, exasperated. "I can't keep going on like this. You know what the first thing I felt when I saw you on the side of the road was? Anxiety. It wasn't relief, it wasn't happiness, it was anxiousness. I saw you and thought, 'God, I wonder if she'll even acknowledge that I'm here. I wonder if she'll even be glad I showed up!'" Doug raised his voice then slammed his back into the wall behind him, crossing his arms, retreating within himself.

Wren held back the tears that demanded to be shown. She wasn't going to let him have that. Not here, and not now. She spoke her words slowly, meticulously. "Well, I'm sorry I made you *uncomfortable*. And I'm sorry that my presence caused your delicate constitution to fall under added stress. I have been in a car wreck, shot at, and watched all three of my children nearly die at the hands of madmen, but by all means, let me make you feel *better*." She spit the last words with a sting of venom and leaned back, wanting to escape through the walls behind her. The rest of the trip was silent, and Wren's mind was splintered with the stress of the day along with how her marriage had become so jaded, pinpointing the moment when she stopped loving her husband.

9

Wren's head jerked up from her shoulder, where it had drifted off to rest, her body taking advantage of the lull in activity to shut down, doing its best to try to recover her nerves.

"Doug," Steve said, the ambulance squeaking to a stop. "We might have a problem here.

Wren squeezed past Doug, investigating the cause of their delay. But whatever she could have imagined in her nightmares paled in comparison to Chicago's skyline. Columns of smoke rose into the sky, glows of fire battling the sun for attention as the beautiful architecture she'd fallen in love with as a college student burned to nothing. A distant explosion caused all of them to jolt and she looked back to Zack who still lay unconscious.

Doug reached for the radio, scanning the channels. "Nathan, can you hear me? Nathan, this is Doug. Come back." Only the rush of white noise answered.

Traffic was roadblocked in all outbound directions from the city, people laying on horns on the highway and overpasses, anger and desperation reaching a crescendo as everyone clamored over one another to escape the chaos of

Chicago. Wren clutched Zack's arm, feeling the warmth of her child as he lay still on the cot. She drew in a breath, a glimmer of strength returning with it. "How far are we from the station?"

Ken, the second paramedic in the passenger seat spoke up. "Ten miles, at least." His gaze was locked on the chaos in their path.

"We don't stop," Wren said. "For anything. You turn the sirens and lights on, and you keep driving. Whatever you have to do."

"I'd buckle up back there. And make sure Zack is secure." Steve shifted into drive, flipping on the lights. Doug climbed back with Wren, helping strap Zack down. The sirens wailed from the roof, and Steve jolted them forward.

Wren white-knuckled the railing on Zack's stretcher, Steve maneuvering the ambulance in and out of traffic. She heard him try the radio one more time, but the efforts were fruitless. Wren forced her concentration on the fire station. The girls were still alive. She could feel it. *I know they're alive.*

"Hang on!" Steve swerved the ambulance hard right, swinging everyone inside. Wren lifted from her seat as they mounted the curb. Smacks and pops echoed through the ambulance wall at her back, and Wren squinted her eyes shut, hoping that whatever they hit wasn't living.

By the time they arrived at the fire station, Wren had to peel her fingers off the railing of Zack's stretcher one by one. She was the first out of the back doors, rushing to the station's entrance. "Addison! Chloe!" Nathan stepped out of the door in the garage, and two small faces poked out behind him.

Tears burst from Wren's eyes as she stumbled the rest of the way and squeezed them so tight she thought they might burst. She kissed their cheeks, running her hands through her hair. "Thank god you two are all right."

Doug came running up behind her, and the moment the

girls saw him, they rushed to their father. "Daddy!" they screamed collectively, and he engulfed them in his arms, showering them with kisses. "We missed you!"

"I missed you too." Doug carried them back over to the door and set them down inside.

"How's your arm, Chloe?"

Chloe lifted her cast, examining the hard plaster around her arm, and shrugged. "I can't really feel anything anymore."

Nathan stepped forward, between Doug and Wren. "The equipment went out about an hour ago." His face was covered in sweat, and dark blotches spotted his chest and underarms. "I haven't been able to hear from anyone. I wasn't sure what to do, I trie—"

Wren touched his arm, and his rambling stopped. "Thank you for watching our girls." The words relaxed him, his shoulders sagging. She stepped out of the garage, the bustle of the city roaring in defiance of the abuse it was enduring.

The thin veil of protection and civility had been ripped to shreds. A hot wind brushed Wren's face and brought with it the din of car alarms, the crash of windows, the echoed terror of gunshots and screams. She turned back to Doug, Nathan, and the girls. "We have to get out of here."

Doug looked to the girls. "You two go inside while Mommy and I talk, okay?"

Addison quickly wrapped herself around her father's leg, clinging on for dear life. "You're not going to leave again, are you?" Chloe immediately mimicked her sister, compelled by the same anxiety, clutching Doug's other leg.

Doug knelt, gently peeling both the girls off him. "You two listen to me. I'm not going anywhere." He kissed both of their foreheads. "Now, go inside so the adults can talk." He gave them a push through the door, and Nathan, Wren, and Doug circled together. "So, what do you have in mind, Wren?"

"We fuel up and head west," Wren answered. "Aurora,

Rockford, as far as we can get without stopping." She looked back over to the ambulance. "Or the first working hospital we see to get Zack's leg looked at."

"What about Steve's wife and son?" Doug asked. "They're not west."

"We split up, then. He goes and gets his kids with one of the trucks, and we take the ambulance."

"Wren, we can't just leave him," Doug said.

"He'll have a vehicle, and it'll be fueled; what more do you want us to give him, Doug? I understand him needing to go and get his family, but I'm not taking ours deeper into that madness than we already have." Wren paced back and forth, convincing herself that this was what needed to be done, regardless of how anyone perceived it. "He'll understand that."

"Doug!" Steve stepped out of the back of the ambulance and jogged over. "Zack's awake. He's asking for you guys."

Doug eyed Wren, and she saw his hesitation. He didn't want to leave the man behind and let him risk going it alone, but he promised his girls. *He promised.*

"Thanks." Doug placed his hand on Steve's shoulder. "Hey, let me talk to you for a second."

"No, it's okay," Steve said. "I heard what Wren said. She's right. I won't make you guys follow me back into the city. It's too dangerous." He nodded to the trucks in the back. "I'll take one of the truck's. I'll be all right. You take care of your family, Doug."

"Thank you," Wren said. "For everything." She kissed his cheek then made her way to the ambulance, where Zack had propped himself up on the pillows. "Hey, how are you feeling?" She moved to his side, wiping the sweaty bangs from his forehead. His skin felt clammy to the touch, and his face was pale.

"My leg," Zack said, his face wincing in pain. "It's really sore." His words left his mouth in a hoarse whisper, his mind groggy and his body fatigued. He swayed his head back and forth lazily, unable to hold it up on his own.

"I know, sweetheart," Wren said, answering assuredly. "We're going to get you some help. Just hang in there."

DOUG AND NATHAN immediately started loading whatever supplies they could: medicine, blankets, medical gear, clothes, food, anything that would fit in the ambulance. The station had a fuel depot on sight, and once everything and everyone was loaded up, the goodbyes were said.

"Take care of yourself, Steve," Doug said, wrapping his friend in a hug. "If the radios come back on, you call me and let me know the moment you and your family are in the clear. You hear me?"

"You'll be the first to know." Steve smiled then hugged Wren. "You take care of yourself, Wren. And your family." Steve left first, the sun sinking lower into the horizon, Wren watching the truck disappear into the city. *What kind of fate have I damned him to?*

"Wren!" Doug said, shouting from the ambulance already on the edge of the street. "Let's go!"

Wren climbed in the back, slamming the rear doors shut behind her. She found a seat next to Chloe on the right, while Addison sat with her father on the left, with Zack still on the stretcher between them.

The second paramedic that Doug had brought with him, Ken, drove, while Nathan rode shotgun. "I'll take as many back roads as I can until we can get onto Interstate 86. The traffic was backed up on the way out, but it looked clear past Oak Brook." They kept the sirens off, not wanting to draw any more attention to themselves than necessary.

Everyone's heads bounced like bobblehead dolls, the ambulance speeding down streets, weaving in and out of the obstacles that dotted the roads: abandoned cars, downed power lines, fallen signs. Looted trash flowed from broken shop windows and into the street. The city was being torn apart at the seams.

"Oh, shit!" Ken screamed.

The ambulance skidded to a halt, slamming everyone forward along with any loose gear they couldn't tie down. Wren's shoulder collided with the wall, and the pain that followed faded her vision to black for a few seconds. When she regained control, she checked Chloe and clawed her way to the gap between the passenger and driver seat. When she saw what had stopped them, her jaw dropped. "Oh my god."

A blockade of burning cars cast flickering flames on at least a dozen masked men, all armed with rifles, marching slowly down the street. "Hang on!" Ken shifted into reverse, the tires screeching from the sudden force.

Wren ducked back into the rear of the ambulance, using her body to cover Chloe as gunshots filled the air. She felt the percussion of each bullet connecting with the ambulance reverberate through the seat, and she placed her hands over Chloe's ears to shield her from the gunfire and Addison's screams.

Time stood still as the engine revved, and Wren felt her center of gravity shift, slowly rotating along with her sense of reference. Gear tumbled back and forth, and a violent force slammed her against her seat belt. Her grip around Chloe loosened from the violent motion and the inside of the ambulance whirled in a blur. Cracks, pops, and the deafening twist of metal suddenly thundered all around her.

One of the medical kits flew into the twirling vortex and smacked the bandage on Wren's head, the sharp sting ringing through her skull and a dull sensation overtaking her limbs. When the motion finally ended, Wren's head still spun in place, her body struggling to find the coordination to move. When she opened her eyes she shook her head, confused. Doug and Addison were below her, and it took her a moment to realize that she was dangling from the seat belt around her waist. The ambulance had flipped to its side, leaving her on top.

CHLOE DANGLED NEXT TO HER, crying, her face red and her arms and legs swinging from the seat belt clung tight around her waist. Wren reached for the buckle, trying to free her. "Hang on, sweetie." She could only graze it with her fingertips. "Doug." He stirred below, his head lolling back and forth as Addison lay unconscious. "Doug!" The scream worked, and he pushed a pile of boxes off himself, first checking on Addison, who groaned, then reaching for Chloe.

Wren rotated her jaw, trying to wedge free the high-pitched din stuck in her eardrums. She shook her head, thinking it was only in her mind, but as the whine faded from her ears, she heard it again. It was quiet but growing steadily. "What is that?"

Doug stopped and turned to look out the window, his jaw dropping. "Jesus Christ." He turned back, his hands and fingers fumbling quickly to free their daughter. "We need to move. Now."

The buckle clicked open, and Doug caught Chloe before she hit the ground. Wren rushed over to Zack, who was awake, and clutched at his leg. The brace had broken, and whatever stabilization it offered the leg had busted with it. "Zack, we have to go." She kept one eye on her son and the other on the growing size of the marching army heading straight for them.

"Uuugghhh." The moan came from the front seat, and Doug stumbled past Wren, pulling Nathan from the passenger seat, scrapes covering his forehead and cheeks. Doug carefully laid him on the floor, checking his pulse and his breathing and opening his eyes. "Nathan, can you hear me?" Nathan stirred but offered no coherent speech.

Wren gathered the girls and sat them at the rear doors. Both were now awake but barely conscious, Addison unable to stand. "You girls stay right here. I need to get your brother."

Doug and Wren worked together on Zack's straps, their son moaning, reaching for his leg, which looked in worse shape than before. But the growing chants outside of the ambulance erased any alternative course of action. They propped him up between their shoulders and made for the rear doors.

"Look for any cover we can run to." Doug panted between breaths, looking up over the black tuft of curls of their son's head. "The closer, the better." He looked down to Addison. "Sweetie, can you stand up?"

Addison frowned, anguish etched upon her tiny face as she cradled her head in her hands. "I don't feel good."

Wren stumbled to the front of the ambulance, trying to get a better look at their surroundings. The driver, Ken, was unconscious in the driver's seat, his head cocked at a ninety-degree angle. But an even more disturbing sight grew in the distance. The mob of terrorists chanted and fired their rifles into the air as they passed buildings and broken down cars, setting to blaze anything in their path.

Quickly, Wren hustled back to the rear of the ambulance, reached for Addison's hand, and pulled her daughter up forcefully. "Chloe," she ordered, "take your father's hand."

Chloe marched obediently to her father's side. The two of them both glanced at Nathan, who lay unconscious, but she knew what Doug was already thinking. "We can come back for him once we get the girls to safety." She spit the lie, her gut wrenching the moment it left her lips.

Doug and Wren each threw one of Zack's arms over their shoulders, wedging him in between. Glass shook from the rear doors as Wren and Doug pulled their family onto the pavement. Wren frantically tried to keep up with Doug's pace, the two seeing the same open shop door, shifting Zack and the girls in the same direction.

Wren turned to look behind them and caught the edge of the mob out of the corner of her eye, the masked men aiming their rifles toward them. Her heart leapt from her chest, a feeling of weightlessness overtaking her as she dug her heels into the pavement, pushing harder, faster, beyond her body's capacity.

Bullets peppered the side of the building, drowning out the girls' screaming. The world passed in slow motion. Bullets impacted the doorway to her right just inches from her head. With one foot inside the building a sudden jerk on her right shoulder pulled her down.

Zack slipped from Wren's hold, and Addison tripped, the entire family smacking against the tiled floor. A sharp crack sounded as Wren managed to get one palm under her, and the pain shot like lightning from her wrist all the way to her shoulder.

More bullets shattered what was left of the store window as Wren became deaf to the world, all of her energy focused on dragging Zack and Addison deeper into the store, crawling forward on the tile, shards of glass and broken electronics digging into her fleshy palms.

Wren looked to her right and saw that Doug was in the same position, dragging Chloe along the floor with him. The shadows of the mob in the street flickered from the surrounding fires as she pulled Zack to his feet. They all chanted, repeating the same words over and over again on their march.

Wren pushed her way through a cracked door, spilling inside, all of them losing their footing in the hurried panic, and crashed to the floor. Wren heeled the door shut, and the room went pitch black. She fumbled for her cell phone in her pocket, using the light to check on Addison, Chloe, and Zack.

Chloe squinted from the brightness, holding her hands up

to block the light, her palms red and cut from the fall, but she was otherwise unharmed. Addison threw up spontaneously in the corner, and Wren held her daughter's hair as she lay on the ground, moaning.

"I think she has a concussion," Doug said, short of breath and keeping his voice low.

Wren stroked Addison's hair then crawled to Zack, whose face was scrunched up in pain. She quickly locked the door and pushed as much junk in front of it as she could muster, piling boxes, shelves, and chairs in hopes of keeping the masked men in the streets away from her family. She looked around for a weapon, anything she could use to try and protect them.

"Wren," Doug said, his voice soft.

Wren shuffled around the small storage room, the light from her phone illuminating a bottle of bleach, some mop heads, scrubs, and brushes, but nothing sharp, nothing that they could use.

"Wren," Doug repeated.

"Doug, we need to get—" She turned around and the phone's light shone on Doug's face. He was propped up against a mop bucket, his complexion white as a ghost. He was panting heavily and clutching his stomach, where black blotches stained his clothes, and patches of red shimmered on his fingers as he peeled them off the wound.

Wren dropped to her knees, crawling over to him and cradling his head. His body was slick with sweat, and he leaned his face into her shoulder, his eyes wandering deliriously. "I don't... You need to get the kids out of the city."

"Doug, tell me what to do." Wren lifted his chin, giving his head a stern shake, trying to bring his concentration back. "How do I help you?"

Doug lifted his hands, revealing a sticky crimson stain that covered most of his paramedic's uniform. He took a hard, dry swallow then gently placed his hands back down, the gold band of his wedding ring covered in blood. "The bullet went all the way through. I think it may have hit my liver, maybe my kidneys. I'm losing too much blood." He closed his eyes, shaking his head.

"The ambulance—there must be something still there?" Wren couldn't let him die, not now, not here. She held his face firmly between her hands. "Tell me, Doug."

He took a few panting breaths, and Wren saw him trying to stand on what resolve remained to him. "The trauma bag. We need to"—he took another dry swallow—"stop the bleeding. Clotting powder and an IV. A blue bag, a red cross on each side."

"Got it." Wren laid him down, and when she turned, Chloe was right behind her, her eyes big, staring at the wound in her father's stomach.

Doug saw her and tried to flash a smile. "Hey, kiddo."

"Daddy?" Chloe's lips collapsed in grief, her lower lip protruded, and her eyes watered.

"I'm fine, Chloe." Doug gestured back to Addison, who still lay on the floor, curled up in a ball.

"I think your sister needs your help. Why don't you go and make sure she's okay? Could you do that for me?"

Chloe nodded and then leaned in to give her dad a kiss on the cheek. Wren kissed the top of her head and then took one of the broomsticks, shoved the handle end in the bottom corner of the room, and then slammed her foot down over the middle, snapping it in half. She knelt and put one of the jagged, splintered ends into Zack's palm. It was the best she could do. "Zack." Her son opened his eyes, his fingers gripped lightly around the wood. "Anyone comes through that door, you stick this inside of him, you got it?"

Zack's fingers tightened around the wood, and he gave a stiff nod. Wren kissed his forehead and took the other end of the broken broomstick. She shoved the junk she stacked in front of the door, and stepped out into the store. The chants of the masked men was now nothing but a faint echo in the distance.

Aside from the massive clouds of smoke that filtered through the air and debris in the streets, it looked clear. Wren held the makeshift spear tightly, keeping her eyes about her on the way to the ambulance, which was still mangled and flipped to its side, some of the gear spilling from the back like guts from a wound.

Wren sifted through the wreckage, looking for the pack Doug had described, when a faint moan came from inside the ambulance. *Nathan. He can help.* She jumped inside, the vehicle creaking in the same distressed manner as the volunteer firefighter, his head lolling back and forth, the blood on his face shimmering with ever shake. "Nathan," she said, shaking him. She looked behind her at the open doors, then through the broken windshield, making sure no one was close. "Nathan, wake up!"

Nathan blinked, shifting his arms and legs around on the floor. "What happened?"

"Nathan, I need to find the trauma bag. Where is it?" Wren grabbed his collar. "Doug's been shot. I need to find the bag!" She screamed the words louder than she intended, but the intensity reignited Nathan's coherence as he shifted his large body to the side, planting four wobbling limbs underneath his body as he pushed himself up.

"I packed it up here." Nathan staggered, stretching his arms. He tossed a handful of clothes and bandages aside, and there underneath rested the blue bag with the red crosses etched on either side.

Wren snatched it from Nathan's hand then yanked him along. "Hurry!" Each pull and jerk, dragging Nathan with her, felt as though her arm would snap in half. She burst through the door, the delicate bundle of junk still blocking her path sent crashing to the floor.

Doug lay unconscious, his hands fallen from his stomach.

Chloe was crying in the corner, and Zack could do little more than drop the broken broomstick in his hand upon their entrance. Wren collapsed next to Doug, clutching his hand in her own. His fingers were sticky with blood and deathly cold.

Nathan knelt on the other side, pressing his pudgy hands onto Doug's neck, then pressed his ear to Doug's mouth. "It's faint, but he still has a pulse, and he's breathing." He ripped the trauma bag open and pulled out a small baggie, tearing the top off, and then ripped the front of Doug's shirt open with a short blade. He dumped the clotting powder in the wound and started rotating Doug to his back. "Help me get him on his side."

Wren let go of Doug's hand and pushed. Nathan finished pulling the shirt off Doug, dumping the same material in the wound on his lower back. "We need to get some fluids in him. Hand me that light."

Wren extended her cell to Nathan, the movement shifting the shadows in the room, when suddenly it went out, casting a veil of darkness over their eyes. Wren pulled the phone back, tapping the screen and the power button, but nothing worked. "It's not..." She shook it in her hands, her fingers digging into the case. "It had a full battery." She groped for her son in the darkness. "Zack, give me your phone, quickly." They fumbled the exchange awkwardly in the dark, but Zack's phone offered the same result as her own. "*Shit!*" Wren's muscles tensed. Chloe's whimpers grew louder, and Wren felt the last shred of sanity slip through her fingers. "What is *happening*?"

Wren felt a hand on her shoulder. Her eyes had adjusted to the darkness somewhat, and when she looked up, she saw Nathan's shape. "Wren, we have to go."

"*Where*, Nathan?" She pulled her hair backward, her nails digging into her scalp. She looked to her husband, only the outline of his shape visible in the darkness, then back to her daughters, and then to Zack on floor. The world had crumbled around her. She felt her heart accelerate along with her breathing, but the quick breaths suffocated her. The overwhelming sense of finality took hold, and she shook her head violently.

Nathan knelt and gently pulled her hand from her hair, holding it in his own. "Wren, the power's not coming back on any time soon. And depending on the range of the device, it may be a while before we run into anything electronic that's able to function."

She heard, but she didn't understand. The words bounced around her head like a foreign tongue, the same jargon that the masked men had spit in their chants. "What… what are you talking about? What device?"

Nathan leaned in closer, his features becoming clearer in the darkness. "An EMP."

10

Ash fell from the sky. On the horizon, the downtown Chicago skyline burned, crumbling the once-proud architecture she had loved so much. The empyrean blue of the atmosphere grew congested and poisoned with black, virulent plumes of pollution.

The combined heat of sun and fires burned the streets clogged with broken-down vehicles, half of them wrecked in twisted piles and the other half abandoned, their owners fleeing on foot. Along the roads, what stores hadn't caught fire were looted. Any goods the criminals left behind were scattered on the sidewalks amidst shards of broken glass. The city had turned to chaos, and Wren Burton was anchored in the eye of the storm.

Wren limped forward, ignoring the pain radiating from her right thigh. She swung her right arm awkwardly, compensating for its companion on the left, which lay wounded in a sling. Dried blood was caked on her right pant leg, and every pound of pressure she laid upon it with her hobbled steps brought forth a fresh coat of crimson that added to the flaking crust already in place.

The sections of the borrowed shirt and pants she wore

that weren't covered in bodily fluids were dirtied with grime. Her pale skin was darkened with the ashes of the burning city, and her black hair was greyed from soot and dust. Her foot kicked away debris scattered in the street: a broken bottle, crumpled papers, shattered glass. She fumbled her fingers over car doors, yanking at their handles fruitlessly, all of them locked, and not even trying the wrecked vehicles stacked in pileups that dotted the roads.

After a few dozen tries, success. Wren flung the door open wildly, sliding into the driver's seat, probing her hand in search of the keys, which the owner had left in the ignition in their haste to flee the burning city. But when Wren turned the engine over, she heard nothing but a click. "No!" She flicked the key again, frustrated, but each try only returned the same impotent noise. She slammed her fist into the wheel and then pulled herself out. She sprinted to the next car, slid into the driver's seat, then punched the dash after the second failed attempt to start the engine.

Wren looked back to the looted electronics store where the overturned ambulance lay twisted and mangled. No working car meant no escape. No escape meant death. What did Nathan say? An older car. Find an older car. She passed the newer models, their paint still fresh and bright, their innards sophisticated with the comforts of technology and efficiency.

The searing pain in the cut on Wren's thigh forced her to stop and grip the rusted pole of a street sign for support. Her legs shook. Her breath was labored. She eyed the small strip mall parking lot to her left, a rusted minivan catching her attention. She pushed herself from the pole, using the momentum to press forward.

Wren patted the side of the rusted van until she arrived at the driver's door. The handle squeaked when pulled, but refused her entry. She thrust her good arm through the cracked window and reached for the lock at the window's base. The lock grazed against her fingertips, and the window dug painfully under her arm as she stretched to position for a better grip. With her face smashed against the door frame and her arm extended as far as it would go, she plucked the lock up and swung the door open.

Bits of rust fell from the hinges as she climbed into the driver's seat. The ignition was empty, but a purse lay over the torn fabric of the passenger seat. She dumped the contents out hurriedly. She pushed past lipstick and napkins, credit cards and IDs until she felt the rigid metal of keys scrape against her fingers.

Wren thrust the key into the ignition, the gaudy key chains jingling together. She closed her eyes, her wrist poised to start the van. Please. Work. The engine choked and stammered. Wren leaned her foot on the gas as the engine struggled to catch its spark. She pumped the pedal. C'mon! Finally, the cylinders kicked into gear, and the old rust bucket took its first breath of life.

"Yes!" Wren slammed the door shut and shifted into drive. The car squealed as she pulled out of the parking space, maneuvering through the minefield of busted vehicles and overturned lampposts, trash cans, and street signs.

The brakes screeched as the car came to a stop next to the overturned ambulance, and Wren left the engine running as she passed by the dead paramedic, half his body hanging out of the front windshield, his head bloodied and the rest of his body limp.

The inside of the electronics store was in no better shape than its exterior, and Wren kicked aside broken boxes and packages on her way to the storage closet. "Nathan! I have one!" Before she reached for the handle, the door swung open, and a large, heavyset man with his belly falling over the front of his jeans stepped out. The mustache under his nose was thick and bristled, and he stroked it nervously as he nodded.

"We need to get Doug in first," Nathan said, disappearing back into the closet.

The moment Wren set foot in the room, her leg was attacked by her youngest daughter, Chloe. The hardened cast around her left arm smacked the cut on Wren's right thigh, and Wren winced from the pressure. "Mommy, I want to go home."

Wren knelt down while Nathan propped Doug up against the wall. "Honey, we can't go home. Not right now. We need to get your dad and brother help." She looked past Chloe to her eldest daughter, Addison, curled up in the corner, cradling her head. "And I need you to take care of your big sister, okay? We need to get her to the van out front. Can you help me with that?" The five-year-old puffed out her lower lip and nodded.

"Wren," Nathan said. "I need some help moving him."

"Mom." The cry came from behind her, where her eldest child and only son, Zack, lay propped up against the wall. Even in the darkness, his face was pale, and Wren saw the beads of sweat rolling off him. His right leg lay mangled and bloodied under his ripped jeans, the shin completely snapped in half, the remnants of the makeshift brace his father had constructed barely holding it together after the ambulance wrecked. The involuntary spasms of pain his muscles offered betrayed the hardened look of courage the fifteen-year-old had etched on his face.

Wren clutched his hand as she walked past. "We're taking you to get help. Just hang on for a little bit longer." She kissed the top of his head, fisting a cluster of black curls that rested on his scalp. *But what kind of help will we find?*

Wren tossed Doug's arm over her shoulder, and together she and Nathan lifted him off the floor. Though his weight was spread between the two of them, she still struggled to keep him upright. And the added pressure only increased the agitation of her thigh. "There." Wren gestured to the van, the heat from the city and the stress triggering a burst of sweat from her brow and neck.

"We'll get his torso inside first," Nathan replied, opening the back doors. "On three. One, two, three!"

Both of them grunted in the coordinated lift, and the back of the van lowered on its rusty shocks as Doug's body thumped on the floorboard. Wren gave him a shove forward but stopped once she saw the streaks of blood smear the van's dirtied carpet.

"The clotting powder will only hold for so long," Nathan said. "We need to get him to a doctor. He's lost too much blood, and he'll most likely need a transfusion. Do you remember his blood type?"

"AB positive," Wren answered, looking at the gritty material covering the hole in his stomach. She grabbed his hand. She shivered; his skin was an unearthly cold. She quickly released his finger and limped back inside to retrieve Zack. "Let's get everyone else loaded—"

An explosion sounded in the north, and Wren and Nathan ducked, grabbing whatever they could for support as the blast rocked the pavement. Wren danced on shaking legs into the center of the street. A fresh column of smoke snaked its way into the sky, and the sharp pierce of the initial explosion faded into a dull roar.

"Wren!" Nathan said.

Wren forced her attention back to the van and hastened her pace. We have to get out of the city. Nathan helped Zack outside, her son spitting groans through gritted teeth, while she carried Addison with her one good arm with Chloe trailing closely behind.

Nathan piled Zack next to his father in the back, and Wren strapped the girls in the second row. Addison rolled her head back and forth, her neck loose as a noodle. She cradled her daughter's cheek, worried about the effects of the concussion, and double-checked her seatbelt. Once everyone was secure, Wren climbed in the passenger seat. "Do you know any hospitals in the south?"

Nathan shifted into drive, shaking his head. "None that'll have any power, and judging by what we've seen so far, they'll be targets as well."

"Right," Wren added absentmindedly. She caught her reflection in the side mirror and didn't recognize the face staring back at her. Dust covered most of her head, and her hair was ragged, her cheeks hollow and dirty. She reached down and touched the cut on her thigh, grimacing, then gently rubbed the dull ache of her left arm in its sling.

"Zack!" Nathan yelled, narrowly missing a ten-car pileup as he veered around the edge. "I need you to check your dad's breathing every few minutes. Just place your hand under his nose and leave it there, make sure there's still an air flow."

Wren turned and watched her son place a shaky hand under Doug's nostrils. The van bounced over a pothole, and he nodded. "Yeah. It's faint, but he's still breathing."

"Good. Just keep checking, Zack." Nathan jerked the wheel side to side. The tires screeched with every harsh maneuver. Stand-still traffic congested the outbound lanes.

"Stay off the highways," Wren said, clutching her seat belt. "If we're one of the only working cars in the city, then I'd rather not advertise it."

"Me either," Nathan answered.

City buildings slowly morphed to the industrial district the farther they drove. A few miles beyond that, they saw the backs of the lines of people who'd left their disabled cars behind, exiting the city. Their heads perked up at the sound of the vehicle.

The greater the distance that separated them from the city limits, the thicker the crowds of pedestrians grew. It wasn't long before Nathan was forced to slow their pace as they came upon a cluster of broken-down police cars. Wren gripped the armrest tight, hoping none of them were desperate enough to try and stop them. But while she drew in her breath, the herd's attention was focused elsewhere. A massive Red Cross station had been erected, composed of flapping tents and folding tables.

Stacks of food and water were unloaded from trucks and distributed to outstretched arms and hands clamoring for help. Police officers formed a human barrier between the workers and the crowd, the hordes growing increasingly bold as the officers struggled to keep the masses at bay. A cluster of soldiers intermixed with the police kept their hands on their rifles, one of them barking orders to the crowd, which only exacerbated the people's defiance.

The line finally broke on the far left side, and the crowd swarmed through the hole like water in a sinking ship. They toppled tables and trampled workers, discarding what decency remained and satisfying the impulsive need of survival. Wren scooted away from her passenger-side window, watching the eyes follow their vehicle with the same lustful intentions they cast on the rations. She clutched Nate's arm. "Don't stop."

Nathan pointed to some of the medical tents. "Wren, this could be the only available medical staff for miles. I don't know how much longer Doug is going to last."

Gunshots rippled through the air, and Wren turned just in time to watch the masses shift like waves in a tide, pulling apart like cotton candy. "Go!" But by the time Nathan tried to accelerate, the masses swarmed the van like locusts, smacking into the doors and windows, climbing on top of the roof and clinging to the hood. Screams flooded in from the left, cut short by more gunfire. Wren squinted through the fleeing crowds, and her heart dropped at the sight of masked men tearing through the masses. They wore the same black cloth as the terrorists that attacked the hospital. "Nathan, go, now!"

The engine revved, and Wren felt the thump of bodies

collide against the van as Nathan pushed through the sea of people scrambling to get out of their path. Nate laid on the horn, and horrified faces gazed through the windows as Wren peered over the heads of the crowd to the skirmish between the authorities and terrorists. One by one the men in masks fell, and as the crowd cleared, only one remained, bloodied and on his knees, reaching for a device at his belt.

The explosion blinded Wren just as much as it deafened her. The van rattled, and the heat from the blast melted through the windows and doors. The harsh, high-pitched whine slowly faded, and as she opened her eyes, she saw the road had cleared and the van had picked up speed.

Wren turned to look back. The tents and tables had been wiped away, the windows in the surrounding buildings shattered, and a small crater rested in the earth where the masked man had knelt. On the outskirts of the blast, what was left of the crowd was scattered in pieces. Random body parts stretched for at least thirty yards. Those who'd survived the blast sprinted in whatever direction led them away from the carnage.

Chloe and Addison huddled on the seat, their limbs twisted around one another with their heads down. Doug still lay unconscious, while Zack looked out the back window in the same direction as his mother. When he finally turned around, she watched his pale cheeks turn a light shade of green. "Girls, don't look out the windows for a little while. Just keep your heads down."

Nathan gripped the wheel tightly, keeping his gaze straight ahead. His eyes watered, but no tears fell. "We shouldn't stop until we can't see the skyline anymore." His voice caught in his throat, and he shifted uneasily in his seat, glancing in the rearview mirror to Zack. "Your dad still breathing?"

The van was silent for a moment before Zack answered with a yes, and Wren felt her mind grow heavy and tired. She reclined her seat as the landscape outside her window shifted from buildings to open fields. The sky cleared the farther south they drove, and only a few sporadic vehicles were left in their path. What people they passed were too few and exhausted to cause any trouble. Wren brought a shaky hand up and rubbed her eyes, trying to rid herself of the fatigue as much as the images of body parts.

"Mom!"

The fog lifted from Wren's mind at the panicked shout, and she turned around to see Zack with his ear to Doug's nose. "He's not breathing." Her son hyperventilated, looking from his father to his mother, uncertain of what to do.

"You'll have to give him CPR, Zack," Nathan said, his eyes scanning the road for any signs for a doctor's office or medical facility. "You need to tilt his head back by lifting his chin to open his airway."

Zack shook his head, tears streaming down his face. "I-I can't. I'm sorry. I can't."

Nathan pulled off to the side of the road, unbuckling his seat belt in the process, and jumped from the driver's seat and into the back. "You drive."

Wren climbed behind the wheel and shifted the car back into drive, peeling out in the grass and gravel as she floored the accelerator. She flitted her eyes between the rearview, where Nathan pumped his hands over Doug's chest, and the road, searching for any sign of help. Suddenly, the horizon offered the small outline of buildings. "We've got a town coming up!"

"We'll have to stop there," Nathan said, puffing another breath into Doug's lungs. "He's not going to last with me working on him like this."

The speedometer tipped eighty. Adrenaline raced through her veins with the same high-octane intensity as the fuel in the van. The town's welcome sign passed in a blur as the first few buildings came into view. She slowed, looking for any signage for the hospital, but soon discovered the town was nothing more than a small strip of buildings on either side of the road.

A white building with a black sign out front toward the end of the row of stores caught her attention. She slammed on the brakes, veering off the road. "I've got something!" She thrust the van into park and helped Nathan pull Doug out of the back doors. Nathan scooped Doug in his arms, sprinted past the veterinary sign, and made a beeline for the door.

Wren flung the side door open. "C'mon, girls." Wren held out her hand, and her daughters sheepishly crawled from their seats. She scooped up Addison, who still couldn't stand up right, and Chloe huddled around her legs. She looked to her son. "I'll come back for you once I get them inside."

Zack nodded, and Wren guided the girls up the steps and inside the office. A series of bewildered faces glanced at her once inside, along with howls and screeches from a handful of animals, some of them caged, others held by their owners. Nathan burst through a door down a hallway. "Wren! Back here!"

Wren placed the girls in two vacant chairs in the waiting room. "You two stay right here and do not move." She kissed their foreheads and sprinted toward Nate. His massive body blocked the doorway, and she tried to peer past him, but the small openings offered no view of Doug.

"Wren." Nathan placed a heavy hand on her shoulder, and she felt her body sink. "He's not sure he can do anything."

Wren shoved Nate aside and stepped into the room. "Watch the girls." Doug lay on a steel table, a light above him, and a shrew-looking man with thinning hair, glasses, and a white coat far too large for his petite frame standing next to him. She thrust a finger at the doctor and then to Doug. "Help him."

The doctor took a step back, shrugging, his hands spread

out in a desperate plea. "Miss, I'm only a veterinarian. The wounds he's sustained, the amount of blood loss—"

"You need blood?" With her left arm pinned in the sling, Wren awkwardly rolled up the sleeve of her right arm, exposing the pale, soft, dirtied flesh underneath. "Take it. He's a universal receiver."

"Ma'am, I—"

"Take it!" Wren's voice shrilled, her cheeks and neck flushed hot red. She stepped forward, her arm jutted out, the lines and curves of her face shifting between tremors of rage and fear. "Try. Please."

The doctor hesitated, wiggling his fingers back and forth. Wren's arm shook the longer the silence between them grew. "Okay." The doctor pulled out a tray of instruments, the metal objects clanging against each other. He thrust an oddly shaped oxygen mask over Doug's face and ripped the fabric of his shirt.

Wren lowered her arm, slowly walking toward her husband on the table. He's not gone. Not yet. She reached for his hand. His finger was cold to the touch. The doctor grabbed her arm, and she felt the cold prick of steel pierce her skin.

"There's no guarantee he'll survive." Blood drained from the veins in Wren's arm, oozing through the tube and into Doug, warming the point of entrance on his skin. "You should prepare for the worst."

Wren watched her blood drain, feeling dizzy and light-headed. "I already have."

11

Addison and Chloe lay asleep in Wren's lap. She felt the steady rise and fall of their chests, and she stroked their hair. Her sleeve was still rolled up, and a bandage had been placed over the puncture wound. The paleness of her complexion only accentuated the dark circles that had formed under her eyes, dragging her downward.

The doctor worked on Doug for an hour, and while his pulse returned, his consciousness did not. And now that he was stabilized, the veterinarian shifted his work to Zack. Her son screamed when the doctor reset the bone, but since then, it'd been nothing but the barking of dogs and the hiss of cats.

The waiting room in the veterinarian's office was dark, save for the sunlight coming through the windows. The EMP had stretched well beyond Chicago's city limits, and she heard the rumblings of the town's citizens in regard to the sudden malfunction of their vehicles, phones, and other devices. A few candles were set out and slowly became the main source of light as the sun touched the horizon in the west.

Nathan stepped around the corner of the hallway, Doug's dried blood caked over his shirt and arms. His shoulders sagged as he leaned against the wall, examining his attire. "The doctor's done with Zack. He's resting now."

"And Doug?" The past hour had seen her mind race down every nightmarish avenue she could imagine, wondering what she would do or say if Doug didn't survive, or if he did.

"He's still passed out. The doctor is checking on him now."

Wren nodded, her gaze cast down to her girls in her lap, then she rested her head against the wall. She closed her eyes, her head swimming. She was surprised that her mind was still dizzy from the doctor draining her blood. I'm just tired.

"Wren." Nathan's bearlike palm engulfed her shoulder. "We need to get out of here. I know of a place that we can go."

The scrape on Wren's leg roared its irritation, and a hot flush ran through her. "We're out of the city, Nathan. We're safe."

"For now." Nathan looked around suspiciously then inched closer. "Wren, if this town was affected by the EMP blast, then we have to assume the entire country was as well. And if that's the case, this power outage is going to last a very long time. What we saw in Chicago was just the beginning."

Wren forced the dizzy spell into submission, gently shifting the girls off her lap. "It's too soon to talk of something like that. We don't know if it's the entire country. We can't base our decisions off our fears, Nathan." She rested the two of them across the chairs, and they fidgeted lightly from the interruption. "Watch the girls for a second. I'm going to go check on Zack."

The first few steps were difficult, her knees buckling twice, and she had to grip the wall for support. But once she fell into a rhythm, a portion of her strength returned. The doctor had just come out of Doug's room when she made it to Zack's door. He'd removed his coat, revealing the true thinness of his frame. His clothes were covered and stained with dark blotches, and his arms were red from fingertips to elbows. "Thank you."

The doctor shook his head, his eyes focused on the blood on his hands. "I didn't do anything. There's still no guarantee that he'll survive. He's alive, but barely."

"You did enough." Wren smiled then stepped inside Zack's room.

Her son lay asleep with his left leg in a cast from knee to foot. An IV bag hung above him, offering what nourishment it could to his young, battered body. She pulled up a chair and sat next to him, her fingers lacing between his. "We're okay." She kissed his palm. "We're going to be okay."

* * *

THE SUN HAD COMPLETELY DISAPPEARED below the horizon, and with the power out the night cast a darkness Wren had never seen before. She rotated her shoulder that hung in the sling from the hospital, stiff from sitting in the van, as she scanned the radio channels for any news, anywhere. But just like her phone, the airwaves remained quiet.

A bead of sweat rolled down her forehead, stinging her eye on its way. She felt the heat radiate from her body, and her mind was dizzy. I just need to rest. Sleep had been in short supply, her mind too busy contemplating their next move. It offered a distraction from worrying about whether Doug would survive.

Indiana was an option if they headed east. Wren's parents still lived just outside of Indianapolis, but if what Nate was telling her were true, then she wasn't sure if their circumstances would improve. While Nathan's option of his secret camp loomed in her mind, she refused to bring her family to people she didn't know or trust, no matter how many times he brought it up.

"Wren," Nathan said, slinking through the dark. "You need to come, quick."

Wren stumbled getting out of the van, which they'd moved into the veterinary's garage to keep out of view from the rest of the town. Having a working vehicle had its advantages, and she wanted to make sure those advantages stayed in their possession.

The candles that replaced the faulty lights down the hallway exaggerated the menacing shadows in the dark. She followed Nathan to Doug's room, where he lay still, the vet hovering over him. At first glance, Wren thought Doug had awoken; his head lolled back and forth lazily, and she heard the murmurs of his voice. But the closer she looked, she realized that his eyes remained closed, and his words were nonsense. The light from the candles illuminated the slick sheen of sweat covering his skin.

"He has a fever," the veterinary said, removing a thermometer from Doug's mouth. "His temperature has spiked three degrees in the past hour. He's burning up."

Before Wren even touched Doug's forehead, she felt the heat coming off him. The bloodied bandage around Doug's stomach was damp with sweat, and the IV was running low. "Can't you give him something?" Wren removed her hand, her palm scorching hot.

"I don't have the antibiotics he needs." The vet gestured to the wound. "If he has an infection, he won't last more than a few days. His organs will slowly shut down. He needs more help than I can give him."

"You have to have something." Wren paced across the shelves in the large animal operating room that were lined with hundreds of different bottles and boxes. "One of these has to be able to help him."

"There's nothing here!" The vet's voice screeched like a scratch in a record. His small body trembled from the exertion, and Wren wasn't sure if the meager man was more afraid of his words, or how she would react to them. He rubbed his brow, and his glasses slid down the bridge of his nose. "What he needs now, I can't help with." He stomped over to the shelves, pulling down boxes hastily. "I know every single pill and powder in my inventory. I have medicine for horses, pigs, sheep, dogs, cats, birds, and snakes, but none of them can fight what he has." He emptied the box, the bottles rolling across the tile, then slammed the empty cardboard to the floor. "I. Can't. Help!" Steam fumed from the vet's ears, and he clenched his small hands into fists.

Wren took a breath, letting her thoughts gather and the vet's temper cool. "Then what does he need?"

"Cefepime, ceftazidime, and ceftriaxone sodium." The vet listed them off slowly, rubbing his eyes. "They're used to fight infections in the organs, bones, and skin. He'll need a steady six-week regimen to eradicate the bacteria."

"You're sure he's infected?" Wren placed a hand on Doug's table. His face was still dripping with sweat.

"If his fever hasn't broken by morning, then it's a one hundred percent certainty."

Wren nodded, her gaze shifting from Doug, who lay motionless on the table, to Nathan. "Then we wait until we know for sure."

"Wren, if we wai—"

"We wait. Until we know for sure." Wren stomped away, her head spinning once more. She wasn't going to let someone else dictate what was best for her family. She'd seen too much. Her family had felt the burden of the chaos in Chicago. She wouldn't be pushed around, not here.

Wren found the girls asleep in one of the rooms, and she leaned against the doorway, lingering at the precipice of entry. The two of them were balled up tight in blankets, their hair tangled and messy. She'd never seen anything so peaceful in her life.

"Wren." The whisper was accompanied by a tap on her

shoulder, and when she turned around, Nathan clasped his hands together, pleading. "You need to listen to me."

Wren grabbed his arm, pulling them both away from the girls. "I already told you, Nathan, we wait until morning. The doctor's not one hundred percent sure."

"He's also not a medical doctor," Nathan replied harshly. "He's a veterinarian."

"All the more reason to stay put." The waves of exhaustion beat their way against her, eroding her patience. The harder Wren fought, the quicker she drowned in her fatigue. She loosened the collar of her shirt, suddenly feeling warm.

"And if the vet is right, it might be too late by morning."

A sudden shock of icy cold mixed with heat cut through Wren like a freight train. She put her hand against the wall for support. The cut along her leg ached. The white bandages the vet had wrapped around the wound upon their arrival already needed to be changed. She shook her head. "How far is it to this camp?" The wound burned like hot coals. She shut her eyes and felt the tiles under her feet shift, as if they were rolling waves on the ocean.

"From here, it's at least a three-hour drive," Nathan answered. "And that's if we don't run into any trouble. Hell, we may not even have enough fuel to get us there."

Wren stepped away from the light; the sight of the flame dancing in the dark hallway only compounded the illusion of the shifting ground. "We'll check for gas in the morning." She backtracked down the hallway, retreating toward the van. "I'm going to go and catch some shut-eye. Wake me up if anything changes."

Nathan agreed, and Wren focused on putting one foot in front of the other on her slow walk down the hall. By the time she arrived at the van, it was all she could do to pull herself inside, collapsing onto the backseat. Her skin flashed from hot to cold, and she found a blanket in the back, which she pulled tight to her chin, fighting off the shivers running up and down her body.

But whatever peace Wren hoped to find in her sleep was disfigured by shifting nightmares. The gunshots at the hospital in Chicago thundered through her mind like a hurricane, rolling her back and forth in the chaos she tried so desperately to escape. She felt the warm splash of blood from the dead as one by one patients fell around her. She ran through hallways of shrieking screams and bloodcurdling cries of the dying. The wicked foreign tongue of the killers barked in her ears. "Yuhzir! Alkhuruj wamuajahat mammatik!" The wailing cries of her daughters shook loose the gripping fear the terrorists' voices had instilled. She sprinted toward the sound of their cries through the hallways, stepping over and around the slain bodies that were spread across the tiles. And it wasn't but a few moments later that she found herself covered in dust, the hospital behind her nothing but rubble, and she was alone. Her girls had disappeared, and when she cried out to them, another voice echoed back to her. Zack. Her son's voice was muffled under the mangled concrete and twisted steel which grew taller the closer she moved. Her son's voice shrank with the growing heap of rubble. She flung rocks and rebar from the pile, digging deeper and deeper into the collapsed mountain until she finally came upon him, broken and unconscious. She scooped her son up in her arms as the unstable structure around her shifted and moaned above them. A searing pain ripped through her right thigh. And just as the rubble tumbled down upon both of them, she awoke.

Wren ripped the blanket off her and clutched her leg. Her entire body was slick with sweat, the blanket damp and her clothes soaked. Her hair clung to her forehead in greasy, matted sheets. The muscles along her thigh felt like they were melting off and she rolled off the seat and onto the floorboard.

With a shaking arm, she pulled down her pants. Every inch was excruciating, and when she peeled back the top portion of her bandage, she gagged. The cut had grown a bright red, and a small amount of pus oozed from the side of the gash. Infected. She pulled her pants back up, gingerly, and lay still on the floor.

A ray of light broke through the high window of the garage, signaling that it was dawn. She rubbed her eyes and pushed herself to an upright position. Fear gripped her as she realized what morning meant. Doug.

Wren crawled forward awkwardly over the seats, doing her best to keep pressure off her wounded limbs. She collapsed out of the van and limped forward, forcing all of her weight on her left leg. The hallway was quiet, no sign of anyone awake. She used the walls for support on her way to Doug's room. When she opened the door, both Nathan and the veterinarian looked at her as if she'd grown a second head. "His fever," Wren said, the words escaping her lips in hoarse rasps. "Is it gone?" Against her will, she slid to the floor, struggling to keep her eyes open. She felt a hand on her forehead.

"Christ, she's burning up."

Wren swatted the hand away. She opened her eyes. Her vision was blurred. Both the veterinarian and Nathan were nothing more than hazy images. "Doug, is he—"

"His fever has gone up," the vet answered. "We're trying to cool him down, but it's only a temporary fix. He'll still need the antibiotics if you want him to live." He left Doug's side and knelt down with Nathan, popping a thermometer into her mouth. "And he's not the only one in need." He peeled back the bandages on her thigh and shook his head. "It's in the early stages of infection, but it'll get worse if it goes untreated." He retrieved one of the compresses from Doug's table and applied it to her forehead.

"It was just a scratch," Wren said. The cool pack broke

through the heat melting her mind, and Wren felt the instant relief. It spread down the back of her skull, through her arms, and gradually made its way to her leg. But the relief was short lived, as the heat from her body quickly melted whatever cool the pack provided. She tried to connect her thoughts before they disappeared into the heat of her mind. "We have to… Doug needs…" But each time she got close, they melted away, dripping into the abyss.

"Wren, listen to me." Nathan gently cradled her head. "We need to go to the camp. They have medicine there that will help Doug, and you. It's safe. I promise."

I promise. Promises weren't strong enough to bet her life on, or her family's. Hell, it wasn't even strong enough to save her marriage. She shook her head. "Somewhere else. A hospital." She swallowed hard, the lack of spit making the motion rough.

"The closest hospital that's not in Chicago is farther than the camp," Nathan explained. "Wren, if we don't leave now, then you are going to die. Doug will die."

With the searing pain pulsing through her body, death sounded like a welcome reprieve. But then her children would be orphaned, and she would not let her own blood wander the rest of their lives alone. Not with the world crumbling around them. "Okay." Wren nodded. "We'll go."

12

Wren watched the fields and bushes fly by her window in a blur. She focused all of her strength on keeping her eyes open, but despite her protest, her mind drifted off to sleep, her unconscious filled with more of the same nightmares as before. She awoke, dripping in sweat, and reached for the bottled water in the cup holder they'd taken from the vet's office now in their rearview mirror.

The water was nearly as warm as Wren, but the liquid helped quench her thirst regardless. She drained half the bottle and took a moment to catch her breath as her body still quivered from dehydration. She pushed herself higher in the seat, the water providing a brief moment of clarity. The landscape had transformed from fields to trees. "Where are we?"

"We're close," Nathan replied.

Wren reached for her leg and nearly fainted from the lightest touch of her fingers. She gripped the armrests for support until the pain passed then shifted uneasily in her seat, turning back around to Zack and the girls. "Hey, guys."

Chloe and Addison offered a weak smile while Zack

simply rolled his head to the side, away from Wren's view.

"Where are we going, Mom?" It was Chloe who spoke, her blue eyes flashing in the passing light between the trees on the side of the road.

"Your dad needs some help. And Uncle Nate is taking us to a place where we can get some." And hopefully for me as well. Wren forced Nathan to keep her infection from them, even Zack. The kids had enough on their plate as it was.

The van squeaked to a stop, beckoning attention. "We're here." Nathan thrust the car into park, and the engine hummed irritably, as if the very prospect of having to start moving again was too much to bear. "I'll be right back."

The structure in front of them was impressive, especially considering the surrounding area. The front gate was at least ten feet high and twenty feet wide and made of reinforced steel. A catwalk stood on top of the entrance, where two guards were stationed, armed with rifles. But after the twenty feet of steel, either side of the fence transformed from metal to wood and stretched farther than she could see, blending into the forest.

At the gate, voices were raised and tempers flared. Nathan thrust his arms angrily at the two men with guns on the top walkway. Once the exchange was complete, Nathan stomped back to the van, and the gate opened, making a gap in the middle as the two doors swung outward. The flustered look on Nathan's face matched his tone as he shifted the vehicle back into drive. "You'll have to meet with the council before they'll administer any medicine to Doug."

The van lurched forward, and Wren shook her head, wondering if the fever had affected her hearing as they passed through the gate. "The council?"

"They're in charge. It's protocol for any member bringing someone from the outside." Nathan kept the van at a slow pace on the way through the camp, which so far was nothing more than trees and a dirt road. "I wasn't supposed to bring anyone that wasn't on my list."

The trees inside the camp were thick, the terrain rockier than she'd expected. The dirt road dipped and wound through the forest, and Wren caught herself looking upward. She wasn't sure if it was the fever or the fact that the last time she was in the wilderness she was with her father as a young girl, but there was something comforting about the canopies above. The rays of sunlight passed between the leaves and branches and into the dirtied windows of the van, and while she was already burning up, it was a different type of warmth from the hellish fever engulfing her. She closed her eyes, and for a moment she could almost hear the sound of her children laughing on a spring day in the park. The car jerked to a stop, along with the brief glimpse of a past Wren wasn't sure would ever be in her future again.

Much of the forest in this area had been cleared and replaced with buildings and open fields. Most were built from the same wood as the trees that once stood in their lots, but one particular building on the back side of the camp held the distinct glare of concrete in the sun. Nathan pounded on the van's hood and motioned for her to get out.

Wren turned back to her children and reached for Zack's hand, which felt oddly cool compared to her blazing-hot ones. "If anything happens, you get your sisters out of here." He offered a light nod, and Wren gave his hand a squeeze, which he didn't reciprocate.

Nathan helped her to one of the larger buildings, and every step forward, she felt the pain from her leg weaken the rest of her body. She examined the eyes staring back at her and the hands that carried logs, crates, cases, and weapons. Despite the heat, everyone dressed in thick, layered clothing, and their expressions looked as heavy as the woven fabric on their backs. A foul stench graced her nostrils, and she wrinkled her face in revulsion.

"They'll ask you questions," Nathan said. "Who you are, how you know me, your family, but the only thing that matters is your job."

"Am I on trial?"

The words were meant in jest, but Nathan stopped the two of them just before the steps to the building. "Yes. And if the council votes to kick you out..." Nathan gripped her shoulders tight. "Everyone was invited and chosen to be in this community. You can too. Your skills as an architect are valuable, and you're a gifted engineer."

"Structural engineer," Wren said, correcting him. "Nathan, what happens if they don't want me and my kids here? We came here because you said we could get help."

"And help doesn't come free," Nathan answered. "Let's go."

Nathan held out a hand to help her up the steps, but Wren shoved him aside. She gripped the railing and pulled herself up by her own steam. It was painful, but the rage and frustration over the situation displaced the symptoms of her fever. Panting by the time she made the ten short steps up, she pushed through the front doors with her head up.

Inside, the building was more akin to a town hall. Backless benches lined either side of a narrow path that fed into an open floor and a raised platform with five seats arranged in an arc pattern. The floors were dusty, and the air inside smelled of the maple and oak that comprised the rafters. There were no windows, and when the door closed behind her, Wren found herself alone and cast into darkness. She stopped halfway down the narrow path to the front platform. "Hello?"

The building's acoustics that echoed back her words were the only answer she received. She shuffled a few steps forward but stopped at the creak of a door opening in the back of the building and saw the light it cast from outside.

Footsteps followed, and the glow of candlelight moved behind the platform.

One, two, three, four, then five people stepped onto the platform, each finding their seats, each with their own candle. Two women and three men from what Wren could tell, and while most of their features were masked in the candlelight, she noticed the distinct scarring on the man who sat in the middle. The candlelight that flickered across his face highlighted the disfigurement, and while he looked only slightly older than herself, the dark eyes that stared down upon her looked ancient.

"Come forward," the man with dark eyes said, his voice booming low and deep. The others kept silent, and despite the man's commanding voice, she did not sway. He leaned forward, the shadows on his face shifting with him. "I do not have time for your cowardice. Step forward, or you will not be afforded an opportunity like this again."

Zack, Addison, Chloe. And Doug. For them. Wren forced herself forward. The faces on the platform grew taller the closer she moved. For the moment, her adrenaline had returned, vanquishing the symptoms of her leg, but the sweating only worsened. By the time she reached the front, she was drenched. All five of them looked down at her as though they were dissecting an insect, determining whether to let her scurry by or end her existence with the heels of their boots.

"You were brought here by Nathan Heiss, yes?" The woman on the far left spoke softly, calmly, a far cry from the hellish looks her peers cast. From what Wren could tell, the woman was older, close to her fifties, but in the dim lighting, it was hard to tell if the strands of hair were silver grey or a vibrant blond.

"Yes." Wren forced her voice to steady despite the nerves running rampant through her body. "Along with my three children and their father."

"Your husband?" The man next to the older woman asked, raising his eyebrow. His lips remained motionless when he spoke, hidden under a thick mustache, which was as bushy as the caterpillars of his eyebrows that stretched over the shadows of his eyes.

"I was told I needed to speak with you in order to secure my family's acceptance into this community," Wren said, ignoring the man's question. "Tell me what you need of me, and I will do it."

"Need?" The man in the center drawled the word for a moment before he let it end. He tilted his head to the side. The dark eyes sucked up the dull light from the candle, and Wren found herself trying to look away, as if staring at the pools of black in his face for too long would suck the life from her. "We have no business for need here. This community was not established for the sole purpose of harboring those who need help. Only those who earn their keep." He thrust his finger at the doors behind her. "Your cities and your government have failed you, and now you come to us with your hands cupped like a beggar's bowl!" He slammed his fist on the table, and the deafening crack wavered the flames of the candles that rested upon it.

Two of the dark-eyed councilman's colleagues curved a smile up the side of their hollowed cheeks, while the other two sank back in their seats. The woman to the dark-eyed councilman's left leaned close to his arm, while the second man remained nothing more than a bystander in the proceedings. "I come with no bowl. I was an architect at a firm in Chicago, where I've been practicing my craft for the past six years. I'm an accomplished structural engineer, and there isn't a building technique or material that I'm not familiar with. There is no one better at blending design and functionality when it comes to erecting a structure from this earth." While her words ignited the interest of Dark Eyes, Wren felt a sudden emptiness at the thought of the city that was her home. The way she left it, she wasn't sure if she'd ever get the chance to see it again.

The two closest to the dark-eyed councilman leaned in to whisper in his ear, and all the while he never took his gaze off Wren. There was something unnerving in his glare, and it wasn't the darkness; she knew the light could play tricks. The councilman's pupils took on a hard callus, as if he could leave his eyelids open in a sandstorm and walk away with his vision unscathed.

Once the two on either side of Dark Eyes had spoken whatever thoughts they deemed necessary, the councilman rose from his seat, and the others followed suit. He made his way down from the platform and stopped only inches from Wren. The scars on his face were sharper, more defined up close, and his scowl only intensified the disfigurement. His height and broad shoulders further compounded his commanding presence. "Come with me." The other council members brushed past quickly, and Wren struggled to keep up.

Outside, she shielded her eyes from the sunlight. She looked for Nathan and the van, but neither was in sight. The lack of familiarity irritated the aches and pains in her body, but she forced herself to the front of the pack, ignoring the stares from those she passed on the way. She yanked the dark-eyed councilman's arm and spun him around. "Where is my family?"

If the man's features were bad in the dark, then in the sunlight they were abhorrent. Four scars covered the majority of his cheeks and neck. One ran along his left jawline, the second from the corner of his lower lip to his chin, the third across the meaty part of his right cheek, and the last from under his chin down beneath his shirt to the collarbone. While the wounds had long since healed, they left canyons on his skin that would never afford him a normal complexion. He pointed behind him to the fence. "We have a wall around our entire encampment, with guards patrolling twenty-four hours a day, seven days a week. You tell me how you would get through, and I'll let you stay."

"Tell you? Or the council?" Wren turned to eye the others; the man and woman that seemed cozier with Dark Eyes than the other two had their arms crossed.

"You don't have any bargaining chips on the table, so I suggest you tell me quickly before I change my mind."

Wren shouldered past the councilman, toward the far side of the compound. While the front gate had looked formidable, the same quality had not been replicated for the rest of the fence. She examined the wall, running her hand over the bumpy logs that rose from the earth like medieval spikes around a castle. "The wood's dry." She peeled off a few splinters and snapped them between her fingers. "A little bit of gas and a lighter, and you'd be engulfed in a ring of fire." She walked farther down, noticing a lean in a large portion of the fence. "You didn't reinforce the foundation. When winter comes around, that portion of the fence will cave after the first heavy snowfall." She turned around to look him in the eye. "But that's not your biggest problem."

"No? And what is?"

"You think you've used the natural landscape to your advantage, sucking up the resources around you to help reinforce your buildings and walls, but you've built your compound on low ground." Wren walked around him, taking in the infrastructure of the community. "If you're planning to live here for the long haul, you'll find you'll have a problem with sewage and plumbing after the first hard rain. It'll flood, and those crops will mix with waste you let build up and then wash away into your soil." Wren limped forward one step. "That's what I'm smelling, right? I'm guessing this is the first time all of these people have been here at the same time for this long. But you don't have to take my word for it. The first outbreak of dysentery should speak for itself. Of course, by then, it'll be too late to stop it from happening."

The councilman clenched his jaw and narrowed his eyes. Wren knew he understood that she was right, but whether or not it was enough to admit her entrance to the camp was a different story. After a pause, he turned back to confer with the rest of the council. They spoke in hushed tones, glancing back at Wren, pointing to the flaws she mentioned then pointing to one another. After a few minutes, Dark Eyes made his way back over to her. "Much of your family is in need of medical care?"

"My husband needs antibiotics, and my girls need to be looked at by a doctor." Wren palmed the side of her wounded thigh where the cut had worsened but kept it to herself, not knowing how much value her skillset would afford her.

"Your family will be treated." He thrust a finger in her face. "But I will tell you this. You try and double-cross me on this, and I promise you the last thing you'll be worried about is your children seeing a doctor." He stomped away, two of the council members following, while two stayed behind.

"You'll have to excuse Edric. He takes some getting used to." In the sunlight, Wren could make out both of them more clearly. The woman had defined age lines carved across her face, and daylight revealed her hair to be grey, but her eyes and smile were a natural complement to the rest of her features. "My name is Iris. This is Ben."

The gentleman with the thick mustache and eyebrows extended a hand as thick as his facial hair. "Pleasure to have you on board, miss."

Iris gestured to where Edric and the other two councilmen exited. "The other two councilmen with Edric were Jan and Ted. You'll rarely find that those three have any differences of opinion."

"My family, where—"

"Nathan already has them with the doctor; he's looking

over them now," Iris replied then smiled, adding, "You really didn't think we'd turn you away in the condition you were in, did you? Edric just likes to play hard to get."

It looks as though he enjoys playing a lot more than that. The architecture world wasn't one many women ventured into, and in her experience, she had noted that not all of her male counterparts shared her belief that she belonged. It was a trait she learned to recognize quickly, and it was one she saw in Edric.

13

The bunk was small, but Wren was grateful to have a bed. It was a huge improvement over the van, and when she woke, she still felt tired and hot, but the dizziness from the previous day had ceased. There were four cots in the small room, with Doug and Zack each having their own, but Doug's remained empty, as he was still under the doctor's supervision. The girls shared one, and Wren had her own, although in the middle of the night, she felt Addison climb into bed with her.

Wren planted two bare feet onto the worn wooden floor and tried applying pressure to her wounded leg. The pain was still there, but it had diminished some, although the same could not be said for her arm, which was furious with her after she had allowed Addison to fall asleep on it.

She let Zack and the girls rest a while longer and hobbled from the bedroom into the living room, which was bare save for the necessities, and even that was stretching it. A few chairs surrounded a table, and a large cast-iron heater sat in the middle of the living room. Other than the main room and the bedroom where Wren's family slept, there was only one other room in the cabin, which belonged to Nathan.

The community didn't have any extra housing, and Nathan had offered to put them up until Wren could build their own place. She burst out laughing at the suggestion but soon realized that Nathan wasn't joking. He, along with the rest of the community, believed that the effects of the EMP weren't going to end. Everyone here was in it for the long haul.

With no one awake, and dawn barely breaking over the horizon, Wren decided to have a look around. The morning was surprisingly cool, and the surrounding woods were quiet. The only noise that filled her ears was the soft crunch of earth underneath her feet.

A mist floated through the air that was so fine she couldn't feel it on her skin. She looked north, half expecting to still see the plumes of smoke and fire of Chicago, but they were too far from the city now. The only view on the horizon were a few clouds that floated above the trees.

Since she was admitted into the camp based off of her career choice, she decided to get a better look at the camp to see where any improvements could be made, but kept a path toward the fence. Along the way, she passed a few people who had already woken, busy about their morning tasks. She watched people hoe their gardens, fill water buckets from a well in the center of the camp, inventory jars of food stacked in crates, and a few clean rifles and pistols.

The reactions to her presence were as mixed as the council when she first arrived. Some offered a smile and a wave, others a grimace, and the rest ignored her completely. Not that she cared. She knew nothing of these people, and they knew nothing of her. All that mattered now was making sure Zack and the girls remained healthy, and that Doug stayed alive.

The deeper Wren followed the fence, the thicker the forest around her became. She looked back a few times, making sure she could still see the majority of the compound from her position. From what she could tell, the community was centered specifically in the clearing behind her. The fence itself grew more decrepit the farther she walked, and more than once she stumbled upon portions of the wooden logs that had been splintered. When she dug her fingers into the cracked wood, her fingers grazed the smoothness of metal. At first she thought it was a nail, but the deeper she dug the more she recognized the thickness of the bullet.

A branch rustled to Wren's left, and the sudden commotion made her heart leap, but it was nothing but a squirrel leaping onto a tree trunk. She backed up against the fence for support, and gently massaged the wounded leg, careful not to get too close to the cut.

"What are you doing here?"

Wren jumped and screamed, covering her mouth as she backed away from the fence. She tripped over her feet and fell to the forest floor, her back scraping against the rocks that littered the ground. "Who's there?"

The voice echoed from beyond the fence, and through the cracks between logs, she saw a body pace back and forth. Portions of eyes, a mouth, and cheeks flitted between, looking at Wren on the ground. "I saw you come in." The man's voice was hoarse, as if he'd screamed his whole life and now could only bark haggard words. "You're not welcome in there."

"The council said I could stay. Whoever you are, you can't overthrow their decisions." At least I don't think you can. From what she'd experienced the previous day, she was under the impression that the council's word was law.

"Hmph. The council." The voice spit the words out as though they were poison on his tongue. "You tell me you trust them? Can't trust them as far as you can throw them."

"And who can I trust, then? You? It seems you're on the wrong side of the fence." Wren pushed herself off the slab of leaves and rocks and took a few careful steps toward the voice, wondering if it was this man who'd caused some of the bullets to be lodged in the wood.

"That's where you're wrong, woman. This forest is full of wolves. More so now than ever."

Gunshots blared to the south, and Wren involuntarily ducked. Her adrenaline heightened, along with her heart rate. She clutched her chest and stumbled backward. Her body broke out in a cold sweat, and flashbacks of the gunfire in Chicago terrorized her mind. She squinted her eyes shut, trying to rid herself of the throbbing visions of the terrorists. *Are they here? They couldn't have followed us. Was that man one of them?*

Wren rushed to the fence, her nails digging into the wood as she desperately clawed over the posts, peering through the cracks in search of the voice, but her investigations revealed nothing but daylight and trees. More gunshots thundered toward the front of the camp, and she shuddered. *The kids.*

Wren sprinted as fast as her legs allowed, using the perimeter to guide her back. Shouts from the camp bounced through the thick trees. When the clearing finally came into view, Wren watched people dash between houses. All of them carried weapons, and once armed, they headed in the same direction. By the time Wren made it within arm's reach of a woman clutching her child, her mouth was so dry that she couldn't form the words to speak. After the third try, she managed to croak out words. "What's happening?"

"An attack on the front gate." The woman's voice hid the fear which her eyes betrayed. "Everyone is going to want what we have." She turned and gave Wren a look that suggested she was a part of the attack, then returned to her cabin with her young boy, bolting the door shut behind her.

The herds of people funneled toward the front gate, and Wren followed. The sight reminded her of an old western. The community members wielded rifles and pistols, a coldness in their gaze that would kill anything that meant to harm them.

With the majority of the crowd gathered by the gate by the time Wren arrived, most of the gunfire had stopped. The guards on duty had their weapons aimed downward toward the outer portion of the fence and were shouting at whoever was on the other end of their rifles. "Turn around, and do not come back here. You're not welcome. This is private property."

Wren weaseled her way to the side of the crowd and discovered that she was the only person not armed, and what was more, their side of the front gate had sliding doors built into the steel. Every person stationed at one looked poised to slide it open and squeeze off a few rounds. She moved left, toward the wooden portion of the fence, and squinted through the cracks.

"What do you have?" Edric climbed to the top of the gate, and one of the guards whispered in his ear. Even from a distance, Wren could still make out the scars. He nodded then bellowed down to the unknown persons. "You have sixty seconds to remove yourself from this gate, or we will kill you."

Wren could only see fragments of the people between the wooden posts, but she was able to make out three cars, all of them old, rusted and worn. Only the driver and passenger of the lead vehicle were outside the protection of their car. "Please, we've tried everywhere, but it's all the same thing. No power, running low on food, water, and medicine." He pointed a shaky hand to the car behind him. "We have people who are diabetic. We'll do whatever we have to. Please, just let us in!"

More footsteps thudded toward the gate, and Wren peeled her gaze from the cracks in the fence to watch the remainder of the council march up the front gate's steps. Iris and Ben were armed, but didn't add their weapons to the arsenal of rifles aimed at the people below like Jan and Ted.

"Wren," Nathan said, pulling her away from the fence. "You shouldn't be here."

"Who are those people?" Wren slid out from Nathan's hands and repositioned herself back at the fence. A few more had stepped out of their cars. Their faces looked familiar, and she saw a dog in the back seat of the middle vehicle.

Nathan gripped her good arm, yanking her backward. "I don't know. But they shouldn't be here." He was more forceful this time, but Wren refused to leave, and she added a shove into Nathan's soft chest in defiance.

"Like me?" The retort came out angrier than she'd intended but afforded her the distance to stay out of Nathan's reach until he was summoned by a few of the other community members.

The driver had moved to the front of his car now, his arms spread wide. "Please, we won't cause any trouble."

"You already have!" It was Edric's voice that boomed down at him as he aimed the barrel of his rifle at the intruder's head. Nearly everyone else mimicked his actions, with the exception of Iris, Ben, and a few others on the ground.

Wren watched out of the corner of her eye as Iris pulled Edric back, a grimace on her face with every hushed word that escaped her lips, until her whispers roared above the crowd and she shoved the barrel of his weapon down. "Edric, this isn't the way!" But before Edric could retort, Wren watched another passenger in the front car step out, holding something in his hands, and before she saw what it was, shouts broke out.

"Gun! Gun! Gun!"

Gunfire erupted in the quiet morning air, and Wren covered the back of her head with her hands, flattening herself against the dirt, but her eyes were still glued to the small spaces between the fence that offered fragmented glimpses of the carnage beyond the wall.

The front car was turned to Swiss cheese while the second tried to reverse, but the windshield shattered like ice after the first volley of bullets, and the car veered off the dirt path and crashed into a tree. The passengers in the backseat of the wrecked car fled but only made it four steps before they were dropped by a hail of lead. Each gunshot, each pained final scream, caused Wren to dig her nails deeper into the back of her skull.

Shouts and curses spread through the camp as Wren watched the dust of the third car trail into the sky as it sped down the road, bullets chasing after it, the driver recklessly taking the curves and turns at high speeds, and jumping divots to avoid the deadly gunshots.

"Help." A bloodied hand followed the weak voice and covered the view from Wren's position. She jolted backward, and she smacked her wounded arm on the compacted earth in the process. Moans and heavy breaths accompanied the light pawing from the dying man. And before Wren had a chance to see his face, another gunshot dropped the man's hand. Smoke wafted from the tip of Edric's rifle as he smiled.

Two hands pulled Wren up, and Nathan dusted some of the leaves off her back. "Are you all right?"

"Those people," Wren said, turning back to the fence, where just on the other side she knew rested a field of corpses. "Were they from the town we stopped at?"

Wren saw the heavy doubt cloud Nathan's face as he answered. "I don't know."

"You!" Edric leapt the twelve feet from the top of the gate's walkway and shook the earth upon landing. The crowd parted to make way for him as he beelined toward Wren and Nathan. "They followed you here. They came from the same town you did." The scars along Edric's face curved and twisted with his rage, which reached a crescendo when he aimed his rifle at Wren's head. "You've been here for less than a day, and you've already compromised our camp!"

Nathan wedged himself between the rifle and Wren. "Edric, we didn't have anything to do with that."

"Shut up!" Edric flung Nathan aside with one quick, easy swing of his arm. With the barrel of a gun once again close to her head, Wren felt the sudden familiarity of death creep up her spine. A crowd was gathered around them now, and judging from their expressions, most of them agreed with their head councilman.

"Edric!" Iris shoved her way through the crowd, Ben following close behind. She knocked the barrel of the rifle away, and while the woman stood at least a foot shorter than Edric, you wouldn't have known it by the look in her eye. "You know better than to point a gun at a community member."

Edric ground his teeth. "She's not a member, Iris. She's a leech that Nathan dragged in with him."

"She is a member of this community now. We voted her in yesterday, or is that thick skull of yours suffering from memory loss?" Iris refused to let up, mocking the man in front of nearly half the community. And while her methods were blunt, they were effective. "And you know the laws of drawing a weapon on a member."

Wren found herself staring at the spot on the fence where the man's bloodied hand had blocked her vision. Iris's verbal assault distracted Edric long enough for Wren to creep toward the fence. She crouched to the same spot as before and peered through the thin cracks of wood. A bloodied arm sprawled out on the ground. Both cars were smoking, their engines shut off. Bodies spilled from both wrecks, the cars riddled with bullet holes and their windows smashed. And there, just a few feet beyond the open and bullet-ridden rear passenger door of the car, was the man who the others had shouted held a gun. But as Wren looked closer at the outstretched hand of the man who'd fallen, she saw no gun, no knife, no weapon of any kind. In place of the pistol they'd believed he pulled, she saw a black phone. It was small and now speckled with the man's own blood.

"Hey!" Edric pulled Wren from the fence and slammed her on the ground. She scurried backward, and Edric stomped after her, the rifle swinging from his arm. "I'm not done with you!"

"It wasn't a gun!" Wren blurted the words, and Edric froze. "It was a cellphone. Go. Look for yourself."

Murmurs spread through the crowd, and Edric's concrete stance suddenly shifted on quaking sand. Iris stepped forward, and she and Nathan helped Wren up. "Take her inside, Nathan."

"You can't—"

Iris held up her hand, silencing Edric. "The laws of leading others here are clear. There will be a trial." Iris turned to Wren, her mouth downturned. "She will give her defense, and the community will hear her words." She turned back to Edric. "But in the meantime, I want our people cleaning up this mess. I'm sure it's something you can handle?"

Edric's cheeks blushed red. "I want a four-man team tracking down the escaped car. It took heavy fire, and one of the wheels was damaged. They won't get far." He brushed past Iris and wedged himself right between Nathan and Wren. "Whatever speech you have planned won't save you. This is my community, and I'll be damned if I let you be the one to bring it to its knees." He stormed off, a cluster of the community breaking off with him, along with Councilwoman Jan. Though, just before Councilman Ted turned, Wren caught him staring at her. His gaze lingered just long enough for her to notice before he quickly joined Edric and the others.

"It's going to be fine, Wren. You didn't do anything. We

didn't do anything." Nathan offered a pat on her shoulder, but Wren's mind was far from the present moment. She drifted back to just before the gunshots erupted, back to when the man from beyond the fence told her about the wolves of the forest, and she began to believe that there might be some inside the walls already.

14

Wren pushed her finger through the clumped dirt on the wooden floorboard as she sat against the rear wall of her "room," which it didn't pass for. It was no bigger than a closet and wasn't long enough for her to lie all the way flat in width or length. The only luxury that was afforded to her was the small window that let her know if it was day or night outside. A comfort she didn't appreciate until after the second day.

The designs in the dirt next to her were nothing more than simple drawings that her youngest, Chloe, would interpret as houses. It was all she could do to pass the time, waiting for the trial. After the events at the gate, there was a lot of talk about what to do with her and where to keep her. While she wasn't a part of the discussion that put her here, she was betting her last dollar that she had Edric to thank for her current accommodations.

No news had been brought to her of either Doug, Zack, or her girls since her imprisonment. The only visitor she received was the guard stationed outside her door, who opened the food slot to shove in a tray of rations twice a day, which barely passed as edible. The worst part of the entire ordeal was the smell of her own waste that lingered in a bucket only a few feet away. After the first night she couldn't hold it any longer and was forced to use the makeshift latrine. The stench filled the small space quickly and by the next day, with the sun cooking the cell, it had festered into something inhuman. While she finished her breakfast, it quickly evacuated her stomach, which only added to the foul stench.

Even now, a day later, Wren's nose had yet to numb against the wretched waste that was so pungent it permeated the walls along with her clothes and skin. But as bad as the heat, the smell, the pain, the fatigue, the hunger, and the thirst became, she still couldn't help but wonder about her family. Every drawing etched in the dirt under her finger brought with it a pillar of strength that she clung to, rising above the filth around her. For them.

The lock on the door ground against a key and opened, bringing a burst of sunlight and a shadowed figure that nearly took up the width of the door. "Wren." Nathan knelt in front of her, his face scrunched as he did his best to hide the obvious disgust at the room's stench. "Your trial is set for tomorrow."

"The girls, Zack, are they—"

"They're okay," Nathan answered, covering his nose with his shirt. "But they've stopped giving Doug his medications for the infection."

"What?" Wren attempted to push herself up but found that sitting down in the cramped space for the past two days had left her legs weak. "If he goes off the regimen—"

"I know." Nathan dropped the portion of his shirt covering his face and nose and grabbed her hand, massaging it in his own. "I'm doing what I can, but there are a lot of people here that don't trust you."

"One is more like it." The distaste she held for Edric was almost as potent as the room's stench. "What am I supposed to do tomorrow? Tell them I'm sorry for something I had nothing to do with? Beg their forgiveness?" Wren shook her head. "I don't know how you came into league with these people, Nate."

"These people are the only reason you're still alive right now." Nathan took a step back, and Wren knew she'd offended him. "These people worked hard for what they have here, and with everything that's happening, they have a right to be skeptical of anyone that tries to take it from them." He thrust his thick finger into his chest. "I'm one of these people, Wren. I brought you here."

"I'm sorry." She rested her head against the back wall, her anger dissipating. "I know you're trying to help. What are they accusing me of?"

"Treason."

Wren couldn't hold back the laugh. "Treason? Am I standing on some sovereign land that no one told me about? I don't remember getting my passport stamped."

"Wren, this isn't a joke."

"Then why is it so fucking funny?" Wren slapped her palm against the floor, the boards underneath offering nothing more than a dull whimper. She clawed her hand into a fist, scraping up dirt, and squeezed until her knuckles flashed white. "These people have my family."

"Then make sure you tell them that tomorrow." Nate brought his large paw over and engulfed her fist with his own. He gave it a gentle pat and rose, grabbing the waste bucket on the way out.

"Nate," she called out after him, the sight of his leaving overflowing the desperate need to speak with another person. "I don't know what to tell them. I don't know what they're looking for. I don't understand these people or the world they live in."

Nate gave a light shrug, tilting his head to the side. "They're just people, Wren. You've done what you've had to do to keep your family safe. That's all we're trying to do here. It's that simple." He smiled, and the door shut behind him, and with it went the light that offered her warmth.

With the cell cast back into darkness save for the small window above her, Wren deflated. Done whatever I had to do. Did Nate know? How could he, when he was unconscious in the ambulance after the wreck. I left him to save my children. Left him to die. A stab of guilt knifed its way through the memory of yelling at Doug to abandon Nate as the terrorists marched down the street. She half expected him to be dead when she came back outside, but there he was, still breathing in the back of the ambulance, his face cut and scraped. But alive.

That's the same thing Edric did at the gate. Was this how it was now? Was this how she was meant to live? Had survival ascended above morality, above laws and ethics? Or had it always been like this, just in a different form? However Wren tried to spin it, one thing became abundantly clear: whoever these people were didn't matter. They held her children's lives in their hands. And for better or worse, her husband's life. The infected wound on her right thigh throbbed, and she placed a gentle hand over the cut. And my life. She would have to make them listen. She would have to make them let her stay.

* * *

THE GAVEL SMACKED against the table, and Wren did her best to hide her shudder. The town hall had transformed itself since the last time Wren had visited. While her first encounter had the space empty and hollow, now it was brimming with the entire community. Everyone had come, even people's children. During her entrance, she'd spied the girls and Zack sitting with Nate. She kept that image glued to the front of her mind as the council presided over her, with

Edric in the middle, tossing the gavel aside as the room finally quieted.

"Five days ago, power and circuitry went down around the country, and upon such news, we as a community enacted our emergency plans." Edric addressed the crowd behind Wren, who stood alone before the raised platform, isolated. "Four days ago, one of our own came to us, bringing with him five others. Five. And not one of them was on his roster of personnel. The day after their arrival, our camp was discovered by a party seeking refuge from the very threat that brought us here ourselves." He finally glanced down at Wren with a pause, letting his icy stare linger until she felt a chill run up her spine. "This community and its survival is all that stands between us and the chaos beyond our fences. In the coming days and weeks, people will grow desperate, more so than we've already seen. What we do now will affect our world, our families, and our lives. Today marks our first trial of not just this woman's fate, but everyone's."

Iris and Ben, who flanked Edric on opposite ends of the long platform, exchanged a look while Jan smiled and Ted retained his stoic expression. Out of the four of them, Iris spoke first, her voice as calm as the steady hand that gripped her pen. "We will hear your defense, Wren Burton, as the accusations that stand against you are conspiracy for treason against the citizens of this community as well as its leaders."

"But first we will hear from the community," Ben said, his voice scratchy as if the words leaving his throat fought his tongue before being shoved from his lips. "Here, everyone has a right to voice their thoughts." His gaze lingered upon her before one of Edric's goons pulled Wren aside and the first community member showed themselves.

All of the testimonies blurred together, as well as most of their faces. Wren listened, but most of the message was the same. We don't know her. We don't trust her. She shouldn't be here. I'm doing this for my family. And what am I doing for my family?

"I know all of you are scared." Wren looked up from the dusty, worn floorboards and saw Nathan standing, addressing the crowd behind him as much as the council. "It's a fear we all share, and rightfully so. Not all of us saw the crumbling of the cities we came from, and some were worse than others, but all I can tell you about are the events that happened to me."

Wren's stomach tightened, and she felt the churn of guilt. I left him to die. She shifted uncomfortably on the stiff bench, where her guard had kept a close watch.

"When we escaped the city, it was chaos," Nate said. "The terrorists who caused the power outage were everywhere. Fires, gunshots, mobs, panic, all of it swirling together in this terrible storm of fear. It wasn't like anything I'd ever seen." Nate pointed a chubby finger to Wren. "Her family was separated, scattered across the broken city with no way of getting to one another. But the odds didn't stop her. She went into a war zone to get her son. She kept her girls safe. She made the tough decisions. She saved my life."

The gut-wrenching knife burrowed deeper into Wren's stomach as Nathan looked her way. She could tell his words were reaching some of them. The lines of judgment across their faces slowly softened. But when Wren looked to the council, she saw that Edric remained unmoved.

"Those people that came to the gates overheard my conversation with Wren," Nathan said, continuing his defense. "I am just as guilty as she is." His spine stiffened, and he lifted his chin. "And whatever her fate is, I will share."

The silenced crowd erupted after Nathan's words, and Edric smacked the gavel to return order to the hall. Nathan smiled as he found his seat, and Wren sank deeper into herself. A few more community members spoke, some of them swayed by Nathan's speech, while the others had determined her fate long before the trial, either too stubborn or too afraid to venture out into a world larger than themselves.

Finally, after the last member had said their piece, Edric turned to Wren then nodded to the guard, who yanked her to her feet. "We will now hear from the defendant. Wren Burton, present yourself to this council and community, and tell us in your own words why this council should grant you pardon."

Treason. It was a word Edric had enjoyed repeating. It was a word familiar to everyone in the room, and it was a word that encouraged complacency and obedience. And judging from the smile curving up the corners of his mouth, those two attributes were exactly what Edric wanted from his subordinates.

Every eye shifted to Wren as she took center stage. The rope binding her wrists together was coarse, rough, and tight against her skin, and she spasmed uncomfortably in the spotlight. Her new environment was a far cry from the drawing board where she felt so at ease, where she could build anything. This was a world she didn't understand. This was their home. And she was an unwelcome guest.

"Everyone here serves a purpose." Wren took a swallow of what spit she found in her throat to stop her voice from cracking and then raised her volume. "Everything you've built has been made from sacrifice and dedication. And those are two words I know well." The drawing board, she thought. My sketches, my profession, my passion and love. My family. "Those people that came to the gate a few days ago, the ones who were gunned down, they came here because of the same reason I did. Because of the reasons so many of you have given yourselves. There is life here. And Edric is right. People will become more desperate. People will seek out that beacon of life and want to take it for themselves. I've seen it. And I've done it myself."

Out of all the faces Wren watched twist in affirmation of

their fears and bigotry, it was Nate's she found first. She saw his confusion, underlined with the fear of knowing that he put his neck out on the line for her, as he had done so many times already since she'd arrived. But she wouldn't leave him behind this time. She wouldn't leave him bloodied and to the wolves once more.

"Nathan, my link to all of you, spoke some very kind words tonight." She smiled at him, her eyes watering. "But unfortunately he doesn't have the entire truth. And neither do all of you." She shut her eyes, forcing the tears back into the wells of grief, finding her grit to continue. "We were in an ambulance, trying to escape the city. I'd finally collected all of my family. But my son, Zack, he was still hurt. Many of you know that his leg was broken." She shook her head. "Is broken. My daughters were tired and scared. My nerves and patience had dissolved." Wren rubbed the coarse fibers of the rope, which suddenly felt tighter, around her wrist. "The terrorists who caused all of this, or whoever they were, had blocked the road on our attempt to escape the city. They opened fire, and the paramedic who was driving the ambulance was shot and lost control. We flipped, the driver was killed, my son's leg had worsened, and my daughters were hurt. There just wasn't any time." She found that she was talking to herself more than the community now. "Doug and I grabbed the kids. I went to the front and saw the driver was dead." She found Nathan's gaze in the crowd once more, and the silence of the hall was quieter than anything she'd ever heard in her life. "I thought you were dead too." She wanted to look away. She wanted to stop. She wanted to tell the people what they wanted to hear, but that wasn't the way. That wasn't her way. "It was Doug who wanted to take you. But you were unconscious. The terrorists were marching closer, and I knew that if we hesitated, we'd die. I'd seen the way those animals cut down everyone and anything. There was no discrimination in who they killed. And I was not going to let them take my family. Or me. Not after everything that we'd been through. Not when we were so close."

Nathan shook his head, his expression failing to comprehend her words. But the crowd around him understood. She saw the disgust in their eyes. It was the same reflection she would have given herself if she'd had a mirror. "I left you, Nate. I chose my family over your life. Once we were safe in the store, I came back, but it wasn't for you. It was for the pack to stop Doug's bleeding. You must have stayed unconscious as the terrorists marched past. They probably thought you were already dead too."

Wren turned back to Edric and the council. If they'd made up their minds, they refused that answer to her through the stoic walls upon their faces. All except for Edric. She saw the finality in his eyes as he gripped the gavel. She pictured his face in an executioner's mask, much like the ones she'd seen the terrorists wear. While she'd never actually seen their faces, she imagined that they shared the same look as Edric wore now right before sentencing their victims to death. But Wren wouldn't let that fate befall her. Not when her children would share the same fate.

"But you're not dead, Nathan." Wren turned back to the crowd. She took a few steps forward, heading toward the center aisle, looking each of them in the eye as she passed, forcing them to see her. "And neither are you, or you, or you." She continued until she made it all the way to the end then circled back, every head turned to watch her, save for one. "Your families are not dead. Nor will they be, because we will not let harm befall them. We are stronger together because I know, just as well as you do, that my family's survival depends on yours." Wren spread her palms open in submission. "I know nothing of growing food, or shooting weapons, or healing broken bones. But I graduated from one of the most prestigious architectural schools in the country. And I worked for the premier architectural firm in Chicago. I have designed buildings that have never been seen before or are likely to be seen again. And while that knowledge may seem useless, I can apply it to making sure that the next group that comes knocking on that gate won't be able to get inside. No matter what weapons they have."

Wren faced the council now, her back to the crowd, and while she couldn't see it, she felt the weight of every pair of eyes on her back, her words entrapping them in their own snare. They wanted to survive, and someone who could help them do that was valuable. Edric's cocky gaze was replaced with the grimace of disgust he wore the first time they met. The scars turned uglier in his distaste of her. "And just as Edric said, those people will come back. They will return in greater numbers, more desperate, hungrier, and dangerous. They will want what you have." She turned back around to the community. The mood in the room had palpably shifted in her favor. "I will help you protect it. I can make it to where no intruder will ever get inside. I will strengthen the homes and structures you've built to survive the harshest winters and the most dangerous storms. I will keep your families safe, because that will keep mine safe. There isn't anyone in this room that should doubt what I will do to protect my family." Wren found Nate's eyes in the crowd. While she might have reached the minds and reason of the mob around her, she'd just lost her closest ally.

"Mrs. Burton," Iris said, the first to break the silence of the hall. "Your testimony has… shown your resolve." She looked down the row to the rest of the council. "You will be escorted from the building and called upon once our decision has been reached. Thank you for your words. And your honesty."

Wren was shoved roughly from the hall and thrown back into her cell, locked in the darkness and foul stench that she'd wallowed in for the past two days. "Wait," she called after the guard, "my wrists." But he only slammed the door in her face.

The moment of courage—or lunacy, the more Wren pondered her speech—evaporated into thin air. She paced the cell impatiently. If she failed to convince those people that they were better off with her inside the walls than outside, then she knew Doug was as good as dead. And even if they let Zack, Addison, and Chloe stay, she didn't think Nathan would keep them, not after what she'd said.

Wren punched the wall, and her fist ached the moment her knuckles smacked the wood, her dry skin ripping from her hand, leaving bits of blood on the wall. She collapsed to the floor. The rot, the smell, the pain—all of it was in her now. She looked up to the bloodied fist print. And now I'm a part of it. Her leg bounced nervously as she lost track of time. All she knew when the guard returned to bring her back to the hall was that it was still night, or early morning.

The hall was empty except for the council, who looked to have remained frozen in their positions since her departure. The guard brought her front and center, looking to the giants on the platform, her fate in their hands once more.

"We have reached a decision, Mrs. Burton," Iris said. "But before we tell you what we and the community have chosen, do you have any final words for us that you wish to say?"

"My children," Wren said, finding it odd that it was Iris who spoke, and not Edric, who sat stone-faced in the middle with a fire in his eyes meant to set Wren ablaze. "They are innocent in all of this. And so are my husband and Nathan. Let them live. Keep them safe for as long as these walls will stand."

Iris raised one eyebrow. "Nothing else? Nothing you wish to impart to us in these final moments?" She leaned closer, edging herself over the precipice. "Nothing you wish to... recant?"

"Everything I told you was the truth," Wren answered. "I

find it better to let that decide my fate than a farcical show of begging. You cannot wish a building to stand, nor can you make it rise from the earth with false tales. There is life in truth, and I found that I never benefitted from lies in my professional life or my personal one."

"Very well," Iris replied, leaning back into her chair. "Wren Burton, this council finds you innocent of treason. You will be returned to your family, and your husband and son's medical treatment will resume immediately. Tomorrow you will begin your new post with engineering." Up until then, Wren had never seen Iris offer any look of coldness, but before she spoke her next words, it was as if vengeance itself had taken human form. "And I hope that your speeches are as effective as your professional skills."

Wren wasn't sure what to say once the gavel was smacked, but luckily the council dispersed before she even had a chance to speak. The guard begrudgingly removed the ropes, and Wren gently rubbed the tender flesh. "Wait, where is my family?"

But her only answer was the slam of the town hall door, leaving her with only the light of a few flickering candles the council had left on the platform. Nathan. They're probably still at Nathan's. She started for the door, and she found her feet shifting from a stumbled walk to a sprint as she ignored the pain in her leg.

"Wren!" The voice echoed through the empty hall, and Wren skidded to a stop. When she turned to look behind her, it was Iris standing there, her body half cast in light and darkness. She took a few steps down the hall but stopped once she was out of reach of the flickering glow of the candles. "It was a dangerous play you pulled tonight. There wasn't any guarantee the community would budge."

"There was no play, Iris. My intention was never to manipulate."

"It wasn't?" Iris asked, taking a few steps closer in the darkness of the hall. "You could have fooled me."

In the darkness, Wren couldn't tell Iris's age, and her voice offered the illusion of youth. She hadn't noticed just how poignant her words were until now. "Is there something you needed from me, councilwoman? From what I heard of your decision, I have been freed from any crimes."

"You have," Iris acknowledged, stepping around Wren until she was side by side with her. "But there are those that lack conviction in their decision. And there are those that don't."

Edric. Wren had never doubted that he'd been one of the council members that voted to exile her, or kill her, or vote for whatever the punishment would have been. But she wondered which of his two dogs had voted to keep her. Jan had never portrayed anything but an icy distrust for her, and Ted had never even spoken a word. "My family is waiting for me. Are they still at Nathan's?"

Iris paused before finally answering, "Yes." And then she disappeared back down to the platform, exiting the same way she entered. Wren lingered in the hall for a few minutes longer, waiting until the flame from Iris's candle had disappeared with her. Wolves. The mysterious voice the day of the attack on the gate returned for reasons unknown. Right now she couldn't tell friend from foe, but she was valuable so long as she delivered on her promises of strengthening their defenses. Weeding out the wolves would have to wait for now.

15

Wren ran her fingers through Addison's hair. Chloe was huddled up next to her big sister, both of them breathing softly. Wren had gently lay down next to her girls, careful to not disturb them. She closed her eyes and felt the warmth from their bodies, the lumpy mattress a welcomed comfort that she'd never take for granted again. She watched the steady rise and fall of their chests as the morning sun rose through the windows behind her. With everything that happened, she was happy with the peace and quiet of the morning. She knew the girls would be excited to see her, though that couldn't be said for everyone.

When she met Nathan at the cabin after she was released, it was like trying to speak to a ghost. He went to his room without a word, offering no hint to his thoughts. Though the cold shoulder was evidence enough that it would be a long time before he trusted her again.

Zack was the first to wake, and when he saw her, his sleepy eyes burst into silent tears. Wren's heart melted at the sight, and at first she thought he was simply overwhelmed, but when she reached out her arms, he violently knocked them away. The angered glare that accompanied the swing stung more painfully than the motion itself. He huddled in the corner of his cot with his back to her.

With no idea of what he was upset about, and too exhausted to investigate, Wren found her cot and pulled the coarse blanket over her body. It was easy for her to fall asleep. Her eyes were so heavy she didn't think she'd ever be able to open them again. How long the rest lasted, she couldn't be sure, but the call of her name pierced the bubble of her dreamless sleep. She struggled to wake, her eyes snapping shut after every attempt to open them. She rolled lazily to her side, pulling the blanket over her head, hoping to shield herself from any more disruptions, but failed. The sheet was ripped from her grip, and the light dispersed the darkness from under the covers. The three cots were empty, Zack and the girls gone, and Nathan hovered over her. "You're late for work." The words were clipped and short, and he disappeared before Wren had a chance to speak.

"Hey!" Wren stumbled from bed, her muscles uncoordinated and shaky. Every flex of her right thigh sent a thousand needles digging into her skin, and the first shot of pain collapsed her to the floor. She grunted, pushed herself up, and limped after Nate. The farther she walked, the more she numbed to the pain, and she caught up to Nate at the well, where she leaned against the stone brick, catching her breath. "Nate," she panted between breaths, "about last night—"

"You should head down to the front gate." Nate pulled the well's rope, lifting the bucket from the center of the walled stone. He kept his eyes on his task, refusing to look her in the eye. "Iris and Ben are waiting for you. Best not have them linger there without you for too long."

"Right." Wren limped away, unsure of what she expected from him. From the very first moment they ran into each other in Chicago, all Nathan had tried to do was help, and she'd repaid him with betrayal during his moment of need.

He didn't have any reason to forgive her. All that was left now was to try and make their situation amiable.

By the time she arrived at the gate, both Iris and Ben's expressions signaled they'd reached the end of their patience. Iris was particularly wroth. "I don't suppose this is how you'll be starting all of your days with us?"

Wren rubbed her thigh and felt the sweat of fever as she had the day before. She wiped the perspiration from her forehead. "I'm sorry." She turned back to where she'd left Nate at the well, then back to Iris. "It won't happen again."

"Good." Iris waved up toward one of the guards on duty, and the front gate opened. Along with Ben and Iris, two guards joined the escort, everyone armed except for Wren.

Wren's first step beyond the wall was planted in a dried patch of blood. The fluid had lost its crimson shimmer but retained the distinct hue associated with claret. She remained frozen in that first step, and her eyes fell upon the other stains that dotted the dirt road. The wreckage of the vehicles had been removed, along with the bodies, and what remains were left behind had been scavenged by animals. All that was left of their lives were the stains on the forest floor.

"Wren," Iris said, looking back at her, the rest of the group stopping alongside.

"Sorry." She limped forward, leaving her footprint on the dead, stained leaves. With no idea of where she was being taken, Wren followed the herd as they kept tight to the community's walled perimeter. Every few hundred feet, Iris and Ben would whisper to one another, but Wren was so concentrated on staying upright that she couldn't hear what they were saying. But before her mind wandered down the twisted corridors of speculation, Iris and Ben stopped. Wren leaned against the fence, her body drenched in sweat and her lips so raw they felt like pieces of flint.

"You said that you could improve our defenses," Iris said,

walking through the tall grass that had overgrown next to the fence. "What do you see here?"

Wren examined her surroundings. The trees, rocks, thick grass, the surrounding hills, and the rotten wood that composed the nearest portion of the fence. "That lumber needs to be replaced." She fingered the brittle bark that flecked away at the lightest touch, then kicked the weeds that came up to her knees. "And you'll want to push this grass back, keep it maintained around the entire perimeter. That'll help keep the integrity of the fence and keep any pests from nesting too close. The biggest problem you'll have with wood is rot." She pointed to a cluster of tall oaks a few dozen yards into the forest. "Oak holds up well against that; it's strong, and I've seen plenty of trees to provide the resources we need." She pointed out the more obvious signs of rot and then to a few showing the early stages. "Eventually we'll want to upgrade to any steel we can salvage from the towns, or what we have on hand, and use it as brace materials. So to start, we reestablish the foundation of the fence and make sure it can't be toppled over by a stiff breeze, as I've seen in some parts." The explanation sucked the wind from her, and she struggled to catch her breath.

"Ben and I took a risk bringing you on board," Iris said. "Your words were inspiring, but what you do with them will decide your fate. Remember that you're only as valuable as what you bring to the table. Once that disappears, so do you."

Wren nodded, triggering a dizzy spell. She fought against the desire to collapse. If she needed to show strength, then now was the time to do it. "Then I'll need a team to help get me started. How many carpenters do you have in the community?" They started the walk back to the front gate, Wren doing her best to not stumble in the tall grass along the way.

"We have three," Iris answered.

"And two blacksmiths," Ben added from behind them.

"That's good," Wren replied. "There's no guarantee that the materials we'll be able to salvage will be of high quality, so they'll need to know how to get the most from what we find." The heat from the sun sapped her strength as she walked. The cut along her thigh burned. She stumbled, and Iris caught her arm. She turned her head away from everyone's gaze to hide the pain etched along her face.

"Wren, are you all right?" Ben asked, coming up from behind her.

"Yeah," Wren answered, trying to straighten her leg. "The past few nights were a little rough, that's all." She forced a half smile, but it was cut short by another searing burn in her thigh. She stiffened her back, avoiding collapse, but the ground started to spin.

"Wren?" Iris asked, the tone in her voice shifting to concern. "What's wrong?"

"I just..." Before she finished, she collapsed to her knees, her leg numb from the fall. And just as quickly as she'd fallen face-first into the grass, she felt her body lift from the ground, her eyes opening and closing, the pattern of the canopy of trees changing each time. "I'm fine."

Suddenly the view of the sky shifted to the wooden beams of a ceiling. Wren lolled her head back and forth. The faces that hovered above her shifted and changed. All of them spoke, but she waved her arm at them. "I'm fine. I just need to lie down." She repeated the words like a prayer. Her whole body ached, and her last bits of coherency melted away.

Every once in a while, a jolt of discomfort ran through her, but her mind and body were so exhausted that her reactions were little more than a soft shudder and mumble. She became lost, wandering in pain, and suddenly she was back in Chicago. Fires circled her, the heat from the flames licking her skin. She saw Zack and the girls beyond the inferno, crying out to her, pleading for her to save them.

But Wren's every attempt to reach them was met with failure. The flames roared in defiance and tossed her back into the middle of the fire. Screaming, she watched her family catch fire. Her throat grew raw from smoke and heat. Wren wrestled the flames, stretching out her arms, the heat so intense she felt herself catch fire. And that was how she slept, burning with her family.

* * *

"WREN."

The voice was faint, nothing more than a tickle in her unconscious mind. She stirred as the voice grew louder, repeating her name over and over. The voice echoed louder, ringing through her ears until she finally opened her eyes. "Doug?" She squinted and for a moment believed that she was back in the hospital in Chicago. She reached her hand up to the arm where she'd been shot and felt the same sling that was given to her after the surgery. But the movement brought to light another pain in her leg. And while the ache had dulled, it still lingered. She ran her palm down to her thigh, and the infected flesh was replaced with a bandage that ran from hip to knee.

"Wren," Nathan repeated once more. "Can you hear me all right?"

Her vision cleared, and the outlines of bodies appeared. She lifted her head from the pillow to get a better look, but the exertion was too much for her neck to bear, and she collapsed back onto the cushion. "What happened?"

"The infection on your leg spread," Nathan answered. "If it had gone any farther, we would have had to amputate. Why didn't you say it was getting worse?"

"Where's Zack and the girls?" Wren lightly fingered the bandage on her leg, the cloth soft under her fingertips.

"They're fine," a voice said.

"We wanted to send them away before you woke up," Nate said. "To make sure you were okay before they saw you. Yesterday was your worst day."

"Yesterday?" Wren asked, confused. "How long have I been in here?"

"Three days," a voice said.

The voice sounded familiar but tired. She couldn't place it, though, and she lifted her head, forcing herself to locate the source. She propped her arms underneath her body to get a better look, and that's when she saw him.

Doug sat at an angle, supported by a dozen different cushions on a cot, and had an IV stuck into his arm. His shirt was removed, and his entire midsection was wrapped in bandages. Dark caverns etched themselves under his eyes, and his face had grown hollow and thin. In all their time together, she'd never seen him so weak. "The girls are back at Nate's place. Zack's been watching them."

Wren nodded then rested her head back on the pillow. Her body ached, and her mind was barely strong enough to formulate more than a few words. "How long have I been in here?"

"Nearly three days," Nathan answered. "You had a fever of one hundred and four. We did what we could to keep you cool. You're on an antibiotic regimen for the infection. Same as Doug."

Wren flinched. "Three days?"

Iris stepped forward. "Your husband will be joining Nathan's cabin once he's able to walk around himself. When the doctor says the two of you are healthy enough to return to work, you will do so immediately. So I suggest you rest quickly and often." Iris left with a few people Wren didn't recognize, leaving only Nathan and Doug at her side.

"We'll bring in some food from the mess hall," Nathan said, taking a look at the IV drip hooked up to her arm. "You'll need to eat quite a bit to help you recover." He rattled a bottle of pills and placed it next to the bedside table. "You need to take these three times a day, with food, until they're gone."

Wren wanted to thank him, apologize, explain, but there were too many words she needed that she didn't have access to at the moment. All she managed to express was a smile, which Nate returned in kind. It could have been out of pity or regret, but either way, she took it as a step in the right direction. Nathan left, leaving Wren and Doug alone in the infirmary. The glow of the sunlight coming through the windows hinted at sunset, and she closed her eyes, hoping to drift off to sleep before either of them had a chance to speak. But Doug had other plans.

"The girls came by to see you the other day. They seemed okay, though I think they were just pretending to keep a brave face. Zack took it hard, though."

Wren kept her eyes closed, her hand running up and down the bandage on her thigh. There was a slight indentation underneath the gauze, and she wondered how much flesh they'd had to remove to save the leg.

"Nate told me what you did," Doug said.

She shifted to her side to look him in the eye. He kept his head down, and his arms hung limp like noodles from his shoulders. "And what did he say?" She remembered the look of betrayal Nate gave her during the trial after her omission. It was a look she never wanted to see again.

"He's not mad at you, Wren," Doug replied. "Not anymore, at least. He knows why you did it. But it was a lot for anyone to process. Especially in the setting you chose to do it."

"There's never a good time to give someone bad news," Wren answered, hoping that Doug would catch her meaning as she spoke. "Did he also tell you what I promised to give these people?"

"Yeah. He told me."

Wren's strength faded, and she closed her eyes once more, repositioning her head on the pillow to get comfortable. "These people will only keep us here for as long as they need us." She yawned, her eyelids turning into heavy pieces of lead dropping over her eyes. "They'll want to have me finish as quickly as I can. I need to… figure… something out." She pulled one of the blankets tight to her chin, and she thought she heard Doug mumble something, but she didn't hear it. Her last thoughts were the howls of wolves. Though she couldn't be sure if they were real or just the beginning of a nightmare.

16

One Month Later

"We need all that material cleared before the afternoon. It's rained like clockwork all week, and I don't want to lose the trench to another slide before we can fill it." Wren walked the line of at least a dozen workers ripping logs from the earth and tossing them aside, replacing them with some of the forged-steel braces she had instructed the blacksmiths to mold. She rotated her left shoulder, still not used to the sling's absence, though glad to be rid of it. All that remained of the bullet wound in her arm was a small scar under the worn T-shirt sleeve.

Wren moved quickly up and down the line, one hand clutching the plans she'd drawn up to reinforce the wall. Nearly half of the fence was reconstructed. She replaced old wooden beams and reinforced the weaker ones with iron studs sunk deep into the ground. Massive braces on the interior of the fence stiffened the wood, adding to its defense. She also raised the wall's height. The surrounding trees were cleared to provide the material for the extension, and every dozen yards contained a small window concealed with a sliding piece of steel. If they were attacked, it would allow patrols to shoot through the fence and to spy on any enemy while safely behind cover. The additions provided the fence with a more formidable presence. And judging by the looks of the council and the community, everyone was starting to believe they'd made the right decision in allowing her to stay.

"Mrs. Burton!" The foreman of the crew, Tom, waved from farther down the fence, where tomorrow's project lay. He was a large man, nearly six and a half feet. He'd spent most of his life in construction, and out of everyone Wren spoke with, he was the only one who understood the plans she created. "I would have done it myself, ma'am, if I had the background," he'd told her. He constructed the first version of the wall, and his acceptance of her work only helped bring the rest of the crew in line. Through his respect of her, the others followed without question.

Tom stood near a thirty-foot section of the fence that had been set ablaze the night before, staining the wood black. If the logs weren't as damp as they were from the week's rain, it could have been much worse. "The second patch of burned wood is another hundred yards down," Tom said, gesturing his massive hand to the north, then pointed to where black and charred bark had ended in a decidedly straight and geometric line. "Looks like the retardant worked. It's a good thing we started applying it when you said."

Before they began any heavy construction, Wren looked for anyone with a chemistry background, and she found it in the form of a retired science teacher. The retardant was a simple varnish, but with the lack of materials at their disposal, she was afraid the substance wouldn't hold up. For once, she was glad she was wrong. "That's the third time in the past week they've tried torching it." Wren ran her fingers between the dead and healthy wood. She looked to the group of guards patrolling the forest behind her. A security detail escorted the crew every day. But since most of them were

Edric's men, she wasn't sure if they were for protection or reconnaissance.

"We could have some of the men start applying the resin to the rest of the fence this afternoon," Tom suggested.

Wren shook her head. "Whoever keeps trying to raid us knows they can't get through by trying to burn us out, not with the rains still this heavy. And I don't want to risk diverting manpower on sections we'll have to replace anyway. We'll just have to tell the council to continue doubling the guard patrols until we're finished." The manpower involved in fortifying the structures was more than most of the community wanted to invest, but two weeks after the first incident at the front gates that had put Wren on trial, others came knocking. And those people had guns.

A heavy hand tilted her shoulder down, and Wren looked up to see the tall giant smiling. "You're doing great, Mrs. Burton. There isn't a person inside those walls that doesn't appreciate it. Me included."

"Thanks, Tom."

Wren stayed with the crewmen all day, as she did on most days. When the sun sank low in the sky, Wren called it quits. After working on the wall for nearly three weeks, their return to the front gate grew longer every day. She wanted to install another entrance at a different intersection of the fence but knew that would cause a security risk and required materials she didn't have.

At the front gate, one of the guards on the catwalk eyed her all the way through while the others passed unmolested. One of Edric's men. While there was still a schism in the community, most of the people took to Wren once they saw how easily the fence was defended with the upgrades. But even with the fence's success, some still found fault with her.

"Burton!" Edric's sidearm hung from his hip, black and the brightest feature of his ensemble. "You didn't coat the remainder of the fence with the resin?"

"We're going to have to replace most of the fence we coated anyway. The rain will keep the wood damp until that happens. I didn't want to waste the manpower."

"You seem content with taking your time on your upgrades while my guards pull double shifts on patrol." He stepped forward, his hounds remaining close by. "Those men and women on my wall stand between you and the bullets meant to kill you when those raiders decide to attack again. They've tried burning their way in here three times already. What makes you think they won't do it again?"

"Because they've failed three times." The long day and hot sun had dried up all of her patience, and she looked to the darkening clouds above. Everything she did left a sour taste in his mouth. But with the fence proving its worth so far against the attacks, she'd seen her value substantiated. "And tell your 'guards' that I don't need them giving me the once-over every time I walk through the gate." She turned on her heel, leaving Edric fuming as she headed for the mess hall.

Every home had their own personal rations, but every family was required by community laws to contribute to a massive stockpile of food, which everyone shared in eating their three square meals a day. At first, it seemed excessive to have an entire building just meant for cooking, but there was a very important aspect of the hall she overlooked, one that Ben pointed out to her after her first week.

"Community." He smiled, his mustache hiding the creases and lines around his mouth. "People weren't meant to live alone in hovels, Wren. We're stronger in groups. It's how we've survived for thousands of years. And what better way to share and commune with one another than through meals?" And he'd been right. Every meal the hall was filled with chatter and smiling faces. She'd find her place on the long benches, wedged between her girls, and listen to them go on about their day. In that setting even she had to admit the place felt like home. Out of all the laws the community offered, this was one she enjoyed. The meal house provided a renewable resource for everyone: hope.

Wren slid into the food line behind one of the fence workers and filled her bowl with rice and stew. Most of the concoctions were crockpot-style meals. They were easily made and mass produced. The hall could fill and feed the entire community all at once.

Addison and Chloe were already sitting down with Zack, and she was surprised when she saw Doug at the table, gingerly bringing a spoon full of meat from bowl to mouth. "Hey, Mom!" Chloe waved, grinning and holding a freshly fallen tooth from her mouth. "Look what I have!" She held out her palm, thrusting her small molar into the sky.

Wren picked it up, smiling. "Well, would you look at that. When did it come out?"

"She pulled it out," Addison said, rolling her eyes. "I told her to wait, and that it would hurt, but she didn't listen. She had that little kid Brent yank it out, and she started crying."

Chloe offered a sheepish smile. "It hurt more than I thought it would."

Wren returned the tooth to her daughter and wiggled between them. Doug still looked down into his soup, and Zack mimicked his father's posture. She shoveled the rice and pot roast into her mouth, savoring each bite as Chloe showed her the new signatures on her cast and Addison complained how much her sister's arm smelled since Chloe had never washed it. But despite the lighthearted laughter between the girls, Zack never so much as cracked a smile.

Her son's disdain and cold mood hadn't changed since they'd arrived at the camp. Dark circles had formed under his eyes, and when he wasn't at school he spent his time lying on his cot, dead to the world. Ever since she was released after her trial, he hadn't said more than three words to her, half of them mumbled grunts. She'd tried multiple times to get him to open up but had failed. "How was your day, Zack? Are you liking the school?"

"He doesn't say much in class," Chloe said, scooping a big spoonful of meat. "I don't think he likes it."

"I'm the oldest kid in the class by four years," Zack said, stirring his spoon in his soup aimlessly. "Everything they're learning, I already know. It's stupid."

"It's not stupid," Chloe said defensively.

"All right, that's enough," Wren said, trying to end the argument before it started. Chloe frowned, furrowing her eyebrows, and returned to her soup, while Zack shoved his away. Wren looked from the bowl to her son. "You need to eat."

"I'm not hungry."

"Zack, there is only so much food here—"

"I'm not hungry!" Zack slammed his fist on the table, and his outburst echoed through the hall's high ceiling, quieting the rest of the crowd as every face turned to them.

Wren leaned forward over the table, the steam from her bowl heating her throat, which was already flushed red. "You do not raise your voice to me like that." Any meaning that may have been misconstrued in her tone was made clear with her eyes. "Finish. Your. Dinner."

Addison and Chloe shrank behind her, but Zack refused to relinquish any ground. He reached for one of his crutches and pushed himself off the bench. He knocked his food over before he left then slammed the door on his way out.

Once Zack was gone, the frozen stares cast toward her family thawed, save for the occasional dirty glance. No words were said, but Wren read the disappointment and judgement etched on every parent in the room, clear as day. *She can't keep her family together, so how is she supposed to keep a wall together? You'd never see my son act that way. She doesn't know what she's doing.*

But, unlike her son, the wall lacked emotions or thoughts.

It bent and molded to whatever form she commanded. Her son was another matter entirely. Wren looked from the steaming pile of rice and meat Zack had left behind to Doug. "You're just going to let him walk away like that?"

"You're the one who wants to leave." Doug blew lightly on the spoonful hovering close to his lips, then sipped.

Wren withheld the sudden urge to fling her bowl in his face right then and there. Instead, she reached over and knocked his chin up with the end of her finger. "I need to speak with you. Outside." She looked down at the girls and told them to stay put. Wren was already out the door by the time Doug finally got to his feet, and she paced the dirt. Whatever their differences had been over the past few years, they'd always agreed on one thing: the kids wouldn't be affected. She'd lost track of the number of times she'd bit her tongue, holding back a verbal lash in front of the children that she knew would cut him. By the time Doug stumbled outside, she was fuming to the point of combustion. "What the hell is the matter with you? Is this funny? Is this some sort of game to you?"

"It's good to see you too," Doug said, his voice calmer than she expected it to be. Like their son, he walked on crutches, his body thin from healing from the gunshot wound in his abdomen. He'd lost at least twenty pounds.

"You do not get to speak to me in front of our children that way. Do you understand me? Never." Wren thrust her finger into his face, and his neck was so thin she could have wrapped her entire hand around it.

"You don't even know what's going on, Wren. I thought that this would be a fresh start for us. I thought there was no way that you could value your work more than your family at a time like this, but it looks like you proved me wrong."

"More than my family?" Wren snapped, and she felt hot rage flood her veins, her voice shrieking to the point of hysteria. "Everything I've done has been for my family! I haven't stopped working for my family since we left Chicago, or while we were in Chicago!" She shoved him in the chest, and he stumbled backward, nearly falling to the ground, but she didn't care. She didn't care about his gunshot wound. She didn't care about his feelings. She didn't care about his life. "You're the one who stepped out, Doug. You're the one who didn't make enough money for us to get out of that shitty neighborhood. You're the one who couldn't hack it in school. You're the one who cheated on me! So don't fucking stand there and tell me I'm the one to blame. You're just a ball-less shell of a human who can't take care of himself or his family." Spit flew from Wren's mouth on her last words, and Doug turned his cheek. If he cried, she couldn't see, but she hoped he was. "You're not a father. You're not a man. You are nothing."

Shame rolled down his cheeks. "You and I both know there was more to it than that. I tried everything I could to reach out to you, but you wouldn't listen." He straightened his spine, exposing his true height to her. "I know I hurt you. I know what I did hurt our family. But this blame isn't all on me."

"Yes it is!" Wren spit it back in his face, refusing to let him twist her words, to try and make her feel like shit. "You say what our family needed was a run-down house in the slums? You think what our kids needed was a bad school that pushed more kids onto the street than kept them off?" Wren stepped back, walking away. "You sit behind your wall of excuses, hiding behind your family. That's a coward's way out. And that might be acceptable for you, but not for me."

Doug leaned forward. "I'm no coward. Call me whatever you want, but not that." He swung his crutches forward, slowly and awkwardly. The sky was a swirl of dark blues, blacks, and oranges as the sun sank under the horizon and Wren lost sight of him in the night.

Just as she was about to call after him, the food hall

started to empty as families, finished with their meals, walked home. Wren found Ben bringing the girls out, their smiles returned as he gripped their hands in each of his. "I made sure they finished their vegetables before I brought them out."

"No, you didn't." Chloe giggled. "You said we didn't have to!" She spun around in his hand, and Ben looked down at her, shocked.

"Well, you're not supposed to tell your mother that," Ben replied, smiling.

Wren did her best to let the boiled rage and stress cool down, but she wasn't sure if it worked when she felt Addison flinch when she took her hand. "Thanks, Ben." He offered a smile and polite nod, and Wren led her girls back to Nathan's cabin before the rest of the crowd poured out. She wasn't in any mood to try and fake pleasantries.

"Burton."

And just when Wren thought the hell storm of the evening had ended, Edric marched toward her, flanked by Councilwoman Jan and Councilman Ted. "What is it now?"

For a change, the scars on his face tilted upward in what she assumed was an attempt at a smile. "I trust your family issues won't affect your work performance moving forward? It would be a shame if the community's confidence in your fortitude wavered."

Jan stepped forward. She was nearly as tall as Edric but slender. Her hair was cropped short but thick and black as the night around them. The only redeeming quality of her face were her eyes, but the angular cuts of her cheek and chin gave them a sinister tone. "Keeping your family together is what matters most in these times, Mrs. Burton." She curled her fingers around Edric's arm lightly. "Or do you prefer your maiden name?"

Wren ignored the jape, taking both her girls in hand. "My family," she said, looking at Jan, "and my job"—she turned to

Edric—"require no inquiries from anyone in this community. The wall will be finished on time. And my family will be fine." She brushed past them before they retorted, pulling her girls with her. Halfway to Nate's cabin she felt a tug on her sleeve.

"Mommy?" Chloe asked. "Are you okay?"

Wren knelt down to meet both her girls at eye level. "Of course, sweetheart. I'm fine. Are you okay?" Chloe nodded, but Addison kept her head down. "Addy?" Wren brushed her cheek, but Addison twisted out of her grip.

"You say that we're okay all the time, but I don't feel okay." Addison retreated into the darkness, her voice crackling as tears broke free from her eyes. "It's never going to be fine."

Wren reached for her daughter, but the sudden burst of gunshots drew her attention to the wall. She clutched Chloe's hand tighter in a knee-jerk reaction and heard her daughter squeal from the pressure. The peaceful exit from the hall turned into a stampede as everyone either rushed toward or away from the gunfire. She looked through the crowds, trying to find her daughter. "Addison!" She lifted Chloe to her chest. "Addison!" Desperation dripped from her lips as she shouldered through the hurried flow of bodies as the pops of gunfire grew more frequent in the night air.

"Wren!" Ben's face appeared in the crowds, and he held Addison in his arms. She rushed toward them against the flow of the crowd. "I saw Edric take a unit toward the south portion of the wall. I'll help you get the girls back to the house."

Wren and Ben joined the exodus and retreated to their homes. When they arrived at Nathan's, he was already loading a magazine into his AR, and he met them at the door on his way out. Wren clutched his arm before he left, her nails digging into his shirt. "Did Zack make it back?"

"I haven't seen him." And with that, Nathan disappeared into the night.

Wren set Chloe down in the bedroom, hoping to find Zack already there, but the room was empty. The noise outside grew louder, and she brought both girls to the panic room underneath the living room floor. "You two just stay right here, okay?" She kissed their heads, and they huddled close to one another, familiar with the drill when the wall was attacked. "You guys know what to do if you hear someone come in the house that doesn't live here, right?"

The girls nodded, then at the same time added, "Stay quiet and follow the tunnel."

"That's right." Wren kissed each of them one more time then rushed into the living room, where Doug hobbled inside on his crutches, his face dripping with sweat. "The girls are already downstairs. Make sure they stay there." She brushed past him, giving him neither time nor comfort.

"What about Zack?" he shouted after her.

"I'll find him!" Outside, the night air had grown alive with screams and gunshots. She watched the lights diminish in each house she passed, per protocol during an attack. The guards had use of night vision, and they wanted to decrease any advantages the intruders might have. Ben kept up as best he could, but Wren's strength had nearly returned to normal, and she sprinted through the community faster than he could keep up. "Zack!" She looked everywhere—the mess hall, the community hall, the school, the infirmary—but every place turned up empty.

Each gunshot that blasted the night air only increased her panic. Flashbacks of Chicago and the factory where he was trapped struck her mind like flashes of lightning. Ben finally caught up with her, and she clutched his arm. "I don't… I can't find him."

"I'm sure he's back at the house by now," Ben said,

catching his breath. He reached into his pocket then grabbed her wrist. "Take this."

Before Wren could protest, she felt the bulky metal of a pistol grip in her hand. It felt oddly heavy as Ben wrapped her fingers around it, forcing the weapon into her palm. "Does Edric know about this?" She'd requested a weapon before but was denied. Since they brought no weapons, and with Edric's rhetoric of her lack of trustworthiness, it was decided that she and the rest of her family would go unarmed. It was a victory he dangled over her in the council's decisions.

"Just take it." And with that, Ben disappeared.

Wren gripped the pistol in her hand awkwardly, and while she no longer ducked in a knee-jerk reaction to the gunshots, she couldn't stop the light shudder running up her spine. She kept the pistol close to her side, avoiding waving it around to attract as little attention as possible. She doubled back to Nate's house, hoping that in the time she was gone Zack had returned, but when she opened the cellar doors, she saw only Addison, Chloe, and Doug, their eyes glued to the pistol in her hand. "He hasn't come back?"

A fiery ball erupted into the night sky near the unfinished south portion of the wall, accompanied by a percussive blast that hummed through her body. The flash of light quickly dissipated after the magnificent bloom of colors, leaving only a faint burn of embers in its stead.

For a few moments, the air was quiet. No screams. No gunfire. Nothing but the silence of the night air, but the reprieve from the murderous sounds of death was short lived, as a single scream pierced her eardrums. And it wasn't long before the screams multiplied, spreading like a virus attacking a host.

Wren walked slowly toward the sounds, the painful tones familiar. She'd heard the same pleas on the streets of Chicago during the car wreck that sent her daughter to the hospital.

She'd heard them in the ER from desperate friends and families of the sick and dying. She'd heard them from her son, from her daughters, from people yearning for security. And now they were here. In a place she was told was safe. Safe.

"Mom!" Zack's voice snapped her out of the flashback as she watched her son hop forward on his crutches from the direction of the blast site. She involuntarily dropped the pistol from her hand as she clutched him in her arms, violently clawing his back in the relief that he was alive and the rage that had caused her to worry. "Mom, they're inside." Zack's pronounced Adam's apple bobbed up and down as he looked back to the source of death slithering inside the camp. "They shot two people. I don't know how many of them there are."

"C'mon." Wren grabbed his collar and pulled him as fast as his crutches would keep up but screeched to a halt once she realized her hands were empty of the pistol. She hurried back to the spot where she'd dropped it. She groped the grass and dirt with her fingers, hoping to find it, but struggled in the dark. She was about to pull back when her fingertips grazed a chunk of metal, and she snatched the gun, sprinting to Zack. "Let's go!"

Gunfire mixed with the pounding of feet and pulse as they headed for Nate's. The community was well over one hundred strong, over two-thirds of that population adults, and from what she'd seen, unlike herself, all of them competent with a weapon. Unless they were swarmed with greater numbers and skill than their own, she didn't think they'd be overrun, but she wasn't going to leave her family's fate to chance.

Nate's house was close to the south end, where the explosion occurred, and when Wren pulled the hidden doors open in the floor and tossed Zack inside, the gunfire grew excessively worse. Doug helped Zack down. Before she shut the doors, Doug thrust his hand up to stop her. "What are you doing?" His gaze shifted between her face and the pistol in her hand.

"I don't know how many of them are out there." She looked to the gun and did her best to steady the light tremor in her hand. Unable to cease the shaking, she moved her hand and pistol out of view. "If they can't be stopped, then you'll need to take the kids back into town. But you'll have to do it fast. If I'm not back in the next twenty minutes, you'll know it's bad. Follow the tunnel underneath, and it'll take you to the garage. Take one of the cars they have stored there. You'll have to break the lock on the key box. Don't stop until you run out of gas."

"Wren, you can't—"

She slammed the doors shut and pulled the mat to cover the hidden compartment's entrance. She stopped at the doorframe of the house as a man hurried by, wielding a shotgun. She raised her pistol and fired, her shot missing its target wide left, sending up a spray of dirt. The recoil from the gun knocked the pistol from her hand, and she dove to the floor after it, ducking out of the way of the shotgun blast that sprayed a cluster of lead balls through the wood.

Wren reached for the pistol's barrel, burning her fingertips as she mistakenly grabbed the searing barrel. She cursed and fumbled the gun in her hands. Her body trembled with adrenaline. She huddled close to the doorframe on the inside of the cabin and slowly poked her head around the corner, only to duck back behind it at the sight of the twelve-gauge staring her down.

The blast splintered the doorframe as Wren rolled to her right, the slivers of wood from the door falling off her shoulders. She aimed the pistol toward the door, both hands on the grip this time and her finger on the trigger. She saw the man take a quick step inside, and she squeezed, the recoil jolting her arms and shoulders, but the pistol remained in her palms.

Bullets redecorated the inside of Nathan's house, and while she emptied the clip, missing her target, the shots were enough to send the intruder running. But even after the clip had been emptied and the intruder was gone, Wren continued to squeeze the trigger. Click, click, click. The hammer knocked against the firing pin until the weight of the pistol grew too heavy to keep lifted, and the pistol thudded against the floor as it fell from her hand.

Wren couldn't tell how much time had passed while she was on the floor, but after a while, the gunfire outside ended. Then, Doug, Zack, and the girls were standing above her, looking at her as though she were a ghost, feeling as cold as one.

But it was Nathan who helped her up, his shirt sweaty and stained with blood and dirt. "C'mon, Wren. You're okay." She watched him pick up the emptied pistol on the floor and tuck it in his belt. He set her on the couch, checked her heart rate, and flashed a light in her eyes to check her pupils. "Wren, do you know where you are?"

"I'm..." She squinted her eyes shut and forced herself back into reality. She pushed herself up from the couch, making her way to the door. "What portion of the wall was hit?" She clung to the life that was her work, and the livelihood of her mind, using it to shift her out of the chaos.

Doug remained quiet for a moment before he answered, slowly. "It was yesterday's work. Just before the south wall."

Wren cursed under her breath, and as if on cue, Edric appeared at the door, flanked by his personal goon squad. His face was drenched in sweat and covered with soot. His arms bulged from his shirt, and his rifle strap clung tight to his chest. "Come with me. Now."

One of the goons grabbed her arm forcefully, and before she even had a chance to wrench herself free, she was out of the house and being marched toward the south fence, where the explosion took place. In the dark, it was difficult to see, but once she was close enough, she managed to make out a lumped shape in the middle of the grass. And the body wasn't alone.

Wren passed dozens of fallen bodies, all of them sprawled out in the dark grass, their limbs twisted awkwardly where they fell, their clothes and the ground around them stained with a dark liquid she knew could only be blood.

Edric's goons brought her to the site of the blast, where only bits and pieces of the fence remained. An entire section at least ten feet wide had been blown apart, leaving nothing but a crater in its wake. To the left of the crater, there was a group of people on their knees, their hands tied behind their backs and guns aimed at the back of their skulls. Edric walked over to the first captive within reach and yanked his face up so Wren could get a good look. "You know who this is?" He thrust the man's head down forcefully, the scars on his face twisted in what light the lanterns offered. "I ask because it seems to me that these people had some inside information. Attacking a portion of the fence that you rebuilt." He turned around to the gathering crowd, the stench of fear and anger thick in the air. "After all," he said, raising his voice, "you said that nothing would break through your designs. You said you could keep us safe. You call this safe?"

"The walls were meant to withstand scaling, gunfire, and battery," Wren said. "We don't have the materials to build something to withstand a bomb."

"You said you could do anything," Edric said, throwing her own words back in her face. "You said that you would do whatever it took to make sure that our families were protected." Edric pointed to one of the bodies on the ground. "What about Steve's family? Are they safer now that he's dead?" He walked to another body, this one face up, with blood still leaking from the hole in her head. "Or how about Martha's children? Her husband died years ago, and now she has two sons who are parentless. They're nine and twelve. Are they supposed to look after themselves now?"

The dissent in the crowd fed off of Edric's words, every one of them growing hungrier, angrier, the pain in their veins clamoring to escape, begging to punish someone. Wren looked at each of the fallen in turn, doing her best to not fall into the trap of words that Edric was hoping she'd slip into. "Everything I have done, everything the team I was charged with have tried to accomplish, has been for the good of this community, for everyone."

"Has it?" Edric asked, looking down at her then back to the line of captives on the ground. "And you said you would do everything you could to protect not just your family, but everyone's?"

Wren felt the edge of the snare, the final blow Edric was seeking to deliver, but with the growing crowd around her and its palpable anger, her options were slim. "Whatever I can do to help." She spit the words out reluctantly, trying her best to keep her voice calm.

"Good." Edric stomped over to the farthest captive and wrenched him up by the collar, dragging him to Wren's feet, where he rolled onto his side. Edric removed his rifle from his shoulder and extended it to Wren. "Shoot him."

Wren looked down at the captive. He was a boy, no older than Zack. The whites of his eyes were prominent in the darkness, the rest of his face dirty. She took a step back, shaking her head. "He's a kid."

"A kid who shot and killed one of our own. A kid who orphaned children. A kid who meant to take what we have and kill anyone who stood in his way." Edric thrust the rifle into her arms, forcing her to grab it, then stepped around her, positioning the rifle under the crook of her arm and aiming the barrel at the boy's head, then whispered in her ear, "A kid who sought to kill your family." He stepped away, leaving Wren with the gun pointed at the captive. "Well? You want to protect this community? Here's your chance."

Wren watched the others, looking everywhere except the face of the boy on the ground. "This isn't who we are," she said, the strength in her voice surprising her. "We don't murder children. We don't kill in cold blood."

"This isn't murder!" Edric snapped back at her. "This is justice."

"Edric, enough!" Iris burst through the crowd, Nathan and Ben close behind her. "You have no right to give such an order. Any sentencing must be done through consultation with the community and then approved through the council. You know our laws."

"Our people don't need laws! They need action!" Edric pulled his sidearm, aiming it at Iris's head. "And you will bite your tongue before you try and interrupt me again." He wavered his aim between the three of them as the rest of Edric's goons raised their rifles. He shifted the pistol's barrel to Wren. "Shoot him. Show us who you value more. Us. Or them."

The boy quivered on the ground, spewing unintelligible pleas, his fellow captives glaring at her with the same look of death in their eyes as half the community around her. Wren raised the sight of the rifle to her eye, positioning her finger on the trigger, and the boy cast his head down, his shoulders shaking violently. For my family.

But the thought struck a chord. Somewhere, the boy at the end of the barrel had a mother and a father. He had once been a child like Addison and Chloe. She looked to the other captives tied up on the ground. All of them have family. All of them were someone. Wren lowered the rifle.

Edric flicked the safety off his weapon and took a step forward, shortening the space between the tip of his pistol and Wren by half. "Shoot him."

Wren tossed the rifle on the ground. "No."

The scars on Edric's face twisted in the same rage she'd seen before, and her eyes wandered quickly over the faces in the dark and the flickering light of the lanterns to see their reactions, and the expressions were mixed. "You pick these people over the community that took you in? The community that gave you food and water? Who helped keep your husband and children alive?" Edric shook his head. "Now we know where your loyalties reside." He tilted the gun down at the boy's head and squeezed the trigger, spraying his blood across Wren's legs.

17

It was abnormally cold just before the sun broke over the horizon. Goose bumps rose on Wren's arm as she sat on the front steps of Nathan's porch, alone except for the nearly empty bottle of whiskey to her left. She'd found it in the cellar where Addison, Chloe, Zack, and Doug were hidden. She didn't remember much of returning to the cabin, but the gunshots from Edric's pistol still rang as clearly as they had nearly ten hours ago.

Wren curled her fingers around the bottle's neck and lifted the rim to her lips, the brown liquid sloshing back and forth inside then sliding down her throat. The whiskey's burn had numbed her senses and slowed her mind. But the one thing it hadn't done was blur the vision of the young man who was killed at her feet, nor the screams from the fellow captives right before Edric's men silenced them as well.

Murderers. They came here to kill your family. But even as Wren repeated the mantra that Edric had used to justify the deaths of the captives, she couldn't rid herself of the trembling boy at her feet, his eyes wide with fear just moments before his death. There was no trial, no talk of their reasons, no explanation of who shot first. Justice. That wasn't justice. It was revenge.

Wren circled the rim of the whiskey bottle with her finger, the glass warm from the heat of her lips. If there was one thing that came out of the altercation from the night before, it was Edric making a point of who was really in charge of the community. While he was gunning down the enemy, Iris and Ben were held to little more than a few words before Edric disappeared with his goons.

A shudder ran through her at the thought of his little army, his disciples that he'd trained so well. They'd listen to anything he said and would follow through with anything they told him. The only question was how much of the rest of the community would? Her wall failed, the people in the community saw her refuse an order from a man they either feared or respected, or both. Whatever little headway she'd made disappeared the moment she lowered her weapon.

A part of her wanted to do it. That much she was sure of, or else the shame from last night would have worn off hours ago, before the bottle between her knees was drained. She'd tried to find a way to justify killing the boy, but no matter what excuse she set in front of herself, she came back to the same conclusion: all those people wanted was help. They asked for it before, and we turned them away. We never even considered working with them.

The community's policy of isolation was one that was well accepted, and if it weren't for Nathan, she and her family would have been in the same boat. She thought about everything she did to keep her family safe back in Chicago, never stopping to think about the repercussions. That's all they did. They were just trying to stay alive.

The first rays of daylight broke through the trees, and Wren squinted into the early sunrise. She grabbed the bottle lazily and pushed herself off the porch, but before she was able to stand fully, she collapsed backward, the world spinning with her. She lay on her back, the wooden planks lumpy and stiff underneath, and rested her head on the porch, her mind wavering back and forth like a ship caught in a storm at sea.

She chuckled, the booze flooding her senses. She hadn't felt this drunk since high school. She shimmied to her side, pressing her palms flat against the wooden planks, and used her two shaky arms to push up from the floor. She used the porch railing for support and stood still for a few moments once she finally straightened.

Her first step forward was misplaced, and she caught herself on the doorframe just before she fell, her fingers cutting into the grooves of the bullet holes. The worries and pain that had plagued her mind the entire night were immediately washed away and replaced with the dizzy sensation that accompanied draining a fifth of whiskey. She made her way to the only piece of furniture in the living room, which was the dining table, and sat awkwardly on the edge of one of the chairs, avoiding the bedroom and risking waking up the kids in her drunken stupor.

She rested her elbows on the table and cradled her face with both hands, trying to steady herself and the room swirling around her. Carefully, she laid her face down on the table, the wood cool against her flushed cheek, and the world went black. When she felt a nudge on her shoulder, she grunted, and when the intrusion refused to relinquish its assault, she knocked it away with her hand, only to have it return with greater force.

"Wren, wake up."

A sudden wave of heat washed over her, and she lifted her cheek from the table, the skin peeling off like Velcro. Her body was covered in sweat, and she smelled the booze squeezing through her pores. She wiped her face. The flavor in her mouth was something akin to what she expected a rotten animal to taste like. The window on the far side of the room showed the day had gone well into the afternoon, which jolted her awake. "Christ." Wren jumped from her chair, wobbling on two legs toward the front door, where she was forced to stop and catch her breath. Whatever aches plagued her body failed in comparison to the pounding in her head. Her brain throbbed against her skull with such a force she slid back down to the floor, pressing her palm into her forehead as if she could press the hammering into submission.

"Are you all right?"

She felt hands on her, warm, thin hands, yet oddly familiar. She shook her head, her eyes still squinted shut. "I feel like was hit by a freight train."

"Whiskey never agreed with you."

Wren opened her eyes and saw Doug kneeling down beside her, his crutches on the floor. Despite the hangover, her rage sifted through the impaired thoughts and memories that clung tightly to their last encounter. "Whiskey wasn't the only one." She rolled to her left, using the doorframe to climb back to her feet, while Doug remained on the floor. "Why didn't anyone wake me?"

"They tried," Doug answered, reaching for his crutches and pushing himself up awkwardly, taking considerably longer than Wren. "You were blacked out. Dead to the world."

Wren squinted into the sunlight. "With the heat of hell beating down outside, who's to say I'm not?" She wobbled back to the porch. The whiskey bottle was knocked to its side, and she scooped it up then headed back inside.

"Iris and Ben came by earlier. They wanted to talk to you about last night."

Wren set the empty bottle on the counter in the corner that was attached to what passed for their kitchen, which was no more than a few cupboards where they stored some of their perishable items to snack on between meals. "I'm sure they do." She leaned her head against the wall. The floor shifted under her feet.

"Wren, they told me what happened."

"And?" She wasn't surprised at the news. Gossip spread like wildfire through the camp. Since they had no real entertainment, she'd taken up the mantle as the community's most desperate housewife.

"And… they're worried about you." Doug paused. "I'm worried about you."

Wren chuckled, peeling her forehead off the rough wooden walls of the cabin, a red mark placed on her forehead where she'd applied the pressure. "You're worried? About me?" The laughter rolled drunkenly off her tongue, her head swimming in a delirium of fatigue, pain, and anger. "You have to be kidding me."

"Wren, I know we haven't been on the same page about a lot of things, but that doesn't mean I don't still care about you."

"We haven't even been in the same book, Doug."

"I still love—"

Wren snatched the empty whiskey bottle on her spin, thrust it high above her head, and smashed it on the ground. The glass erupted into thousands of pieces that flew in every direction, the thundering crash silencing Doug's next word. "You have no right to say that. No right! I don't love you, Doug. Not anymore." The alcohol-induced wrath came down on him like a fiery hell storm. Every step she took forward, every verbal dig she cut his way thrust him backward. "You wanna know what I wanted to talk to you about? Before the shit storm in Chicago? I wanted a divorce. I'd spoken to the lawyers; I already had all of the paperwork drawn up. I was going to leave you." The weight she'd carried with that on her shoulders lifted the moment the words left her lips, but something else replaced that burden, something she didn't expect. Anger.

Doug remained quiet for a moment. The sunlight caught the back of him, casting his front in shadow, making it hard for Wren to see his reaction. "I didn't realize..." He slumped low between his crutches. "I didn't know I'd hurt you that badly."

"You didn't hurt me, Doug." Wren stepped over the broken glass, the bits crunching under the soles of her boots until they stopped just before knocking into Doug. "I didn't care about you enough for that to happen." Wren was close enough to see his reaction that time, and the wounds across his face were all she needed to see to know the cost of her attack.

Without a word, Doug turned, his crutches thudding against the floor and his head hung low until he was out the door and out of sight. Wren uncurled her fists; she hadn't realized how tightly she'd been clenching them. She walked back to the table, kicking the glass from her path along the way. She collapsed in a chair, but with her body still numb from the alcohol, she didn't feel the impact. How did I get here?

Wren lay with her head on the table for only a few more moments before the needs of food and water compelled her body to seek nourishment. She headed toward the mess hall in hopes of finding some water and any leftover lunch. There were a few people walking about, but Wren kept her eyes forward, not wanting the trouble of having to explain herself to anyone. Not now. Not yet.

By the time she arrived at the mess hall, the doors were locked, and she tugged against them fruitlessly. The walk had only worsened the dryness in her mouth, and when she wiped her brow, she saw that salt had crusted on her skin. I don't even have any water left in me.

"Mrs. Burton?"

The voice was sheepish, and for a second Wren thought she'd imagined it until it repeated, and she turned to the sight of three people huddled closely together. An older man stood in the front, someone she'd seen before but never learned his name. The two behind him were his wife and daughter. Ella and Mary, if she remembered correctly. "Yes?"

The old man fiddled with his hands nervously, rubbing the liver spots on his skin hard enough to scrub them off. "We have some leftovers in our cabin if you're hungry. Water too." He offered a half smile, and the girls behind him nodded in agreement.

The offer took Wren aback. Did Edric convince them to do this? But her stomach grumbled, and her tongue scratched the dry patch in her mouth. In the end, her body's desires overrode her concern for an ambush and she followed them to their home, keeping her distance from the old man and an eye out for any of Edric's goons. But they arrived at the old man's door with little incident.

The inside of the cabin was even smaller than Nathan's but more adequately furnished. The walls were decorated with pictures and a few paintings. Wren stopped to examine one as the old man offered her a glass of water. He gestured to the picture, smiling. "My little Ella did that when she was only five." He turned back to his daughter, who blushed. "She was always so talented."

Wren nearly drained the glass in one gulp. Even at room temperature, the water felt cool against the hot desert that was her mouth. She turned from the painting and back to the old man. "I'm sorry, I never learned your name."

"Edison," he answered, smiling. "But I know who you are, Mrs. Burton." He gestured to the sofa and took her glass from her, looking to his wife to refill it. The couch was small, and the proximity both of them were forced into was cozier than Wren would have liked, but the old man did his best to keep his distance at a respectable measure. "How are you feeling?"

The past eighteen hours had left Wren jaded to the sincerity of the people around her, and if she hadn't seen the old man's genuine expression firsthand, she would have waved it off as a slight. She took the refilled glass of water and gave it a raise. "Better now."

"What you did last night. It was brave."

Mary offered her a small plate of jerky, and Wren tore at it hungrily, the water whetting her appetite. "The boy still died. It would have been braver for me to take the bullet myself." Half the plate disappeared in two handfuls as she stuffed her mouth. After a few bites, she forced herself to slow, making sure to chew instead of swallowing the pieces whole.

"If you had taken the bullet yourself, then your children would have been left motherless." Edison reached his hand over and gently touched her forearm. "And we wouldn't have a chance to talk."

Wren looked up to see both Mary and Ella standing over them on the couch. She slowly set the plate of jerky down on the coffee table, her eyes moving wearily between the three of them. "And what would you want to speak with me about?"

"Edric." Edison said the name firmly, and the two women nodded their heads in agreement. "This isn't the first time he's gone beyond the laws of our community. This place is not a castle, and he is not a king. He can't be allowed to do whatever he sees fit."

"Apparently he can." Wren stood up. She neither wanted nor needed a lecture. "If you wanted to stand up to him, then you should have done it last night. He wasn't the only one that was armed. If you wanted to make a statement, then you missed your chance." She headed for the door, her stomach irritated at the abandonment of the jerky.

"He wants to dissolve the council," Ella blurted out.

Whether it was the desperation in the girl's voice or the hatred Wren had for Edric, she stopped at the door. "What are you talking about?"

"It's okay, Ella," Edison said, encouraging her. "You can tell her."

The woman was young, her hair a light blond. She was thin, but the wiry muscles along her arms and legs revealed a strength in her frame. Wren noticed the muscles in her hands as well, a side effect of someone who always had a pen or a brush in their hand. It was a side effect Wren was familiar with herself after spending hours at a drawing board. "How do you know that?"

"I was... talking, to one of the men in his guard unit. David," Ella answered quietly.

Sleeping with the guard was more like it. "Go on," Wren said.

"Edric pulled him aside when we were together, and I didn't mean to listen, but their voices were loud. They were angry with each other over something. And when David came back, he told me that Edric had been trying to eliminate the council to streamline the decision-making process. But David told him that it was a bad idea, that the only way to keep us all together was maintaining a balance in the community."

"Did he say how he was going to do this?" Wren asked.

Ella shook her head. "When I tried to talk to David about it more, he told me I shouldn't probe into it. That it didn't concern me. But after last night..."

"If Edric thinks he can kill anyone on a whim, then I think it's obvious what he'll do," Edison replied.

Wren let out an exhausted sigh. "Why didn't you bring

Ben and Iris in on this? If he's going to dissolve the council, then those two will be the first to go."

"They did." Iris stepped through the door first, followed closely by Ben, who shut the door behind him, locking all six of them crammed in the small living room. "Wren, we need to talk."

18

The effects of the alcohol wore off by evening, but Wren's head still swam with confusion. She sat silently in Edison's living room, the orange glow of the setting sun shading the drawn curtains a beautiful orange. Iris and Ben waited for her response, but Wren had no idea where to even start. "You realize that this idea is ludicrous, right?"

"We have to make a move, and we have to do it soon," Iris answered. The soft, kind features Wren remembered on their first day together hardened to stone. The councilwoman had made up her mind, and Ben was with her. "Edric won't waste any more time. He has the numbers."

"And guns," Wren added. "And bullets, and training, and a raging thirst for power that doesn't seem to be satisfied in his current role." Wren jumped from the couch, needing to move around. "You saw what happened last night, Iris. You all did. If Edric wants to take control of this camp, he doesn't need to do it in secret meetings. He controls the guards. He has access to the garrison. All he has to do is say the word, and the camp is his. You think going to him with a resolution telling him that he will be kicked off the council will persuade him?" She laughed. "The world beyond those walls is providing him with everything he needs to scare the people here into doing whatever he wants them to. They want security, and he's already convinced them that he can keep them safe."

"He's not the only one," Ben replied.

"The fence didn't work." Wren paced around, her arms flailing about in animation that she'd normally reserved for arguments with Doug. Christ. Doug, the girls, Zack. Edric will kill every single one of them the moment he thinks I'm planning something against him.

"You're right," Iris said, her voice low and solemn. "But what you did last night proved that you're not afraid of him. It showed the people here that he can be stopped." Iris moved closer, her small frame growing larger with every word. "Do you know how many people came to me after what they watched him do last night? Nearly half of the community. Half. If that isn't cause for a call to action, then I don't know what is."

Wren grunted in frustration. "Then where are they now? Edric doesn't talk. He shoots. And anyone that disagrees with him will get a bullet to the head. That's what your people saw. And that's what will keep them in line. Edric knows it. You know it. I know it." She waved them all off, having reached her fill of foolishness, and headed for the door.

"You cut off the head, and the body dies," Iris said, just as Wren's hand was on the handle. "And we could kill him without ever having to squeeze the trigger. All we have to do is catch him off guard."

Wren released the door handle and turned around. Everyone was standing now, all of them gathering around Iris. Wren lingered at the door, entertaining the thought. "He's always armed. And it would be foolish to think he doesn't keep himself protected at night. You'd never get close to him in here."

"That's why we're not going to do it in here." Iris pointed south, to where the explosion the night before had destroyed a large section of the wall. "You go to him and tell him that you want to take a team out to scavenge for more material. Tell him you need to make the wall stronger, and that the only way is to get better material. Steel, iron, concrete, whatever you have to do to convince him that we can't get the materials from the forest."

"I've been saying that since day one," Wren answered.

"Exactly. Despite his looks and brute force, he's smart. Anything out of the ordinary, and he'll smell it. But you coming to him, wanting to try and make amends for the failed wall..." Iris raised her eyebrows. "Now that's something he'll believe."

"But he'd have no reason to go," Wren replied.

Iris looked to Ella, who quickly turned her head down. "It's all right, Ella. Tell her what you told me."

The girl stepped forward, and though she must have been twenty, the way she twiddled her hands and twisted her ankles made her look no older than Addison. "Edric said... He told David that..." But the girl stuttered, unable to spit out her knowledge.

"Edric wants to kill you, Wren," Iris said, finishing the girl's words. "That's why he'll go with you."

And suddenly Wren realized why they'd chosen her in the first place. Why Iris was betting all her chips. "You want to use me as bait. Draw him away from his protection, away from any prying eyes."

"A lot of things can happen on a supply run these days." Iris shrugged. "With all the attacks that have happened over the past few weeks on our camp, what's to say we don't run into trouble?"

It was amazing to Wren how innocently the words left Iris's mouth. She'd heard the same strategies and talk at board meetings at her company, though the end goals were building acquisitions, not murder. "It's some sort of game for you, isn't it?"

"This is no game, Wren," Ben said, stepping around Iris. "This could be our only shot at successfully getting rid of this man. Iris said before it's only a matter of time before he finally makes his move, and with the events of last night, he has more reason than ever to finally take control. This has to be done quickly."

There was no denying that having Edric gone would be a burden lifted from her shoulders and a reason for her to stop looking behind her everywhere she walked. "When are you planning on having this… run?"

The mood in the room shifted from anxious to relieved, and Iris walked her through the plan. "Ben and I have a meeting with him tonight. It's a regular affair, so he won't suspect anything. I'll bring up the proposal for the run, saying it was your suggestion. Edric already knows how close we are, so it would be natural for you to come to me about it. Once he agrees, I'll make sure to stack enough of our people on the run to give us a chance. Then… we'll kill him."

"And the men he brings with him?" Wren asked. "You know he'll be sure to take his own people."

"He's the head," Iris reminded her. "I don't think they'll put up much of a fight once he's gone."

"Right." It was dark now, and Wren knew that her girls would be worried about her. As for Zack and Doug, they probably wouldn't mind Edric getting away with whatever he had planned to kill her. "Let me know how it goes."

Once outside, Wren suddenly felt tired. Her legs, arms, and body were sore. She couldn't figure out why, until she remembered her alcoholic adventures from the night before. After wasting away the day still reeking of whiskey, she was surprised she'd forgotten. But she forgave herself due to the casual conversation regarding her planned murder by a cold-blooded lunatic.

Wren kept on a path to Nate's away from most of the buildings. The fewer people she ran into at that moment, the better off she'd be. Compared to the night before, the forest surrounding them was disturbingly peaceful.

With Nate's house only a few dozen yards from the thick of the trees behind the main buildings, Wren turned back toward the main portion of the camp. Her foot snapped a twig, and a rustle in the bushes to her left caused her to freeze. She squinted in the darkness, trying to make out any further movement or shapes, but the dense trees made it difficult. Maybe another member of the raiders? They could have easily snuck through now, with the majority of the guards focused on the massive gap in their defenses.

The rustles grew louder, and Wren coiled her body, reaching for a rock on the ground to defend herself with, but the body that stumbled out from behind the bushes walked on three legs. She dropped the rock in her hand and let out a sigh. "Christ, Zack, what are you doing out here like that?" But her son ignored her, keeping his head down as he changed his direction toward the cabin. Wren caught up to him easily and stepped right in his path. "Zack, what are you doing?"

Zack tried sidestepping her, but any attempt was too slow with the massive cast around his broken leg. "Mom, get out of my way." His voice was irritated and pathetic, sounding like nothing more than a sniveling toddler on the verge of a tantrum.

"No, not until you talk to me. You've hardly said more than a few sentences to me since we've arrived here, and the times where we do speak to one another are cold and nasty." Wren waited for a reply but received none. "Zack, I can help."

"You can't!" Zack's throat cracked at the sudden burst of volume in his voice, his scream just as shocking and violent as the explosion she'd heard the night before. The outburst sapped his strength as he hung from the two crutches like a lifeboat. "They're dead," he said between sobs. "They're dead because of me."

Wren placed a gentle hand on the back of her son's head. "Zack, what happened last night isn't your fault, it's—"

"No," he said, sniffling. "It's not from last night. My friends. In Chicago." He looked up, and even in the darkness, Wren saw the tears running down his cheeks. "My friends are dead because of me." He collapsed forward, leaning all of his weight into Wren, who was caught off balance by the sudden fall.

Wren pulled his head up, wiping the tears from his eyes. Her heart broke in two as she watched her eldest fall apart in her arms. She helped him over to a log, where the two sat down, his head leaning against her shoulder as she gently stroked his hair. They'd never spoke about what happened at the abandoned factory she pulled him out of before they escaped the city. "What happened at the factory, Zack?"

He took a few deep breaths, trying to force his composure, but struggled with finding any strength in his voice. "It wasn't the first time," he started, pulling up from her shoulder, wiping his nose with his shirt sleeve. "We'd gone there before. The place was shut down a long time ago." He shook his head. "It was stupid, I know. The day of the attacks, we had talked about going, but some of my friends had a test they said they didn't want to miss. They wanted to stay. But I made them go. I told them that the class was a waste of time, that one test wouldn't flunk them out. So they went. We took Jesse's car, since he was the only one with a driver's license. When we got there, everything was fine. We were just hanging out, joking around like we always did. It was getting later in the afternoon, and they wanted to get going, since school was letting out soon, but I told them to lighten up." Zack grimaced, the tears returning unabashedly. "And then the explosions went off. It was like bombs were dropping all around us, and I knew it was down the street, but the building and the equipment inside were so old that I guess all it took was a light tremor to bring most of it down. Everyone was screaming, running, trying to get away. I turned around and saw them reach out their hands for help just before the vats crushed them, then my leg." Zack uttered a few more words, but he was so distraught that Wren couldn't decipher what he said.

Wren cupped her son's face in her hands, pulling him up from the despair he was sinking into. "I want you to listen to me very carefully. What happened in Chicago was not your fault. Your friends being with you in that warehouse was not your fault. Some sick people with a twisted agenda killed them." She lifted his chin, looking him directly in the eye. "Your friends did not die because you skipped school, or because you convinced them to come with you, or because you told them to stay. They died because of murderous thugs. You had nothing to do with it. Nothing."

Zack nearly broke down again then and there. He nodded quickly, trying to hold tightly to the pillar of strength she offered him. He wiped his eyes and his nose. "I still have nightmares about them. About that day. I can see them. I hear them. Every night. No matter what. They always find me."

Wren heard the torment in her son's voice as he gazed off into the night, looking as though the ghosts of his friends would pop out from behind the trees. She thought about all of the death she'd seen and looked down to the bloodstained pants she still wore from the night before. She wondered if the boy's face would haunt her tonight. "It will get better, Zack. It's just going to take time. And you're going to have to talk about it. The more you keep it bottled up, the more you're afraid to talk about it, the more it will control you."

She placed her hand on his back. "There is no shame in being the survivor. God knows I'm glad you are."

Zack offered another light nod, accompanied by a sniffle. "Yeah, I know." He reached for his crutches, and Wren helped him off the log. "I'm sorry, Mom. For, well, me."

"It's all right." Wren took him in her arms, thankful he had finally let her inside. "Remember that I love you. And I will always love you no matter what. Never think you can't talk to me about what you're going through. No matter how bad or evil you think it is, okay?"

"Thanks, Mom."

Just the sound of his voice was enough to lift her spirits, let alone the thank you. She squeezed him tightly one more time and threw her arm around his shoulder as they walked back to Nate's cabin. "Did you eat anything today?"

"I had some lunch."

Wren patted his back. "We'll head back over to the mess hall, see if there's anything left from dinner." They had just stepped out of the thickest portion of the forest when Edric blocked their path. Wren instinctively stepped in front of her son, spreading her arms out to cover as much of him as she could. She looked for a weapon on him, but it was hard to see in the darkness. He said nothing at first, just stood there, silent, menacing. Does he mean to do it here? Kill me in front of my own son?

"I need to speak with you," Edric said, his voice as deadly quiet as the woods behind them. "Send your son to the house. It's a conversation I wish to have in private."

Wren looked around to see if any of his goons had followed him, but when she saw nothing in the clearing before them but Nate's house, she nodded to Zack. "Go on. I'll only be a minute." The two of them remained quiet as Zack hobbled away, and it wasn't until her son was in the house that Edric finally broke his silence.

"I just had an interesting meeting with the council." Edric

stepped around her, keeping his hands behind his back. "Was the death toll last night not enough for you? Do you wish for more of our community members to die, risking their lives only to make another pathetic wall?"

"The wall I inherited was already pathetic," Wren said. "I did what I could with what I had." She took an aggressive step forward. "If you want to keep the community safe, then I know what we have to do. And taking the risk to find better materials to reinforce our defenses is the only way it can be done."

Edric studied her in the darkness for a long time. And while she couldn't see his eyes, she felt the cold rush his gaze cast over her body. And despite Wren's attempt at courage, in that moment she knew he could see her tremble in the night air. "You are right about one thing, Burton. It is the only way it can be done. I suggest you get a good night's rest. We leave first thing in the morning." He turned swiftly on his heel and disappeared.

Wren exhaled and made her way back to the cabin. But despite Edric's advice, she knew that tonight's sleep would be just as restless as the one before it.

19

Wren spent most of her morning staring at the girls as they slept under their blankets. She wanted to wake them, pull them from bed, and squeeze them tight until they pushed her away. But in the morning light, they looked so peaceful she couldn't bring herself to disturb their slumber.

Zack was awake by the time she left, and she nearly broke down when he told her he loved her, but forced back the tears. None of them knew what she was being sent out to accomplish, and if the plan worked, none of them ever would. She didn't see Doug, but after their exchange the other day, she found herself disappointed with how they separated. Whatever their marriage used to be, it saddened her to know it was no longer worth saving, to either of them. But as morose as the outcome was, the closure offered her some peace.

Before the teams chosen for the run departed, Iris made sure to point out which of the scouts were on their side. The numbers were at least even between Iris's people and Edric's, though she found it odd that Councilwoman Jan was staying behind. Lately, the two had been inseparable. And Councilman Ted was nowhere to be found. Though Wren was thankful to have some familiarity in Tom, her foreman on the wall. Iris offered a hug before Wren joined the rest of the team in the back of the truck and whispered in her ear, "Tom will give the signal when it's time. When he says 'it's getting late,' that's when it'll start."

They took two vehicles, the mixture of Iris's men and Edric's men spread out between the trucks evenly. The ride in the back of the truck was rough, and for each dip and bump, Wren's knuckles flashed white against the black rifle in her hands. The weapon felt thick and bulky, but she kept the rifle tight against her body. She rode in the same truck as Edric, something she couldn't avoid, as he didn't pick a vehicle until she had already chosen hers. She kept a watchful eye on him from her position, but he offered no movement or hint as to his actions. Whenever a moment of doubt or fear crept into Wren's mind, she clung to the consequences of her failure. If Edric survived, then her family would be the first to die. She knew the bastard would do it out of spite, maybe even drag her along to watch if she was still alive afterward.

Another path came into view up the road, and the lead truck veered onto it. When Wren felt them slow and follow, and the icy grip of panic took hold of her heart. "What's going on? The town is to the east. That'll take us north."

Tom banged on the window to the truck's cab, and Edric turned around, sliding the dirty glass window open. "Where are we going? The town's in the other direction."

"A little detour," Edric yelled above the howl of wind and the hum of the truck's engine. "We're stopping at one of the food caches. With the increased number of the attacks over the past few weeks, we didn't want to risk missing an opportunity to grab it." He looked to Wren. "Better safe than sorry." He slammed the window shut, and Wren jolted from another bump in the road.

They traveled for another twenty minutes. When the truck came to a stop, she jumped out eagerly, the butt of her rifle pulled tight in the crook of her arm. She watched Edric exit the truck, but he never even looked her way, and neither did his men. Wren tugged on Tom's sleeve as they hung back. "Is there really a food cache out here?"

"Yeah," Tom answered. He shook his head uneasily, his motions as angular as the square jaw that encased his face. "But I don't like the change in plans."

Some of the men carried shovels, and Wren watched Edric examine the trees, leaning in close to their trunks, looking for something. "All right. Should be just… about… here." He stopped, looking straight down, smiling. "Jackpot." His men dug up the earth where he planted his foot, and the crater grew deep quickly.

Wren watched Edric carefully. She watched his eyes, his hands, his feet, arms, legs, neck. She looked for any inkling or the slightest hint of trickery. But the one time he locked eyes with Wren, all he offered was a smile.

One of the diggers struck a crate, and the men lifted the sealed boxes and bags of food to the edge of the hole until the pile stood as tall as Wren and six feet wide. Everyone grabbed a box and loaded the truck, piling the rations in the bed.

When the last box was shoved into place, everyone dusted off their hands and tossed the shovels in with their bounty. Edric looked into the sky, smearing some of the dirt from his hand onto his forehead as he wiped his brow, and when he looked Wren in the eyes, the same rush of cold that she felt upon their first encounter shivered up her spine. A smile burst onto Edric's lips as the next words from his mouth sounded like he spoke them in slow motion. "Looks like it's getting late."

It took Wren half a second too long for the words to process, and by the time she realized what happened, gunfire erupted. She raised her rifle, nearly dropping the weapon in the process as she shuffled her feet backward. Her shaking finger found the trigger and squeezed. Her eyes shut involuntarily from the rifle's kickback, and she had no idea of the projection of her bullet. Her back slammed against a tree, and she grasped the trunk, pulling herself behind it for cover. She tilted her head out from behind the grooved bark and saw both sides had separated, and Edric's men had the trucks.

Bullets struck the tree, and Wren jerked back behind the safety of the thick trunk. The rifle rattled in her shaky arms, and though she wanted to shut her eyes again, she forced them open. Her breath was labored and quick as she looked left and saw one of Iris's guys a few trees down. The sight of allies caused her to grow bolder. She wasn't alone. Not yet.

"Wren!" Tom waved his arms from behind a small embankment between a cluster of trees to get her attention. "Are you all right?"

"Yeah." Wren gripped the rifle a little more firmly as the beacon of strength in her voice spread to the rest of her body. She tucked the weapon's stock back under her arm, the thunder of gunshots no longer causing her to flinch.

Tom ducked from a round of bullets that sent a spray of dirt over his back. "Just stay there!" He jumped to his feet, shell casings ejecting from the rifle as he returned fire, then pressed forward.

Wren inched her way around the trunk, the gun in her hands poised to shoot. She felt her muscles coil and harden with every step. Just before she completely removed herself from the cover of the tree, she paused, and her heart rate spiked, the muscles along her face twitching with adrenaline. If I die, then my family dies. She clung to that thought like a war cry and jumped from behind the tree, firing into a cluster of Edric's men near the tailgate of one of the trucks.

Combat washed over her in a blur. All Wren felt was the

steady thump of the rifle's butt against her shoulder and the smooth, hot metal of the trigger against her fingertip. Her legs and feet numbed to the ground beneath her, and after the first round of gunshot blasts all she heard was a high-pitched din that silenced the sounds of death filling the afternoon air.

Edric's men scattered from the truck, and despite the vulnerability of her position in open space, she continued to push forward. The fear in the pit of her stomach churned into rage with every squeeze of the trigger. The heat from the rifle flushed hot against her arm, and she felt her cheeks redden from the mixture of sun, adrenaline, and fury.

Wren glanced to her right. Only a few of Tom's men remained in pursuit. The gunfire thickened, and Wren sprinted to a cluster of rocks on her left for cover. The dead foliage was still slick from the previous day's rains. She slipped on the rock and smacked her elbow hard on a stone upon landing. The pain numbed her limb all the way to her shoulder, but the ricochet of bullets on the other side of the rock offered the incentive to push through the pain.

One of Tom's guys had sought cover behind the rocks as well, but found no such asylum as Wren shoved the corpse aside to make room for herself. She turned to fire, but the magazine was empty. She threw it on the ground, grabbing the dead man's rifle to replace her own. The high-pitched din had faded, and in its place the screams of dying men filled her ears. She crawled to the top of the rock cluster to get a better view, but when she crested the top, the landscape had grown still and quiet. No bullets. No screams. Nothing, except:

"Wren!" Edric's voice roared louder than any of the previous gunshots, shattering the ice-like calm that had descended on their battle. "Give it up. It's no use trying to win this. You'll just make things worse."

Wren's voice caught in her throat as she looked to the

facedown man next to her and the bloody gunshot exit wound on the back of his skull. She swallowed hard, her palms fused to the rifle. "The only thing that'll make my life worse is one more second of you being alive, Edric." She shimmied along the rocks, doing her best to stay low and quiet.

"I have two of your men," Edric replied. "The rest are dead. You want these two to live, you come out right now. I'm only going to offer this once."

Wren slowly lifted her head above the rocks for a better view. Tom and another one of their guys were on their knees with their hands on their heads. "Let them go!"

"Only if you give yourself up quietly." Edric placed the barrel of his pistol on the back of the man kneeling next to Tom. "And quickly."

"Don't do it, Wren!" Tom yelled. "He'll just kill you too!"

"Shut up!" Eric said, pistol whipping Tom. "No more games, Burton! You come out now."

"The moment I step out, yo—" Wren ducked involuntarily from the gunshot, and her body trembled long after the ringing in her ears subsided.

"That's one dead," Edric said. "You want more blood on your hands?"

Wren peered through a crack in the rocks and saw Tom still on his knees with his dead comrade facedown in the dirt on his left. She looked around, searching for anything or anyone that could help, but she was on an island, alone. Tom was right, the moment she gave herself up she'd be dead, and Tom with her. And if she died, her family wouldn't be far behind. Her veins boiled with rage, and she smacked the back of her head against one of the rocks in frustration. "You won't win, Edric. You hear me? This will solve noth—"

The gunshot silenced Wren's voice, the forest, and everyone around her. It shook loose the sanity in her mind. Her grip loosened on the firm foundation of reality, and she felt herself slowly drift into chaos. Possessed by nothing more than the urge to kill, she jumped from the rocks, firing wildly into Edric's men. Two quickly went down as she sprinted forward, her finger glued to the trigger. She didn't stop running when the magazine emptied, nor did she stop thrashing against one of Edric's men when he slammed her up against the truck. The rage in her blood boiled so hot that she was deaf to her own screams, which she was only aware of because of the hoarse pain in her throat. The next few minutes were nothing but a white-hot flash of anger, but when it finally subsided, she found herself in the back of a truck, her wrists and ankles bound together, and Edric sitting directly across from her.

"You trusted the wrong people, Burton," Edric said, his body wobbling back and forth with the turn of each bend on the dirt road. "If you had just done what you were told in the beginning, listened to me, then all of this blood wouldn't be on your hands."

"I wasn't the one who pulled the trigger on a defenseless boy," Wren retorted.

Edric laughed. "Don't travel the high road with me, Burton. I know what you were planning today. I just beat you to the punch. It's amazing what you hear over pillow talk."

Ella. The foolish girl must have told her boyfriend what they had planned. That's how Edric knew. "The plan isn't over yet." Wren narrowed her eyes, knowing that she had nothing up her sleeve. But any shadows of doubt she could stir in the back of his mind was reason enough to keep prodding. "What do you think is going to happen when you head back to camp? They'll know what you did. Whatever control you think you have will disappear the moment the community sees you walk in with half the group missing."

Edric leaned forward, and grazed the scars on his face, his fingers digging into the grooves and divots that ran along his cheeks and jawline. "The same people who gave me these tried something like you did. Although, as you can see, their plan was slightly more effective than yours." He reached for his belt and plucked a grenade. He held it out between the two of them, cradling it gently in his hands. "Have you ever been hit with shrapnel from an explosive, Burton?" He tapped the side of the grenade against his cheek. "It's nasty business. The metal comes flying at you with a velocity faster than a bullet, tiny shards tearing through your flesh like a disease burrowing itself into your body until you bleed out." He pointed to his scars. "Transport detail. Afghanistan. Roadside car bombs had become the weapon of choice for the enemy, and any suspicious vehicles were thoroughly inspected. It was my second tour, so I had a pretty good intuition when it came to spotting something meant to kill me. A skill I still use today." He pulled the pin on the grenade, clutching the lever tightly in his fist, and Wren drew in a breath as he waved the grenade around like a conductor's wand. "The enemy was a master of deception. You could never be entirely sure if the man in the robes walking down the street had a pack of C-4 strapped to his chest, or if the woman in the burka to your right had a machine gun underneath her garb." He frowned. "Every person there looked like they wanted to kill us. No matter what we tried to do about it."

The truck smacked into a large divot, and Wren's heart jumped as Edric's fist wobbled, but the grenade clung tightly to his palm. Her worry broke out in the beads of sweat along her face and neck. "And that's how you see everyone now? Your enemy? How long before that enemy turns into the kids at the community? Or someone who says something you don't like?"

"You know why we lost so many men in that war, Burton?" Edric leaned forward, but her eyes were still glued to the explosive in his fist. "We couldn't fight the battles the way we needed to in order to win. The administration was so caught up in red tape and public opinion that we couldn't kill them the way we needed to kill them. I'm not going to let that same bureaucratic nonsense destroy what I've built here."

"So that's why you've planned your little coup?" Wren asked. "You think the community is better off living in fear of you?"

"I think the community is better off living." Edric slammed his back against the side of the truck, stretching his legs. He tilted his head to the side. "You know, I heard you speaking with your husband that night." He leaned forward, then gave her a look up and down, the same look she'd seen from catcallers since she was a teenager. "It's a shame you couldn't pick a man to handle your spirit."

"Well, real men have been in short supply lately." Wren's nostrils flared, and she grimaced at Edric's stench. "But I'll let you know when I find one."

Edric grabbed her throat, choking the life out of her with his left hand. The pressure compounded in her head with every second he kept hold. "I've thought about the different ways I could kill you. I wanted to see how long I could draw it out. You people, in your cities, standing atop your ivory towers, you have no idea what it's like for the individuals whose backs you stand on. You have no idea of the sacrifices it takes to keep security." He pulled her closer, Wren's face shifting from red to purple. "But you will." He shoved her back forcefully, releasing his grip.

Wren collapsed to her side, gulping in giant breaths of air, hacking and coughing, her throat sore and raw. Her head rattled against the truck bed, and with her hands bound, she struggled to push herself to an upright position as she watched Edric place the pin back into the grenade. "You're not protecting people, Edric. You're nothing more than a prison warden now."

The truck came to a stop, and Wren suddenly realized that the forest had disappeared behind them as they pulled into an abandoned parking lot on the outskirts of town. "In a few minutes," Edric said, "you'll be wishing you had some bars of your own to keep you safe."

Two of his goons grabbed her roughly and flung her to the pavement. Her shoulders and arms smacked against the concrete, a portion of her face scraping against the grainy gravel, and she felt the warm burst of blood trickle down her cheek. More arms scooped her off the ground, the air stinging the fresh wounds.

They'd stopped at the town she could only guess was their original destination. Edric walked over to her while the rest of his men unloaded some of their food. "I just want you to know that I will not pass judgment on the rest of your family for your crimes. Unless they defy me, no harm will come to them." Those scars formed another wicked smile. "And besides... by the time your two girls come of age, women will have their uses. And if they share your looks, then I know I'll enjoy them."

Wren spit in his face, thrashing against her captors. "You fucking bastard! You lay one hand on them, and I will find you. You hear me? I will fucking kill you!" She kicked, screamed, and flailed her arms, but no matter how hard she fought, she couldn't break free.

The outburst depleted what was left of Wren's strength, and she hung limply from the hold of one of the guards. Her mind raced through the horrors her family would encounter back at the camp. I've failed them. I've given them up to this monster. She fought back the desperation welling up in the corners of her eyes. She would not give them the satisfaction of seeing her cry.

"Sir, we have movement. Three o'clock."

Wren perked up at the noise, a brief flash of hope that it was someone from camp. Maybe Iris had another team. A backup. But when she looked, all she saw were a few men she didn't recognize slithering out from behind an old lumber warehouse. They held rusty pipes and tire irons. Their faces were thick with scruff, their clothes dirty, and their hair as wild as the overgrowth creeping in from the patches of grass along the streets.

"You're late," Edric said as he approached the three men, his tone as rough as his peers. No handshakes were given, and no smiles were cast. "Where's the rest of your men?"

"Where they can see you, but you can't see them." The man who spoke had yellow-stained teeth, and she smelled the sour stench coming off him from ten yards away. When they made eye contact, he flashed a wicked smile. "That her?"

"Yes." Edric led the self-appointed leader over, while his other two henchmen stayed put, patting the ends of their rusted weapons in the palms of their hands.

The man with the stained teeth stopped just inches from Wren's body as the guard holding her still stiffened her back, standing her up straight. He stroked her hair then moved his hand down to her chest, where he fondled her right breast, smiling. "She'll do just fine."

"And two weeks' worth of rations. Just like we agreed upon." Edric motioned to a pair of his men, who dumped half of the sacks and crates of the food cache. "We have a deal?"

The man released Wren's breast, and she felt a shudder run through her body as he nodded. "My men will not attack your compound for the next month. After that, should your contributions prove... worthwhile"—he glanced over to Wren—"we will come up with a new arrangement."

Wren watched the bastards shake hands as if she were a product to be sold, and her new captor summoned his own goons. "We'll have some fun with you," he said as Wren was dragged against her will. She watched the trucks drive away, leaving nothing but dust in their wake, and she felt foreign hands dig into her flesh. She jammed the front of her forehead into her captor's jaw, knocking loose his grip but leaving her head ringing. "Hey!" But before his partner could interfere, Wren slammed her heel into the toe of his left foot then drove her knee into his crotch, sending him to the ground with his friend.

Wren sprinted. Her arms were tucked tight behind her from the restraints, but less than ten feet into her escape, she tripped and violently smacked onto the concrete. The pavement was hot and coarse against her body, and she lay there, moaning from the impact.

"Dammit, Coolgan! Can't you keep hold of one woman?" The voice lashed the words harshly, and when Wren looked up, she saw Stained Teeth glancing back down at her. "Look what you did. Her face is all fucked up."

Wren spit out a wad of blood, her cheeks on fire and a sharp pain cutting up the left side of her back. The man jerked her up and gripped her throat, forcing her to choke on her own spit. "You listen to me, bitch. We can do this the easy way, or the hard way. There are at least thirty men here who haven't fucked anything but their own hand in over a month, and you're their prize for behaving so well. So are you gonna play nice?" Wren answered, but the man's grip was so tight that her words gargled incomprehensibly from her lips. The man leaned closer. "What was that?"

"Go fuck yourself." Wren strained the words through her throat and spit a wad of blood in the man's face. She received a backhand for the comment that sent her to the ground once more, the world spinning underneath.

"Wrong move, bitch."

20

The chants and screams from the men watching Wren as she was paraded through the camp were frenzied and tilted off the edge of lunacy. The vulgar taunts paired with a few choice words told her everything she needed to expect from her stay. But when the man with the yellow-stained teeth led her inside a dimly lit room with nothing more than a few candles burning in the corner, something felt wrong.

"Boss gets to have you first when he gets back." Yellow Teeth prowled around room, sniffing at her, flashing his stained smile. "But don't you worry. When he's done with you, I'll get my turn. And I'll make sure you get everything you need, baby." He blew her a kiss, and hysterical laughter trailed behind him as he slammed the door shut on his exit, the rush of wind blowing out the few candles inside, sentencing her to darkness.

Wren pushed herself to her feet, running for the door he'd just closed, and wiggled the handle in a fruitless effort to escape. Outside, the chants and echoes of the men permeated the walls of her cell, all of them relishing in whatever sick fantasies they hoped to use her for. The thought forced her to swallow a retch of vomit, and she collapsed against the wall for support. She slowly slid to the floor, her dignity and courage falling with her as she sobbed silently in the quiet of her own solitude.

The salty tears stung the cuts on her face, but it didn't deter the tears from falling. She curled up into a defenseless ball, clutching her legs close to her chest, letting the fear run its course. She wanted to get it out now. She wouldn't cry when they raped her. She wouldn't give them anything but cold, stoic indifference.

When the wells of her grief ran dry, she pushed herself up from the floor, forcing herself to sit upright. Her eyes had adjusted to the darkness a little more, and the shapelessness of the room cleared. All of the walls were barren, and from what she saw, there wasn't a single piece of furniture in the room. Nothing she could fashion into a weapon, nothing to help her escape.

I can't die here. I can't let Edric hurt my family. Wren shuddered at Edric's last words, knowing full well that he wasn't the type of man to offer empty threats. She had to escape. Wren leapt to her feet as quickly as her bruised body allowed and pressed her hands against the wall, running them across the grainy surface until she found the candles, nothing but small nubs, the pooled wax around the shafts still warm to the touch. But they sat on no holders of any kind, and the mushy wax itself offered no defense against what she would have to fight.

Think, Wren. She shut her eyes, trying to drown out the hum of voices beyond the walls, which had grown louder. With her ear tilted to the side, she inched closer to the back wall, the chants building in volume with every step. She crouched low, running her hands against the bottom of the wall until they stumbled upon a vent.

Wren nearly screamed in elation but managed to keep her calm. The vents of the lumber yard were large to help with ventilation from the sawdust. If she could crawl inside, she would be able to find a way out. She fumbled her hands to the corners of the vent where the screws protruded. She squeezed her fingers around them, trying to twist them free. Her skin pinched against the rusted metal, and she felt flakes of rust fall from the screws with every attempt.

After a few tries, blood dripped from Wren's fingertips and rolled down the back of her hand. Every droplet that splashed into the growing pool of dark crimson beneath the air vent sent tiny droplets onto her pant leg. Each turn of the screw shredded her skin. Her fingers ached, and the screw she struggled with rusted with defiance as it neared the end of its length. With a shaky hand, she palmed the metal, where it sat stained in blood, and then placed it in her pocket. She peeled the free corner back, but it wasn't enough to make room for her to maneuver inside.

Wren winced in anticipation of the pain to come as her raw fingertips touched the next screw. Sweat rolled down her forehead, cheeks, and neck. It collected under her arms and rolled down the sides of her ribs underneath her shirt. She turned the stubborn metal fervently, but despite the effort, it withdrew painfully slowly. She smacked her forehead into the wall. Fatigue and frustration were catching up with her. She felt her grip on reality loosen, and each laugh and cheer that echoed through the walls from the dozens of men outside only slickened her fingertips as she dangled over the edge.

Wren punched the concrete wall, the only reaction from the room a dull thud that was quickly lost in the chants outside. She brought her left hand to the screw, its fingertips not as raw and bloody as her right, but her grip not as strong. She focused on returning to Addison and Chloe. She thought of her only son, alone and broken, and what that madman would try to do to him. She gritted her teeth and heard the rusted screw squeak on its turn. Her entire arm shook from the pressure, but she pushed through the pain as fresh skin tore from her fingertips and clustered in the screw head's grooves, spouting a fresh well of blood that stained her hands and the metal underneath.

Every tenth of an inch the screw protruded, Wren felt her heart race. So close. She looked back to the door behind her and the menacing intentions that lay beyond. The pain reached a crescendo on the last turn as the screw clanked against the floor. Wren took hold of the opened side and pulled backward with all of her might, the old metal vent straining against her will. With a final yank, the metal bent ninety degrees and opened a path large enough for her to wiggle through. The weight under her bloodied palms caused the metal to buckle, and with it a noise loud enough to pierce the celebrations outside.

Wren froze, slowly turning to the door behind her, waiting for it to burst open with the men who meant to rape her. But no one entered. She turned back to the vent, crawling, feeling her way through. The space was tighter than she anticipated, and her shoulders scraped against the sides while her stomach slid across the bottom. She ducked her head, and her legs stuck out straight behind her. Each movement forward was as slow as pulling the screws from the wall.

Built-up sawdust, dirt, and grime smeared across her body and limbs as she pressed forward. If the room was dark, the vent was as void of light as a black hole. Twice she smacked her head against a wall as the vent reached a dead end, forcing her to go left or right. And with no schematics to the facility, every turn through the airshafts was a gamble. She had no idea where she would end up, but with no option other than forward, she pressed on.

Finally, the glow of firelight through one of the vents offered the first look at freedom, but along with the light came the grunts and voices of the men who'd captured her.

She approached cautiously, doing her best to avoid the loud bumps and pops of the sheet metal that comprised the airshaft as she crawled forward.

The yellow-and-orange light flickered through the vent's open grates on her left. When she peered through the narrow slits, she saw the large fire that was the source of the flames. Six men sat and circled the inferno, all of them with bottle of liquor in their hand, save for one, whose face remained hidden on the far side by the fire.

"This deal is temporary, and it shows just how desperate they are. They truly believe they are safe behind those walls. It's only a matter of time. We're gaining more men along with the weapons to arm them. The food they bartered with us will be put in reserves for when we need it." The hidden voice spoke with an elegance that contradicted the Neanderthal-like faces that surrounded him.

"And the girl?" one of the men asked and spilled some of the liquid from his bottle as he sloshed his arm drunkenly back and forth. "The men are waiting for your word. They want you to have her first."

Wren held a curse under her breath, and for a while the only sound from the scene below was the crackle of the fire. Every face around the flames looked to the man she could not see. She tried moving to the right, reaching as far as the grate would allow her, and for a moment she saw a sliver of his profile. Unlike most of the men, the man's right cheek was smooth and shaven, his hair combed and slicked back. "I care nothing for the woman. But if it lifts the men's spirits, tell them to have their fun. They could use a distraction. A reward for their loyalty."

The men around the fire sniggered, and Wren had to keep the bile in her stomach from spewing through her mouth and nose. They spoke of her like an object to be used and disposed of, and they did so with candor. As the others departed, Wren lingered behind to see who their leader was, but he remained seated behind the fire.

Knowing her escape would soon be known, Wren pressed on. She crawled quickly, her heart racing, the adrenaline coursing through her body numbing the pain in her fingers and hands. After two more turns, the glow from the fire through the vent had disappeared, eclipsing her in darkness once more. She knew there was an exit point, but each grate she peered into revealed nothing more than a dark room, and she couldn't risk dropping herself into a locked room like the one that acted as her cell. Suddenly, angered shouts echoed through the long shaft behind her. She was running out of time.

Wren double-timed it, her knees and elbows smacking against the sides of the shaft. She abandoned her attempts at a quiet escape as she raced against her captors now in full chase. The air grew hotter, and she noticed a faint glow down the shaft. It wasn't the orange-and-red flames of a fire, but something softer. Moonlight.

Wren gripped the sides of the vent, which led to her freedom outside. The ground was at least twelve feet below her, and she smacked the vent violently, savagely, desperately as the men's voices grew louder. The top right corner of the vent broke loose, the small screw falling to the dirt below. Wren palmed the corner, leveraging the vent down, the weak and rusted metal crumbling from the pressure until the other screws snapped off and the vent crashed to the ground.

Wren squeezed through the tight opening, a wave of vertigo washing over her as half her body dangled twelve feet in the air, trying to grip the sides of the vent running along the building with her fingertips. The rusted corners of the side tore the fabric of her pants as she pulled her legs out, her entire body dangling from the side of the vent. She looked down, making sure the ground was clear of debris before she dropped, but as she did, the air vent buckled under the strain of her weight, shaking her loose, and she tumbled to the dirt, her limbs flailing awkwardly.

Her back smacked against the packed earth, knocking the wind out of her. She gasped for air and for a moment received nothing but the smother of suffocation. She rolled to her side, the muscles along her lower back spasming in defiance from the fall, and finally she sucked in air, filling her lungs greedily as she clawed the dirt. Angry shouts exploded into the night air, and Wren made a beeline for the woods, sprinting as fast and far away from the town as her legs would take her.

While the moon was out, the lighting it provided was poor as she shuffled through the trees and brush, her clothes snagging and tearing in the thick branches. Dogs howled behind her, and their eerie din sent a chill up her spine and added a spring to her step.

Wren searched desperately in the darkness for anywhere she could run, anyplace where she could hide. The barking grew louder, and the flames of torches flickered between the thick tree trunks as she glanced behind her. She reached into her pocket and pulled out the bloodied screws she'd removed from the vent. She palmed one of them, the end sharp enough to puncture skin.

An ache roared in her stomach, and her breath grew shorter the farther she ran, the howl of the dogs still fresh on her tail. She removed her shirt, fumbling with the buttons awkwardly on the sprint. She tore the blouse from her body and balled it up and flung it away from the trail, hoping to divert the dogs from her scent long enough for her to put some distance between her and the madmen in pursuit.

With her shirt gone, the night air felt cool against her sweat-stained body, and the chill coupled with the adrenaline that pushed her forward into the night air. Her feet and ankles bent awkwardly on the rocky, uneven ground, and more than once she stumbled to her hands and knees, the earth scraping her skin with every fall.

But the farther she ran into the woods, the slower her pace grew, and with her lethargic crawl, the men and hounds grew louder. She ducked behind the largest tree she could find, knowing that she couldn't outrun them any longer, and with the dogs tracking her, she couldn't hide. All that was left now was to fight.

Wren pinched the screw head between her fingers. The coarse bark of the tree scraped against her bare skin as she crouched low. She slowed her breathing, quieting herself as much as possible. Branches and leaves rustled nearby, and she raised her fist high, ready to strike. Luckily, the first man around the tree didn't have one of the dogs, only a spiked baseball bat. Taking him by the arm, Wren jammed the tip of the screw into the side of his neck repeatedly, each blow covering her in a fresh coat of warm blood on her face, shoulders, arms, and chest. The man gargled, choking on his own fluid. The dogs barked wildly at the scent. He clawed at her arms as the life drained from him and he slowly collapsed to the dirt. She ripped the homemade mace from his grip just as another man rounded the corner.

With a backhanded blow, Wren brought the mace's spikes into the man's cheek as both he and the hound howled at the sight of their prey. When she yanked the bat free, he dropped the dog's leash, and the beast lunged at her, jaws snapping viciously as she fell backward. The hound sank its teeth deep into her left forearm, and her mind blurred with pain. In a panicked flurry, Wren brought the side of the mace to the dog's ribcage, and the beast whimpered, letting loose her arm and limping away with its tail between its legs.

When the dog fled, the mace was yanked from her grip, and Wren was left defenseless as a swarm of arms snatched her up. She fought, clawing, kicking, screaming, and cursing as they dragged her backward. Their hands slipped on her sweaty and bloodied skin. She thrashed wildly and broke free of their hold, smacking hard against the ground. She clawed forward with her good right hand, the other arm too mangled and hurt to perform any function.

The men laughed at her on her hands and knees, her body so drained of energy it was all she could do to crawl. "Look, Jim, the bitch already started taking her clothes off."

Wren listened to his friend snigger back. "What's the matter, honey? Weren't getting enough loving at home?" They both thundered with laughter, the dog continuing its barking until she heard the smack of a boot against the hound, and the snarl transformed into a helpless yap. "I say we take her now before the others ruin her."

The man's partner agreed, and Wren felt her legs tugged backward, her belly scraping against the dirt, roots, and rocks as she kicked in defiance with what was left of her strength. She tried to hold back the hot burst of tears in her eyes, but the more she struggled, the more they fought to pin her down. She felt their foreign hands tuck under her bra and slide her pants down to her ankles.

"Hold her still, Jim." Wren looked up to see one of them with his pants down, his manhood tucked firmly in his hand. "Flip her over. I like to ride 'em like a cowboy."

Wren slammed her fist into the man's groin, and the man let go of her shoulders, but her outburst was retaliated against quickly as the man grabbed the back of her neck and punched her nose. The warm, metallic taste of blood rolled onto her lips and tongue, and her thoughts clustered together like a traffic jam. "You stupid bitch!"

"C'mon, Randy, quit screwin' around."

Once again, they grabbed her by the legs and flipped her over to her stomach as she choked on the taste of her own blood. The ground shifted unevenly, and she felt fingers pull the waistline of her underwear down. She offered another feeble kick, and then her face was slammed into the ground, dirt running up her nostrils and mouth, adding a gritty texture to the liquid swarming around her tongue.

A gunshot rang out, and she felt a body collapse on top of her, followed by the manic howls of the hound. She was too weak to push the body off of her, but with her cheek pressed into the earth, she saw a pair of boots shuffle through the grass and heard the pleas of the second man who'd punched her. "No, please, listen. I don't want any trouble. Look, you want her? Go ahead, take a turn. I don't care. I don—"

A second gunshot rang out, the dog barking wildly now, then a third silenced the forest, leaving nothing but a ringing in her ears. She felt her heart pound against her chest and then back into the dirt underneath. A brief surge of adrenaline pumped through her as she pushed up from the ground, and the man on top of her fell clumsily to the side. He landed faceup, a hole through the front of his skull, his eyes cross-eyed and lifeless.

Wren looked up to a man towering above her, and she was suddenly aware of the nakedness of her own body. She trembled despite her protest, and crawled backward, shaking her head. "No." She wanted to say more, but it was the only word that escaped her lips. "No. No. No."

The man followed, his steps methodical. Ragged and soiled clothing hung loosely from his body. His face was thick with beard, and his eyes were hidden under the shadow of his cap. He gripped a rifle in his right hand. "I told you there was wolves."

Shouts from the fallen men's comrades echoed through the woods, and Wren saw at least a dozen more torches. She flipped to all fours, trying to push forward, but her limbs refused to cooperate, and she fell face-first back into the dirt. When she turned around, she put a hand up as the man raised the butt of his rifle and smacked it against her forehead, turning the world around her black.

21

It was the pungent smell that woke her, but it was the throbbing in her head that kept her awake. She gently cradled her forehead and felt the rough stitching of cloth around her head. Her vision was blurred, but when it came into focus, she noticed that her raw fingertips were wrapped as well, bits of dried blood staining the fabric a ruddy tinge, along with her right forearm.

Wren forced herself up, the room spinning as she noticed the bed underneath her and the foreign clothes draped over her body, far too large for her frame. She squinted from the sunlight piercing through an open window, and judging from the color, they were the first rays of a new day. But which day? She tried retracing the events, but pain roared so loudly in her mind that she lay back down against the lumpy mattress.

Again the smell grazed her nostrils and forced her awake, but when she opened her eyes this time, a bearded, crazy-haired man stared back at her. She screamed and crawled backward until she slammed against the wall. The face brought back flashes of the men in the small town, the air ducts, and running through the woods. "What do you want?"

"To live." He drawled the words lazily but gruffly. He eased back into a wooden chair next to the bed and brought a pipe to his mouth, which he puffed from greedily then blew rings of smoke from his lips. But while he maintained the leisurely aura of a retired grandfather, his eyes betrayed him with the look of wild intelligence.

His voice. I've heard it before. Wren leaned forward, her curiosity slowly overtaking the fear of the unfamiliar and the throbbing pain in her head. "It was you that spoke to me my first day by the wall at the community. You said there were..." She furrowed her brow, trying to remember his words. "Wolves," she remembered suddenly. "You said it last night." Last night. Wren shuddered and curled her legs to her chest.

"I didn't touch you," he said, knocking loose the old tobacco in his pipe that spilled onto the floor. "Can't say as to what happened before I got there, though." He pushed himself out of his chair, and his heavy feet thudded against the straining floorboards. "But from what I could tell, I shot the pecker head who was about to stick you before it happened." He opened a wax casing and pulled out some more tobacco, stuffing it into his pipe.

The small cabin was roughly furnished. What chairs and tables Wren saw looked homemade, fashioned from the very trees of the forest that surrounded them. On the far wall, a cluster of rifles lay stacked neatly on a rack, and a table full of pistols and knives lay underneath. She eyed the rifles and then found the grizzly-bearded man staring her down as smoke puffed from the pipe. "You could try and get your hands on one of them guns. But I doubt you'd be able to shoot me before I'd gun you down. I may have saved you, but I don't mean to die by your hand."

Wren brought her feet from under the blanket and placed them on the floor, every muscle in her body sore and irritated from the movement. "And am I your guest, or your prisoner?"

"Depends on how long you expect to stay, and what your plans are after you leave." He narrowed his eyes, taking another long drag from the pipe.

"The community where you first saw me. Do you know those people?"

The man grunted. "I know 'em. They think they're out here surviving. The bastards don't know shit about livin' and even less about the land they sat their plump asses on." He gave her a look up and down. "Still can't figure out what you were doing there."

"They have my family." Wren stood, her legs wobbled, and she leaned back against the mattress for support. "My children. They're going to hurt them. I have to get them back." She wasn't sure what the man would say, but he stayed quiet for a long time, taking puffs from his pipe, the sunlight from the window illuminating the worn fabric of his long-sleeved shirt with different-colored patches over the holes, with the same patchwork over his knees on his pant legs. From what she'd seen so far, the man could handle himself, and whatever honor he possessed stayed intact, as he could have done whatever he wanted to her after he'd taken her. "All I need is for you to point me in the right direction."

The man set the pipe down and strode across the floor to where his rifles lay. He plucked one from the rack and opened a drawer, pulling out a magazine of ammunition that he clicked into place. His hands moved effortlessly with the weapon, and before she could blink, the barrel was aimed right at her. He took a few slow, methodical steps, his left eye shut as he stared down the sight of the rifle with his right, and he didn't stop until the barrel was less than an inch from her face.

"If you're going to kill me, then do it. But if not, get the fuck out of my way." Wren stood her ground, not relinquishing an inch.

The man finally lowered the weapon and extended it to her. "I believe I will."

22

Wren peeled back the bandage on her right index finger. Tiny fibers clung to the dried blood as she pulled the fabric to expose the wound. The flesh underneath was still pink and raw, and the fresh air only heightened the sting of her shredded fingertips. She frowned, then rewrapped the bandage. She shifted uncomfortably on the bed, which rattled the chain that tethered her ankle to the wall.

Two sleepless nights had passed since she woke up in this place. And what little sleep she did manage to catch was tormented with nightmares. Every time she closed her eyes, Edric appeared alongside Chloe and Addison. Each instance was different. Sometimes there was a gun or knife, but no matter what he used or what he did, she awoke drenched in sweat and with her heart beating out of her chest.

The door burst open with a crack, and the hermit stomped inside. Rabbits and squirrels swayed from his belt. Dirt and time weathered his thick clothes. Noticeable patchwork lined his shirt, pants, and jacket, which he never removed. Wild brown hair protruded from beneath a wool cap, and his face fared no better, with a beard that covered his cheeks from ear to ear and rested in long tangled mats down to his chest.

"You have to let me go." Wren crawled to the edge of the bed, and the chain pulled tight, stopping her right at the edge. "My family—"

"Enough." The hermit dumped the dead game onto his workstation in the corner along with his rifle and the ammunition and rations he always carried with him. "You're lucky to be alive. And you're in no shape to go prancing through the woods. Or do you not remember your last trip?" Dirt caked the portions of his face that weren't covered in beard, and at first glance he always looked as though he meant to kill you, but his eyes betrayed the effort of malice.

"I can give you food, water, whatever supplies you need. The camp has plenty." Wren clasped her hands together. "You help me get my family back, and you can help yourself to as much as you like. Please, Reuben." It'd been an uphill battle to earn his trust since she arrived. It'd taken her a day just to learn his name.

The hermit lifted one of the rabbits by its ears, his massive fist dwarfing the animal. "I have food. I have water. I don't need your help." He spit on the floor, adding to the filth that smeared the wooden boards in a greasy film.

Wren rattled her arm as violently as she could, which shook the very bed she lay upon. "You have no right to keep me here!"

"Shut up!" Reuben's voice cracked like thunder. He marched toward her, his steps shaking the walls and floors like an earthquake. "If your family is still back at that camp, then they're dead. I know those people. Take it from me and let them go."

Wren turned her head away from the hermit's rank breath as he drew closer, her body shaking in anger. "Just let me go. They're not dead. I know it."

"No, you don't!" He stomped his foot, sending another

tremor through the floorboards. His expression softened. "I'm doing you a favor. Trust me. They're dead. Move on. If someone would have—" He stopped himself, shaking his head. He plucked the game from his belt and headed outside, slamming the door behind him.

Wren deflated. She leaned against the wall the bed bordered, the wood grainy and coarse against her shirt. A part of her believed the hermit's words. Edric had no reason to keep her children alive. But despite the reason and logic she relied on so much, she still felt them. *They're alive.* She shifted her eyes to the rifles locked in the case on the far side of the cabin.

When she wasn't thinking of the ways to kill Edric, she spent her energy trying to find a way to free herself and get one of the hermit's guns. The rifle he handed her on their first encounter wasn't loaded, and the moment she turned the weapon on him the chains came out. It was a test she failed, and she'd been trying to free herself ever since.

The splinters she peeled from the wall by the bed had yet to offer the strength needed to pick the lock on the shackle around her wrist, but it wasn't for lack of effort. Wren picked at the wall, but the bandages around her fingers had diminished her dexterity. Still, the thousands of hours at the drawing board, sketching buildings, had made her hands strong, and it didn't take long before she had a fresh piece of oak between her fingers. She found the lock and inserted the pointed edge inside. She guided the splinter like a blind man's cane, fumbling in the dark recess inside the lock.

The door had remained open, and Wren kept an eye out for Reuben. A breeze drifted inside, and with it came a light jingle of cans. She perked up at the noise, the metallic clanking an unnatural sound in the forest. Reuben suddenly burst through the door and she dropped the splinter. He snatched a rifle from the cupboard and loaded the ammunition. "They're coming." He opened a drawer and pulled out a ring of keys. "They're roughly one hundred yards away right now."

"What? Who?" Wren watched him scurry through the cabin, gathering weapons, shoving them in his belt, pulling packs from shelves stored close to the ceiling, mumbling to himself.

"The gang from town," he said. "Doesn't sound like more than three or four." He pulled a knife from the sheath on his belt, the steel cleaner than any part of him, and brought the tip of the blade only inches from Wren's eye. "How bad do you want to see your family again?"

Wren froze. Her gaze shifted from the sharpened tip to the hermit's eyes. "I'll do whatever it takes."

Reuben lowered the knife, then shoved a key into the lock at her ankle. One quick twist, and she felt the metal relieve its pressure. He flipped the end of the blade around, shoving the handle toward her. "It's you they want," he said. "I'd take it." Wren curled her fingers around the knife, and before she even had a chance to consider using it against him she was staring down the barrel of a rifle. The hermit kept the weapon steady, and spoke calmly. "You have two options. Kill me, and run as fast as you can, with no idea where to go, and hope those scouts don't catch you, but I promise they will. Or help me kill them."

Wren slid from the bed and planted her bare feet on the floor. Even when she was standing up, Rueben had a good half a foot on her. She lowered the knife and tucked it in her belt.

"All right, then." Reuben flipped the rifle around and handed her the stock. "You know how to use one of these?"

The weapon looked more sinister than what she was given at the camp. She ran her fingers down the bulky metal until she found the grips. "Nothing like this."

The hermit snatched the rifle back as quickly as he'd given it to her. His hands worked over the weapon deftly, and she tried to keep up with the instructions. "Trigger. Safety. Magazine ejection when you're empty. The slide will open here when you're out of ammunition." He removed the magazine, showing her the empty chamber. "You reload in the same position, and—" A gunshot sounded. "Fifty yards," Reuben whispered to himself. He finished loading the rifle without explanation, shoved it back into Wren's arms, then rushed outside.

Wren fumbled with the rifle awkwardly. It was heavier than the previous weapons she'd held. She took a few careful steps toward the door. Another single gunshot froze her in her tracks. Her knuckles flashed white against the rifle's midnight-black stock. She steadied her hands and brought the tip of her finger to the trigger. The curved metal felt awkward under the bulky fabric of her bandage, but she forced herself into familiarity with the weapon. The wound from the dog bite on her left forearm weakened the grip on her left hand, causing her to cradle the rifle like an infant. She remained quiet and hidden at the cabin's entrance, looking into the woods for the enemy that had come to kill her, or worse.

Wren fell backward as Reuben sprinted back into the house, sealing the door shut behind him. He smashed the front window with the butt of his rifle and scraped away any remaining jagged pieces. "There's only five of them. One on horseback in the rear. A scout team, just like I thought." He stomped to the opposite side and broke the second window. "No rifles from what I could see, and the bastards have the stealth of an elephant." He kicked the glass on floor away with his boot and turned back to Wren. "You shoot anything that's not me that steps within twenty yards of this cabin. Understand?"

Wren looked from the rifle to the hermit, who stood defenseless right in the line of fire from her weapon. The air stiffened between them, and all Wren had to do was squeeze the trigger. *I could make it if I ran.* But once in the forest, she wouldn't know where to run. Without him, she wouldn't be able to return to her children. "All right."

Reuben positioned himself at the front window, while Wren watched the rear. The smaller bits of glass he didn't clear away pressed into the naked sole of her foot, but her adrenaline numbed what would have normally been uncomfortable. Outside, the forest was still and quiet. All Wren heard was the sound of her own breaths, and all she felt was the warmth of the rifle's metal against her cheek as she eyed the scope. The tunneled view through the scope magnified the world and divided it into small, round segments. Details once lost in the forest became clear.

Wren jolted at Reuben's first gunshot, shaking her from the concentration of her post. She looked back and watched the discharged shell roll across the floor and come to rest against the thick leather of his boot. She returned her attention to the crosshairs and maneuvered her aim through the thick trees. An odd branch stopped her sweep, the scope blurring in and out of focus. When the lens finally focused, the branch transformed into the rounded shoulder of a man. She lined the crosshairs over the target and drew in a breath.

One quick pull of the trigger and the recoil of the gunshot disrupted her aim. The bullet missed the shoulder and splintered tree bark. She cursed under her breath, and just before she realigned her aim, a hail of gunfire descended upon the cabin.

Wren ducked, covering the back of her head with her hands, as she felt the vibration of every gunshot transfer through the thick oak of the cabin walls. She looked over to Reuben, who was in the same position, a slow rainfall of dust shaken loose from the walls by every gunshot, slowly covering his head and back. Upon eye contact, he motioned for her to stay low.

After a while the thunder of gunshots ended, and the

storm was replaced with silence. Wren slowly lifted her head and reached for the rifle. She looked to Reuben who moved his lips softly as though he were whispering a prayer. When his eyes opened, he gave a firm nod and leapt to the window, firing wildly into the forest.

Wren joined the assault, thrusting her rifle's barrel through the broken window. She peered through the scope and watched two bodies sprint between trees. They moved to fast for her aim, and she watched bullet after bullet miss, hitting everything but the flesh of her targets.

The enemy returned fire and Wren ducked. The heavy din of gunfire filled her ears, and she felt splintered pieces of oak fall over her body. She clamped her hands tight over her ears. But with each gunshot, she felt the foundation of her conscious mind crack. Fear and apprehension escaped from the deepest caverns of her mind, bringing to life the nightmares that had tormented her the previous nights. She watched Chloe cry as she was cut, she heard Addison scream with a man on top of her, and she watched the tip of a barrel press against Zack's head and his body go limp at the sound of a gunshot. The images replayed over and over in her mind. Wren hyperventilated. The gunfire reached a crescendo. Her grip on reality slipped away. She couldn't take it anymore. She rose from behind the window, the sunlight warming her face, and she closed her eyes.

A body crashed into her and she was driven to the floor. The violent blow shook the evils from her mind, restoring her senses. When she opened her eyes Reuben stared down at her, his face scrunched in bewilderment, the stink of his body flooding her senses. "What's the matter with you?" He pushed himself off her and returned to the front window, shooting anything that moved.

Wren caught her breath, and reached for the rifle she dropped. Her skin felt clammy, and despite the blazing heat, a shiver chilled her spine. But she tightened her grip on the rifle and the heat from the weapon warmed her. She huddled below the windowsill, and the moment there was a lull in gunfire, she rejoined the fight.

The constant discharge of ammunition filled the cabin with a smoky haze. The acrid cloud stung her eyes, but Wren forced them to remain open. She drifted the tunneled vision of the scope and crosshairs through the forest and stopped once she saw flesh. Before she fired, the gunman zigzagged on a path toward the cabin.

Wren kept her stance in the open window, her finger over the trigger. She took a deep breath, calmed herself. *If you don't kill him, they'll kill you.* She guided the crosshairs along the man's path, then glided ahead of him to anticipate his next steps. She followed the pattern, and then just before the gunman veered left, she aimed the scope into his path and fired.

A fine red mist spewed into the air nearly simultaneously as she pulled the trigger. The man's hurried sprint ended, and the bullet's velocity knocked him backward. He rolled lazily back and forth in the dirt, the bloodstain on his chest growing larger with every motion. More than once he tried to stand, but each attempt was met with the same defeated collapse.

Wren remained motionless, watching the man die like the animal he was. He raised the rifle in his hand and squeezed off one last round in defiance. Blood foamed at the corners of his mouth, and Wren lowered her weapon, refusing to put him out of his misery. *Let the bastard suffer.*

Finally, his head collapsed and his body lay motionless. But while her victim's body was still, Wren's trembled in excitement, adrenaline, fear, and anger. She'd killed men before, but this was different. Every other time had been quick, in the heat of the moment. This was calculated, this took patience. The beast that awakened inside licked the lust dripping from her heart. And what frightened her most was that it craved more.

"Hey." Wren jolted backward at the touch of Reuben's hand, aiming the rifle at him in a knee-jerk reaction. He held up his hands in defense. "Take it easy." He extended a slow but steady hand and pulled the rifle from her grip. She watched her hands tremble then clenched them into fists.

Wren followed the hermit outside and squinted into the sunlight. Her first step onto the ground reminded her that she was barefoot, and the dirt felt soft and cool under her feet. The forest was quiet now, and she looked to the bodies that had been silenced.

The man she'd shot lay by a cluster of trees. The earth around him was stained a crimson red, his eyes still open. Blood dripped from his chin and the back of his jaw. She knelt by his side and examined the wound over his chest. She stretched her hand and felt the warmth of the blood on his shirt. Just before her fingers grazed the wound, Reuben's heavy footsteps caused her to jerk her hand back.

He panted and pointed between the trees. "Their partner on the horse took off as soon as the shots were fired. If we're lucky, he'll get some weather to slow him down, but it won't be long before he comes back. And with more men. I can't stay here anymore. This location is compromised."

Reuben didn't wait for an answer from Wren, nor did she try and give him one. Some of the man's blood had collected on the leaves and rolled toward the tip of her large toe. Just before the blood touched, she withdrew her foot. *Everything is compromised now.*

23

By the time Wren stepped back inside the cabin, Reuben nearly had the entire place packed. She stood in the cabin's center, watching him shove a pack of MREs into a bag. "You can't leave." He ignored her and continued his manic pace. When her words failed, she reached for one of the rifles and aimed for his head. "Hey!"

The hermit stopped, staring down the rifle's barrel with the same indifference he'd treated her with since her arrival. "Put that down before you hurt yourself." His tone was strict, like a father addressing a child.

"I'm not letting you leave until you help me get my children back." Wren moved her finger to the trigger and took a step forward. She noticed that her arms had stopped trembling. "I need you to take me to the camp. I know you know where it is."

Reuben squinted. The kindness she'd seen in his eyes since her arrival was suddenly gone. He leaned closer to the tip of the barrel. "I'm not taking you anywhere."

Wren aimed the tip of the rifle at Reuben's arm and squeezed the trigger without hesitation. But the thundering crack of gunfire was replaced with the light click of the hammer snapping against the firing pin. She looked down at the weapon, and the moment her eyes were off him, he snatched the gun from her hands, flipped the end of the barrel into her face, and flicked off the safety. Wren thrust her hands up defensively as Reuben took an aggressive step forward, and she took one back.

"You think you can use my own gun to kill me?" He walked both of them out the door with only the length of the rifle between them. "I don't take kindly to threats, woman." He spit on the ground and continued to press them deeper into the trees.

Wren dug her heels into the dirt. "Stop!" She thrust her hand in front of her, the tip of the rifle just out of reach, and Reuben grimaced. "I didn't..." She searched for the words, but when she looked to her left all she found was one of the dead bodies that still littered the ground. "I don't have a lot of options right now. What you've done for me, I'm truly grateful. I wouldn't be alive if it weren't for you."

"No," Reuben agreed. "You wouldn't." He lowered the weapon and cradled the rifle over his shoulder. "I can't help your family. What's coming I won't be able to stop, and you can barely fight yourself. If your family is still back at that camp, then they're as good as dead. If you thought your fate would have been cruel staying in town, it'll only be worse if you head back to that community. I warned you that first day. I told you there were wolves. Well, now they're hungry, and the scent of blood is in the air." He turned and headed back inside, leaving Wren barefoot in the trees.

Wren followed him inside and she stopped once she saw him staring into the rifle case. From the angle she couldn't see what had caught his attention. He went to reach for it, but stopped himself. He slammed the cabinet doors shut and zipped up his bag, everything he planned on taking with him strapped to his back. Before he walked out she stepped in his path, blocking his way. "I lived in that camp for over a month. I know what it looks like. I helped reinforce most of the defenses, and I know where they're vulnerable."

Reuben shoved her aside, heading around the cabin, the very top of the pack teetering back and forth high above his head. "The world you want back is gone. Make do with what you have. If you choose to live, then you will. That's all there is now."

Wren stepped in his path and shoved him hard in the chest, but the force barely moved his massive frame. "I'm not leaving my family to die in that hellhole. You want to know why the world is shit now? It's not because of some attack, but people like you! You sit behind your walls, or hide in your forests, and tuck yourselves away thinking of nothing but yourself!"

"And what have you done?" Reuben thrust a dirty finger in her face and stepped closer. "The world was always like this. The only difference now is that thin veil of protection that you treated like a trash can was torn down, and you got a taste of what really goes on in people's minds. You sat in your homes, in your cities, thinking of nothing but what was right in front of your faces." He took a step back. "Look at you. What did you do before all of this, huh? Sit behind some desk, watch the world pass out some open window while your eyes were glued to the faint glow of a computer screen? Yeah, you look the type. What'd you do, sweetheart? Marry rich? You got a grit that tells me you didn't come from money, but that fair skin, that air of superiority when you turn your nose up to me, yeah, I know who you are, you stuck-up bitch."

Wren flung her hand back in an attempt to slap him, but the hermit caught her wrist faster than she could swing. She stood frozen, her hand curled into a fist thrust toward the sky, trying with all of her might to free herself from his grip.

"Is that what you did to your family? Did you just leave them because it got too hard?"

Reuben thrust her arm backward with a hard shove, and she landed with her back in the dirt. She clawed her bandaged fingers into the earth and flung a lump of the cool soil at his body. His retaliation was shoving the tip of the rifle's barrel in her face. "You ever speak to me like that again, and I'll replace the brain matter in your head with lead. Do I make myself clear?"

The hermit's eyes were bloodshot as Wren lay on her back. "Yes." She lay frozen on the ground with him staring her down, his finger on the trigger. The anger pulsated through his shaking arms, and the reddening of his cheeks. It took a moment for the realization of his words to work its way past her own anger. "So you did have a family." Reuben pulled the barrel of his rifle away and marched past. She scrambled to her feet, chasing after him. "If you've lost someone you cared about, then you know what I'm going through. You know how much—"

"How much it hurts?" Reuben stopped dead in his tracks. "I'm not going to get into an argument with you about who has dealt with more pain. We all go through trials. We all have demons that torment us in our sleep. There isn't one that's worse than the other. They're all bad. And they all end up killing you if you let them. Your family is gone. The sooner you can come to grips with that reality, the better off you'll be." He shoulder checked her on his way past, and this time Wren stayed. Whatever pain the man spoke of had broken him. He wouldn't help her. He wasn't coming back.

A trail of footprints was all that followed Wren back to the cabin. She glanced at the bodies that still lay lifeless near the trees. Shadows hovered around the corpses, and she looked up to the vultures circling overhead. Nature pitied nothing, and life always moved on. But she wasn't ready to do the same. Once at the cabin, she rummaged through what the hermit left behind and found a few cans of food, a knife, and a compass that no longer worked. Aside from the furniture, the cabin was empty.

A few shelves lined the cupboard that Reuben had stored the rifles in, and she removed the longer pieces. The first shelf she pulled out dislodged a piece of paper that drifted to the floor. Wren knelt down and picked it up. It was a picture. The faded colors and thick layer of dust told its age. When she brushed the dust off, a woman and two young girls were revealed. All three of them were crouched low, looking at something, unaware that the picture was even being taken. Wren looked out the broken window in the direction that Reuben had disappeared, but she couldn't see him anymore. She set the photo down on the windowsill then returned to her search for supplies.

Wren knew that Edric would keep the camp well guarded, but she also knew he'd kill anyone who wasn't loyal, which meant his numbers would dwindle. And unless he'd managed to recruit more people into the camp while she'd been gone, the patrols around the camp would be sporadic. Even still, she knew she'd need a weapon, and since Reuben took all of his guns, she'd need to fashion her own.

Wren took the long planks from the cabinet and used the knife to sharpen the ends. The bandages around her fingers fumbled the plank awkwardly, but she kept them on since her fingers were still healing. The shavings from the wood collected at her feet as she sat on the steps of the cabin, sharpening the ends of the boards into spikes. She looked up periodically, making sure she was alone. She kept the supplies close at hand in case she needed to run, though she still wasn't sure which direction she should flee.

With the sun nearing its highest crest in the sky, signaling midday, and the pile of shavings nearly up to her ankles, Wren picked up the crude spear she'd fashioned and grabbed the cluster of nails she pried from the furniture inside. The metal was rusty, and most of their points had dulled over time, but she knew she wouldn't need much force to puncture the neck or eyes.

Wren took one last inventory, spreading the supplies on the steps. Aside from the clothes on her back, all she had was the spear, six nails, four cans of cooked meat, a spool of gauze, and the sheet on the bed that Reuben left behind. The food would hold her over until she made it to camp, and the spear would offer her some form of protection if anyone or anything moved too close, but then what?

Her parents' house in Indiana was still an option, but it was almost two hundred miles away, which wasn't a distance she thought the girls could walk. Once they were on the road they'd need food, water, and shelter, all of which were in short supply, save for the camp. She could steal a car once she made it back to the community, but that only complicated the escape.

"Dammit!" Wren slammed her fist into the cabin's front steps, running her fingers through her hair, remembering the antibiotics that Zack and Doug still needed for their wounds. The only way around the problem she faced was to retake the community, but she'd need more firepower than the feeble stick at her side to accomplish that. And that was if she could ever even find the camp. Every tree looked the same, and she had no idea how far away from the community she'd strayed.

Maybe I should have gone with Reuben. Maybe he's right. The realization unsettled her mind just as much as her stomach. *No. I can't give up. I won't abandon them.*

Wren combed through the cabin one last time and found she'd overlooked another can of food that had rolled beneath the bed along with a half-used box of shotgun shells. If anything, she could use them to barter later on down the road. She eyed the picture she'd left on the windowsill, unsure of taking it with her. She knew Reuben had seen it, and he'd left it behind on purpose. In the end, she tucked it in with the rest of the gear and bundled everything save for the spear and her knife into the sheet from the bed and picked a direction from the cabin.

When she took that first step into the unknown, she wasn't sure if she'd live or die, or even find the camp. But she knew that if she didn't attempt to retrieve her family, it would haunt her for the rest of her life. There wouldn't be a night where she didn't see their faces, and there wouldn't be a single moment she didn't spend tormenting herself. The choice was as clear as the skies above her. Get to her family, or die trying.

The first few miles were easy enough, but as the sun sank lower into the sky, Wren felt the fatigue of the rocky terrain. Her mouth grew dry even though the temperature had cooled as the sun faded. She needed to find water. Every few minutes she stopped, remaining still in hopes of hearing the rush of a stream or river, but only gusts of wind greeted her ears.

By nightfall her lips were chapped, and she stopped to rest under the large cavern of a tree that remained partially uprooted. She kicked a few rocks inside to make sure it wasn't already occupied, and once it was determined the coast was clear, she crawled inside. She sprawled her exhausted body against the dirt, which was cool from the tree's daylong shade. Her stomach grumbled and she clutched it tenderly. But despite the fatigue and hunger, her thirst rose above all else. She knew the canned meats would have liquid inside them, but she resisted the urge to open them, in fear of running out of food. She'd already eaten that day, and while she knew her body wouldn't object to the calories, there was no telling how long her hike would last.

The night grew cool, chillier than Wren had expected. It was a restless sleep, shivering underneath the cover of the thick roots that twisted and turned overhead. She wondered what had caused the massive trunk to fall. Age, weather, storm, it didn't matter, because when the night sky thundered rain, she was glad for its protection. And as the first beads of water pelted the ground beyond the small cavern, Wren realized what caused the tree to topple. *The foundation grew weak.*

Some of the traits that make a good architect include studying topography. The earth beneath the building is just as important as the material that's used to construct it. The architect that ignores the natural environment that surrounds their structure will not last long.

It was a subject that many of her peers in school had ignored, though in all most of her peers didn't put in a fifth of the effort she did. Wren was surrounded by students who already had a job waiting for them the moment they graduated, regardless of their schoolwork. It didn't matter how hard they studied or what grades they received so long as they passed. And once that sheet of parchment was handed to them, they'd run to their daddy's office, hang the diploma on their new corner office, and be given a team of those less fortunate enough to not have a father with his own firm.

For ten months Wren searched, but there wasn't a single firm in Chicago that was hiring. When she tried looking beyond the limits of her own city, she was met with obstacle after obstacle of trying to relocate her family. The one firm that offered her a position was stationed in Los Angeles, but it was only a low paying intership, and they wouldn't provide any relocation funds for uprooting her family and traveling across the country.

After another month of nothing, she tried talking to Doug about the position in L.A., but he brushed it off. He was born in Chicago, his job was in Chicago, and the kids' schools were in Chicago. He wasn't going to budge. But in the end it didn't matter. When she tried calling them back, the position had been filled, so the matter was settled.

Wren's first year out of school was one of the hardest years of her life. It was harder than balancing work, school, and the kids, it was harder than her childhood, and it was harder than finding out about Doug's affair. But she knew the alternative if she failed.

The deferment period on her loans had ended, credit card companies were calling, the bank was calling, they were behind on their mortgage, the power bill, the water bill, and it wasn't uncommon for them to go a few days without any heat or AC in the house. With a diploma and zero job offers, Wren had to face the fact that the dream she chased in school was never going to be real. She returned to her old job at the telemarketing firm and thought she'd live out the rest of her life in that dimly lit office, packed like sardines in a can with eighty other people, selling products to clients who didn't want them.

But in that darkest hour, a ray of hope broke through the clouded distress. After an exceptionally difficult day, she came home to a message on their answering machine, which had been restored the day before along with their power and water after paying two months' worth of backlogged bills.

One of the first firms she interviewed with nearly a year before had reached out to her with an opening at one of their smaller locations. She went in for the interview the next day, took the job offer on the spot, quit the telemarketing firm immediately, and never looked back.

It was one of the proudest moments she'd ever had in her life. She was beaming when she came home that day and had picked up a pizza for the kids for dinner and hired a sitter so she and Doug could go and celebrate. But when she told Doug the news, his reaction lacked the excitement she thought he'd have. He wasn't angry or upset, just... shocked. He looked at her as though she had been replaced by someone he didn't know. And what was supposed to be a night of celebration turned into their first of many fights. *That's where I lost him.*

Doug never handled being the secondary breadwinner well, nor did he take kindly to the fact that it was Wren whose name was on the mortgage to the new house, or the paperwork for the cars, or the kids' schools. All she wanted to do was bring him up with her, take them both to a place they'd always talked about. But it was apparent that in those conversations they had during their first years of marriage, it was supposed to be Doug who provided them the funds for a better life. Except he didn't. He never even tried. And when Wren grew too tired of waiting, he became resentful.

With her mind lost in memories, Wren almost didn't feel the sudden burst of warmth from the first rays of light. She crawled out from under the tree, the collapsing behemoth clinging as tightly as it could to the earth. *Foundations.* She'd always believed that hers was the same as Doug's, but it wasn't. She rose on granite, while he sank in sand.

"Rough night?"

Wren jumped, thrusting the spear in the direction of the voice, but lowered it when she saw Reuben, his big body blocking the sunrise. "What are you doing here?"

The massive pack on his back shrugged in the same motion as his shoulders, and he looked beyond her to the small cove where she'd slept. "Must have been cold in there without any insulation. You didn't sleep at all, did you?"

"Sleep's a luxury I don't get anymore." She took a step forward. "And you didn't answer my question."

Reuben looked down to his feet then paced back and forth in the same rut. "My second location was looted. Someone stumbled across it and took everything. It's compromised. All that I have left now is the cabin." He looked back into the direction Wren came. "If you're trying to find the camp, you're heading the wrong way." He pointed. "That's where you'll want to go."

"That would have been helpful before you left." She started walking, unsure of why he'd chosen to find her again.

"I have a proposal for you!" Reuben shouted. Wren stopped and turned. A brief surge of hope rose amid the hopelessness of her own fears and limitations. He took a few steps forward. "But first I need something from you."

24

The march back to the cabin seemed infinitely quicker than when she left. They returned before sunset, which afforded them more time to prepare. Reuben set his pack on the ground at the cabin's front steps. "They know where we are, and they already know the layout of the land." He pulled item after item from his pack, and Wren wondered how he managed to carry all of the gear in the first place. "What they don't know are the resources we have. They know we have rifles, but they don't know how much ammunition." He stacked box after box of bullets on the table until the sack was completely empty and their bounty lay in front of them. "From what I've seen in town, the group is only thirty large. We should have enough bullets to kill them, so long as we choose our shots wisely."

"You're sure they'll come back?" Wren asked, opening one of the ammunition boxes. She picked up one of the empty magazines and started loading.

"They will."

"When I escaped, I saw a few of them speaking with a man. I think it was their leader. I didn't get to see his face, but from what I heard, he sounded… different." Her mind flashed to the voice hidden behind the fire.

"Different isn't how I'd describe him. I saw him once. It was years ago, before all of this. I was tracking a deer, followed it for nearly four miles before I lost it. He was standing in the middle of the forest, dressed from head to toe in a suit. I'd never seen anything more out of place in my life. It was a few moments before he spotted me, and when he did, he just smiled." Reuben shook his head. "I've seen some things that have sent shivers down my back, things I wouldn't wish on my worst enemy, but when he looked at me, I felt my blood run cold."

Wren nodded. She'd experienced the same sensation when she heard him speaking to the gang. His words glided through the air with a sweet, poignant stench. She could understand how he'd pulled together so many people: he was a wordsmith.

Every spare magazine was loaded, and once they were stacked and distributed evenly between the two of them, Reuben pushed his way out the door and gestured for Wren to follow, a rifle in his hand. He stopped just before the clearing where his cabin stood and extended the gun to her. "You can't shoot worth a damn."

"Thanks for the vote of confidence," Wren replied, falling in line behind him.

Reuben set up a few targets, ranging from rocks and old cans to leaves on branches. Each target offered a different shape and was positioned to provide a specific difficulty in aim. Wren raised the tip of the rifle and lowered her head to the scope. She lined the black crosshairs over the old soup can, but the weapon grew heavy in her hands. By the time she squeezed the trigger, her arms were shaking so badly that the bullet skipped wide right. She let loose a defeated sigh, and the barrel of the rifle fell to her feet.

"You're not giving the weapon enough support," Reuben

said, lifting the rifle back up and tucking it firmly between her shoulder and arm. "You're letting your arms do all of the work. Let your shoulder stabilize it for you, and never bring your head down to the scope, always raise the sight to your eye. Widen your stance and try again."

Wren adjusted her body and rifle to the correct positions. She lined the crosshairs over the rock and placed her finger on the trigger. She fired, and the bullet nicked the left side of the target.

"Better, but your trigger action is jerky. Squeeze," Reuben said, flexing his hand into a fist. "Don't pull. You want to keep your motions fluid so your aim stays true. Now, do it again."

Wren brought the sight to her eye once more. The rifle felt sturdier in her grip, and when she squeezed the trigger, the rock fell from its perch.

"Good," Reuben said, clapping her on the shoulder. "Now, let's see if you can hit a moving target." Reuben put Wren through every scenario he could think of. And after the tenth rock Reuben thrust into the sky, she finally shot a moving target. With her confidence in the weapon improved, Reuben moved on to self-defense techniques. It wasn't flashy, but it was effective. "You want to aim for the soft spots," Reuben said. "Eyes, neck, and groin. Gouge, squeeze, and twist anything in those areas and then run. You won't be able to overpower these guys, no matter what I try and show you, so keep it simple. If you can, shoot them once they're incapacitated."

Wren practiced a few times, gently, on Reuben as he put her in different holds and she did her best to squirm away. It was easier than she thought, and it didn't take long for her to feel comfortable with the maneuvers. When finished, Reuben brought her inside. "They'll have more numbers than we can deal with, so we have to make them play by our rules. If we can make them come to us, then we'll have a good shot."

"A good shot at what?"

Reuben removed a stack of brick-like explosives and set them on the table along with wires and placed them neatly together. "We'll only get one shot at using these. This is our last stand."

Wren reached for one of the bricks. It was small but heavy, the metal around the claymore thick. Reuben emptied the remaining portions of his pack and started arming them on the perimeter's outskirts. Wren watched him carefully, forcing Reuben to go through the process six more times even after she was sure she understood the steps.

They engirded the entire cabin with wires, hiding them under rocks and next to trees, and covered them with clumps of dirt and leaves. Once it was finished, there were enough explosives to blow apart anyone that came close twenty times over. Reuben clapped the dirt from his hands and motioned toward the cabin. "C'mon, let's get back inside."

Wren lingered outside a moment, her eyes scanning the forest, wondering when they'd arrive and how many there would be. She never really saw the full scope of their numbers when they held her captive, but however many there were didn't matter. They had a plan. They had weapons. And she wasn't going to let them take her again. That gang was the only thing standing between her and saving her family, and she wasn't going to let them stop her.

"Wren," Reuben said, calling from the doorway. "Let's go."

Once inside and the preparations completed, Reuben set the fuse detonators in the middle of the room, so either of them could reach should they need to enact their final blow. Wren looked over the device carefully, the wires protruding from the detonator like weeds in grass. "Once we use the explosives, that's it?"

"If we time it right, we can use it to wipe most of them out," Reuben answered, pushing aside some of the glass from the day before when they were attacked by the small scout team. "The blasts will cause a lot of confusion. And we have the high ground, so we shouldn't need to use them until after we've already killed a few." He handed Wren a cluster of magazines and gave her a quick rundown of which worked in the three rifles she had laid out. "They all work the same way I showed you with the one in practice. The rifle on the far left is slightly heavier than the rest, but they'll all have the same kickback when you squeeze the trigger."

Wren nodded and chose to start with the one she'd used training with Reuben. The steady tremor in her hands subsided once she felt the familiarity of the weapon. The cabin grew quiet as they waited and waited. And waited. After a while, the adrenaline subsided, and she felt her eyes grow tired. The sleepless night on the ground had caught up with her, and she felt fatigue take hold. "What'd you do before all this? Before you moved here?"

Reuben stayed quiet for a moment, and for a second she didn't think he'd answer, but a few grumbles later he finally spit it out. "My brother and I owned a hunting lodge. He kept the books, and I found the game."

"Sounds right up your alley." She turned to see if Reuben was listening, but his gaze remained out the window, looking into the forest. "What brought you out here?"

"Another story for another day," Reuben answered.

"I may not get another day." Wren shifted on the floor, positioning herself where she could see Reuben but still keep an eye on the forest. "You mentioned you had a family before." Her mind drifted to the picture in her pocket, the one he'd left behind.

Reuben remained quiet for a while, and Wren didn't think he'd speak. "I've lived in this cabin for twelve years, eight months, twenty-two days, fourteen hours, and seventeen minutes."

"So why'd you move out here?"

"You already know the answer to that."

A stab of guilt ran through her as she remembered the verbal lashing before he left, and her expression softened. "I find it difficult to believe someone like you would just up and leave your family without any reason."

"I didn't leave my family. They died." Reuben spit the words out robotically.

Wren remained quiet for a moment, searching for the right words. "I'm sorry for your loss. Were they—"

"It was Labor Day weekend. My great-uncle left me a cabin on Lake Michigan when he passed twenty years ago. My wife and kids loved it, but with the girls getting older, I wasn't sure how much longer that would last, so I took them every chance I got. I remember we left later in the day than we usually did when we drove up there. My wife was tired from working her shift at the hospital. She was a nurse and pulled a lot of overnighters. She slept in the backseat of our van, and the girls took the middle row. We were playing some kind of game; I Spy, I think. My youngest wanted to ride up front and sit with me to get a better view of the road." Reuben paused, and the whites of his eyes grew red and glistened. "The woman that hit us was drunk. Didn't slow down coming out of her turn. Didn't even look. Savannah was thrown from the car through the front windshield. She died on impact. My oldest, Rebecca, made it to the hospital with a broken back and a busted blood vessel in her brain. She died in surgery. My wife held on the longest. Two weeks in the ICU before her body finally gave out. I can't even remember what the last words I said to her were." He shook his head. "It was probably something stupid. Something about bills or work. I know we had an argument the day before about something like that. And that's how she left me." A tear rolled down the corner of his left eye and into the thicket of his beard. "That's how they all left me. I didn't get to say goodbye. To any of them."

Wren remained quiet for a long moment before she gathered the courage to speak. "I can't even begin to imagine what that's like. If I lost my kids..." She wondered if she would slip into the same madness that cast Reuben into solitude if she discovered her children dead. "I'm so sorry, Reuben."

A hysterical chuckle erupted from his lips, and he wiped the few tears that had run down his cheeks and hidden in his beard. "You know what the kicker is? The woman walked away with a couple of scratches. That was it. Fucking scratches. She was leaving a bar and heading to some party when she hit us." He buried his eyes in the palm of his hand. "A fucking party." His shoulders sagged and then shook violently as sobs escaped him.

Wren reached into her pocket and pulled out the folded picture she found earlier. She extended it to Reuben, who eyed it with the same red eyes he had telling the story. "It's important to hang on to the memories that made us who we are."

Reuben stretched out his hand and gently took the paper from Wren. He looked at it for a long time, neither crying nor smiling, then when he was done he folded the paper up and tucked it into the front pocket of his jacket. A while passed before he spoke, and when he did, he acted like nothing had happened. "If things turn south quickly, you'll want to head east." Reuben pointed to her left through the window and into a thicket of trees. "That's where your camp is. You might be able to make it there before these goons catch you. If you do, then keep quiet. Don't go in guns blazing. You'll die before you even get to see your kids' faces."

"We're not going to run." Wren's voice had an edge to it as she scanned the trees. "The only way my children live is if I get them out from under Edric's thumb, and I can't do that without your help." She turned back to him. "So don't go running off and trying something stupid."

The cabin and the woods were quiet, and the only signals

of the passage of time were the moving shadows cast by the sun. Wren watched them grow along the forest floor, shifting and waning as the sun descended. Wren rested her cheek against the rifle's cool metal, watching a squirrel climb a tree. He ascended gracefully and quickly. But the squirrel, along with the rest of the forest, was suddenly interrupted by the mechanical thunder of gunfire.

25

Puffs of sawdust sprayed from the logged walls. Dust covered Wren's head and shoulders as she fumbled her fingers nervously for another magazine. The bullets cracking against the cabin roared like cicadas in the summer, a never-ending background noise that refused to quiet. She felt the vibrations of each bullet through the thick slabs of oak. The magazine clicked into place and she jumped from behind her cover. The crosshairs of the scope scanned the horizon, searching for her next target.

"I count twelve on my side!" Gunfire burst between Reuben's words. He squeezed off the rounds methodically, his feet surrounded by a field of empty shells. "How many do you have?"

"Three so far!" She spied an arm sticking out from behind the thick trunk of a tree, but her bullet only splintered the bark as the body shrank back behind its cover. *Shit.* A series of return fire forced her back under the window, and despite the number of gunfights she'd found herself in over the past month, she still flinched with every bullet fired.

"They probably have more on the sides where we can't

see," Reuben said. "Make sure you keep an eye on your peripherals. We don't need any surprises right now."

They'd barricaded the door with enough furniture and nailed enough planks across it to give a rhino trouble breaking inside. Wren swiveled to the far corners of her window, looking down the side of the cabin for anyone crouching close, but so far the space was clear. She looked back to the center of the floor, where the explosives' detonators rested, now covered in sawdust from the rain of lead hammering the cabin. Empty shells rolled along the floor. The barrage of lead was relentless in every direction, and Wren felt the overwhelming finality of their situation. They were outnumbered and outgunned.

Wren leapt from the cover of the window, thrusting her rifle through the open gap. She stiffened her back and widened her stance. Bullets missed her by only inches, but she stood her ground, finding the shooter to her left, crouched low in the brush. She exhaled and lined the crosshairs over the center of his skull and squeezed. Through the tunneled vision of the scope, she watched the man's head fling backward and then collapse in the dirt, his body lifeless. But the moment of triumph was short lived as another series of bullets ricocheted off the wall to her right. She quickly redirected her aim and found him sprinting toward her, pistol in hand and firing wildly.

Wren aimed and squeezed the trigger, this time barely feeling the recoil of the gunshot. And just as her shoulder had numbed from the repeated gunfire, so had her reaction to the deaths by her own hand. A coldness accompanied the sensation, and she moved on quickly, looking for her next target, but suddenly realized through the high-pitched whine in her ears that the gunfire had ended. She turned around, and even Reuben had quit shooting. "What's going on?" She ducked back behind the wall, one eye on Reuben while the other scanned the forest.

"They pulled back," Reuben answered, though the tone in his voice was just as skeptical as the grimace on his face. "There's no way we scared them off this quickly." He raised his rifle back up to the opened window, his finger on the trigger, and scanned the horizon with the fluidness of water.

"Hello!" A voice boomed through the trees and the cabin walls. It was loud, but Wren recognized the smooth calm in the brief introduction, and she knew it was the man she saw hidden behind the flames. The leader of the gang in town. "I think we can agree there has been enough bloodshed today."

"The only blood shed has been from your men!" Reuben said. "And if you don't turn back around and leave us be, there will be more of it before the sun sets."

The man's voice echoed in all directions. Wren looked out her window, though the view offered nothing but trees. She slunk back from her position and crawled along the wall to see if Reuben's window offered a better vantage point, but he waved her away.

"I'm hoping it won't come to that," the leader said. "But it will if we must. I know what you want, my friend. You want to be left alone. You want the quiet of the forest that you've lived in for so long. You came here to find peace, and we've disrupted that tranquility. I only come for the woman. Give her to us now, and we'll leave you to return to that endeavor."

Wren watched Reuben's face, looking for any sign that he'd betray her. He'd done more than anyone else would have in his position. She wouldn't blame him for calling it quits. He owed her nothing.

"So she can be made a slave?" Reuben asked, shouting back. "The only deal is you leave, or you die."

Wren searched the forest, looking for any movement, but only came across the fallen men she'd already killed. *If he's trying to bargain, then he thinks there's a chance he could lose. Or at least lose more than he wants.* The thought hardened her resolve.

"That's disappointing." The leader's voice seemed to travel from every direction. "Perhaps there's something you'd be willing to trade for her? Something you need? Or want? If it's companionship, I can bring you a new girl, something more akin to your personal tastes. I'm sure it gets cold at night. Nothing wrong with a little warmth in your bed."

Reuben's gunshot was his only reply, silencing the man's voice. Quiet filled the forest air, and Wren drew in a breath, the steady ringing in her ears from the gunfire yet to subside. And just when she thought the fight had ended, a storm of gunfire blew through the trees and collided with the cabin like a never-ending hurricane of hail.

The walls opposite the open windows turned into Swiss cheese as the bullets chipped away at the barricade and interior. She looked up from the floor and saw Reuben ducked low by the window, his eyes glued to the detonators in the middle of the room, the film of sawdust growing thicker with every bullet that eroded their sanctuary.

Wren crawled forward but froze when she saw him shake his head then mouth, *Wait.* He slid on his stomach toward the back wall and pushed off the floor just high enough to see through the window at his angled position then quickly ducked back down. He screamed something at her, but Wren couldn't decipher the words through the gunfire. He repeated it a few times, but it was just noise.

Wren used the wall closest to her vantage point to prop herself up once the lead storm had softened. She poked her head around the edge, hoping to find a cluster of easy targets for her to bring down, but was offered no such luck. Her jerky movements were too fast to catch anything, and she was forced to inch her nose close to the window's pane to get a better look.

Gun smoke had left a hazy fog that circled the cabin and the surrounding forest. Wren peered through the mist-like clouds, squinting to home in on any movement. Gunshots fired to her left, and she swung the rifle in that direction, holding back her shot and waiting for a clear view of the target she watched sprint through the grey smog.

The enemy fired at will, but his sprint hindered his aim, and he missed wide left and right. Wren's eyes grew dry and tired, but she kept steady. The target fell between her crosshairs, and she watched the bullet slice through the man's chest as though it were a freight train. A burst of red cut through the gray haze, and before the body hit the ground, Wren had another target in sight.

The gunman hid behind a cluster of thick, low-lying branches. She caught him in the arm, and though wounded, he managed to scramble back behind a tree before Wren could finish the job. She followed the blood trail and fired off three more rounds, but he was too well hidden. Heavy gunfire from her left forced her from the window and back behind the cover of the wall.

Reuben was still at his post, relentless in his assault. His screams intermixed with his gunshots, though Wren couldn't tell which was louder. The cloth along his left shoulder was ripped, and she saw the damp trace of blood shimmer off the light through the window. She wasn't sure if he'd been shot or if it was a ricochet, but the wound didn't hinder his offensive.

Wren rejoined the fight, nearly catching her own wound in the process. The smoke had worsened, and so had the number of targets. They had sprouted from nowhere, and what had been two or three had transformed into at least a dozen.

All of them hovered close to the bottom of the small hill that gave the cabin its high ground. The uphill climb was free from cover for at least twenty yards and would offer Wren an easy shot for anyone who ventured within its range. But the gang continued to fire from the safety of the tree line. She shot anything that moved, keeping the bandits from advancing, but suddenly stopped. *They're waiting for something.*

Wren pulled her weapon back, but it was too late. The rifle jerked forward and pulled left, jarring her elbows and shoulder. Hands gripped the weapon's barrel, and she squeezed the trigger, which shook loose her assailant's hold. She fell backward, pulling the gun with her. Her vision blacked upon impact but returned in time to see the face and pistol that peered down at her, and instinct kicked in.

Even though she could barely see, her numbed and clumsy fingers found the rifle's trigger and squeezed. The bullet connected with his chest, but still he aimed his shaking arm. She fired again, the second shot opening a hole through his shoulder, which caused him to drop the pistol. Blood dripped from his mouth. He tried to speak, but all that came out were wheezed gasps. He kept his eyes on her the entire time as he slipped away, until there was nothing staring back at her except finality.

Reuben shouted, catching Wren's attention, but in the frenzied gunfire, she couldn't hear. She shook her head, trying to make sense of the motion of his lips. A brief lapse in gunshots finally allowed his voice to break through. "Shove him out of the window!"

Wren leapt to her feet and shouldered the body off of the windowpane. Three bullets pierced the dead flesh before the opening was finally clear, and she quickly turned from the window before she shared the same fate. Blood covered her hands, the fluid warm and slick against her fingers. The rifle slipped from her grip when she picked it up, but the second effort steadied the weapon. *Keep pushing.*

Wren pivoted on her toes, dropping herself to one knee in the process, and used the windowpane to support the rifle. All that protruded from the opening now was the top of her head. The crouched position made it harder to shoot, but it also made her harder to hit.

The gang's shots grew more frantic as she picked off her targets under the cover of trees, rocks, bushes, and branches. Most of the shots only wounded them, but a few were killed. And while they sat there bleeding, struggling to keep themselves alive, it provided one less bullet meant to kill her. "They've stopped at the clearing!" Wren said, shouting over to Reuben, who shoved a cluster of empty shells away from his foot. She looked down to the stack of magazines on the floor, growing scarcer with every bullet she fired.

"Mine too!" Reuben's voice and rifle thundered together, as if they were one and the same. He dropped the empty magazine and reloaded a new one effortlessly in the same motion. "They don't have anything bigger than their guns, or they would have used it by now." He looked her in the eyes. "We're gonna make it."

And for the first time since she was thrust into this world, Wren believed it. She had to believe it. The alternative wasn't an option. She chose her shots more carefully now, only shooting when the enemy grew bold enough to venture from their cover. The sharp edge of their assault had been filed down and dulled, the wind sucked from their sails. It was a waiting game now, to see who would grow more impatient first and make the wrong move.

With the adrenaline of battle subsiding in the stagnant climate, her fatigue returned. Her hands ached, and her back had stiffened. Her joints cracked and popped like rusting metal. Her concentration grew hazy as she sat in the same frozen stance at the windowpane, the end of her rifle wavering back and forth.

"You can't win this." The voice sounded as if it came from Wren's side of the cabin, and with the words came a surge of adrenaline. She scanned the forest but only saw the same faces she'd seen for the past hour. *He's out there somewhere.* And as if she were in the cabin with her, some of Iris's last words came to mind. *Cut off the head, and the body dies.*

"You will eventually need food and water," the voice said, the echo giving him an omnipresence. "We will outlast you."

"You'll need medical attention before we need food," Wren replied, her voice hoarse from the smoke. She peered through the scope and saw some of the men squirm from her words. "And I can tell you right now that I already had a big breakfast."

A light laughter was carried on the wind. "You're just making it harder on yourself. The longer you try and fight here, the more your family will suffer."

Wren's heart dropped, and she felt her skin grow cold. *How could he even know that? Did Edric tell him? Was her family part of whatever deal they made with one another?* She tightened her grip on the rifle, the dull ache in her hands replaced with anger. "You're bluffing."

"Addison, Chloe, Zack." At each name the voice rattled off, Wren felt her stomach flip and her cold blood boil. Wren swiveled the rifle to one of the men clustered behind the rocks and opened fire. Puffs of dust and granules of rock exploded as she squeezed round after round into the granite, hitting nothing but rock. She pushed herself up from her knees, her gunshots and screams overpowering the man's voice. She pulled the trigger until the magazine emptied, and she panted heavily, her body just as empty as her weapon.

A bullet splintered the wooden log to the left of her head, and Wren spun out of the way then slid down with her back against the wall. She knew Reuben was watching her, but all she could focus on were the names the madman in the woods rattled off. *How does he know?*

"Wasteful," the voice said, a chipper bite to his tone. "Whatever atrocities you think could befall your children would be prevented should you cooperate. Look around you! I have more men. More guns. More bullets. You are on your last stand. You will not win this fight. You will lose. You hear me? You will *lose*!"

Wren eyed the detonator in the middle of the floor then looked to Reuben. The crooked lines on his face exposed his feelings about the idea, and he shook his head. But if this man knew her children's names, then he knew where they were, and if she let him get away now, there wasn't any guarantee that they'd survive. "All right!"

"Wren." Reuben barked in harsh whispers. "Don't do this."

"I come out and give myself up peacefully, and you keep your end of the deal," Wren said, her voice growing breathless as her adrenaline once again returned. "No harm comes to my friend here, and no harm comes to my children. Agreed?"

The silence that followed was almost more than Wren could bear. Perhaps she'd pushed too hard then given up too easily, but with her children's lives hanging in the balance, she didn't have time to contemplate the decision.

"Agreed," the voice finally echoed back. "Come out with your hands on the top of your head. If your friend shoots, or even breathes too loudly, you're dead, and he'll be next along with your kids."

Reuben scurried across the floor, blocking her path to the door. "This is suicide. They're not going to let your children go. You're only feeding them exactly what they want!"

"I'll stop halfway to the bombs. Wait until they cluster, then hit the detonator." Wren grabbed hold of Reuben's large, dirtied fist and squeezed tight. "If I don't make it find my children. I know you've seen them. Get them out of that community and make sure that psycho doesn't touch them." She touched the pocket where he'd hidden the picture of his family. "There are still people you can help."

Most of the barricade was nothing more than dust after the gunfire, and Wren had to do little more than yank at the top board for the rest to crumble. Before Reuben stopped her, she burst from the door, the sunlight of the evening warming her face as she squinted. She held her hands above her head, and one by one the gang emerged from the depths of the forest, their rifles aimed at both her and the cabin. She looked for their leader, but as her eyes fell upon the lurking shadows, none of them held the demeanor and sophistication that she had seen on display behind the fire. Wren stopped in the middle of the clearing, with the circle of explosives only a few feet away.

The gang mimicked her motions, freezing in their positions as she stopped. They looked to one another questioningly, and then one of the filthier members, his arms and legs covered in soil, opened his mouth. "You come to us."

They were too far out of range for the explosives to be useful. Wren looked to her left and right, the rest of the goons slowly stepping out from behind their cover, all of their rifles and pistols aimed at either her or the cabin. She stepped forward, slowly. Her pulse quickened, and she felt the nervous beads of sweat roll down her back and neck.

The explosives were only five feet from her now, but the goons had moved closer as well. *Just a little further.* She looked to her left and saw the gang's boldness grow with very step. Only three feet separated her now from the explosives. Two feet. *What's he waiting for?* The circle of goons had nearly engulfed the cabin now. Her foot grazed one of the explosives, and she shuddered. *This is it.*

"Wren, run!" Reuben's voice thundered from inside the cabin, and she turned on her heel and sprinted back toward the door. A brief series of gunshots filled the air, cut short by the explosives. The ground rumbled and shifted under Wren's feet, and she felt a hot blast of heat brush her back, coupled with a force that thrust her face-first into the dirt, and she felt the warm taste of blood upon impact.

The roar of the explosion was deafening, and as Wren lay in the compacted earth, she heard nothing but a high-pitched din. She brought her finger to her left ear and cupped it gingerly, a splitting pain running up the side of her head. Her ear felt wet, and when she examined her fingers, they shimmered red with blood in the sunlight.

Wren looked around at the bodies spread out on the forest floor, some of them twitching, some lifeless, and some of them in more than one piece. Wren looked to the cabin and saw Reuben rushing outside, rifle in hand, firing into the bodies on the ground. He seemed to find her without ever even looking down. She felt his massive hand yank her up by her collar and drag her inside, his one free arm still firing. Reuben flung her onto the cabin floor, and when he pointed down to her she watched his mouth move but still heard nothing. She collapsed to her back, her body hot and achy. She clawed the floor, dragging her body to the rifle next to the window where she'd left it. She glanced behind her to the open door. The ground was lumpy and uneven at the points of explosion.

Wren wrapped her fingers around the rifle, but when she tried to stand, she collapsed. The cabin spun along with her brain. She released the rifle and squinted her eyes shut, trying to hold back the brewing volcano in her stomach, but failed. Vomit spewed from her mouth. Her throat burned from the bile, and the foul, pungent stench filled her nostrils, adding to the sour taste that lingered on her tongue.

The second attempt at standing resulted in a more vicious bout of gagging, and Wren was reduced to standing on all fours, watching the puddle of puke beneath her grow larger with every heave. With her arms shaking and the contents of her stomach emptied, she collapsed to her side, the ceiling above her shifting from side to side. She wasn't sure how long she lay there, but after a while she felt the thump of footsteps shake the floorboards. This was her end. Lying on the floor, surrounded by her own retch, the thoughts in her shaken mind adrift like a small boat in the vastness of an ocean.

Hands grabbed her by the arms and pulled her backward.

Any thoughts of trying to fight back were useless, as she no longer had the use of her limbs. She felt her body be leaned up against the cabin walls, and just when she thought her time had come, it was Reuben's face that greeted her. She squinted at him like he was something out of a dream. "What?" She felt herself mouth the words, but couldn't hear her own voice. Panic gripped her at the thought of deafness.

Reuben shook her by the shoulders, his face highly animated, reddening from raising his voice to a scream. But no matter how much he yelled, Wren just shook her head. She buried her face in her hands, the fear of the disability taking hold of her senses, of her reason. Her palms grew wet with tears, and her shoulders trembled with Reuben's continued agitation.

"We have to go!"

The words were dulled and muffled, but she perked up at the noise. "What?" she heard herself ask.

"We have to go, Wren! Now!" Reuben lifted her off the floor with ease, and she managed to keep her legs under her, even though the floor still felt tilted. Reuben hurried around the cabin, more mumbles escaping his mouth as Wren moved her jaw and shook her head as if water blocked her ears.

By the time the spinning subsided, Reuben was already out the door with the remainder of their gear, and she stumbled forward. She felt her heartbeat thump in her chest, vibrating like a bass drum. She looked down at the bodies littered in the clearing, the few survivors of the explosions dead with a bullet lodged in their heads, bleeding the soil red. She hurried after Reuben, struggling to keep up, not knowing whether they were running from someone or after someone.

26

The longer they ran, the more Wren's hearing sharpened. She brushed past a branch and heard the light snap of wood, followed quickly by the angered hush of Reuben in front of her. Out of the two of them, he'd remained stealthy, tracking the few men who'd escaped after the explosions. She did her best to remain silent, but her feet had the stealth of bricks, and her coordination was still warped from the blast.

"Wait." Wren stopped, her breathing labored as she bent over and rested her hands on her knees. She wiped her mouth with the back of her hand, her chapped lips scratching the dirty skin. She shook her head and felt the dried, crusty blood in her left ear. She pawed it nervously. While her right ear had returned to normal, her left had not.

Reuben glanced up ahead and walked over to a branch, bits of blood staining the leaves. He rubbed the liquid between her fingers. "It's still wet. They're close."

Wren forced herself to stand. The exertion had sapped her strength and left her body drenched in sweat. She ran her tongue over her upper lip and rolled some of the salty moisture back into her own dry, cracked mouth. "How many?"

She tucked the rifle under her arm. The quicker they ended this, the quicker she could get her children back.

Reuben bent down, running his fingers over the prints in the soil. "Three. One of them is walking with a limp." When he turned to look at her, it was the first time she had really seen his face since the cabin. Specks of blood dotted his cheeks and beard. The red tinge provided him with a more sinister appeal in the sunlight, but his eyes still remained the calm pools she remembered seeing upon their first meeting.

"You should have let me die," Wren said.

Reuben remained stoic. "It's hard to find life in a place like this. And when I recognize it, I do my best to keep it alive."

Wren watched him press forward a little farther before she followed. They tracked for what felt like hours, though she knew that was false due to the setting sun. She wasn't sure what would happen if they didn't find the men before nightfall, or what would happen if they found the men at all, or if Reuben could even track them in the dark. Lost in her thoughts, she slammed into Reuben's back, stumbling them both forward a few steps. "Sorry."

The sun set, and the forest blurred in the darkness. With her left ear still deaf to the world, Wren panicked at what was left of her diminishing senses. She kept her eyes focused on Reuben's silhouette, stopping when he stopped, turning where he turned, placing her feet in his footsteps.

A gunshot broke the silence of the night, and both Reuben and Wren hit the ground. She lifted her head from the dirt and waited for Reuben to move, but he remained still. When no other shots were fired he crawled backward on his stomach until he was side by side with Wren. He leaned in close enough for her to feel his hot breath in her one good ear. "The shot missed far left. They can't see us."

"Can we see them?" Wren asked.

Reuben gestured left. "I saw the muzzle flash in that

direction. About one hundred yards out. They must have heard us coming. We'll follow the trail for a little while longer, but we'll have to stay low. They'll be actively looking for us now. Just do exactly as I do."

They pressed on, hunched over, which Wren found difficult with her center of gravity tilted from the explosive. She was amazed at Reuben's stamina. He never tired, no matter how far they walked, while her body clung together with duct tape and gum.

They continued in silence for another hour, their movements slower. Every once in a while Reuben would tell her to wait, then move ahead alone. She wasn't sure what he was doing but knew better than to try and follow. He'd had multiple opportunities to leave if he wanted, and now wasn't the time to question his methods. This was his world out here, and Wren was merely a spectator.

Reuben came to an abrupt halt and gunfire erupted ahead. Wren crashed into the bushes on her right and she crawled through the sharp twigs and branches until she burst out of the other side, her face and arms stinging with fresh cuts. In the darkness, white flashes burst from the enemy's barrels with each gunshot. When she tried to shoot, she realized she'd dropped the rifle and she scrambled back through the bush, searching for the rifle.

Reuben returned fire, and Wren tried to keep one eye on his movements, but after a few moments, she lost him in the darkness. Her foot smacked against something hard, and she reached down through a thicket of brush and felt hardened steel.

"Wren!" Reuben burst through the trees on her left, and she nearly shot him on sight. "C'mon, stay with me." All she saw were the whites of his eyes and then the back of his head as he quickly returned to chase their prey.

Wren struggled to keep up. Every step numbed her legs, sending a tingling sensation up her back. Gunfire was exchanged on both sides, and more than once Wren and Reuben were forced to stop. But with every two steps forward, they managed to gain a half step on the enemy. Reuben maneuvered through the forest as if it were broad daylight. He came alive on the hunt, and as she followed, Wren couldn't help but feel a certain adoration for the man. She'd never been a violent person, and if she'd seen this a month ago, man hunting man, it would have made her stomach turn. But here, in the wild, in the dark, she knew she was witnessing a man who'd mastered his craft. And from her countless hours at the drawing board mastering her own, it was something she admired.

A brief lull in the chase provided Wren time to catch her breath. She leaned up against a tree while Reuben changed out his magazine and then dropped his pack. For the first time since they departed, she heard him out of breath. "I'm going ahead a little bit on my own. Their gait's shortened. They're tiring. Probably looking for a place to make their last stand."

"Do you know where we are?" Wren asked, trying to rub the feeling back into her thighs. "Is there someplace here where they could find shelter? Did they lead us back to town?"

Reuben shook his head. "They started in that direction but then veered off about a mile back. I don't know where they're going now." He pulled a new magazine from the pack and tucked it into the waist of his pants. "Don't venture far."

Wren propped herself up against a tree. Her muscles ached with fatigue. The rest only worsened the desire to close her eyes. But she forced the rifle under her arm, staving off the weariness, and focused on scanning the different sections of the woods around her in case she needed to move quickly.

The trees were shorter here, with the majority of the greenery consisting of shrubs and bushes. The terrain was rockier and the soil loose and silky, almost like clay. It was a peculiar patch of forestry for the area, and Wren wondered how much farther the small biosphere would stretch.

"Wren!"

Gunfire erupted, and she pushed herself up in what felt like slow motion and sprinted toward the firefight. Her ankles and feet wobbled unevenly over rocks and pebbles, and twice she felt her right ankle buckle, but she managed to stay upright.

Reuben hadn't ventured very far, and he saw her before she saw him. In fact, she nearly stepped on him on her way past. He yanked her down behind the cover of a rocky shelf as bullets ricocheted and echoed off stony earth. "They've cornered themselves. The bastards thought they could lose me on the rocks. They've got nowhere else to go."

Wren stuck her neck out to get a better look, then ducked. The bullet that nearly killed her originated from a dark portion of the rocks, a cave carved by millennia of rain, wind, and eroding earth. "How do we get them out?"

"They weren't carrying any supplies, so unless they stumbled into a cave with running water, which I know they didn't, they'll have to come out for water." Reuben pointed to a small clearing of trees. "We'll keep watch there. It'll offer a good view of the cave, and the trees will provide us cover. We'll take shifts. My guess is they'll try and make a run before morning."

Reuben started a fire and, once it was blazing, handed Wren a container of water. "Sip it. But make sure you drink till it's gone." Wren cradled the canteen as if it were made of gold. The water rushed over her chapped lips and wet her tongue. She fought the urge to drain it in one gulp, heeding Reuben's advice, and sloshed the liquid back and forth in her mouth, savoring every drop.

After the water and a bit of jerky in her stomach, Wren inched closer to the fire. The night air had cooled quickly, and she was thankful for the flames' warmth. She shut her eyes, trying to picture her children's faces, to hear their voices, afraid their memory would fade from her own.

"How's the ear?" Reuben kept his gaze on the cave's entrance.

"What?" The tone in her voice caught his attention, and she smiled at her own joke, which he reciprocated. "The right ear's fine, but I don't think the left is coming back." She poked at it half-heartedly, hoping to prove herself wrong.

"One's better than none," Reuben replied. He paused a moment before he added, "It was stupid, what you did. You're no good to your children dead."

"And my children are no good dead to me," Wren spit back. "I'm not a soldier, Reuben. I'm not a fighter or survivalist. I'm an architect from Chicago and a mother of three. And the latter is all that matters to me. I'm not going to let my kids die. No matter what the cost."

Reuben returned his gaze to the cave's entrance. "I'll take the first watch. You get some rest."

Wren didn't object, and she used a portion of his pack as a pillow. The moment her eyes closed, she drifted to sleep. When Reuben prodded her awake for her shift, it felt as though she'd just lain down, but the plummet in temperature and the bags under Reuben's eyes told a different story. She kept the rifle close and tried to get comfortable for her watch.

Flames glowed from inside the cave's depths. No doubt the gang had someone on watch as well. Two pairs of hidden eyes peering through the darkness, each of them locked onto one another in a stalemate of wills. She raised the rifle's scope to her eye and peered through the magnified lens. Her vision ascended to the pinpoint accuracy of crosshairs, and she saw the faintest outline of a man's silhouette at the edge of the cave. She placed her finger on the trigger, her arms surprisingly calm. *End it now.*

But before she squeezed the trigger, another gunshot rang out, this one coming from inside the cave. Wren ducked, trying to elude the bullet meant to kill her, but as a second shot thundered, she realized she wasn't the target. Reuben was already at her side, gun in hand, staring into the same darkness as she was. "Did you shoot?"

"No," Wren answered. After the two gunshots, only silence and the shadows of fire filled the night air. She wanted to investigate, but with Reuben frozen like a statue, she stayed put.

"Don't shoot!" The voice echoed from the cave, and a silhouette appeared at the entrance. "I've chosen to give myself up. And if you take me alive, I can help get your children back, Wren."

Wren peered through the scope to get a better look, but the man had stopped at the edge of the shadows. She recognized the smooth, casual voice of the leader, but in the darkness his features still eluded her. Reuben, who remained in the same position, with the rifle's stock tucked closer to his shoulder, stared down the tipped sight of his rifle, but Wren placed her hand over the barrel and lowered it. "I want him alive."

"Could be a trick," Reuben answered.

"He shot his partners," Wren interjected.

"He fired his weapon. We don't know if he shot anyone."

The voice responded as if he had heard their whispered conversation. "Come check the bodies if you'd like. I've placed the weapons in the opening a few feet from the cave. I'm unarmed."

Reuben rose from behind their cover, still peering through his rifle's scope. "Step out of the cave, slowly. Keep your hands up and walk toward me." Wren popped up beside him, and the two walked toward their new captive in sync. The weapons he spoke of were right where he said they would be, but he remained in the shadows of the cave. "Show yourself. Now." Reuben and Wren both had their rifles aimed at the silhouette, only visible from the waist down in what little moonlight the night provided.

Wren watched him step out slowly, the line of moonlight traveling up from his waist, to his chest, his raised palms level with his shoulders, neck, and finally... "Ted?"

The councilman curved the left corner of his lips up in a smile. "Hello, Wren."

27

Reuben gathered the weapons Ted had discarded and, after a thorough pat down, made him drag the bodies of the two men he'd shot from the cave to confirm his story. The first victim took a bullet to the back of the head, which was caved in and hollow from the sudden expulsion of bone and brain matter. The second victim received his through the neck, choking to death on his own blood.

Ted stacked the bodies on top of one another and dusted his hands as though he'd just taken out the trash. "Unfortunate. They were good men. Loyal." He nodded in affirmation then looked to Wren. "It's good to see you again."

"Did Edric put you up to this?" Of all the people Wren expected to see, he was the last. In camp, she'd never even heard him speak. He was nothing more than a placeholder in the background, one of Edric's silent cronies that followed him around like a lost puppy.

But when Wren brought up his name, she watched Ted's face grimace. "The toy soldier?" He scoffed, taking a step around the bodies and closer to Wren. "He doesn't even know I'm here."

Wren found a seat on one of the larger rocks and sat

before she collapsed. "Why? You sided with the man with all the power at camp. If you had just stayed there, you'd have everything you needed. Why risk turning Edric into an enemy?" The rifle rested on her side now, but Reuben kept his aimed, refusing to give Ted any opportunities to make a move.

She watched an unearthly calm wash over Ted in the darkness. The day it took to travel to Reuben's cabin had replaced his smooth cheeks with a stubble that ran across his neck and jaw. His hair was disheveled, and she noticed the tears and unkempt clothes he wore. It was the first time she'd seen him look so disordered. "Have you ever been anything more than just yourself, Wren?" He paced back and forth like a professor during a lecture, the tips of his fingers lining up with one another as he slowly became lost in his own thoughts. "Have you ever imagined what the world could be if we stopped getting in our own way? If we set aside our egos, our pride, our unstable emotions? What if we acted on what needed to be done for the betterment of our future, not as an individual, but as a whole?" He looked up into the night sky, his eyes closed, and smiling.

"Whatever end goal you think you're going to find won't do you any good with a bullet to your head." Wren pushed herself off the rock, aimed, and flicked the safety off. "I don't have time for whatever twisted fantasy you've created for yourself. Are you still working for Edric? Where are my girls? Where's Zack?" She took an aggressive step forward. She thrust the weapon into his cheek, and it rattled from her adrenaline-filled arms. "Tell me!"

Ted kept his hands up and took a step backward, separating his cheek from Wren's rifle. The barrel left a circular dot on his skin that smoothed quickly after he smiled. "I'm not working for Edric. Last I saw, your girls were with their father, your husband, in case you've forgotten." He twisted the lines on his face into an overexaggerated look of sympathy. "Though I did hear about that ugly outbreak the two of you had before the explosion at the camp. I can't imagine what that's like, especially now, in a time like this. All alone, the entire weight of your family on your shoulders, only adding to the pressures the camp offered." He clucked his tongue lightly. "That's something you should have never had to bear. I can help you with that. Edric still thinks I'm working with him. I can get you on the inside. I can get you close to your children. I can help you save them." He whispered with the hiss of a snake, a hypnotic cadence with his words.

Wren shoved the rifle back into his face. "No more games, Ted."

"I'm not—"

Wren aimed the rifle left and fired into the open air, only inches from Ted's head. But despite the proximity, he didn't flinch. The only sign of irritation he offered was the closing of his eyes. She returned the end of the rifle to his cheek, and he flinched his head back to avoid the burn of the smoking barrel.

"Determined," Ted replied, glaring down at the rifle as he spoke. "I should have spent more time recruiting you, although I hoped you would have gotten the message after the trial. You needed at least three votes. Iris and Ben were the obvious two, and you know Edric would never side with you, which left only me and Councilwoman Jan."

The cold rush of realization rushed through Wren's veins, and the rifle dipped slowly from Ted's face. She'd always wondered who it was, knowing it had to be Ted or Jan. "You? Why?"

Ted smiled. "I wanted to see what you would do. We had a common enemy, and I had never seen anyone get under Edric's skin the way you did."

"Why would you risk everything you helped build at the camp?" The questions tore through Wren's mind like a freight train. "You had everything you needed. Food. Water. What more did you want?"

"The camp?" The laughter that rolled from his tongue was stressed and hurried, as though he were a young child who'd just discovered the art of crude humor. "That little outpost in the middle of nowhere guarded by a few dozen country boys? If I had a part in building the camp, then it would have been a much more formidable endeavor." His amusement slowly subsided, the hysterics fading. "The only resource I offered that camp was false counsel. Whatever negligent advice spewed from my lips was meant to weaken it, not strengthen it."

Wren dropped the rifle and took a step back. She retraced the moments upon her arrival, the bullets in the fence, the random torchings when they tried to rebuild, how the assailants always knew exactly where to attack the weak points, how the guards on patrol always seemed to miss the raiders. As one of Edric's confidants, Ted had access to all of the knowledge regarding their defenses. "You planned all those attacks on the camp. It was you who helped place the bomb. You wanted everyone behind those walls to die." Her pulse quickened. *My family was behind those walls.*

In the time it took for the rifle to drop from Wren's hands, she had already landed her fist into Ted's mouth twice. Her mind didn't even process the assault. All she felt was the harsh knock of her knuckles on Ted's jaw. Each blow sent a ripple of pain through her arm that shook her entire body. The hot burst of rage seared through her muscles. Her cheeks flushed red from boiling blood.

Wren mounted Ted on the ground, beating his face senseless. He offered no resistance, only laughter. All of the pain and frustration and fear and uncertainty had unleashed a raging beast from its cage. For the first time since she could remember, she felt the unbridled power of certainty. She knew exactly what she wanted. *Kill him.* But before Wren could realize her prophetic vision, hands and arms pulled her backward. "NO! He did this! He did this to my family!" Her shrieks pierced the sky and puffed a chill into the night air. She kicked and flailed her arms, but Reuben finally managed to subdue her rage.

Ted gargled blood as he laughed, and the claret dripped from his nose and mouth. His right cheek was swollen and red, and his clothes and hair soiled from the dirt where he landed. Ted never took his eyes off her as Reuben dragged him to the nearest tree and tied him up. "You would have done well, Wren." He spit a wad of blood. "You have the makings of greatness and a foundation of stone. I didn't think you'd crack, no matter what Edric threw at you." He grinned, and the black space of a missing tooth where his back molar used to sit disrupted the coy smile he had sported earlier.

Reuben knelt in front of her and gently grabbed her by the chin. He examined her face then her knuckles. "Hell of a jab, Wren." He wiped the blood from her skin, and she winced from the pressure.

The adrenaline had worn off, and the repercussions of her outburst set in. "You should have let me kill him." She offered the same defiant glare to Reuben as she had to Edric and Ted. But his response differed from theirs.

"I know." Reuben removed some gauze from his pack and wrapped her hand, his massive fingers surprisingly gentle and nimble. "But if I let you kill him now, we wouldn't know what he knows. And if we're going to get your family back, we'll need all the help we can get."

Wren cocked her head to the side. "What changed your mind?"

Reuben concentrated on wrapping her wounds, keeping his voice casual. "I was always going to help you. I don't think I realized it until now though." He looked up at her, his eyes glowing under the night sky, surrounded by dirtied cheeks and the mangled beard that covered most of his face. "You remind me of someone."

At school, Wren had studied and graduated with some of the brightest minds in her field. She'd been a part of meetings with men who commanded respect and awe from their peers and subordinates. But never had she seen anyone dwarf them until now. "Thank you."

Once the bandages were wrapped, Wren took a step back. She allowed her mind to regain its footing in reason before she slipped back into chaos. She and Reuben approached Ted together, the blood from his nose and lip crusted dry onto his face and shirt. "Who are you?"

"A question many have asked themselves upon my introduction," Ted answered. He straightened himself as best he could with his arms bound. "But one that you should know the answer to by now, Wren. After all, you've met so many of my friends."

Wren furrowed her brow. "I doubt that."

"No? But you spoke of them so fervently at your trial and so openly with anyone that would listen back at the camp."

Reuben backhanded Ted, and a fresh spout of blood erupted from Ted's lip, and he spit another wad of crimson into the earth. Wren stepped backward, and a cold shiver crawled up her back. *It can't be.* "You're… You're… with *them*?"

"What are you talking about, Wren?" Reuben asked, holding Ted up by his shirt as he howled in excitement at her realization. "Wren!"

The events in Chicago flooded her mind, drenching her memories and thoughts in fear and despair until she was soaked to the bone. The car wreck, the hospital, the factory, the riot in the city, the march of death that consumed everything she had ever known. The black masks that concealed the enemy, casting the true nature of their intentions under a veil of secrecy. But here it was unmasked, bloodied, and psychotic. "You're one of the terrorists."

"I am," Ted replied. "I helped destroy your city. I helped detonate the EMP. I'm responsible for your family's misfortunes. And I am the only person that can retrieve your children in one piece. So I suggest you take these ropes off me before it's too late."

Reuben released his grip on Ted's collar, dropping him to the ground with a thud. Wren watched the confusion spread across the hermit's face. "Wren, what is he talking about?"

It was almost too much for her to comprehend, but all of the information was there. She just refused to connect the dots. "You wanted me because you knew I could help bring down Edric. Because anyone that's not on your side is the enemy. Anyone that's still alive you mean to kill."

"The enemy of my enemy is my friend. Once the EMP was detonated, we knew pockets of resistance would form around the country, so we started the long process of recruitment to our side long before the device was detonated. We're everywhere, Wren." Some of the crusted blood from Ted's face flaked off his upper lip as he smiled. "And I don't mean to just kill the camp, no. I mean to purge this entire country of its useless bodies, its backward thinking that has limited our potential for the past three generations." Ted leaned forward, the fresh cut under his lip dripping new blood. "Edric may be a Neanderthal, but he is well stocked with weapons and men. I don't have any doubts he managed to secure the compound after exchanging you for the false peace my men promised. You don't have the resources to take him down. You don't have the bullets. You need my help. Take me back to town, and I will tell my men to attack the camp."

"Wren." Reuben tugged on her sleeve, pulling her out of earshot from Ted. "You can't trust him. He'll do whatever he needs to get out of those ropes. We take him back to the town, and he'll double-cross us."

"We're not taking him back to town." Wren pushed past Reuben and marched toward Ted, their eyes locked on one another. "You don't care about my family. You don't care about me. But I know one thing that you hold above everything else. Even your sick ideals. And that's your life." She leaned closer. "You didn't kill your comrades to try and buy some favor with me. You did it because you knew there was only one way out of that cave. So I'll make *you* a deal. I'm going to take you to Edric in exchange for my children. You keep your mouth shut, maybe you can weasel a pardon with him after I'm gone. You talk before I have my kids, I put a bullet through your head."

The charismatic indifference vanished from his face. An uneasy tingling stirred in the back of her mind. But despite the icy fear gripping her heart, she didn't break. Ted leaned forward as far as the restraints would allow, until the two were nearly nose to nose, and then he smiled. "Now you're talking like one of us."

28

Wren allowed Reuben to handle Ted on their trek back to the community, though she didn't expect a problem from him with a gun to his head and his hands tied behind his back. When she wasn't watching her footing over the terrain hidden by the cover of night, she stared at the back of Ted's head like a hawk. More than once she had to remind herself that he was of more use to her alive than dead. While she and Reuben kept quiet, Ted was nothing short of chatty on their journey, only stopping his mouth to catch his breath.

"It's a missed opportunity." Ted stepped over a fallen log, balancing awkwardly with this hands tied. "For both of you. I don't think you understand the influence I have with the organization."

Reuben smacked the back of Ted's knee, and he stumbled, but caught himself after a few steps forward. "I said enough." He bared his teeth like an angry dog. Ted's incessant chatter had tested his patience since he opened his mouth.

"No reason to get nasty," Ted replied, shaking the leg Reuben had struck. He looked back at him. "You know, I still remember you from that day in the woods."

Reuben grabbed Ted by the back of the neck and slammed him against the nearest tree. He pulled a knife and pressed it against Ted's cheek. "It might work out better for us if he can't talk. I can take out his tongue now and save us the trouble of wondering when he'll give us up to Edric to save his own skin."

"Reuben, enough." Wren caught up to him and saw that the blade had drawn blood. In the dark of night, the fluid ran black down his skin. "I'm sure we could come up with something more creative than that."

Ted moaned as Reuben released him. "The lady has my thanks."

"I don't want it." The longer they walked, the more her legs turned to lead. Never in her life did she want a bed to lie down on, but the thought of her children fueled the fire within. And the more time she spent in the forest was more time Edric had to breathe.

Ted remained quiet for a short time, but the compulsion to listen to his own voice overrode his fear of the rod. "I'm surprised you haven't asked more about what I'm trying to do. About my organization."

"That's because I don't want to know." Wren tried to keep the energy in her voice high, but even she tasted the dullness on her tongue.

"I think you'd fit in more than you think." Ted looked back at her then to Reuben, who brought his free hand to the hilt of his knife tucked in his belt. "Though I'm not sure about him." He gave Reuben a look up and down. "Too much of an idealist in him. But you," he said, turning back to Wren, "you're pragmatic. You do what's needed to survive. And with the number of my men that you've killed, I could use a little more pragmatism."

"You don't know a goddamn thing about me." Wren shook off his words, which triggered the nightmares and horrors that she committed to keep her family safe. The mirage of blood flashed on her hands. She felt the warm, sticky, metallic feel of the lives she'd taken on her fingers. And those she'd left to die.

"I know you're determined. Who else could have convinced this behemoth to help you?" Ted shook his head. "No way he would have joined my cause, unless maybe you were to persuade him yourself. Throw in a little something extra." He gave an obnoxious wink, and Reuben knocked him in the back of the head with the butt of his rifle, though Wren caught him blushing at Ted's words.

"Right now I'm just wishing that the explosive had taken the hearing in both of my ears."

"Although I have to commend you," Ted continued, ignoring Wren. "It seems that you've managed to sway your large friend here with nothing but your stunning personality. Though no one would blame you for trying other avenues. You wouldn't be the first woman to use what's between your legs to get what you want."

The next blow from Reuben knocked Ted out cold, and the man collapsed to the dirt. Wren rushed over and sagged her shoulders in exhaustion. "I hope you know that I'm not carrying him."

Reuben refused to look her in the eye, casting his gaze anywhere but her. The redness in his cheeks only worsened as he kept his head down. "We should kill him. I know you think he'll help you get your kids back, but he won't." He finally turned to look at her, the features along his face hidden in oddly shaped shadows. "He'll just end up killing your children out of spite."

"You don't think that hasn't been running through my mind?" Wren threw up her hands in exasperation. "I don't know if he'll be able to help us. I don't know if Edric will even want to trade for him. I don't even know if my kids are alive!" A few birds took flight, awoken by the boom in her voice. "I have no idea what I'm doing! All I know is that I have to do *something*. I have to keep moving. I have to try, Reuben." She pointed to Ted's lifeless body. "And if there is a chance we can use him to get my children back, no matter what else it might cost me, then I'm going to take it. That's my absolute. That's my compass. And I will follow it until my last breath." Wren panted, her fists clenched. The cool night air calmed the hot sweat on her skin.

Reuben remained quiet, his eyes darting back and forth between Wren and the ground. Without a word, he scooped Ted up and threw him over his shoulder then continued his trek toward the camp.

Wren followed silently, though her brain was loud with chatter. Her outburst had brought back the blaring doubt that she hoped to have rid herself of, and reminded her how little control she truly had. It was nothing more than a façade, a veil pulled back to reveal the strings on her arms and legs, some puppet master telling her where to go. *Helplessness.*

The word soured her mouth, and she spit to rid herself of the taste. She'd devoted her entire life to the destruction of that word. It was a hate that burned deep in her bones. It was the same hate that fueled her to go back to school. It kept her awake into the early hours of the morning as she finished her assignments then caught a few hours of sleep before the start of her shift at work. The hate provided a warmth and a fire she desperately needed.

She wondered if Ted had that same hate. When he'd spoken of her drive, their similarities, it had angered her because a part of her knew it was true. Not everyone had that switch in their mind. She could turn it off and on when needed, though she understood how taxing it was to live a life in those extremes. Yet, still, she persevered. She'd made it farther than anyone thought she would, even her own husband.

Doug had told her that she had tunnel vision, and he was

right. She loved her job. She loved that she was good at it. She loved the fact that she was responsible for pulling their family out of financial ruin. And even though she saw Doug slipping away, she never reached out a hand to help him. All she focused on was the endgame, and it didn't matter what was lost along the way. If she had given her marriage that same burning devotion, then maybe he wouldn't have cheated on her, and maybe they wouldn't hate being in a room with each other. *Maybe, maybe, maybe.* She shook the doubts from her mind. *I'm not like him. I'm not like any of them.*

She watched Ted's unconscious body swing lifelessly on Reuben's back as he huffed and puffed through the forest, unsure of how long he'd be able to carry the man. While Ted wasn't big, he was by no means small. He was nearly as tall as Reuben but slimmer, more toned and agile. She just hoped the hermit would have enough in the tank to help her once they reached the camp. "How much longer?"

Reuben panted heavily between words. "Shouldn't be... more than... six or seven miles. Should get there... before sunrise."

"Seven miles?" Wren jogged up and fell in line with Reuben's long strides. "Reuben, you won't be able to carry him for that long. You'll pass out before we arrive."

"I've had worse." Reuben wheezed, his feet thumping heavily under Ted's added weight. Sweat collected on his forehead and glistened under the moonlight. His shoulders sagged, and his back started to hunch and curl like a cane. But Wren let him walk. There was no sense in trying to hurt his pride.

The rest of the journey, Wren kept to herself. She stayed a few feet behind Reuben, every once in a while checking on Ted to see if he was still unconscious, but after a while she fell into another haze of fatigue. Most of her energy was focused on putting one foot in front of the other, doing her best to stay upright. *Addison. Chloe. Zack.* She repeated the names to herself like a mantra. Keeping them alive in her thoughts, the fuel driving her forward. *Just hang on. I'm coming.*

A sudden thud cleared the fog from Wren's mind, and the two shadows that were Ted and Reuben rolled over rocks and tree branches, a dark storm of limbs flailing about. Wren raised her rifle, but the bodies were too close to one another. She couldn't hit Ted without risking Reuben's own life. And if she wanted to trade Ted to Edric for her children, then she'd need him alive.

Ted slammed his shoulder into Reuben's gut, causing the hermit to release his grip, and Ted sprinted into the cover of the forest. Wren followed suit, rushing past Reuben, who struggled to rise from the ground. Wren rounded the cover of the large trunk that Ted had disappeared behind and saw nothing but the light shake of leaves.

Wren squeezed the rifle as if she meant to bend the steel and iron out of frustration and continued to scan the horizon. "Come out, Ted!" She took a step forward, her eyes straining to identify anything human in the darkness. "You've got nowhere to go."

"Actually, I have everywhere to go." Ted's voice bounced around the trees, its origins as numerous as the leaves on branches. "You're the one who has only one path to follow."

Reuben appeared on her left, rifle in hand, scanning the trees as she was. She looked to him for any guidance, any sign of where Ted might have gone, but the hermit was still catching his breath. It looked as though the day had finally caught up with him. Once his breathing steadied, Wren followed him into the darkness. "Give it up now, and I promise Reuben won't hurt you."

"I'm afraid that's a promise you won't be able to keep." Again Ted's voice ricocheted through the forest, providing the same illusion of omnipresence she remembered at the cabin. "Though I don't know if it'll be much of a challenge now. It's harder to beat a man into submission when his hands aren't tied behind his back."

Wren shivered. There was no way he got loose. "But it's still easy enough to shoot him." Reuben motioned forward, and Wren followed. "We've tracked you before. We'll be able to do it again."

"Who says I'm running?"

His voice solidified to the right, and Reuben and Wren both aimed their rifles in the same direction, their sights landing upon the trunk of a thick oak. Wren curved her finger over the trigger, and she stiffened her shoulder and arm, forcing the rifle to steady. She went right, and Reuben went left, circling around the tree, her feet pushing aside dirt and grass. She paused just before rounding the final turn, her heart caught in her throat, and the quickened beat of her pulse pounded like a jackhammer.

She sprinted the last few steps and came to an abrupt halt as she stared down the end of Reuben's rifle. She dropped her arms and looked around. She peered into the darkness, looking for any sign of where Ted had disappeared.

"Wren," Reuben said, kneeling down into the grass. He grabbed something and held it up for her to see. *The rope.* "If he's free, then he'll be able to move more quickly." Reuben tucked the rope back into one of his pockets and searched the ground for tracks.

Shit. Wren gritted her teeth and followed Reuben. She kept most of her visual resources to the left, since she couldn't hear anything on that side, and relied heavily on her right ear to pick up anything that meant to kill her.

"You're wasting your time, Wren." Ted's voice sounded as if it were cascading down from the sky. "You're in over your head. It's too much for you and your hound to stop. Even if you manage to kill me, others will come. I'm nothing more than the small tip of an iceberg, jutting from the ocean's surface."

Motion blurred to Wren's far left, and she swung the rifle's barrel quickly. She fired, the bullet exploding the tree bark as she and Reuben took chase. She poured her remaining energy into the run, but her body stiffened in slow motion. Her legs filled with lead. Her lungs wheezed with every breath. Her body was crumbling right before her eyes.

They stopped where her bullet disfigured the tree, but Ted was nowhere to be seen. Wren maneuvered the rifle hastily in her grip, swinging it from side to side. "Dammit!" Spit flew from her lips and dribbled down her chin as her frustration spewed through the fault lines of her soul. She squeezed the trigger, the bullet thundering randomly and chaotically into the night air.

"Wren!" Reuben called after her.

She ignored him, pivoting to her right and firing again. The recoil of the shot smacked against her shoulder. She aimed left and squeezed the trigger once more. The hot shell that ejected smacked her cheek, the searing metal burning her skin before it fell to the ground. She pulled the trigger repeatedly, screaming until her throat was on fire and her lungs were about to burst.

"Wren!" Reuben took the rifle from her hands, and she collapsed to the ground, her chest heaving up and down with every breath. He slung his own rifle over his shoulder, his head on a swivel as she sat there dead to the world, then checked the magazine she nearly emptied.

"I'm not like him. I'm not like him." Wren rocked back and forth, repeating the words to herself like an inmate in an insane asylum. She clutched her legs to her chest, shaking her head. "I'm not like him."

"No, you're not," Reuben said, pulling her up with one hand. "But right now I need you to get a grip on whatever ledge you're dangling from."

Wren shut her eyes. "Yeah." Her shaky voice didn't evoke the confidence she would have liked, but it was a step back from the abyss. She took the rifle back from Reuben and gave a stiff nod, but whatever foundation she thought she stood upon slowly crumbled at the sound of the slow cackle that whispered through the trees.

"Ha-Ha-HA-Ha-HA-HA!" It lingered on the light breeze that brushed Wren's face, and she aimed the shaking barrel in what she thought was the direction the ominous clamor originated. "You're starting to see it, aren't you, Wren?"

The voice echoed to her right, and Reuben fired at the shadowed figure that darted between the trees. But while Reuben stepped forward, Wren remained frozen in place, paralyzed.

"You and I are two sides of the same coin. You justify your choices with the protection of your children, and I justify mine with the salvation of the world." Another chuckle followed. "We're the saviors of the world, Wren."

Reuben followed the voice, which circled all around them. He spun, rifle in hand, trying to pinpoint Ted's location. It was like being haunted by a ghost. Wren took a step forward and whispered to herself, her voice as shaky as the legs beneath her. "I'm not like you." The ominous laughter grew more boisterous, echoing louder and louder every time Wren repeated the words to herself. Her mind flooded with the nightmares that had plagued her restless sleep, encroaching on the sacred ground that was her waking consciousness. "I'm not like you!"

The vein in Wren's neck pulsed, and the forest grew quiet. The wind no longer carried Ted's manic laughter. She jumped as Reuben touched her shoulder. He said nothing but pointed toward a cluster of low-hanging branches, swaying and scratching the earth in the breeze.

Wren nodded, her rifle raised, and the two approached slowly, carefully. She squinted into the circle of trees, searching for any movement. Her palms grew slick as they burst with sweat the closer she moved to the branches. Only a few steps away, she drew in a breath. The tip of her rifle penetrated the first few leaves, and she entered the waterfall of branches head first.

"AHH!"

The shout and gunshot came from the other side, and Wren sprinted toward the commotion. She skidded to a stop at the sight of Ted with Reuben in a choke hold, the edge of a knife to the hermit's jugular. "Drop it." Ted raised his eyebrows, the air of sophistication he touted replaced with savagery. He applied a small amount of pressure, and the blade drew a trickle of blood. "Do it, or I gut him right here and now."

"Shoot him!" Reuben said, his words choked by Ted's vice grip.

Wren kept the rifle aimed at Ted, but with Reuben so close she was just as likely to hit him. "Let him go." She took a step forward, and Ted dragged himself and Reuben one step back, the knife still wedged into Reuben's neck.

"You shoot me, and I kill him," Ted replied. "Drop it, or I do it anyway, and the only person you have left to guide you back to camp is me." His face reddened with stress and rage, the once-childlike playfulness turned vicious. "You know I will."

Wren placed her finger on the trigger. When she looked down the sight, all she could focus on was the knife point digging into Reuben's neck. Ted's words repeated in her mind like a broken record. All of her justifications, all of her reasoning, all of it made her more like him, more like the very people she condemned in Chicago, and the people like Edric back at camp. She saw Reuben's decision in his eyes. He wanted her to do it. They both did.

Wren lowered the rifle, and she watched Reuben deflate as she set the gun down and put her hands in the air. Ted shoved Reuben to the ground, giving him a kick in the ribs, laughing while the hermit groaned in pain. "You're one stupid bitch, you know that?"

Once they'd been frisked and stripped of their weapons, Ted kept one gun aimed at her while he restrained Reuben's wrists. Once the hermit was secure, he walked over to her, circling her like a shark that had just caught the fresh scent of blood. He knelt down and brushed her hair over the back of her ear. "My men will be glad you've decided to come back." His words were hot and soft against her ear and lingered long after he'd distanced himself.

But as they marched back toward the town, with their own weapons used against them, Wren held on to one thought. *I'm not like him.*

29

Wren tried getting Reuben's attention more than once, but the hermit wouldn't even look her way. He kept his vision straight in front of him, his head tilted up, and walked with a limp. She looked back at Ted a few times, and each instance was met with a nudge from the end of her own rifle.

"Too late to turn back now, sweetheart," Ted said, finally breaking the silence of the past twenty minutes. "I'd stop to let you get some rest so you're refreshed for your big debut, but I know the boys are eager to see you again."

Reuben suddenly flung himself toward Ted, but with his hands tied behind his back, it was a cumbersome sight. Ted knocked him down with the rifle before he even got close. Wren stopped and tried to help him up, but Reuben pushed her away. When he lifted his face, his cheek was scratched and his beard was bloodied. When he rose to his knees, Ted kicked him in the back once more, and he tumbled forward, rolling over a few times before landing on his back. Dirt caked into the gash on his face, and the bloodred tinge was replaced with grey.

Ted laughed, but Wren charged him. "Enough!" While she

didn't manage to hit him, her attempt ended his hysterics. He simply smiled, pressed the end of his rifle against her forehead, and placed his finger on the trigger.

"It's not polite to shout, dear." He shoved her head back with the weapon's barrel, and Wren felt the hard scrape of the metal run across her forehead. "Now, let's move."

Wren complied, and she helped Reuben up, who continued his silence. Whatever psychological wound had opened in him wasn't one that she was prepared to fix at the moment. The only thing that mattered now was making sure they didn't return to the town. But with Reuben injured, no weapons, and her barely able to keep up the pace Ted had set them, she didn't know how. She looked to Reuben, casting her eyes down to his gait, the limp in his left leg glaringly apparent. "We need to stop," she said, calling back to Ted.

"We're not stopping. I want to make it back to town before sunrise."

Wren gestured to Reuben. "He won't make it at this pace. He's hurt. Let me take a look at him." It was all she could think of to do. If she could get close to him, then maybe they could come up with something.

"Learned some new tricks, did you?" Ted asked.

"A few." Wren wasn't sure if Reuben planned it, but the moment the words left her mouth, he stumbled to his knees. She stopped, stepping between Ted and Reuben. "We'll make better time if you let me look at him."

Ted paused, examining her like a rancher purchasing cattle at auction. Once finished, he moved close enough for her to smell the stench of his breath. "Make a move, and you'll have to crawl your way back to town." He gestured toward Reuben then backed off.

Wren helped Reuben to a rock, Ted close behind, the gun on them the entire time. Just before he sat down, they exchanged a look. She set him down easily on the rock, and he cradled his ribs with his arm protectively, sucking in short, quick breaths. She placed her hand over the same area, and he shook his head. She furrowed her brow, trying to make sense of the request. She glided her hands to his shoulder, and again he shook his head.

"My hip," Reuben said, the words coming out like a whisper. "It hurts on my hip."

She fumbled her fingers over his hip and felt something hard over his waist, but when she lifted his shirt, she only saw a belt.

"Yeah," Reuben said, nodding. "Right there."

She ran her fingers over the area but felt nothing but the stiff leather.

"No, lower." Reuben grimaced, doing his best to sell the ruse.

Wren glided her nails under the belt, and Reuben nodded, grunting. She felt a small bump, and when she picked it with her nail, she felt something give way. It was no bigger than her thumb, and she quickly concealed it in her fist, hoping Ted hadn't seen.

"Well?" Ted asked, tapping his boot impatiently. "What's the diagnosis, doctor?" He spewed the words condescendingly, complementing them with a light chuckle.

Wren stood. "Nothing feels dislocated." She looked Reuben in the eye. "But we need to slow the pace so it doesn't worsen." She tucked the small object between the coarse rope and the tender flesh of her wrist before she turned around and was met with the stare of a rifle barrel.

Ted eyed her through the sight. "From this range, there wouldn't be anything left of the top of your head. It'd be blown clean off, splattered all over your friend." He twitched his finger over the trigger and made a fake gunshot noise with his mouth.

Wren's mouth went dry as she tried to swallow. "I'm sure the boys back in town would be disappointed." She remained rigid, a sudden itch begging to be scratched under the rope on her left wrist.

Ted cracked a smile and lowered the rifle. "I know they would."

Once they started their journey again, Reuben returned to his isolation, ignoring her, but keeping up the limp. She knew he really was hurt, and didn't think he'd be able to do much when she made her move. She kept her hands low and out of sight as best as she could. She practiced wiggling the piece she'd taken from Reuben's belt down the flesh of her wrist and into her palm. She examined it in quick glances, doing her best to not draw attention to herself. One of the edges of the square piece opened and revealed a small razor blade, only about half the size of her pinky. The way it was tucked into his belt, she understood why Ted didn't find it during his search. She gently touched the tip of the pointed edge with her finger, and even with the lightest pressure, she drew blood. A few stabs at the neck, and he'd be dead.

After a while, the quick glances Wren cast to Reuben transformed into long stares the farther they walked. And with the grey of dawn lighting the sky, and judging by the distance they'd covered, she knew they had to be close to the town. But not once did Reuben stop, nor did Ted lower the rifle. He kept it tucked under his shoulder, his aim switching between the two of them.

They ascended a small hill. Ahead was a cluster of trees on either side, the only way through a narrow path that would force them into a single-file line. Reuben slowed his pace and fell in behind Wren. Her boots crunched loudly on twigs, dead leaves, and dirt, but the only thing she heard was the steady thump of her pulse. She uncurled her fingers from the small blade, gripping it between some of the calluses that had sprouted on her hands since she'd left Chicago. The hands holding the weapon no longer felt like her own.

They'd grown tan and rough and more accustomed to holding a gun than a pen.

Once they reached the path's narrowest point, Ted complained of Reuben's pace. She glanced behind her and saw the hermit hunched over on his knees, groaning and wheezing. If he was faking it, Wren couldn't tell.

"Hey!" Ted said, pointing the rifle at her. "I don't need you trying to run off anywhere."

Reuben looked up from his knees, the same cold hardness in his eyes from when they first met stared back at her. Then, without a word, Reuben flung himself backward, knocking into Ted and sending both of them to the ground. Ted and Reuben grappled over dirt and rocks, but with the hermit's injuries, he did little more than sit down, and Ted easily knocked him aside.

In the same instant, Wren sprinted forward, her fingers tight around the blade. The fatigue caused the ground underneath to swallow her legs like quicksand. Wren raised her fists together, bound in rope, the tiny tip of the blade aimed for the vein pulsing on Ted's neck, but as she brought the weight of all her force down, Ted blocked her blow with the rifle's barrel, her arms clanging against the weapon's iron. One quick swipe and the rifle's smacked across her face, knocking her to the dirt and the blade from her hand. She scrambled to all fours, disoriented from the blow, searching the dirt for the weapon. A sudden crack smacked under her chin and popped her head up, knocking loose a tooth and filling her mouth with blood. The world spun, and her vision blacked in and out and then fell into shades of grey.

"You stupid bitch!"

A pair of hands wrapped around the back of her neck and twisted her violently to her side. A sudden jab of pain connected with her ribs and rippled through her body, knocking the breath from her lungs. She gasped for air as another blow struck her lower back. She flailed her arms and legs flimsily in a poor attempt at retaliation, but her strikes did little to lessen her attacker's blows.

Dizzied with pain, Wren rolled to her back and watched Ted tie Reuben to the tree, his face covered with a fresh coat of blood. She pushed herself from the ground but collapsed. She shut her eyes, trying to control her breathing, which only worsened the pain in her chest. Hands gripped her once more, and she opened her eyes.

Ted flung her against a tree trunk, the jagged bark digging into her back, and the knifelike pain in her stomach intensified. "That was easily one of the dumbest mistakes you've ever made." Ted slapped his hand across the right side of her face, knocking Wren's head hastily to the side. The red print of his palm formed on her cheek and burned like fire. "The boys aren't gonna be happy with me after this, but you know what?" He paused, leaning in closer. "They're so depraved, they'll fuck anything I toss them so long as it's still alive."

The next punch connected with her eye. The force of the blow slammed the back of her skull into the tree, and she collapsed. She raised her hands in a poor attempt to defend herself, but two more shots to the face, and the strength in her arms gave out. She felt the next few hits, but after that everything went numb. Suddenly she became aware of Reuben, still tied to the tree. He was screaming, his throat raw, fighting against the ropes binding him to the tree like a madman. And then the world went black.

30

It started with a dull ache, slowly waking her from the restless coma. But once the dullness had passed, the pain grew sharper and spread. Everywhere. The swelling had ballooned her face, nearly making her unrecognizable. When she grazed her cheek, she winced. It even hurt to blink. But when she looked down at her hands, she suddenly realized they were no longer bound. Though the pain coursing through her veins was just as paralyzing.

She pushed herself up from the concrete and leaned against the wall. Her spine and joints cracked. The simple movement left her exhausted. She looked down at her clothes and scrunched her face in confusion at the light-green sundress with a floral pattern around the bottom hem. The fabric was weightless and revealing. Her shoulders and back were bare, save for the bruises and scratches. What was meant to entice lust only revealed the abuse she'd sustained.

The unfamiliarity of her surroundings triggered panic. She rose to her feet, driving her heels into the floor, and what felt like shards of broken glass shredded her insides. The pain pulled her back to the concrete. She tried again, making it a few inches farther before falling once more.

"I know it's painful."

Wren jerked her head to the right. A man stood by a door, his face blurred beyond recognition. But the voice. The voice sounded familiar.

"You shouldn't have angered me like that." The blurred figure stepped forward. "You shouldn't have tried to escape."

Lightning struck Wren's mind. The forest. The knife. Ted. The pain. The fear. Reuben. Another stab tore through her as she gasped. *Reuben.*

"My goodness, you look even worse up close." Ted crouched to meet her at eye level then pulled his collar down and exposed his neck. "I didn't escape without my scars either. You nearly ripped out my jugular, and Reuben did the same." Her flinch betrayed her thoughts, and Ted answered the very question running through her mind. "He's not here, Wren. But don't worry. You'll see him soon."

Wren attempted to speak, but the words were choked from her before they had a chance to be heard. Her jaw was swollen and stiff with the rest of her, but after she gathered some strength, she cracked the corner of her mouth open. "Let him go."

Ted laughed. "The two of you are quite the dynamic. You know he said the same thing about you when we got here?" He gently pinched the end of her dress, rubbing the fabric between his fingers. "You should have heard him scream when I beat you. It was like I was hitting him. I didn't realize you two were that close." Ted rose, stalking around Wren slowly. "He's big, but he doesn't seem your type, though to be fair, I actually don't know your type. Perhaps you don't even know yourself. Stemming from the divorce you were planning on dragging your husband through, I would say that would be a valid point." He gently rubbed the scratch on his neck, stretching his jaw, flexing the wound.

As Wren's vision cleared, Ted's features crystallized. The soiled clothes had been exchanged for a new button-up shirt and pants, complemented with a pair of dress shoes that clacked loudly as he walked, and he had combed his hair.

He caught her examining his clothes, and he spread his arms and smiled. "You like it? I never found the wear of tactical clothing stylish, nor did I believe that the end of the world meant I needed to sacrifice some of the finer things in life. And of course today was a special occasion, what with your grand return." He looked past her thoughtfully at the closed door. "The men were so excited to see you. But don't worry," he added quickly, "I didn't let them lay a hand on you."

The left dress strap on her shoulder fell halfway down her arm, and Ted knelt and dangled it from his index finger. "Though I did have to give them something. I wasn't sure if they were more excited to see you with or without the dress on."

His laugh triggered shudders through her body, and she looked away, grinding her teeth, using the pain as a distraction from the nightmares to come. With her body broken, she felt the slow dissolve of her will.

"Wren, Wren, Wren, Wren." Ted repeated her name as though he were speaking to a child. "I know the end is difficult to bear." He nodded, the affirmation akin to a principal counseling a student. "But we are broken down and rebuilt to return stronger than before. It's something I've done to all of the men that work for me. And I can tell you none of them were half as difficult to break as you've proved to be. I hope that's some comfort to you."

Wren watched him smile, the missing tooth she'd knocked out the only missing element in his otherwise perfect ensemble. "If you keep me alive..." She took a hard swallow, her belly growing full of her own blood as she forced her jaw open wider. "I will kill you."

The smile vanished from Ted's face. "And I promise you that by the time my men have had their fun, you won't be able to sit for a week." He yanked her up by the back of her hair, her body spasming in defiance as he dragged her through the room then out the door, where she was blinded by sunlight.

Dust flew from the ground as Ted dragged her across the gravel. Wren choked on the dirt and grit that filled her nose and mouth. When he finally released her, her head smacked against the ground, sending another stab of pain that ran from the base of her skull and crept down her spine. She rolled to her right, her ear catching the sound of raucous shouting. At first she thought the maddened hysteria was for her. But when she lifted her head, she saw that the men's attention was elsewhere.

"C'mon," Ted said. "Let's go see how your boyfriend is faring." He forced her up, and Wren hobbled forward, wincing with every step. Every breath felt like stabs of glass shards. Ted forced his way into the circle, the men giving way.

The half-dozen men that remained in Ted's gang leered at Wren as she passed. The massacre at the cabin Reuben and she had unleashed had depleted his forces. And if she had it her way, the rest of them wouldn't be around for much longer either. Wren shifted and turned, ineffectively fending off their hands as they reached for whatever part of her they desired. As much pain as her face and body were in, none of it compared to the screaming madness that was her dignity. The bodies of men finally ended, and Wren had a front-row seat to the source of the chaos.

Reuben lay on his back, panting, heaving his chest up and down. His arms and legs lay spread out, and his entire body was covered in dust. Flashes of red glimmered when he moved, and fresh blood gushed from the cuts along his face, offering a glaring contrast to the black and grey that covered the majority of his clothes. He rolled to his side, and Wren wasn't even sure if he saw her or not, but he stumbled to his feet, much to the crowd's chagrin.

The man who was in the ring with Reuben threw his hands up in defeat. The contender bowed out and was replaced with another man from the circle. He raised his fists, dancing around Reuben, who couldn't even raise his own hands to defend himself. The fighter taunted Reuben, sending light jabs into his stomach and face, Reuben's delayed reactions too slow to dodge the attacks.

Wren tried to step forward in the ring, but Ted pulled her back by the thick of her hair. "You'll get your turn soon enough."

The fighter ended the taunts and landed a vicious blow to Reuben's right cheek, knocking the big man to the ground. Wren's stomach tightened as he watched his arms and legs spasm in the dirt. *Stay down.* But her heart sank as she watched Reuben push himself to his knees, the dirt caked around his mouth so thickly that with every exhale a fine cloud of dust erupted from his lips, then spit a fresh wad of blood. Just before Reuben had a leg under him, the fighter drove the tip of his boot under Reuben's chin, and the crack of bone broke through the thunderous roar of the crowd.

Wren shuddered, and she looked away, thinking that Reuben's jaw had shattered. But the clamoring ruckus soon turned to laughter as the fighter who'd kicked Reuben's jaw bounced awkwardly on one foot, cursing as he hopped out of the ring.

Ted slapped her back, and she jolted forward. "I have to say, even I'm impressed. The man is built like a tank. You know he's been in that ring for the past two hours? The moment we stepped into town, I let the boys have him. I can't believe he's lasted this long. Though he does have some powerful motivation. Hell, the guys could get tired before he does!"

Just lie down, Reuben. Don't do this to yourself anymore. But

Reuben rolled to his stomach, his arms trembling as he pushed himself from the dirt, blood drooling from his mouth. Wren spun around and gripped Ted by the shoulders. She forced her mouth open, every syllable spoken a challenge. "Please. Let him go."

"I'm afraid I can't do that. I made a deal with him, and despite what you may think of me, I'm a man who honors commitment." Ted removed her hands and turned her back to the scene as another fighter stepped in. But this time Reuben lingered on the ground. She listened to the pain-induced gasps wheezing with every breath. He looked over to her direction, and for the first time since she arrived, they made eye contact. She shook her head, trying to tell him to stop. But Reuben looked away, pushed himself off the ground, and faced yet another opponent.

Wren cringed with every blow. The crack of bone against bone thundered between applause and chants. All of them egged on the new fighter to end it, all of them wishing for victory and the hermit's death.

"Do you want to know the deal I made with him before he stepped into that bloodbath?" Ted asked, whispering into her ear. "I told him that as long as he fights in that ring, the men won't be able to touch you. It's quite admirable, really. I certainly wouldn't have let myself be pummeled to death for your sake. Hell, I probably would have joined in on the fun."

Wren's blood ran colder with every blow Reuben received. Every hit he took, she felt in her bones. *He doesn't have to do this. Not for me.* A fist landed against Reuben's ribcage, and Wren tightened her stomach. The next combination rocked his head left to right, then right to left, and Wren's head ached. An uppercut struck him on the chin, flinging him to his back, and Wren's body numbed.

A cheer erupted from the crowd. "The men are particularly riled up after a fight," Ted said, keeping the distance between them as intimate as he could without touching her. "I hope you're ready for what's coming."

The hot madness simmered through the crowd as Reuben lay motionless. For a moment, Wren couldn't see his chest rise and fall, and her knees buckled. A second later, a gasp erupted from his mouth, then he drew in a ragged breath, shifting to his side before he choked on his own blood.

"C'mon! Finish him!"

"Yeah, he's done!"

"Get it over with!"

The jeers and madness reached a crescendo. Everyone smelled the stench of death that hovered over Reuben like a cloud. Blood dripped from his lower lip, puffed from the vicious blows he'd taken, and he found her in the crowd. The stoic calm and righteousness she remembered from their first encounter was replaced with pain and fear.

"Stay down!" Wren added her own voice to the growing chorus but couldn't be heard through the tumult of the crowd. The tears she struggled to hold back as a show of strength burst shamelessly from her eyes. She felt the warm liquid run down her cheeks, the salty tears stinging the cuts along her face and neck as Reuben pushed himself to his knees, his face lifted toward the sky, his body caked in earth and blood.

The ruckus reached a fever pitch. The contender in the ring circled Reuben, the scent of victory in the air. He fisted the top of Reuben's mangled and matted hair and raised his fist.

"Once he's dead," Ted whispered in her ear as she gazed upon Reuben's final moments, "you'll wish it had been you who died in that ring. Bitch."

A gunshot silenced the crowd, and the fighter in the ring dropped to the ground with a bullet lodged in his skull. Confusion lingered, the men's faces left expressionless at the sudden death. The air grew intensely quiet, and then chaos erupted. Every man screamed and sprinted in frenzied directions at the sound of more gunfire.

Before Wren could reach for Reuben, Ted yanked her backward, and she lost sight of him in the chaos of dust and bodies. The gunfire echoed in all directions as she was dragged through the dirt, the thin fabric of her dress tearing from rocks and sticks. Ted held her by the wrist, and Wren dug her nails into his skin, clawing as hard as she could until she felt blood burst upon breaking skin. He backhanded her but loosened his grip in the process just enough for her to yank her arm away and stumble on all fours toward the nearest building.

Every motion forward throbbed pain through Wren's body. Her face pulsated, and her cheeks felt as if they would explode with every step. She glanced behind her, afraid that Ted was close, but all she saw were trails of dust. She stopped, suddenly alone, and looked for Reuben. Sporadic gunshots echoed in every direction, and Wren squinted under the glaring sun. And there she saw him, lying next to the dead gang member, his body lifeless. She sprinted back into the chaos, her eyes peeled for any of Ted's men, or whoever had descended upon the town. With the growing desperation of people since the EMP it could have been anyone, but all she focused on was the large body covered in blood and dust on the ground.

"Reuben." Wren skidded on her knees, her skin breaking upon contact with the pebbles and rocks in the dirt, her dress riding up her dirty thighs. His face was beaten and swollen almost beyond recognition. She cradled his head in her lap, the tears dripping from her face and landing on his dust-covered cheek.

Reuben gargled, and Wren gripped him tighter. Blood and spit spewed from his mouth as he lifted his head up and rolled to his side, clawing the dirt and gasping for air. Wren quickly helped him sit up, and the sound of more gunshots sharpened both their senses. "C'mon. We need to go."

Wren acted as little more than a cane for the large man as she struggled to bear his weight. She aimed for the nearest building and kept her eyes open for any pursuers and found two heading right for them. She hastened her pace, pulling Reuben with her. "Hurry."

Reuben lowered his shoulder and heaved his body weight, and the force was enough to burst through the door of the abandoned building. He collapsed after the quick exertion, and Wren barricaded the entrance. She hit the floor just as bullets punctured the structure's decrepit wood. She crawled along the grimy floorboards, the dress covering her stomach catching exposed nail heads. She looked and saw Reuben had collapsed to his side and lay still as death.

The desk and chairs she'd thrown against the door buckled with every thud that their pursuers thrust against it. "I know you're in there, bitch! Don't think you can hide from us!"

Wren opened old drawers and padded through the darkness, trying to feel for anything that could pass as a weapon. Her head throbbed, and the pains and aches along her body were no longer subdued by the rush of adrenaline. Every pulse-pounding beat from her heart triggered an agitated roar from her body. Her arms and legs shook uncontrollably, whether from fear or fatigue she wasn't sure.

Bullets exploded through the door, turning the old wood into Swiss cheese. Round after round penetrated, making the hole grow large enough to fit a hand through. Wren felt the cool of metal and wrapped her fingers around a pair of scissors. The door cracked open, and Wren hid in the corner, keeping her body in front of Reuben's unconscious one. She wasn't going to let him suffer any more because of her. If he died, she died.

The snarling face of one of the shooters appeared in the

crack. He hooted raucously at the sight of her and vigorously beat against the door, widening the opening with every smack. Finally, he squeezed through, rifle first. "Well, well, look at this." The gunman's clothes were soiled and grimy, and the body that wore them wasn't any better. He flashed a grin, his teeth caked in plaque and turning yellow. His wild hair added to the ensemble of insanity. "The big man can't give you lovin' anymore, sweetheart. But why don't you let me give it a try?"

The gunman's friend slithered in next, flashing a similar grin, though his had far fewer teeth. He lunged forward, yipping and howling in excitement. Wren kept the scissors open and jutted out at arm's length. She mirrored their actions, jerking side to side as they each took turns taking a swing, laughing in the process.

"She's still got some fight left in her." The first gunman set the rifle down, raising his fists playfully. "Your man lasted a while in the ring. Let's see how long you fare."

"Don't mess up her face any more. It's swollen enough as it is." The two hyenas bobbed up and down, the second gunman keeping his rifle aimed at her while the first gunman swiped his hand a few times as Wren fended him off with the scissors.

"You know, you're lucky we'd rather fuck you than shoot you. It'd make this whole process a lot easier if you wasn't breathing." He sprinted forward, trying to barrel into Wren, but she sidestepped, slashing the scissors' open blades across the goon's forearm. He cursed and clutched his arm. "Fucking bitch!"

Wren smacked into a chair as she shuffled backward, aiming the blade between the two thugs. The first gunman she'd wounded grimaced, then lunged forward. Wren drove the tip of the scissors into his path. She felt the tear of metal on flesh, but the brute kept coming, wrapping his arms around her neck. He squeezed, choking the life out of her, and she felt the scissors drop from her hand as she struggled for air. Her head throbbed, and the room started to fade to black, but through the pain she felt the hot tickle of the man's breath against her ear as he whispered, "I'm going to enjoy this."

Another crash at the door turned the gunman's attention to the intrusion, and before the second gunman could shoot, his body was riddled with lead. The goon on top of Wren loosened his grip, and she wriggled free, picked the scissors up from the floor and rammed the tip of the blades into the man's ribs. She felt the metal scrape bone and catch on the wiry muscle. She kept her eyes on her attacker's face as she pulled the scissors from his side and rammed them into him again and again, each blow triggering a scream until the man could no longer stand on his own feet. He collapsed, gargling blood and clutching his side.

Wren hovered over him until his very last breaths. Blood dripped from the tip of the scissors in a slow, steady drizzle onto the floor. Her knuckles flashed white over the grip, and it wasn't until he lay completely still, the blood, breath, and life drained from his body, that Wren dropped it from her hand.

"Wren."

At first she thought it was Reuben, but when she turned, she saw that the man behind the rifle was Nathan, the thick mustache under his nose wiggling tirelessly from his heavy breaths. Her gaze lingered on him for a moment, but she was so hysterical with delirium that the words she yearned to speak were lost on their way to her mouth.

Nathan stumbled forward, the rifle in his hands falling across his chest, the strap clinging tight to his body. "My god, are you all right?" He looked behind him, screaming out the door. "I found her!"

"He needs help." The words left Wren's throat scratchy and raw. Nate looked at her, confused, and she lifted a shaky hand to Reuben in the corner. "Save him." The room started to spin, and she stumbled forward a few steps, her center of gravity shifting from side to side.

"Easy, Wren." Nathan gently grabbed her waist, stabilizing her for the moment, then helped her to the ground next to Reuben while Ben examined her face. "What did they do to you?"

They beat me. Groped me. Cut me. Whatever they wanted to do to me. But she was too weak to speak. It was all she could do to keep her concentration on Reuben's face, and though he lay unconscious, she felt her spirits lift as she noticed the slight rise and fall of his chest.

31

Iris and Ben screamed at one another, but Wren couldn't decipher their words. She barely felt Nathan prod at the cuts on her face. Every once in a while, a light sting would detract from her concentration, but for the most part all she could focus on was Reuben.

Nathan and the others had tried to convince her to let the doctor work on him alone, but their requests fell on deaf ears. They didn't know. None of them understood. Everything was paid in blood now. Nothing else mattered but the people who took care of you, and who you took care of in turn.

"We need to gather what supplies we have here and head back to the camp." Iris's voice had reached a crescendo. Her flushed cheeks revealed the hours of frustration she and Ben had exchanged since their arrival. "Every second we wait here is one more we give Edric to regroup and strengthen his defenses."

"You heard what Wren said, Iris." Ben dug his heels in, thrusting a heavy hand in her face. "It was Ted that was running the goons here in town. He'd been attacking us. And we don't know if he was working with Edric or not. If he was, then he could be telling Edric exactly what we've done. They'll know we're coming!"

"He doesn't know." Wren turned her head to the conversation, and the room went quiet. Nathan ceased his work on her cut lip. Her voice lacked animation and enthusiasm, but even she felt the sharpness of her words. "Ted is playing both sides. He was a member of the terrorists that caused all of this. I don't know if he'll go back, but if he does, he'll keep Edric in the dark about what he's doing." She looked back to Reuben. His eyes were closed, and his breaths were sharp and quick. The doctor had washed away most of the blood and dirt, leaving nothing but the cuts, bumps, and bruises that mapped his face. "He'll tell Edric whatever he has to in order for them to kill us. And then he'll destroy the camp." It was the silence that finally forced her to shift her gaze from Reuben to Ben and Iris. Everyone in the room was looking at her, and she read the uncertainty on their faces. "This isn't politics anymore. There is no council. There is no order. We need to kill them all. Anyone who steps in our way." She pushed herself up. Nathan offered his hand, but she knocked it away. "The moment the doctor is done with Reuben, I'm heading back there to get my children. And I don't give a damn if you all decide to come or stay. It's your lives."

Wren limped out of the room and took a few steps onto the cracked pavement of the sidewalk outside the abandoned lawyer's office they'd taken shelter in. The group of thirty that had defected with Iris and Ben were gathered outside. The moment they realized it was her, they stood. She wasn't sure if they'd expected a speech, or advice, or an update on what Ben and Iris had decided, but she didn't care. Every one of them had abandoned her children, and she didn't give two shits about how she was supposed to make *them* feel.

The windows Wren passed were shattered or cracked. All of the stores that had offered anything of value were stripped bare. Nothing but shelves and dirty floors remained. They were empty. The town was empty. She was empty.

An old park rested on the town's outskirts. It was overgrown with weeds, and a rusted playground was falling apart in the center. A pair of swings drifted forward and back in a lazy cadence until she stopped their aimless purpose. She sat and kicked her legs, and the rusted chains squeaked with each pump. As she swung, she tried to imagine the park before the EMP went off. She tried to listen for the squealing laughter of children but heard nothing. She tried to picture the small hands and arms swinging from the monkey bars, the short legs pushing off the teeter-totter, but couldn't see beyond the rusted steel and motionless toys.

Nathan took a seat in the empty swing next to her, the support beams groaning louder from the added weight. He kicked in time with her own strides, no sounds between them save for the whine of the chains. It wasn't until Wren stood from the swing that Nate finally spoke. "We tried to get them out, Wren."

Her face and jaw were still swollen, but she could open the left side of her mouth more easily now that the doctor had given her some anti-inflammatory meds. Though she still sounded like she had a mouth full of gauze. "You tried? What the fuck does that even mean? People usually *try* to pay their taxes, or *try* to do well at their job. Tell me just how much you *tried*, Nathan."

"About as much as you tried to help me in that ambulance in Chicago!" He thrust himself up from the swing, the seat dancing wildly upon his exit.

The verbal slap was more than Wren had expected, though she knew it wasn't out of line. "How long have you been holding that in?" She sat on one of the steps of the jungle gym and carefully rubbed her temples. While the swelling had reduced, the pain hadn't.

"I'm sorry." Nate kept his back to her, his head down. A

puff of grey dirt clouded the air around his ankles as he kicked the ground aimlessly. "I know you did it to save the kids. I was too much of a liability." He turned around, the anger wiped from his face and replaced with despair. "Wren, Edric had the girls and Zack under lock and key. We would have lost everyone that tried to get them out."

"I'm going to get them back, Nate. I'll go by myself if I have to. And if Ted's there—" She clenched her fists, cracking her knuckles. The thought of that animal anywhere near her girls was warrant for murder.

"You won't have to go alone." Nathan grabbed her fists, and she loosened her grip. "I can promise you that. Iris and Ben need you, though. The people that came, a lot of them came because of you."

"Me?"

"That night when you stood up to Edric after the attack on the fence, it was all anyone could talk about." Nathan pointed back to the main portion of town, where she'd passed their group. "Those people saw you as something more than what they were offered. They respect you. They'll follow you."

"I don't want anyone dying for me. It's not my place to ask them. I'm not the leader they think I am." *I'm not a leader at all.* Reuben's broken body flashed in her mind, and she shuddered to think what would happen to the rest of those people if they followed her. The knowledge that he'd endured so much savagery for her well-being had tipped her over the ledge of sanity. "I'm not going through that again."

Wren left Nathan at the playground and returned to the cluster of people who'd defected from the camp. She was short of breath by the time she arrived, and once again everyone stood, looking to her, wanting to hear what she'd say. "I'm not the person you think I am. All I've done, all I've ever done, has driven the people around me to pain." She felt blood collecting in her mouth as she forced her jaw open wider, projecting her voice. "That man inside? He followed me. He tried to help me. And he nearly died for it. Save yourselves. Save your family. There still might be someplace that's safe, and if you leave now, you'll be able to find it."

"We're not going anywhere." Iris stepped out of the building with Ben in tow. She circled Wren, and the crowd drew nearer. "You think those people are going to risk their lives just for you?" She shook her head. "Edric drove us from our homes. He took everything that we had worked so hard to build. There is more at stake than just your children. The camp was designed to keep us alive. It's our future."

"You said that we needed to save our families?" Nate asked, stepping through the crowd. "We are. You are our family, Wren. You kept your word more than Edric and the rest of those back at camp. We're not going because of you. We're going because we *are* you."

Everyone nodded, their decisions made. Iris and Ben stood on either side of her, and Iris thrust her rifle into the air. "We will not fail!"

Every rifle, pistol, knife, and fist lifted into the air, joining Iris's symbol of perseverance. And in the center, with both hands by her side, stood Wren, engirded with her own military. But if she was going to extract her children without Edric hurting them, she'd need more than brute strength on her side.

THE TABLE WAS CLEARED. Nothing but the Frankenstein-like pieces of paper taped together in an oddly shaped mass rested over the old wood. Wren had to grip the pencil tightly, or she found that her lines would slant. Every muscle burned, but it felt good to return to a familiar post. "I doubt Edric managed to rebuild the gap in the wall since I left, which means he has a back door he's forced to guard, with even fewer men to do it."

Wren constructed the entire compound from memory, save for some of the details Iris and Ben provided. They revealed two important secrets no one outside the council knew: Edric didn't have all of the lock combinations to the individual weapons vaults in the garrison, and an underground fuselage on the east side of the camp.

"Now, the ammunition and weapons in Edric's and Jan's vaults are well stocked, and we have to assume that Ted has joined up with them by now, adding his arsenal." Iris pointed to the only concrete structure in the camp, which acted as their garrison. "Ben and I had been pulling ammunition and weapons out in secret for the past week in anticipation of Edric's behavior."

"You're sure Edric can't access your vaults?" Nathan asked.

"No, he can," Ben answered. "But it'll take some time for him to break his way inside. And it may not even be something he'll try. But regardless, as of right now, they do have more weaponry than us."

A burning fatigue cramped Wren's shoulder as she hovered over a few of the previous sketches, doing her best not to smear the lines. She took a step back and rested her arm. She massaged her hand. While the grip of the pencil felt good, not all of her dexterity had returned, which was evident in the schematic. "It's done." Wren cocked her head to the side. "For better or worse." She planted her finger on the gaping hole in the fence. "I don't think Edric will have any guards on that portion of the fence. He'll keep it open and booby trapped for anyone that comes through."

"We have to go in at night. It's our best chance of surprise," Ben said.

"Agreed." Iris looked to Wren, the others following her lead. "I doubt Edric will have your girls far from his side.

Especially if Ted regrouped with him and told him you're in the mix. Wren, I don't know what he'll do once he smells the ambush."

"I do." Wren glanced down at the portion of the sketch that outlined Edric's house. "I'll need to go in first. And I'll need a distraction big enough to make the whole camp turn into chaos." She dragged her finger across the map to the underground fuel tank. "There's enough gas in that tank to wake up the entire state of Illinois. It'll be big, it'll draw attention and confusion, but it will give me enough time to get my kids and you guys a jump start on the offense. We'll need teams at different points of entry. The more we can use the chaos of the explosion to our advantage, the better. Once that blast goes off, we'll have a good ten minutes before Edric has a chance to reestablish any kind of order. That's where we can even the odds."

"Nathan, Jim." Iris pointed, and the two stepped forward. "You start assigning teams. Then start dividing up the ammunition and explosives we have. Make sure everyone has what they need. Now's not the time to ration."

"Got it. All right, guys." Nathan clapped his hands together, raising his voice, and started breaking everyone into teams.

Iris pulled Wren aside, and she and Ben cornered her out of earshot of everyone else. "I don't want you going in alone. You'll have your own team, a few people to watch your back."

Wren shook her head. "No, I'll be able to move quieter by myself, and it'll be easier to stay hidden if I need to." *And I won't have anyone else's blood on my hands.*

"It's not a good idea, Wren," Ben said. "At least head in with the explosives team, and then you can break off while they rig the fuel tank."

In the end, Wren reluctantly agreed, then left Iris and Ben to hammer out the details with the rest of their people. *Their people. Not my people.* She found her feet guiding her back to the lawyer's office where they'd let Reuben rest. When it was all said and done, the doctor said the hermit had four broken ribs, a collapsed lung, a broken cheekbone, and more lacerations than he had fingers and toes.

Wren stepped in the room quietly as a ghost, gliding across the floor. The doctor didn't even see her until she was standing right next to Reuben's cot. "How is he?" She gently grabbed his thumb, which was large enough for her to wrap her entire hand around.

"If he makes it through the night, he should be okay, but that's his first big test." The way the doctor spoke was as if Reuben and she were lovers. The doctor excused himself, and Wren chuckled at the thought but wondered if he'd felt the same way.

Reuben had been beaten to within an inch of his life, all to keep her from being raped. "Why did you do that?" Her face reddened with anger as Reuben remained silent. She let go of his hand. "I never asked you to do that. It was stupid." A tear broke through the pain, and she leaned closer to his face, the thick musk of his beard piercing her nostrils. "You should have stayed at your cabin. You should have left me in the woods." More tears cascaded down her swollen cheeks. Was this what drove Doug to cheat? Had she always knocked away every outstretched hand? "I'm sorry." Reuben and Doug blurred together in the distress of her mind as the admission escaped her lips. "I didn't want this to happen." She hunched over, her back curved like the handle of a cane, and wept.

All of the pain, fear, apprehension, and unknowns that had plagued her consciousness flooded from her soul, escaping through the ducts of her eyes. She let herself feel the weakness, let it soak her bones until they dissolved. The walls within crumbled with every tremble of her body. She was exposed, naked and vulnerable. She stayed in the room with Reuben until her sorrow had run its course, and then she left.

Outside, Nathan waited for her. He gripped two rifles, one in each hand, and extended her the assault rifle. "Everyone's set. We're going to leave a few behind here to keep an eye on Reuben and make sure the town remains secure in case we need it later."

The rifle sagged in her arms. It was heavier than she remembered, taking what remained of her strength just to keep the weapon upright. "We won't." The fatigue in her body betrayed the confidence in her voice as the rifle slipped from her grip and smacked to the ground. She knelt to retrieve it, and Nathan lowered with her.

"You know you don't have to do this. You've been through enough, Wren. We can get your kids out."

"No." Wren raised the rifle and tucked it back under her arm. "They're my children. It's my job."

Nate sighed and gave a reluctant nod. "Go and get something to eat before we take off. Ben's handing out the rations now. We leave in twenty."

"Okay." It'd take them all night to make it back to the camp, and her muscles whined at the mere thought of the long trek. When she found Ben handing out the rations, she made it a point to grab an extra pack for the journey.

* * *

THE SMALL TEAMS of three and four huddled closely in the dark, everyone as quiet as the trees around them. When people spoke, it was in hurried whispers, which were few and far between. It was an eerie sight, all of those bodies moving soundlessly through the forest. They moved like the undead toward the last beacon of life in the world, ready to consume it for themselves. Wren didn't object to the silence. Even though she was surrounded by nearly two dozen others, she might as well have been walking through the forest alone. It was a needed solitude, time to prepare herself for what could happen. From the moment Iris showed up, Wren had been a nervous wreck, knowing that only Doug was there with the children, if he was even still alive. And if he was, he wasn't in any shape to keep them safe. He could barely walk.

She slowly processed all of the atrocities that Ted and Edric could inflict on her children. She forced herself down every dark alleyway of her mind, overturning every stone, peeking through every crevice. She needed to see it. She needed to prepare herself. By the time they stopped a few hundred yards from the compound, she couldn't stop herself from shaking.

"Hey." Nathan placed his hand on her shoulder. "You all right?"

Wren nodded quickly. Sweat broke out on her forehead, and she wiped it off with her sleeve before it stung her eyes. She'd forgotten about the swelling in her cheeks and pressed too hard with her forearm. The pain swelled her adrenaline. "Where's our point of entrance?"

"We'll head east, circle around the front gate, and head sixty yards before we make the jump. John and I will head for the fuel depot and start digging. You find your kids and wait for the explosion, and then you head out the same way you came in. We'll spread out the fighting between the north, south, and west corners."

Wren closed her eyes and whispered the only prayer that mattered. *Let my children live.*

"Wren?" Nathan asked. "You don't have to do this if you're not ready. We can—"

"I'm ready." With her assault rifle and the extra magazine of ammunition, Wren followed Nathan and John through the trees. Every few yards, she glanced toward the wall, the proximity to her children enough to drive her mad.

After ten minutes Nathan held up his hand, freezing all three of them in place. Wren drew in a breath, every muscle hissing pain. She kept her good ear toward the fence, her eyes peeled, and slowly exhaled when Nathan motioned them forward.

The roots that penetrated from the earth were slick with the morning's rain, and Wren slipped twice, catching herself with her right arm and cursing under her breath. Her feet dug into the moist dirt, flicking patches of soil behind her with each hurried step. The beating from the previous day had taken its toll, as she panted for breath by the time they reached the fence.

The section of the wall they'd chosen hadn't been completed before Wren's exile. It was weakly reinforced, and most of the wood had rotted away, but more importantly, it was short. She'd never added the height extension like the other sides, though it was something Edric knew as well.

Nathan walked slowly along the walls, keeping low, while John and Wren hung back, waiting for the signal that it was clear. Wren's heart caught in her throat, each thick beat sending a shiver down her spine. Beyond the fence, her children were scared and alone. She dug her fingers into the rifle's grip. The knuckles in her hands cracked. *I'm coming.*

John patted her on the shoulder, and the two bounded soundlessly over the wet earth to Nathan's location. It was Wren who went over first, her belly sliding against the moldy bark. The skin between her fingers pinched in the crevices between poles. Her arms shook violently as she lifted her legs over the side, and she smacked her cheek on her way over the top. The pain numbed her limbs, and she slipped from the top, crashing into the dirt with a dull thud.

Wren clawed at the ground, the first few seconds of breathless gasps heightening the adrenaline-induced panic. The first breath wheezed into her lungs as Nathan landed next to her. "Are you all right?" She nodded and pushed herself up. John lowered himself next as she brushed dirt from the front of her shirt and pants.

"Let's go." Nathan led the pack, careening through the trees inside the compound. The heightened risk elevated everyone's awareness, and Wren felt her mind come alive in the darkness. Her vision grew clearer. The pain in her body faded, and she felt the strength of the moment. Her rage that had gathered in her veins finally hardened. Her muscles flexed in fluent coordination with her commands. The compound had become her drawing board, and the rifle in her hands the pen.

The first buildings came into view. John and Nathan broke off to the north while Wren slowed. She knelt by one of the last trees before the clearing and peered through the scope. The crosshairs focused on two guards, and she nestled closer to the base of the tree, with only the black of the rifle visible around the trunk's corner.

The sentries moved silently, cloaked in darkness. Wren knew they had night vision. She'd seen them use it against the raiders that had come before. The moment she stepped from behind her cover, she'd be caught. Never had she cursed her deafness more than now.

Patience grew thin with the knowledge that her children were so close, and seconds turned into hours. With the rope holding her back fraying, she pivoted slowly, creeping around the edge of the trunk, lifting her scope. She exhaled. Nothing but empty space.

With the guards past, Wren hurried to the first building. She hugged the back side of the house, knowing Edric's residency was close. She hastened her speed, with nothing ahead but open ground. If she was caught here, her cover was blown.

The late hour had tucked most of the residents to bed for the night, but even still, Wren was mindful between the houses, knowing that anyone could wake in the night. When Edric's home finally came into view, she slowed.

A cluster of trees thrust itself inconveniently from the

clearing, challenging the open space the camp had inflicted upon the forest. Wren smiled at nature's defiant act, knowing it had been a point of contention with Edric.

Wren lingered a few dozen yards from the house, waiting for any sign of motion, scanning every corner and crevice before her first step. She'd only get one shot at this, and if she was wrong, or if she was caught, her children were dead.

Once she'd double-checked her surroundings, she planted her right foot forward then froze. She looked from side to side. Another step. And another. She kept the methodical, steady pace until she arrived at the window and crouched low.

Slowly, Wren craned her neck to the window's corner. At first, nothing but darkness stared back at her. She blinked away the emptiness a few times, and the room took shape. A dresser appeared on the far wall. With a point of reference, she slowly mapped the room in her mind, her search catching the shape of a doorknob, a bedpost, and a pair of shoes.

Wren kept her eyes on the bedpost and craned her neck to try and get a better look at who slept, but all she managed to catch a glimpse of was the ruffle of sheets. She glued her back to the cabin's wall and looked to the east, where the fuel deposit rested. *What is taking them so long?*

The cabin itself was raised slightly off the ground, and Wren positioned herself by the front door and started digging. She burrowed out a hole and slithered underneath, her lips grainy with soil as she nestled inside. The space was so narrow that she could barely lift her head. Every breath squeezed her harder against the confined space, and she fought against the growing claustrophobic panic. She focused on slowing her heart rate, and inhaled slowly through her nose and exhaled out her mouth.

Wren positioned herself to face east, and she kept her eyes glued to the sky, waiting for the plume of fire and smoke that would wake the entire forest. She tucked the rifle close to her body, and she stiffened as time passed. She stretched her neck a quarter inch to the right and half as much to the left. It was all the movement the space afforded. And just when her impatience tipped to the edge of action, she felt the ground rumble under her belly. A sudden burst of fire and earth greeted her gaze to the east, the plume rising for only a split second before extinguishing into the night.

Pounding feet thundered on the floor overhead, and Wren recognized Edric's voice as he shouted to someone inside. The words were muffled and indecipherable, but the panicked and hurried tone told her all she needed to hear.

The door burst open, and Wren watched Edric's legs sprint toward the sight of the explosion. Shouts erupted in the night as the quiet of the camp ended with every confused order barked from the lips of Edric's men. She lingered under the building a minute longer, looking to her left and right, waiting for the rest of his goons to flock to the explosion.

With the coast clear all around, Wren wriggled her way to the front of the building. She brought her hands from under the bottom of the house, digging her fingertips into the siding to pull herself out, when the door burst open again. She jerked back underneath, frozen in the hopes that whoever left hadn't seen her. She watched feet hurry across the grass and waited until they were out of sight.

Wren exhaled and returned to her escape. Her stomach scraped along the house's undercarriage, and she rolled across the dirt with her final heave from the cramped coffin. She knocked the dirt from her rifle and stepped inside the house. She squinted into the darkness, every motion a knee-jerk reaction in her heightened state of awareness.

"Chloe! Addison!" She whispered their names, her voice barely rising above the creak of the floorboards. *Please let them be here.* She smacked her knee on the corner of a table, and a crash followed the sharp curse as she limped forward. "Zack! Chloe!"

Scratches sounded to her right. She froze, silencing the creak of the floorboard. She lowered her weapon and saw the outline of a door. She pulled the handle. *Locked.* The scratching intensified, and Wren rattled the doorknob viciously. "Chloe? Addison? Can you hear me?" Again, nothing but scratches answered, and Wren stepped back. She thrust her heel into the door, and the joints along her leg jarred painfully as the wood did nothing more than slightly bend.

Wren raised the butt of her rifle and smacked it against the knob. The wood around the lock splintered, and she quickly struck it again. The third blow broke it free, and she shoved the door open, her heart sinking as she saw Doug bound and gagged in the small closet space. "Oh my god." She pulled him out, his body limp, his breathing labored, and his clothes and skin soaked with sweat. She tore the gag from his mouth, and he let out a gasp. "Where are the girls? Where's Zack?"

Doug shook his head. "I don't know." He coughed violently, wheezing between breaths. "I haven't seen them since you left." His neck gave out, and he rolled his head, exhausted from the interaction. "I thought you were dead."

Wren hyperventilated. She clutched her chest. A tingle ran down her left arm, and her shoulder ached. "Fuck." She pulled her hair. "Jesus fucking Christ." If the girls weren't here, then she didn't have enough time to find them now. She gripped Doug's shoulders and dug her nails into his shirt, pinching his flesh. "Think, Doug. Where was the last time you saw them? You must have heard something Edric said. *Anything.*"

"I-I don't know. I don't remember him saying anything." Doug shut his eyes. He shook his head, drips of sweat flying in every direction. "H-He mentioned more guards someplace. It sounded important."

"Where?" She pulled him closer and tightened her grip, hoping she could force him to hold onto the thought on the tip of his tongue.

"The infirmary." Doug opened his eyes wide. "I think he's keeping the kids at the infirmary."

Without another word, Wren sprinted out of the cabin, shoulder checking the door open. The muscles along her legs burned, but she kept long strides, and her body whined from the exertion.

Gunfire grew louder in its orchestrated chorus in the night air the farther she ran. The rhythm of bullets beat in time with her steps, and she raised the rifle to her shoulder, her finger on the trigger. A shadow darted from the side of a building, and Wren aimed but hesitated, unsure of whether it was friend or foe. But the bullets fired in her direction answered the unknown.

Wren returned fire and glided right, her aim sloppy from her movement. Dirt flew up with every bullet that skipped left and right, short and long. The two grew closer, and Wren planted her foot, dropping to one knee, and steadied her aim. The outlined figure centered in the crosshairs, and Wren squeezed. A cry rang out, and the shadow dropped to the ground. The farther she ran, the more shadows appeared, attempting to take her deeper into the darkness.

Flashes burst from Wren's muzzle and lit up the night with every hurried squeeze of the trigger. She felt the rifle mold to her body, become an extension of her arm as she sprinted through the hail of gunfire. Two figures guarded the infirmary's flank, and Wren brought the first down easily, but the second caused her to roll left behind the cover of one of the houses.

Wren caught her breath and hocked the thick phlegm that had collected in the swollen pockets of her cheeks. The tip of the muzzle wafted smoke, and she flattened herself to the dirt. She saw the man's feet frozen in place, no doubt waiting for her to show on either side of the house. But she burrowed forward underneath, shoving aside dirt, grass, and cobwebs as she crawled toward the last obstacle between her and her children. The cramped space made it difficult to position the weapon, but she managed to raise the barrel high enough to get the needed projection, and by the time the sentry realized where she'd gone, he had two bullets in his chest.

Wren squeezed herself from under the house, her eyes never leaving the sight of the infirmary. A wave of dirt trailed her after the final push, and she sprinted toward the door, rifle up, every cell in her body in overdrive as she burst inside. The scene upon her entrance overwhelmed her, but she kept her rifle up. Her finger itched carefully over the trigger, and her whole body tensed. "Let them go!"

Both Zack and Addison were tied up in the corner by their ankles and wrists, with gags over their mouths. Ted held Chloe by the scruff of her neck, shielding himself with her body, the gun in his hand aimed at her youngest daughter's head. "Oh, I don't think you're in a position to be bargaining." Chloe's head tilted at an angle from the pressure of the gun.

Wren glanced behind her then shut the door with her foot, providing her back with a barrier. She took a step forward, but it only caused Ted to press the gun harder into Chloe's cheek, which was red and wet with tears. "Take the gun off of my daughter. *Now.*"

"Or what? You'll shoot me?" Ted pulled Chloe closer, covering more of his body. "You don't have the skill to shoot me without the risk of killing your daughter. We both know that. But..." He repositioned the gun under Chloe's chin. "You have three kids. So I could easily plow through two of them and still have a bargaining chip to get whatever I want. You want this one to live? Put down the rifle, Wren."

Wren's eyes flitted between Chloe and Zack and Addison tied up on the floor. She shifted her weight side to side. The shouts and gunfire had grown increasingly hectic outside, adding to the screaming match in her head. "You'll kill them out of spite."

Ted threw his head back, his maniacal laughter flooding the infirmary. "You've learned so much. But even still, you're out of cards to play. You don't have any move left but to put the gun down. I've seen you in fights. You don't pull the trigger. You don't have the training. You don't have the grit. And you don't have the nerve." A few drops of spit landed on top of Chloe's head as she continued to cry in his arms.

Wren sidestepped to her right, her eye glued to the scope. The crosshairs wavered between Ted and Chloe's head. Wherever she moved the barrel of her gun, he moved Chloe. Her muscles caught fire, but she steadied her arms, forcing them as still as the metal gripped in her hands. *I can't let him win.* Her right arm spasmed involuntarily, and the steady confidence she'd accumulated vanished.

"I'm running out of patience, Wren." Ted's voice dropped an octave, the playful laughter erased from his face. "You won't be able to win this. You and I both know that. Your distraction is wearing off, and Edric's men will beat back whatever resistance they come across. Time's up."

Wren shut her eyes, focusing on nothing but her breathing. Her heart rate slowed. Her muscles relaxed. The shaky tremor in her right shoulder disappeared, and she felt her body steady. She opened her eyes, and the world through the view of the scope passed in slow motion. The point of the crosshairs lined up perfectly with Ted's left eye, and she felt her right hand squeeze the trigger.

The blast of the gunshot and Ted dropping to the floor flashed faster than the blink of an eye. Wren dropped the rifle and sprinted toward her daughter, her piercing cries eclipsing the gunfire outside. She scooped Chloe in her arms and scrambled on her knees to Zack and Addison. Clutching her youngest daughter to her shoulder, she ripped the gags from her other two children, and they scrunched their faces in grief. She squeezed all three of them in her arms, and she could have stayed there holding them forever, but the thunder of gunshots beckoned the return of her senses. She set Chloe down and pulled a knife from her pocket. She sawed through the restraints, tossing them aside. Zack grabbed his crutches, and Addison clung to her leg. "Zack, here." She handed him the knife and scooped the rifle up, keeping Chloe in her right arm. "You three stay with me, and do not stop moving for anyone or anything. Got it?"

Three nods answered in unison, and Wren led them out the front door. She kept Zack and Addison in front, scanning behind them to make sure no one ambushed their rear. Shudders accompanied every gunshot, but Wren marched them forward. "Don't stop!" They sprinted into the forest, heading for the fence. The farther they ran, the more the gunfire faded, and it was soon replaced with Chloe's steady crying.

32

Zack slammed up against the tree's trunk, wheezing and panting for breath. "I can't... I need to stop." Wren hadn't let them rest for twenty minutes, putting as much distance between her and the camp as possible.

Wren stopped, Chloe still clinging to her neck, and looked back for the first time. "All right. Just for a little bit." Wren peeled Chloe off and set her down next to Addison, and the two huddled close to her legs. Wren unloaded the empty magazine from the rifle and replaced it with her spare. Sporadic gunfire continued to disrupt the stretches of quiet, and Wren peered through the tunneled view of the scope. Only trees and darkness fell across her gaze, and she lowered the weapon. "How's the leg holding up?"

Zack regained control of his breathing, but his face and body glistened with sweat under the moonlight. "The leg's okay. I haven't moved this much since it was broken." He lowered his head, drawing in a long breath.

Wren tilted his head up. "You're doing great." She kissed his cheek and ran her fingers through his hair. "We need to find the others." She stepped over a few of the roots, looking into the darkness, hoping Nate or Iris and Ben would return soon.

"Mom, what about Daddy?" Addison let go of her sister and walked to Wren. "Is he coming with us?"

Wren knelt and tucked Addison's hair behind her ears. "Dad wanted to make sure you got out safe. He's helping keep the bad guys from getting to us." She kissed her forehead. "He loves you so much." Her voice caught in her throat, and she wondered how long her answer would satisfy her daughter's worry.

A twig snapped in the darkness. Wren pivoted toward the sound's origin. Zack and the girls cowered backward. Leaves rustled, and she took a step forward. Shadows moved, and Wren placed her finger on the trigger just before a pair of hands thrust themselves into the air.

"Wren?" Ben's figure withdrew from the darkness. Blood splattered his shirt and arms, with some smaller speckles on his cheeks. "Thank god." He let out a breath and wrapped her in a hug. "I'm glad you made it out." He turned to the kids, palming the top of Chloe's head in his hand. "And I'm glad you're safe too, young lady."

"What happened?"

The answer spread across his face before the words left his mouth. "Edric pushed us back after the attack. We didn't have the manpower to finish him. But Iris managed to retrieve some of our gear from the vaults before we retreated. We're going to mount another offensive at dawn."

Wren paced wearily. She bit her lower lip until she tasted blood. She couldn't risk keeping the kids around for that. She needed to get them as far away from the camp as possible. "I need someone to take Zack and the girls back to the town."

Ben shook his head. "Wren, we don't have that kind of time. We need to hit Edric hard again before he has a chance to come after us. We have to stay on the offensive."

"I just pulled them out of a warzone. I'm not going to

keep them around for another confrontation like that." Wren thrust her finger into Ben's chest. "They go. Or I disappear before you can rally the troops behind my figure."

"Wren—"

"It's not a discussion, Ben." She stood her ground as Ben wavered back and forth.

The gunshots in the distance broke the monotony of silence until Ben finally spoke. "All right, but we can't afford more than one man to go back. We'll need everyone to bring him down."

"Then it's your best man." Wren walked away but caught Zack's glance as she turned to the fading sounds of battle. He hobbled around until he completely blocked her view. Even in the darkness, she saw the distressed lines across his face. "You need to be strong for the girls." She gripped the back of his neck and pulled him close, squeezing him tight. "If something happens to me or your father, you need to take care of them, okay?"

"Don't go back." Zack's words were nothing more than a whisper against her ear. "I know what he did. I know he cheated on you. You don't have to go back for him."

Wren forced his eyes to hers. "He's your father. No matter what he's done to me, he has always loved you. And you're stronger than he is. He knows it, and so do I." She kissed his cheek then embraced him in another hug. "I love you so much."

The rendezvous point was only a mile away, and Ben helped round up the girls as they trekked through the forest. By the time they arrived at their destination, the gunfire had ended, and most of the survivors had returned. The number of casualties for their group were a quarter of their total. Iris and her team were some of the last to return, though what they brought with them raised the group's spirits.

"Ammunition. Knives. Explosives. Rations. And NVDs that were stored in my faraday cage." Iris dumped the loot in the center of the group who'd circled. The booty was distributed evenly, and Wren made sure to take one of the grenade belts. She wasn't sure if she could be as accurate on this round as her previous shots.

Ben pulled Iris to the side, telling her about Wren's demands. When the conversation ended, Iris simply looked Wren's way and gave a soft nod. When she walked by, neither of them exchanged any words.

Once the children's escort was chosen, Wren pulled them aside, away from the ears and mouths of the group. "You guys are going on a trip with Mommy's friend Donny. He's going to take care of you and make sure you're safe, okay?"

"You're not coming with us?" Chloe's eyes widened. She puffed out her lower lip.

"I'll only be gone for a little while longer." Wren stroked her cheek, but Chloe jerked away.

"You just came back, and you're leaving again?" Addison thrust her arms out animatedly. "You can't do that! You can't leave us! You promised!" Her voice shrieked. "You promised!" Her face reddened, and tears burst from her eyes as she stomped her feet and kicked the dirt and leaves.

Zack reached her before Wren could and scooped her up. "Hey, listen. It's not Mom's fault that she has to leave. She's going to get Dad. She's trying to help, and you're not making the situation any better. You need to be brave. Like Mom."

Addison buried her face into her brother's shoulder, and the tantrum ended. Zack rocked her back and forth, using the tree next to him for support. A tear broke through the wall holding them back and rolled down her cheek. Chloe tugged on Wren's pants, and when she knelt down she squeezed her youngest daughter tight, hoping the night concealed the tears.

Before they left, Wren pulled Zack aside, making sure the girls couldn't hear. "When you get to town, there will be a man in the care of a doctor. If he's awake, tell him who you are and that I told him to take you to the cabin. If I don't make it back, you stay with him. He'll keep you and your sisters safe."

"Mom, you shouldn't talk like that."

"Promise you'll listen to what he says." Wren kept her voice stern and grabbed his shoulders. "Promise me." After a pause, he agreed, and Wren hugged him. "I'm so proud of you. And I love you so much."

Wren kissed all of them as many times as she could before Don led them through the woods. Her heart was pulled with them, and she kept her eyes on them until they disappeared into the trees. She lingered on the last spot she saw them and didn't look away until Iris placed her hand on her shoulder.

"They give you something to fight for," Iris said. "Let them be your fuel. You don't stop until they're out of harm's way."

"And when does that happen?" Wren looked back to the empty forest. "The world doesn't stop being dangerous just because I want it to. It's never listened to me before. There's no reason for it to start now." She walked away, leaving Iris and the group. She didn't need to be lectured. She needed to be alone.

A fallen tree provided the quietness Wren needed, and she felt the weight of the past few days fall on her. She rested the rifle across her lap, and the soreness and pain returned in full force. She gingerly stretched her body, every muscle irritated. She poked her cheeks and was reminded of the swollenness in her face. Her eyes felt heavy, pulling her downward. All she wanted was to lie down and sleep.

Wren wrestled with the thoughts in her head, wondering if the driving force behind her return was for Doug's rescue or Edric's death, and whether her motives even mattered. Her broken body didn't have much left in the tank. And while she knew she couldn't rid the world of every evil meant to harm her children, she knew that she had to try and cleanse it of this one horror in her own backyard.

Footsteps triggered a reach for the rifle, but when she saw Nate emerge from the darkness, she lowered the weapon. "I could have shot you."

"It wouldn't have been the first time you tried to kill me."

Wren couldn't help but chuckle as he took a seat next to her. "This one would have been more deliberate."

"But just as fatal." Nate rested the rifle against the log and folded his hands, resting them on his gut, which had shrunk over the past month. "You did good getting those kids out of there. Doug would have done the same thing."

"I know."

"I'm just saying if he were in the same position—"

"Nathan, I know." She clipped her words, cutting him off. "Just because our marriage fell apart doesn't mean our commitment to our children did. He knows why I didn't come back for him, and by now he knows that they got away." She picked at the dirt under her fingernails. "I don't know if he's even still alive."

"And what if he isn't?" Nate elbowed her arm. "Could you handle that?"

Wren exhaled, her body collapsing within itself as she did. "One thing at a time, Nate." She rubbed her palms together, feeling the calluses that had grown over the skin. Every fiber of her being had either broken or hardened. She wasn't the woman she used to be. And she wasn't sure if that was good or bad. "Reuben. The hermit who saved me. I want him to stay with my kids if I don't make it. I'm going to tell that to everyone before we leave."

"You don't have to do this, Wren. You don't have anything else to prove. Let me talk to Iris and Ben. They'll understand."

"No. I'm not going back because of the deal I made with them. I'm going to kill Edric. One way or the other, this will be finished for me." She looked him in the eye. "And I'm not leaving anyone else behind. No matter what."

Nathan nodded. "All right. You need anything?"

"I'm just gonna sit here for a while. I'll be back in a minute."

"Okay." Nathan squeezed her hand and disappeared.

Once his footsteps faded, Wren was left in quiet. She closed her eyes and listened to the light breeze rustle the leaves overhead. She felt her muscles relax, and while the pain in her body lingered, she was able to block it out. The world around her felt like a graveyard, and she was nothing more than a ghost floating through the headstones.

It was a feeling she'd never experienced before, and she found a level of euphoria in the moment, and a peace that she hadn't known since before the events in Chicago. Home had never felt so close and yet so out of reach. Her thoughts drifted to the terrorists, and Ted, and she wondered how many more of them were left. How deep did their network go?

Wren tucked her rifle under her arm and returned to the group. Upon her arrival, Ben and Iris already had everyone huddled together. All of their faces stretched long. Everyone was fatigued, and the slouched shoulders and low-hanging heads lacked the confidence she knew they needed. "We're not dead." Heads perked up at the sound of her voice. The group sat a little straighter, and she felt the light burst of energy rush through them. "Not yet." A few smiles cracked over the stoic faces. "Edric has hurt all of us. And the camp he occupies is everything you've worked for to stay alive. You put your blood and sweat into that place. And now it's calling for more." Heads nodded, and Wren circled the group. "He won't give it back willingly. He's a fearmonger. Some warlord sitting high on his chair."

Iris rose, followed by Ben, and they both stood next to Wren. Iris placed her arm on her shoulder. "Edric has no right to what we've built. We've sacrificed too much. That's our future he holds. And we're not going to let him take it!" She thrust her hand into the air, and the group erupted. Fists and rifles were raised. The anger spread like an airborne pathogen, and Wren felt her blood boil.

33

The sky lightened just before dawn, and beyond the gaping hole Ted's people had blown in the fence, Wren and the rest of Iris's people waited in the trees. They'd arrived an hour earlier, and with the aid of the night vision goggles Iris confiscated after last night's attack, they didn't find any traps set in the fence's opening. They'd determined that the majority of Edric's men were not on the wall. And with the forest bare of any tracks, it told them that Edric had stacked all of his chips in a concentrated effort within the community, most likely the garrison.

The fatigue that had plagued Wren the majority of the early morning had vanished. A steady alertness had replaced the weariness in her eyes, and she felt a slow and steady burn of fuel course through her veins. She looked left, and Nathan held up his hand, signaling the continued order to hold. It wasn't until the first rays of light peeked over the horizon that they were to strike.

Wren glanced behind her and felt her pulse accelerate. The sun had nearly reached the horizon, the clear morning sky now a light pink. Her muscles tensed, and she drew in a breath as the first ray of light broke through the trees. Before she even looked to Nathan, he was already on the move. Wren sprinted into action. She kept the rifle tucked close and her eyes peeled on her way toward the gap in the fence.

Wren stopped at the fence's edge, her shoulder rubbing up against the broken and charred logs that composed the gap's edges. The dozens of bodies that survived the initial onslaught during the first assault hurried through the fence's weak point, the steady thump of boots breaking the monotony of the silent morning air. Wren peered around the corner, looking, listening, waiting, and soon the thump of boots was replaced with gunshots. After the first bullet rang through the crisp morning air, all hell broke loose. Edric's forces burst from their homes. Gunfire exchanged, screams echoing between the pop of rifles. But Wren silenced all of it, focused on locating Edric. He was all that mattered. *Cut off the head, and the snake dies.*

Bullets connected with earth and flesh everywhere Wren looked. She watched one of their own fall with a bullet to the head, body limp and limbs tangled awkwardly on the ground. Wren passed a house, and a woman burst through the front door wielding a rifle. Before she raised it to fire, Wren felt the recoil of two shots smack her shoulder, the bullets penetrating the woman's chest, and she collapsed in a bloodied pile on the steps of her home. Through the scope of the rifle she examined and filtered every detail of the camp, her mind processing the heightened speed of battle. She moved with a fluidity she'd never experienced. No disconnect existed between her mind and muscles. The stakes of life and death elevated her performance.

"Wren!" Nathan pointed over her shoulder, and Wren dropped to a knee, pivoting in the same direction as Nate's finger. A man opened fire, his aim off by less than a foot. Wren brought the shooter between her crosshairs and killed him before he squeezed off another round. When she pushed herself from the ground, she felt the whine in her body return, the protective armor of adrenaline was slowly fading.

The water well up ahead signaled the center of camp, and three of Edric's men grouped in formation appeared from behind the side of the well's nearest house. Wren skidded to a stop, her boots sliding in the dirt and leaves. The slip caused her to hesitate on her aim, and the enemy fired before she could. A wall of lead forced her to roll behind the stone walls of the well, her back and hips cracking from the sudden motion.

With her back against the rocks, she felt the vibrations of bullets through the stones on the opposite side. She dropped her rifle and reached for the cluster of grenades at her belt. She plucked one and pulled the pin, squeezing the lever tight. She peered over the top and saw all three shooters clustered together. She released the lever, paused, and then jumped from behind the well, aiming the grenade at their feet.

One of the assailants managed to squeeze off a round before the explosion, but Wren ducked back behind the wall, and the bullet ricocheted off the stone. She smacked hard on her stomach and felt the ground rumble after the grenade's detonation. The explosion returned the ringing in her good ear, and the thud of gunfire dulled as she reached for the rifle in the dirt. Feet and legs hurried past, leaving behind a wake of bloodied footprints. She pushed herself up, rifle raised, and rejoined the fight.

The view was the same everywhere she looked, and through the rifle's scope, Wren watched the carnage unfold. Bullets dropped bodies. Screams intermixed with the echo of gunfire. Blood spilled. Hearts stopped. Final breaths were drawn, and one by one the field of war grew smaller. It was hard to tell who was winning. For every one of Edric's men that fell, so did one of theirs.

A spray of dust blew over Wren's feet from a missed bullet aimed for her leg. Wren turned in the direction of gunfire and stared down the barrel of a rifle with Jan behind the trigger. The mess hall was the nearest building, and Wren sprinted toward it. The thump of bullets trailed her as she circled the structure, hoping to flank Jan in the rear. But when she turned the corner near the mess hall's back doors, there was nothing but open space.

Wren lowered her weapon and took a step forward. But before she lifted her foot gunfire erupted from inside the mess hall. Wren jolted forward as the back doors splintered with a dozen bullets. Through one of the windows, Wren caught the back of Jan's head, and she fired. Glass shattered, and Jan burst through the broken doors, tumbling to the ground, the rifle in her hands slipping from her grip.

Wren aimed for Jan's head, but the councilwoman pulled a dagger from her belt, and with one flick of her arm, Wren was on the defense, using the rifle to deflect the blade as Jan sprinted toward her and tackled both of them to the dirt.

Arms and legs flailed wildly through the clouds of dust kicked up by the altercation. Wren felt every roll, punch, pull, and squeeze, her previous wounds clamoring for protection. Hands wrapped around Wren's throat, and fingers choked the air from her lungs. Her vision blurred, but she could still make out the snarl etched on Jan's face, which was accentuated by her angular cheekbones. Wren thrashed on the ground, but the harder she fought, the harder Jan's vice locked down on her neck.

"You should have quit while you were ahead, stupid bitch!" Jan's face reddened. Sweat dripped from her chin. "I've wanted to do this for a long time." Her grip tightened, and black spots clustered over Wren's vision.

Wren kicked, punched, writhed her body on the ground, bucking her hips, but nothing worked. She felt the strength in her arms subside and numb. Her arms fell lazily to the side and scraped across the dirt. A sharp point grazed her forearm, and she fumbled her fingers in the grass. *The knife.*

Wren curled her fingers around the hilt of the blade that Jan had thrown and rammed the tip into Jan's chest.

The blade scraped Jan's breastbone, and she wailed, releasing her grip on Wren's throat. Wren gasped for air, clawing at the dirt, her cheeks red and a pounding in her head as snot and spit drooled from her nose and mouth. She looked over and saw Jan pulling the blade from her chest. Blood spurted from the wound, and before the blade was completely removed, Wren punched Jan across the jaw. The hit roared a dull ache in Wren's right hand, and a tooth flew from Jan's mouth. Wren straddled her on the ground, shoving the knife deeper into her chest.

Jan screamed, clawing her nails and drawing blood with vicious strikes across Wren's cheek. Blood foamed at the corners of Jan's mouth, and the clawing ended. Jan heaved her chest up and down with her last breaths, and Wren felt the body go still.

Wren's knuckles flashed white as she kept her grip on the blade's handle. With dead eyes staring back at her, she finally uncurled her fingers from the hilt and collapsed next to Jan's dead body. She gently grazed her neck, which was tender from the dead woman's grip.

Gunshots returned Wren's attention to the fight, and she scooped her rifle from the dirt and left the blade lodged in Jan's corpse. Her fingers grew sticky the longer Jan's blood lingered on her skin. Every time she flexed her hand, they peeled off the rifle like Velcro.

"Wren!" Nathan fell in beside her, his shirt bloodied and his arm wrapped in a bandage. What wasn't covered in blood was drenched in sweat. "We've pushed them back to the garrison. Edric's there with Doug. C'mon."

Before Nathan took off, Wren was already ahead of him. Weightlessness overtook her, and she sprinted toward Iris and Ben at one of the houses near the garrison. A line of prisoners sat with their hands tied behind their back and rifles aimed at their head. Most of them kept their faces cast toward the dirt, but the few that looked up at Wren held an expression she didn't expect to see: relief.

The sun had risen higher into the sky now, and the light shimmered off the only concrete structure in the camp. It was a fortress, and Edric had barricaded himself and locked the door.

"His men have surrendered," Iris said, rubbing her thigh. "But he won't let us get close."

"He started shooting anyone that fled the garrison," Ben said, his thick mustache blowing under his heavy breaths. "He's alone in there. All he has left as a hostage is Doug."

Wren examined the building, squinting in the sunlight. The black spots from Jan's attempted murder had yet to fully disappear. She'd studied the structure before. Only one door inside. No windows, and the only structure in the entire community with a concrete foundation. Edric had picked a hell of a spot for his last stand. Wren backtracked to the rear of the house and slithered up the opposite side, hoping for a better perspective but finding none. It only offered a better view of the dead bodies near the garrison's locked door.

"There has to be some way to get him out." Ben slammed his hand against the house's wall. "Does he plan to live in there for the rest of his life?"

"No," Wren answered, gazing at the fortified compound. "He expects to die there." She knew Edric wasn't one to play games. He was a purist. He only dealt in absolutes. There was win or lose, but there was never compromise. She'd learned at least that much from her time with him. "We have to give him what he wants."

Iris scoffed. "We're not giving up the compound. Not now. He's beaten!"

"Me." Wren kept her eyes on the garrison. "I'm his link to all of his failures. He thinks I'm the reason he lost control of the camp. That's why he still has Doug."

Iris and the others remained quiet for a long time. It was Nathan who finally spoke, breaking the silence. "Wren, he'll kill you."

"All he has to do is let me inside." Wren's hand drifted to the grenades around her waist. "He does that, I can take care of the rest." She found herself praying that Reuben was still alive. She knew he would keep her children safe. She stepped forward, and Nathan pulled her back.

"No. Wren, you can't do this!" Nathan's cheeks flushed red. The sweat and blood on his shirt clung tightly to his chest and arms. "What about Zack and the girls? What about Doug?"

Wren placed a gentle hand over Nathan's and delicately peeled his fingers off. She slowly removed the grenades from the belt until there was only one left. "Those walls are at least two feet thick of concrete. The only weak point in that structure is the door. The length of the building is one hundred feet. I drop the grenade by the door then sprint to the back. The moment you see smoke, you ride in with the cavalry." With the one grenade still on the belt, she strapped it around her waist, hiding the belt underneath her shirt with the grenade hidden in the back.

Nathan shook his head. "You don't have the right to do this." He picked up one of the grenades on the ground. "You go. I go."

"He wants me, Nate. I already told you I'm not going to let anyone else die for me." She edged herself to the corner, and the others held Nate back. She looked to Iris, knowing full well she'd understand. "This is your chance. Don't miss it."

Iris nodded. "We won't."

Wren shut her eyes and stepped around the corner of the building slowly, her hands held high. "Edric!" Her voice cracked through the calm morning air, echoing through the compound. "Let Doug go! You do that, and you can have me!"

She continued to inch forward carefully. She glanced behind her and saw Iris and the others poised behind the house. Nothing but the tips of their rifles inching around the sides.

The garrison door cracked open, but no one stepped outside. Wren froze in place, peering into the dark void that was the sliver of an opening. She felt her muscles twitch anxiously.

"You come to us!" The voice shouted through the crack in the door.

Wren tilted her head to the side. "I want to see Doug first! Show me that he's alive!"

Nothing but deafening silence answered back for the next few minutes. Just when Wren was about to take a step back, Doug's face was suddenly thrust through the crack in the door. Duct tape covered his mouth, and dried blotches of blood were spread over his face in crimson patches. And just as quickly as he was shown, he was pulled from view. "He goes out when you come in!"

Wren stepped over and around the fallen bodies. Their faces were frozen in the last expressions of fear, their eyes lifeless, and they stained the ground red where they fell. She looked to the door that remained cracked, her arms still raised and surprisingly still. She took one last look behind her and the sight of at least a dozen rifles aimed at her direction. She felt the stiffness of concrete under her foot as she neared the garrison's door, and she closed her eyes one last time, whispering a prayer. *Keep them safe for me. Like they were your own.*

A hand snapped at her arm like a snake bite and yanked her inside. She hit the ground hard, and she heard the slam of the door shut behind her. Inside, the garrison was only a single hallway with locked doors on either side, a few of them opened with their contents spilled into the hall, crowding the already narrow space. When Wren turned to face Edric, she stared down the barrel of his rifle, and Doug was still bound by ankles and wrists in the corner by the door.

"I'm impressed you came yourself." Edric was covered in sweat and the blood of his former subordinates. The red veins in his eyes were more prominent from the strain of battle and gave off an ominous bloody tinge. "I didn't think you'd have it in you. But then again, you have been pretty fucking stupid."

Wren kept her arms raised, and with her back on the ground she felt the grenade digging into her spine. She slowly moved to her knees, her eyes locked onto Edric's. "It's over, Edric. The fight is done."

"It's never done!" Edric's voice thundered through the hall, and he jammed the barrel of his rifle against her cheek, and she felt a tooth knock loose. "I'm not dead yet. I'll take this whole fucking place down with me if I have to!" His face reddened in his madness. "Those people don't know what needs to be done."

Wren slowly backed her head away from the barrel of the rifle, pushing herself to her feet, moving at a snail's pace. "No. But you do. Don't you?" In her peripheral she saw Doug in the corner, silently struggling to push himself up. "You've always known what's needed to be done. That's why you tried to get rid of me. Because you knew I was weak."

Edric nodded quickly, his eyes wide like that of a child. "I did everything I was supposed to." Tears streamed down his face, and he tightened his grip on the rifle, his arms trembling from the pressure. "Everything! But you fucked it all up. You fucking cunt! We were fine until you showed up. We were safe. I kept them safe!" Spit flew from his mouth, and the roar sent a blast of hot breath in Wren's face.

Wren's pulse quickened as she saw Doug push himself against the wall, straightening himself. She felt the sting of sweat in her eyes, and the moment Doug lunged forward, the world turned to slow motion. Edric shifted his gaze from her to Doug, and she sprinted forward, her hands reaching for the gun. And when her fingertips grazed the barrel the slow motion ended, and time shifted into a breakneck pace.

Doug could do little more than use his body weight to slam Edric against the wall, and once he hit the floor it was unlikely he'd be able to make it back up. Wren pinned the length of the rifle against Edric's neck, using the momentum Doug had provided to loosen his grip on the weapon. She yanked it free, and before her finger reached the trigger, Edric barreled into her, slamming both of them against the wall then onto the floor.

The rifle landed out of reach from both of them, and she watched Doug scoot toward the weapon. She tried reaching for the grenade, but with Edric on top of her she couldn't squeeze her hand underneath her back to grab the explosive.

Edric punched her cheek, the blow numbing her already swollen face, immunizing her to the next vicious hit. He grabbed her collar, lifting her up, and she saw two faces circling around in her field of vision. "You're a dead woman." He shoved her back down, and her head slammed against the concrete. He kicked the end of Doug's chin and knocked him away before he could reach the rifle. Edric picked it up and tucked it under his arm. "And once I kill you and your husband, I'm going to hunt down your kids. I'm not going to rest until I've erased every last shred of your family from this earth."

Wren lifted her head, rolling to her side, and brought her hands to her back, looking as though she was cradling the pain Edric had inflicted, but her hand wrapped around the lump at her waist. She looked to Doug, whose mouth bled, and the two made eye contact.

"And when I kill them, I'll be sure to let them know that it was their mother that let this happen to them." Edric aimed the rifle at Wren, his finger on the trigger. "I can't wait to see the look on their faces."

"You won't get the chance."

Doug lunged at Edric once more, and he spun around, shooting Doug in the head. The distraction lasted only a few seconds, but it was enough to give Wren time to pull the pin on the grenade. She released the lever and tossed it toward Edric and then scrambled in the opposite direction. She heard him shout something, but in her frantic pace she couldn't decipher it. She made it two steps when the sounds of the gunshots suddenly intermixed with a pain in her back, and she felt her body run cold as she collapsed to the ground. The adrenaline subsided, and the last thing Wren remembered hearing was the explosion that ripped Edric to pieces.

34

One Month Later

Iris paced the floor restlessly. Ben sat in the corner, frozen. Nathan drummed his fingers nervously on the table's surface. All three of them had the same anxiety etched on their faces, though the roots of their apprehension differed.

"I don't like it." Iris stopped, saying the words aloud to the room as much as herself. "I don't like the idea at all. It's too soon for something like this."

"Everybody's for it," Ben replied. "It's what she would have wanted." The mustache on his upper lip curved downward. "And if we're going to do it, then we need to start now."

"Ben's right," Nathan replied, chiming in, ceasing the percussive drumming. "We haven't had any contact from anyone on the outside since Edric was killed. We don't know who's out there, and we need to find out. We need to start establishing a connection."

"And what happens when people want what we have?" Iris raised her eyebrows. The grey in her hair had whitened, and the age lines across her face had grown more prominent. "We've just got this place back on its feet."

"All the more reason to start now." Nathan stood. "We're stronger than we were before. We can help."

"It's what she would have wanted," Ben said.

Iris lowered her head. "I know." She rubbed the creases on her forehead, the loose skin rolling between her fingers. "All right." She drew in a deep breath and let it out slowly. "We'll start sending scouts to look for people. But we do not make contact until we've observed them. I don't want us taking any chances with anyone until they've been fully vetted."

"Agreed," Nathan said.

Ben nodded and softly repeated to himself that it was what she would have wanted. The three of them left their chambers and stepped back out into the town hall. Their population was less than half of what it was when they arrived, but the fence had been finished, supplies had been recalculated, and they still had more than enough to last for a few years.

Iris smacked her gavel, calling everyone to order. "We have listened to and heard everyone's opinion. And based off of the community's voice, we shall start looking for others to bring to the camp. Anyone that comes to us will be given asylum, but thoroughly vetted and closely monitored." She reached for the gavel but hesitated. She twirled it in her hands then set it down. "I know many of you were moved by what Wren Burton did for this community. By all she sacrificed. Humanity should never be something that's lost in times of crisis. It should only be strengthened. Our actions shape us. How we conduct ourselves will shape the future. And though she is gone, we will keep her spirit within all of us." She lowered her head, a smile gracing her lips at Wren's memory, then smacked the gavel.

* * *

Reuben cracked his knuckles then turned the spit outside the cabin. The four rabbits crackled, and the grease from the meat sizzled into the fire below. Chloe sat on his right, while Addison was on his left. "Should be done soon."

"I'm starving." Chloe threw her head back and overexaggerated the throwing of her arms. "It smells so good." She leaned closer, but Reuben pulled her back.

"Easy now. We don't want to cook you." Reuben patted her on the back and reached for the spit, slowly, still recovering from his fight back in town. He tore into the charred flesh, and determined with a satisfied grunt that it was done. "All right. Time to eat. Zack!"

A log split in two, the axe wedged right in the middle. Zack looked over from the logs of firewood and limped over, his leg still acclimating to the freedom from his cast, not all of his strength completely returned. "Smells good." He took a seat next to Addison, wiping his hands on his jeans, then playfully wiped them on Addison's hair, which triggered a squeal and a giggle.

"All right. That's enough, you two," Reuben said. "Chloe, why don't you run inside and get the rest of the party, huh?"

"Okay." Chloe jumped to her feet and sprinted as fast as her tiny legs allowed. Before she went inside, she ran her fingers over the old bullet holes in the cabin walls and then pushed the door open. The cabin had grown even smaller from the sudden increase in occupants, but never had it felt more like a home. "Mom, food's ready."

Wren looked up from the pistol on the table and smiled. "I'll be out in a minute." Chloe disappeared back outside, and Wren tucked the pistol in her holster and pushed up from the chair gingerly. Bandages protruded from the collar of her shirt and she walked slowly, the effort of breathing still difficult from the gunshot wounds.

Outside, Wren found a seat next to Zack. The girls split one of the rabbits, while Reuben, Zack, and she had their own. She closed her eyes as she bit into the meat and cleaned every last morsel off the bones. Once they were done, the kids played, and Zack returned to the firewood. "If you get tired, sit down. Don't push it too hard."

"I know, Mom."

"He'll be okay," Reuben said, tossing the bones into a pile. "You're sure you still want to go tomorrow?" He raised his eyebrows. The wounds on his face had mostly healed, and the beard helped cover up what hadn't.

"Yeah. It's time." After the attack on the camp and Edric's death, she awoke in the infirmary with her kids surrounding her and Reuben sitting in the corner. It was nearly an hour before all the tears had dried. Once Doug was buried, they left the community and returned to Reuben's cabin. Though Iris and the others were more than supportive of having them stay, she couldn't. It was a part of her life she needed closed. And with Reuben's help and a large supply crate from the community, they had everything they needed. And even if they didn't, the community was only a day's journey. "We'll start with some of the smaller towns. See what we find there."

"It's risky. We don't know what it's like out there anymore."

Wren watched the girls play, chasing after one another with sticks, then looked to Zack splitting wood. Everything had changed. But they needed to move forward. "It doesn't matter what we'll find. Whatever it is, we'll be okay. If it's broken, we'll rebuild it." She turned to Reuben and smiled. "It's time to start putting the pieces back together."

Printed in Great Britain
by Amazon